PIECES OF Kalyn

PIECES OF *Kalyn*

KALIOPE

Prologue

JONAH

Arriving at the diner, I feel restless, eager to catch sight of her. My leg shakes involuntarily as we pull into our usual spot, front, and center outside, providing me with an unobstructed view of the area where she'll spend her entire shift attending to those five tables.

Unbeknownst to her, I observe her every move. While she might sense a gaze fixed upon her, she remains oblivious to who it could be.

I watch her approach, rounding the corner to the diner, quietly singing to the tunes playing through her headphones. She always braids her long blonde hair and prefers to let it hang over one shoulder. Despite having a car, she chooses to walk the short distance to work. A subtle rosy tint graces her cheeks, accentuating her flawless white complexion. She's in shorts and a baggy T-shirt with her purse hanging across the front of her, delicately pressing against her cleavage, revealing the curves of her chest.

Soon, I'll witness the rhythmic movement of her full breasts as I eagerly grasp handfuls of them while she straddles my cock, moaning with pleasure from me stretching her pussy as I penetrate and devour her.

However, in the present moment, all I can do is observe her through multiple layers of glass that keep us apart.

She doesn't know me yet. If I were to give in to my desires with her, it would only scare her, as I am still a stranger in her world. Yet, she holds a significance far beyond just being a stranger to me.

She's my heartbeat.

Each breath in and out of my lungs.

The one.

I memorize the way she moves, her interactions with others, and the warmth of her smile. Yet, I've never heard her voice. It could be nothing short of perfection, flowing from her beautifully plump lips.

I find myself tormented as I watch her share laughter with other men, even though they're just her customers—my blood boils with an unmistakable twinge of jealousy, an intense desire burning within to be the one who brings genuine laughs from her. The ache in my chest grows, fueled by the longing to be with her.

It's been two years, six months, and twenty-one days since I first laid eyes on her—a moment when the world seemed to stand still, and my universe began to unravel. Despite having another woman's mouth on my cock, she shattered me. Not only did my dick stop working at that moment, but my mental state also seems paralyzed as I linger here like a fucking creep, watching this angel from afar.

Enduring each extended business trip, I reassure myself that I will see her again soon. When the moment finally arrives, I find comfort in convincing myself that the next time I am here will be the right time to sweep her off her feet and bring her home. Yet, each time, I am rendered spellbound and motionless.

Her work shift always passes in the blink of an eye, and I discreetly follow her home, maintaining a safe distance to ensure she remains unaware I am following her.

But I need to ensure she makes it home safely. She's always so absent-minded, walking in the dark with her headphones on, never bothering to look around and see if there's anyone else nearby.

I watch as she walks into her apartment and closes the door behind her.

"Drive," I instruct Jonathan, my driver, my right-hand man and best friend.

"Until next time, baby." I press the back of my knuckle against the cold glass, longing to touch her.

CHAPTER
One

KALYN

"Wait, you're letting me go?" A wave of confusion washes over me. I've always prided myself on being the most reliable waitress in this small, family-owned diner. I stand here, completely stunned, wondering if I somehow forgot to clean my ears while getting ready this morning.

"It's not personal, Kalyn. We're just not getting enough business right now and we can't afford to keep extra staff," Mr. Milo, the owner of the diner, explains apologetically. "I promise you, once things pick up again, you'll be the first person we call back," he hands me an envelope. "This is for you," he adds, with a pained expression in his eyes. "I'm really sorry, kid."

A couple walks through the door, chiming the bell attached to the top, signaling the end of our conversation. Mr. Milo's lips form a thin line before he heads towards the counter to wait on the couple.

I grab my coat and bag, making my way to the door, shoving the envelope containing my final paycheck into my back pocket. "This is just great," I huff, roughly pulling my coat on.

Leaning against the side of the brick building, I release a heavy sigh. "Why me?!" I mutter under my breath, feeling annoyed with the universe. "Just because it's been a while since I've gotten laid, doesn't mean I want you to fuck me," I inwardly laugh at myself.

"I can help with that," Sam smirks, approaching me from behind.

Sam is my only friend, and I commend him for sticking around when I'm such a mess. He's always there for me without fail. I know he's had feelings for me since middle school, and even though he's undeniably attractive, I just don't feel the same way. I've made it clear to him multiple times I don't have romantic feelings for him, and he eventually gave up trying for a relationship.

"Hey, Sam," I try my best not to sound annoyed. "No need to help. I am getting some from every direction in my life. I am completely full at the moment."

"Well, the offer still stands if you ever change your mind," he jokes. "Are you done with work already?" He nods his head towards Milo's Diner.

Sam knows my schedule and knows I should be working today. But I really don't want to have this conversation right now. I don't have the energy to spend the whole afternoon with Sam trying to solve all my problems.

So, I take the easy way out.

"Yeah, Milo let me off early today. I need to catch up on laundry and clean my apartment."

"Cool, I was headed that way—I'll walk you home," he offers as he starts walking in the direction of my apartment.

We stroll the entire way with Sam talking incessantly. I can't really catch what he is saying because my mind is consumed with thoughts of what I am going to do.

My income barely covers my rent, and the apartment complex has warned me multiple times that failing to pay would lead to eviction. Each reminder of this dire situation brings my mind back to him—Wyatt Broderick—and the job I once held at the prestigious Amaryllis firm.

The women in the office were infatuated with him, and I was the "lucky one" who caught his attention. Every fiber of my being screamed at me to run away as fast as my high heels could carry me, but at twenty-five, I was naive and thought things were finally falling into place for me. How laughable that seems now, huh?

"Here we are," Sam interrupts my thoughts, stopping in front of my door with a smile. It's clear that he's hoping for an invitation inside, but all I want right now is some alone time.

"Thanks for accompanying me back, Sam. Text me once you're home so I know you made it safely." I struggle with my apartment key, trying to get it into the lock before finally managing to unlock the door and step inside.

Despite Sam seeming to search for a way to ask if he can come in, I wave goodbye and shut the door.

I stay put, eagerly anticipating the sound of his footsteps fading away, but there's complete silence. He remains on the opposite side of the door, pondering whether to knock or not.

After an amusingly prolonged pause, I pull the door back open wide enough for him to step inside. Taking his hands out of his pockets, he looks relieved as he enters.

"Apologies for the mess," I gesture around my empty apartment. "Please, take a seat on my bed," I suggest awkwardly.

In my small living space, I've chosen a non-traditional arrangement, placing my queen-size bed in the living room and designating the one tiny bedroom as a closet. The bulk of my possessions comprises clothing from my corporate days.

I step into my closet and swap my attire for shorts and a loose-fitting T-shirt. Glancing at my reflection in the full-length mirror, my natural long, white-blonde hair appears messy, braided, and draped over my shoulder. It seemed presentable when I left for work, but now, with a shirt change, it doesn't look as polished.

The cold outside has left a faint pink hue on my cheeks, more noticeable against my pale complexion. Around others, I tend to gravitate towards wearing baggy clothes, a habit formed as a result of my ex's hurtful comments.

I used to take pride in my full breasts, curvy hips, and round bottom. However, over time he went from loving and complimenting me, to name-calling and constant insults, which resulted in me wanting to conceal my body.

Returning to my bed, an old metal-framed piece that creaks as I climb on, I attempt to make light of it being less than ideal for sexual encounters. "Good thing I never have company over." I cringe thinking of the noises it would make while having sex with someone on it.

Sam doesn't show any signs of finding me funny. Instead, he shifts into his usual serious demeanor, transforming a joke into a genuine conversation.

"Kal, I have plenty of space at my house. We could be great roommates. I'm quiet and will respect your personal space." His eyes reflect optimism.

"Thank you, Sam. Everything is fine here," I lie, suppressing the urge to retch as the words are leaving my mouth.

The reality is far from good, given the two warnings about potential eviction I've already received. Since losing my job at the firm, I've struggled to pay rent on time. The property manager is aware of my difficulties and, rather unhelpfully, offered me a "deal" to cover all the late rent.

However, when I visited his office to discuss the terms, he crossed boundaries, pushing me against the wall, feeling my boobs, and making his best attempt to kiss me. My adrenaline kicked in, and I kneed him in the groin and slapped him across the face, making it clear that if he ever touched me again, I would have him arrested.

Despite standing up for myself, he insinuated that my late rent troubles would disappear if I complied with his inappropriate demands and acted like a "good girl." The next day, I received my first written warning about the late rent.

This is a situation I wouldn't dare share with Sam, as I'm certain he would take it upon himself to pack up my belongings and move me out of here.

"I just think we'd both be happier living together," Sam suggests. Noticing the expression on my face, he quickly adds, "As friends, of course."

"I truly appreciate your offer. Thank you again." I recline on my bed, wanting this conversation to end.

Perhaps I'm twisted enough to find some strange satisfaction in life constantly kicking me while I'm down. Why else would I turn down such a generous offer from my best friend?

Retrieving my phone from the nightstand, I start texting my therapist.

"Hey, Maeva, it's Kalyn. Do you have availability tomorrow? It's urgent," I type, aware I'll need her help to navigate the impending downward spiral I can already feel beginning.

A reply comes almost immediately. "Sure, Kalyn. Can you meet me at my office tomorrow at 11?"

"Absolutely, thank you," I text back and then place my phone on my chest. Taking a deep breath and exhaling slowly, I soothe myself using a breathing technique Maeva has guided me through during our sessions, especially when I find myself too overwhelmed to speak.

"There's a new season of *American Horror Story* we can start," Sam says with enthusiasm.

I think I have responded to him out loud, but I'm so lost in thought, that I realize I didn't vocalize my 'yes' when he pulls it up on his phone, presenting the screen in my direction, asking again, "Do you want to watch it?"

"Oh, sure," I manage to say.

Sam quickly shifts his position, inching closer to me, causing the bed to dip with a loud groan as he settles in next to me. He stretches his arm out to hold his phone so we can both see the screen, even though I can tell it's putting a strain on him. But he doesn't let that stop him. He keeps holding it in the same position for five entire episodes.

I can't recount a single episode's plot. My mind is busy coming up with a thorough plan for my conversation with Maeva. '*You need to actually talk about your problems with her, Kal,*' I scold myself.

Taking a quick peek at the clock, realizing it's only 7:30, and being aware that Sam knows I'm a night owl, I can't help but fake a yawn. A subtle hint for him to leave so I can be alone with my thoughts.

He doesn't pick up on my cues and starts the next episode.

"I'm feeling pretty tired. Do you mind if we call it a night?" I look straight ahead but my peripheral vision focuses on him. I can tell he isn't ready to go yet because his arm falters, and he turns to look at me and just blinks.

You know that feeling when you just want to wallow in self-pity? That's how I feel. I want to sulk alone without having to pretend everything is fine when it isn't.

"I guess." A worried look crosses his face. "Is everything alright, Kal?"

"Yes, just tired," I assure him, turning my head toward him, softening my demeanor.

Throughout the night, sleep eludes me. I wake constantly, completely drenched in sweat. Thankfully, living on the ground floor has its advantages—I can exercise in the middle of the night without disturbing anyone below me. I dedicate the next hour to activities like jumping jacks, jogging in place, ab workouts, and various other exercises, working up a sweat.

Afterward, I indulge in a hot shower, washing away the sweat before returning to bed.

The following morning, I contemplate whether I ever managed to fully fall asleep. I more so feel like I spent the entire night living in a different make-believe dimension in my mind.

Feeling sore from my workout and lumpy mattress, I ease myself out of bed, slowly getting myself ready for my therapy session. Instead of driving, I decide to walk the two miles, enjoying the brisk cold air. I remind myself repeatedly if I want Maeva's help, I need to tell her what's going on.

Upon reaching my destination, the receptionist, a delightful brunette named Tori, welcomes me warmly.

"Feel free to head on back, Kalyn. Maeva is expecting you," she says cheerfully, pointing gracefully towards Maeva's office. I return a smile to her and make my way towards the open door.

I meet with her every week... correction, I'm supposed to meet with her every week—but I'm a flake and cancel more times than I care to admit. Our sessions always follow the same routine. We talk about how I'm doing, if my eating habits have improved, and what activities I'm doing to keep myself busy. But there's one question she asks that I dread the most.

"How are you sleeping, Kalyn?" she asks, sitting across from me with her legs folded.

Instantly, my mind reels back to the previous night. My dreams consistently commence in the same way—Wyatt. Memories flood in, from stolen glances at work, to the escapades in the copy room, staying late for intimate encounters in his office, my office, or the conference room. It was magical until it wasn't.

He used to express an insatiable desire for me, praising how my full breasts were hardly contained in my form-fitting dresses. Every chance he got, he would explore my body, touching and kissing me. We spent so much time at his place that it felt like I practically lived there. Everything seemed perfect until Wyatt changed. His attitude grew curt, and he began hurling derogatory names at me.

During outings with friends, if any other guy even dared talk to me, Wyatt would spend the entire night branding me with hurtful accusations and insisting I go sleep with the guy. It was a toxic cycle that I couldn't escape from. But then, one day, as I entered the copy room, I discovered Wyatt with the new intern, in a position reminiscent of the countless times he had me before. By the end of the workday, I found myself terminated due to alleged poor work quality. No doubt Wyatt had a hand in my termination because I am a damn hard worker. Instead of standing up for myself, I gave in without a fight.

I recall packing up my belongings from my desk, hoping Wyatt would come in and apologize. I even went as far as hoping he would come groveling into my office, begging for forgiveness, but he never did. For three consecutive days, I cried nonstop until I couldn't bear the heartache any longer.

In the pouring rain, I walked to his house, pounded on the door, and *she* answered wearing nothing but his work shirt. The woman I had seen having sex with him in the copy room just days before. She looked at me, mid-laugh, and asked, "What are you doing here?" as if I was the one who shouldn't be there.

When Wyatt appeared at the door, he greeted me with the same coldness, telling me to leave and declaring that he never wanted to see me again. He called me a whore, the nickname I had become so accustomed to being called and slammed the door in my face. I stood there trying to grapple with what had just happened until I could feel my brain urging me to move.

As I turned away from his door and started walking down the steps of his house, time seemed to stand still. A cyclist whizzed past, dinging a bell on his bike, alerting me to watch out, a couple laughed in the distance, a blacked-out SUV idled at the green traffic light, and the car behind it honked incessantly, causing me to quicken my pace.

Tears streamed down my face, and I tried my best to hold myself together. As I walked by the SUV, I couldn't shake off the feeling of being watched, intensifying my self-consciousness. It seemed as though those eyes had witnessed what had transpired at Wyatt's, and I feel they are probably amused, hidden within the comforts of their vehicle.

I felt like a complete fool, with the whole street witnessing my life falling apart right in front of me. The vehicle behind the SUV honked again, startling me and forcing me to quicken my pace. Determined to distance myself, I tightly wrapped my coat around me and hurried back to my apartment.

I can still feel the rawness of the entire incident, even though it happened almost four years ago.

"Kalyn?" Maeva asks again. I assume she must have repeated my name a few times, judging by the look on her face.

"Fine, I have been sleeping fine," I lie. These are moments where I dislike myself. I never speak up. Last night, when I made this appointment, I promised myself I would be honest with her about everything. She should start calling me Pinocchio because here I am, lying. Not wanting to burden her, I've chosen to handle my problems on my own, convincing myself that I can manage them independently, even though I recognize that it's her job to help me navigate through them and find solutions.

Our session ends and I pretty much wasted an hour of both of our time. She urges me to schedule the next appointment before I leave. However, I tell her that I'll need to check my schedule and get back to her like I always do. Lately, instead of our usual weekly sessions, I've been going weeks between visits, only reaching out when I'm at my wit's end.

On my way home, I notice a bakery sign that reads NOW HIRING. This is exactly how I got the job at Milo's. I went in, filled out an application, and he had me start on the spot. Maybe I can get lucky the same way twice. I walk in and ask for an application. The woman promptly hands it to me, and I complete it. Before leaving, I ask about the hiring manager's availability, learning they are in every morning. I make a mental note to come back tomorrow and speak with them.

I continue my journey home, checking out a few more places and asking about any job openings. Even if they say they're not hiring right now, I still ask for an application, just to be prepared.

Returning home, a feeling of accomplishment fills me for applying to so many businesses. But I don't stop there. I grab my phone and keep on submitting online job applications for the next couple of hours.

A week has gone by since I was laid off from Milo's Diner. I have spent countless hours applying for jobs, following up on applications, and not getting a single response.

But today, I've had enough. I'm taking matters into my own hands. I climb off my bed and quickly throw on my coat, sling my bag across my chest, and head out the door.

Just as I am locking up, I notice a flyer taped to my door.

"Live-in-maid needed urgently. In-person interview," the headline reads, with the date being just two days away.

"This could be my chance," I think to myself, clutching the flyer tightly.

With little left to lose and minimal possessions to my name, I make a spontaneous decision at that moment—I am going for it. And just like that, I load my car with everything I deem indispensable, aware that I am leaving this dismal place behind. Deep down, I can feel that I'm finally on the right path.

I stop by the apartment complex office to turn my key in. The manager all but celebrates right there as I place it on his desk.

"A trade," he says, handing me a folded piece of paper. "I planned on dropping it by today," he proudly adds, attempting to hike his pants higher, but his large belly gives no room for movement.

"An eviction notice," I read out loud as I unfold the paper.

"And the back rent is still due. You have seventeen days to get it to me at my apartment or you'll go to jail," he says smugly, tossing out a random number, thinking he was really doing something there.

"Oh, okay," I respond, "I was hoping you could also charge me double interest for every day that I might be late," knowing my sarcasm is completely lost on him. I turn and make my way out the door, leaving him standing there, absentmindedly scratching his round belly.

CHAPTER
Two

KALYN

Anticipation courses through me as I embark on the extended journey to the live-in maid interview. Fueled by the assurance that this opportunity would be a fresh start, I am determined to abandon the heartbreak of the past behind. The lengthy seventeen-hour drive is a soundtrack of my favorite tunes on Apple Music, with the windows down and the wind tousling my hair.

My hand playfully dances in the breeze, creating a sense of liberation and affirming that this journey marks a pivotal moment in my life. The open road becomes a symbol of new beginnings, drowning out the echoes of the past.

My tires hum against the worn asphalt, the landscape gradually transforms into a canvas of untamed beauty down winding back roads to the middle of nowhere. The road is flanked by weathered wooden fences and overgrown foliage. Rustic barns with fading red paint, their roofs sagging under the weight of years gone by.

As the road extends farther, the signs of human presence dwindle, and the landscape blurs to blends of rolling hills and endless skies.

My phone alerts me that I will reach my destination in fourteen miles. Although it seems unlikely that anything remarkable will unfold in such a short span, I keep driving.

A wave of excitement courses through me, prompting me to grab my phone and fling it out of the sunroof. I watch it shatter on the ground through my rearview mirror, grinning at the realization that it was the ultimate tie to the past, and I've now severed that connection as well.

C'est la vie.

Nearing the fourteen-mile mark, a hint of confusion creeps in.

With only dense trees on either side of the road, the only visible sight of maybe something is a paved road to the left, flanked by two open double gates and thick trees on both sides. Even though there is no sign of a house, I decide to follow the driveway.

Lengthy asphalt stretches ahead, and towering trees that create a natural canopy of shade are all I can see. Beyond the trees, meticulously manicured grass peeks through. The driveway gracefully leads to a vast, rectangular-shaped roundabout with a grand water fountain at its center, with eight spouts gracefully arcing in the air.

Slowly emerging into view is the most massive mansion I have ever seen. Around twenty cars are neatly arranged along the driveway, and it occurs to me that they must all be here for interviews.

Another driveway catches my attention, splitting off and curving to the right, vanishing from sight. Farther ahead, another drive veers to the left, extending toward the left side of the mansion. Its expanse has me struggling to gauge its complete width. I am intrigued by an arch between the house and a separate part of the house, what seems to be a spacious garage. Although I can't see what lies beyond the drive in that direction, it seems like no one else is over in that area.

Finding a suitable space to park amidst the row of cars, I carefully position my vehicle right behind the car in front of me, allowing enough space for them to pull out if they leave before me. Stepping out, I make sure I'm generously spaced off to the side, providing ample room for two vehicles traveling in opposite directions to pass without any risk of contact. Even in this remote location, I instinctively lock my car, safeguarding my belongings, similar to a raccoon trying to protect its junk.

Two individuals wearing chef coats are chatting near a side area to the left of the front door. They continue their conversation, gradually heading towards a steep walkway that seems to be the designated spot for food deliveries. Since there are no other signs or instructions mentioned in the flyer about where to enter for the interview, I decide to follow them up the walkway. The lack of clear instructions leaves me relying on their movements as the only apparent direction in this unfamiliar place.

Stepping through the entrance the two other employees just took, I find myself in a grand hallway. On one side, walk-in freezer doors line the wall. Continuing down the corridor, a large open doorway to the right unfolds into a staff lounge that is just as shocking as the rest of the house. The lounge has plush seating, a pool table, and round tables surrounded by soft chairs for the staff to comfortably eat their food. There are recliners and couches arranged strategically around a large flat-screen TV at the far end.

One wall stands out with a row of four massage chairs, each with button pads allowing individuals to customize their massage to personal preferences. Walking past, I gaze longingly at the massage chairs, imagining how incredible they must feel. I recall sitting in similar ones at the mall, although not as luxurious as these, and I doubt they were ever cleaned. The level of comfort and sophistication in these chairs suggests they cost way more than a mall is willing to spend.

Approaching the end of the hallway, I'm met with the entrance to a grand chef's kitchen—a space capable of preparing meals for parties hosting a hundred or more people. The sheer size of this entire kitchen has my mouth hanging open. It has multiple cooking stations, each equipped with ovens, grills, and large pots neatly arranged on the counters. The room is filled with the sounds of sizzling pans and rhythmic chopping. Everything is well-organized with a variety of utensils neatly placed for easy access. On another wall, there are enormous refrigerators that I imagine are stocked with an abundance of fresh and healthy ingredients.

Turning slowly in circles, I try to take in every detail of the room. I'm completely captivated, causing me to miss someone approaching.

"Hello, dear," a kind older woman greets me, presumably aware that I am not in the intended area. She has an air of authority about her, making me think she might be in charge. She's wearing a long black skirt that elegantly falls past her knees, paired with a chef's coat. Her hair is neatly secured into a clip, and a subtle touch of makeup enhances her features.

"Hi, I'm Kalyn," I greet her warmly, raising the flyer. "I'm here for an interview. I wasn't entirely sure where I was supposed to be going, and I didn't want to disturb the owners by walking in the front door," I explain awkwardly, attempting to maintain a friendly demeanor.

"I see," she responds, her hands clasped in front of her skirt as she smiles. "I'm Gladys. Do you have any experience in a kitchen?" she inquires, her question leading me to believe that I am indeed in the right place, and she will be the one conducting my interview. Yet, the flyer specified a live-in maid position, and it seems I might be interviewing for a cook position, which makes me nervous and should absolutely make her nervous.

"Kitchen experience… I have kitchen experience," I mention, as she hangs on to my every word waiting for me to continue. I inevitably admit my lack of kitchen experience but proceed by trying to convince her that I am a quick learner and enjoy being in the kitchen. She must pick up on this lie instantly. With a playful wink, she takes hold of my hand and gives it a pat, commenting on how I look like I know how to clean—which is true. Cleaning has always been my go-to when dealing with any kind of emotion, whether it's happiness, sadness, or especially anger.

"Come with me, dear," Gladys says in a sweet tone, "You can handle cleaning." She leads me away from the kitchen, guiding me through the mansion. We traverse a labyrinth of hallways, large rooms, spiral staircases, and more hallways. It's unclear whether she's deliberately pacing herself to allow me a chance to take in my surroundings or if she naturally moves at a slow pace. Either way, I sense she's allowing me to appreciate the remarkable home.

We reach a generously sized room where the chairs, though aesthetically pleasing, appear more designed for visual appeal than comfort. In one corner, a grand piano sits beside large windows that stretch from floor to ceiling, with curtains that match the entire height. At the center of the far-left wall is a massive fireplace, although it appears untouched. The marble floor, pristine throughout the house, continues the same impeccable pattern in this room.

This house drips of money.

As I scan the room, my eyes fall on a tall, slender brunette wearing high stiletto heels, a knee-length green dress that hugs her figure, and her hair is tightly pulled back into a bun. She's engaged in a conversation with other potential housekeeping candidates.

Just looking at her makes my skin prickle.

"Miss Jenevieve," Gladys says curtly. "This is one of your new girls, Kalyn."

Jenevieve pauses talking. She stands as still as a statue for long enough I think she may not have heard Gladys speaking. But the other girls staring at us lets me know she heard just fine. She pivots on her heel, her eyes scanning me from head to toe, and simply says, "All positions have been filled," then redirects her attention to the other girls she was just chatting with.

Gladys interjects, "Full or not, she's part of your staff now." I am picking up on an entirely separate heated conversation taking place between the two of them that I am not quite privy to.

"It seems like YOU have extra space on *your* staff," Jenevieve remarks. "Hire her for the kitchen," she shoots me a disdainful look before refocusing on Gladys.

Gladys persists once again. "Miss Jenevieve."

I instantly notice a subtle twitch from her every time Gladys refers to her as "Miss." It seems there's more to these pleasantries than mere politeness.

"Kalyn will be joining your staff. Will that be an issue for you?" Gladys questions, her tone leaving no room for disagreement.

Jenevieve shoots a piercing look at Gladys, her eyes narrowing into thin slits before she shifts her attention to me. "Go sit over there, Kara," she mistakenly calls me by a different name. "We'll head back to the maid's quarters shortly," she tries to sound unfazed as she dismisses both Gladys and me, but she is visibly angered.

I exchange questioning glances with Gladys, both of us aware that Jenevieve isn't thrilled about my presence. "Come, sweetie. I'll show you to your room," Gladys wraps her arm around mine and guides me away. "Pay no mind to her."

I notice that Gladys isn't walking as slowly as before, which clears up my earlier confusion. She can actually move quite fast; she was purposely pacing herself. The distance from where we were before is quite significant, making me realize that I might need a map to navigate this home.

The maid's quarters are located far enough from the main section of the house, I don't think there would be any way for us to disturb the owners, which is obviously the intention. The house has an almost L-shaped layout on this side. We round a corner proceeding down a lengthy corridor, eventually reaching a pair of large double doors to the right.

Upon entering, I'm struck by how spacious it is. It's a mansion inside of a mansion. Walking down a wide corridor, it opens to a lounge area on the left, with a fancy flat-screen TV, oversized couches, and a staircase that leads to an unknown destination. Continuing ahead, various rooms unfold—a gaming room, an exercise space, and finally the grand hallway extending straight ahead, with two other hallways branching off from it. Doors line either side, reminiscent of a luxury hotel. As we pass, I peer down each hallway, curious about all the rooms.

Gladys leads me down the hall to the room at the very end. Pausing at the door, she beams, "Here we are," she gestures as if presenting the door to me. "It's unlocked, dear. Go on in."

It feels like she must have been waiting for me. Yet, that's impossible as I have never met her before, and she had no idea I would drive seventeen hours just to come interview.

I push the door open, entering a room covered in soft pinks, silvers, and gold. The sheer size momentarily stuns me. The main area alone dwarfs the size of my entire apartment. As I take a few more steps inside, I marvel at the beauty. The presence of a king-size bed strikes me as unsuitable for someone in a modest housekeeping role, leaving me genuinely confused. "I don't get it?"

Gladys, too, surveys the room, appreciating its aesthetics before redirecting her gaze towards me. "What were you expecting, dear? A cot in a dusty dungeon?" she quips, proceeding further in continuing the tour.

A small laugh escapes my lips, and I admit, "Yes, honestly, that's pretty much exactly what I was expecting."

Exploring the room with Gladys, I'm amazed at the luxurious details. The walls feature identical hues of pink, gold, and silver, complemented by mirrors and other decorative elements. There's a cozy sitting area with plush pink chairs and a small coffee table. The window coverings, matching the overall color scheme, drape gracefully from ceiling to floor. The sheer contrast between my expectations and the reality of this room is nothing short of astonishing.

"Rest assured, dear, Mr. Everett upholds a standard of treating his staff with the utmost dignity," she affirms, gesturing for me to follow her.

She leads me to a petite kitchenette and a spacious master bathroom, complete with a roomy walk-in closet. This all seems a little extreme for someone who will be paid to live here.

"I don't want to come across as unappreciative, but it seems you may have mistaken me for someone else," I admit, all the while enchanted by the inviting glow of the well-lit bathroom.

"While I'm certain you're exceptional, all accommodations offer the same amenities," Gladys explains. "Your official start date is Monday if you accept the position, but you're welcome to move in immediately. Your designated suite number conveniently corresponds to your parking spot in the underground garage. Once all your documents are signed, there will be a sign-on bonus for you. You're encouraged to gather any supplies you may need for the week leading up to Monday," she nearly continues her guidance until Jenevieve enters, accompanied by a group of girls.

"What's going on in here?" Jenevieve questions Gladys, glancing between her and me.

"I was showing Kalyn her room and giving her a quick rundown of what to expect," Gladys beams.

"Her room?" Jenevieve raises an eyebrow, annoyed.

"Yes," Gladys asserts firmly.

"You may go, Gladys. I'll take it from here," Jenevieve says dismissively.

Gladys gives my hand a reassuring squeeze and winks before leaving. This subtle gesture makes me instantly feel calm.

Jenevieve gathers the group of girls and informs them that following dinner, they are expected to go back to the maid's quarters until work begins promptly at 8:00 each morning. Abruptly halting her instructions, she turns her attention towards me.

"Why are you just standing there? Are you not a new hire?" she questions, clearly irritated that I was still captivated by *my* new room.

"Sorry," I respond, swiftly joining the end of the line.

"I didn't ask you to speak," she retorts, shooting a sharp glare in my direction.

I catch the hint and offer a nod of acknowledgment, making it clear that I understand her expectations.

Jenevieve's demeanor gives a drill sergeant-like authority, but fortunately, I've mastered the art of knowing when to keep my mouth shut. "*Thank you, Wyatt,*" I silently share my sarcastic gratitude.

As we enter a conference-style room, Jenevieve continues to pepper us with rules. There are already five other girls seated inside. She instructs us to find a seat and the six of us who just arrived quickly find empty spots. Jenevieve takes her place at the front, guiding us through a stack of papers laid out before us— our year-long contract. Without much thought, everyone signs the documents without reading them, and she moves around the table to collect the papers. I sense her stopping behind me, her hand outstretched to retrieve my signed papers.

"I'm still reading through the contract," I mention, anticipating that she would continue collecting the remaining contracts.

"Do you want the job or not?" she inquires sternly. "The door is unlocked if you don't," she nods her chin towards the exit.

Reluctantly, I cave and quickly scribble my signature across the papers, handing them over to her. She rolls her eyes in response, clicking her heels around the table with an air of impatience. Passing the piles of papers to a girl positioned at the front, Jenevieve instructs, "Get these filed," before addressing the rest of us.

"Monday through Friday, until your shift concludes, you're expected to remain on the premises. Any necessary departures during this time require permission from your assigned leads. Your weekends are your own, but remember, you're an extension of this mansion, representing Mr. Everett's reputation. By Monday at 8:00 AM, you're to be back for work. We pride ourselves on reliable staff. Your weekend activities are your business, but while here, work diligently and avoid creating drama. It's not ladylike," she emphasizes, casting a pointed glance in my direction.

"I strongly advise against getting involved with other staff members. While it may happen, if feelings get hurt, it's your problem. You'll still be required to work with said staff member. This area is exclusively for the housekeeping staff. There's a shared space for all staff members across the way. I'm sure you'll become familiar with it," she remarks, subtly implying something less than "ladylike" about us.

"If you have any further questions, seasoned housekeepers are available to assist. Thank you and welcome," she concludes her speech before briskly stomping out of the room.

Stillness blankets the area, leaving us unsure of what to do next. The silence is broken when a stunning blonde with a sleek, shoulder-length A-line cautiously peeks through the doorway.

"Everyone can relax now; she's gone. Make yourselves comfortable," she reassures us with a welcoming smile.

I stand from the table, taking the initiative to walk towards the door.

"I've got my car parked out front, I think I'm supposed to move it to the parking garage?" I mention, hoping she can tell me the correct procedure, as I'm unsure whether I should keep it along the driveway.

"I'm Shayla," she introduces herself happily, extending her hand toward me. "My friends call me Shay, so feel free to do the same," I reach out to shake her hand, and she continues, "I'll show you where to go. Do you know your suite number?"

"Yeah, it's 19," I answer, pointing toward the door at the end of the hallway.

"Well, neighbor, that's easy enough—I'm 18," she says cheerfully.

"I'm Kalyn, by the way," I acknowledge her earlier introduction.

Shayla guides me through the house, leading us out a side door and down the lengthy driveway to where my car is parked. She accompanies me as we make our way to the underground parking area, providing clear instructions on where to park. She also generously helps me carry all my belongings inside. It may not seem like much, but it would have taken me at least four trips on my own.

"I can always come back for the rest of this," I mention to Shay, who is piling her arms full of my belongings.

"Nonsense, we're not weak. I'd rather have my arms fall off than make two trips," she laughs, stacking more items into her overflowing arms. "After you've settled in today, I'd love to take you into town so you can gather supplies for the week, and I can give you a tour of the area," she offers. "I have some errands to run as well, but would enjoy the company."

"Thank you," I feel grateful for her unexpected kindness.

"It's a lot, right? But don't worry, you'll get the hang of it," she reassures.

"I guess I don't have a choice. I just got strong-armed into signing a contract I didn't even read," I say, as we stand outside our bedroom doors after dropping all my stuff off on my bed.

Down the hall, a shorter girl with curly auburn hair appears, carrying a huge box that hides her face from my view. She stops at the door to her room, located right across from Shay's.

"Shay!" she cries out after struggling with the door for a few moments.

Shay pushes herself off the wall with the leg she was leaning against. "I just wanted to see if you could do it," she jokes as she swings the door open for the girl.

Disappearing into the room, she returns breathless, but this time without the bulky box. Her face is round and bright red as she wipes her hands down the front of her dress, extending her hand in my direction.

"Lilly," she introduces herself with a friendly smile.

I shake her hand, instantly noting its clamminess. "Kalyn," I respond. "Is it your first day too?" assuming it must be since she was carrying boxes as well.

"Oh no, I went shopping," she exclaims excitedly. "Want to see what I got?"

"Well, of course, why wouldn't I?" I rhetorically ask, seeing how happy she is over whatever she bought. In turn, it sparks my curiosity and excitement for her.

She shows a box full of different colored wide-brimmed hats, like ones you would see from the Victorian era or of someone going to the horse races. They are beautiful, really, and would match with her vibrant-colored poofy dress she is wearing.

I dedicate the remainder of the day to unboxing and organizing my belongings, feeling accomplished as I set up my room.

The following morning, Shay energetically knocks on my bedroom door and strides in before I can respond, exclaiming, "Let's go, we're going shopping!"

I struggled to sleep last night, so I woke up early and got ready for the day. It makes situations like this a breeze because she won't have to wait on me. Stepping out of my room, Lilly and another newcomer, Amber, engage in conversation outside Lilly's room. "Where are you two off to?" Lilly asks.

"We're heading to town. Do you guys want to join?" Shay offers, prompting Lilly to eagerly respond with "I'd love to," as Amber follows behind her.

During our twenty-minute drive, we find ourselves surrounded by breathtaking landscapes as we are led down winding roads.

The town we arrive at is unexpectedly larger than I imagined, with charming buildings and beautifully arranged storefronts adorned with colorful flower boxes. The streets are spotless, making it look even more pristine. Lining the streets are cute cafes with inviting outdoor seating, and locals move about, contributing to the town's lively feel.

Shay expertly parks her jeep by the curb in front of a lingerie store. "C'mon," she urges, gracefully stepping out.

"Special occasion?" I tease as we approach the vibrant pink entrance.

"Uhh, why are we going in here?" Amber asks, a hint of discomfort in her voice.

Shay grins and opens the door. "Relax, we're just here for some cozy pajamas."

The store unfolds into a treasure trove of silky fabrics and vibrant colors. This is my first time coming to a store like this and it instantly ignites my excitement.

"Get whatever you want," Shay says to me, "Mr. Everett, our boss, owns this place. He owns the majority of the town," she adds, trying to recall what other places he owns. "Anyways, they know me here. Our purchases are put on his nonexistent tab," she air quotes nonexistent.

At the storefront, an array of pajamas and loungewear greets us. Within the pajama section is a collection of comfortable sleepwear, ranging from silk nighties to plush robes and matching sets.

Towards the back of the store, there's a discreet area for more intimate items like lingerie.

We peruse the store, and I pick out some silk nighties and a few matching bra and panty sets.

Just as Shay promised, checking out is a breeze. Satisfied with our selections, we decide to continue our shopping spree and head to a clothing boutique just down the road.

The boutique isn't too far from our current location, so we walk to it. I find myself captivated by everything inside. The wooden floor echoes with the soft patters of our footsteps. The air has a delicate hint of floral-scented candles, creating a soothing ambiance. Illuminated with a mix of natural light filtering through lace curtains and strategically placed vintage-inspired lamps. Soft music plays in the background. Floral wallpaper covers the walls, and ornate mirrors give an elegant touch. Divided into various rooms, the store offers diverse shopping sections. Racks of clothes showcase an array of styles, from dainty dresses to fashionable tops, each piece meticulously arranged to create an aesthetically pleasing display.

Shay holds up a dress and turns it in my direction. She looks it over, inspecting it, and then up at me, "This would look amazing on you!"

"You should get it," I encourage her.

Slightly leaning towards me wearing an expression of mock defeat, her arms fall to her side, still holding the dress.

"Why do you choose baggy clothes when I can see you have a nice figure drowning underneath?" she exaggerates her expression. "Wanna have some fun? Let's pick out an outfit for each other," she suggests excitedly.

It seems entertaining, so I agree.

Browsing through the racks, I pick out a couple pairs of shorts, a set of pants, and three tops for myself. For Shay, I come across a pair of distressed skinny jeans, a crisp white blouse, and a stylish tan cardigan. Although I might not be entirely certain of her style, I can envision her effortlessly pulling off this ensemble—it's difficult to imagine her not looking fantastic in anything.

I find Lilly captivated by a section of the store with chic plus-size clothing, holding onto an armful of clothes she has already picked out.

"Can I help you hold some of that, Lilly?" I offer, extending a hand to assist her in managing some of the clothes.

"This is the only spot in town where I can find clothes that fit me. I get overly excited every time I come here," she shares, continuing to gather more clothes, beaming from ear to ear.

Lilly's arms become even more full, and an employee approaches us with a rolling cart rack, taking the clothing and freeing up Lilly's arms to continue gathering more items. She mentions the rack will be near the checkout counter for easier browsing.

Shay joins us, a mischievous grin on her face, "Do we want to wear our surprise outfits now?"

"Let me see it first," I raise a brow at her.

She lets out a laugh, "It will fully cover all your private parts... and your knees. Come on," she insists, tugging at my arm. "Can we have two fitting rooms, please?"

The employee agrees, leading us to the dressing area with oversized purple curtains for walls. We exchange outfits, and I take mine into my room to examine it. Shay didn't do too bad. It's something I would have worn pre-Wyatt: a thin-strapped floral dress meant to fit snugly around the chest and waist, flowing gracefully just below the knees. It's paired with a lightweight cardigan that perfectly matches the dress, along with tan wedges.

Slipping into the outfit, I'm pleasantly surprised by how well it fits.

"This is adorable!" Shay exclaims from the other side of the curtain. "Let me see you," she yanks open my curtain without checking to see if I'm dressed. Her mouth animatedly hangs open as she stares at me. "Damn, Kalyn, why are you hiding those under baggy shirts?" she points to my chest, eliciting a laugh from me.

"Do you like your outfit?" I note she looks just as good as I expected.

"I love it!" she holds up the tags. "I already removed them. Do you like yours?"

"I actually do," I admit, turning to admire my reflection in the mirror once more.

Shay leans over and swiftly removes the tag from the dress. "Good," she announces, leaving before I can change my mind. My amusement bubbles out, and I shake my head, gathering my previous clothes in my arms before stepping out. The employee has already bagged each of our items separately. Shay holds an empty bag for her changed clothes. "Hey, want to toss your clothes in with mine?" She suggests, pointing to the open bag.

I approach and combine my clothes with hers.

Leaving the boutique, we carry all our findings to Shay's jeep and stow them in the very back.

"Can we get lunch already?" Lilly asks, her forehead beading with sweat.

"I'm pretty hungry too," I respond, nodding in agreement.

We walk along the sidewalk, absorbing the immaculately kept surroundings of this town. The sidewalks are so clean we could probably eat off of them, and the buildings are meticulously maintained. It feels like an ideal place to live. In the town's center is a spacious circular park area with a fountain. Fortunately, the park is encircled by restaurants, making our search for somewhere to eat quite convenient.

Arriving at the restaurant Lilly chose, we are seated on the patio to enjoy the vibrant view of the town. "You know what this place reminds me of? Disneyland. It feels like we stepped into Disneyland, minus the characters," I mention, glancing around, feeling at ease.

"It really does, doesn't it?" Amber agrees.

We enjoy a delightful lunch, and the food lives up to my expectations. Shay insists on paying for our meals, a gesture met with adamant protests from both Amber and me. Eventually, we give in and let her treat us.

I take in every part of the impressive surroundings. The town appears even larger than I initially thought, with some buildings stretching up to six stories. I notice apartments down the road from the main town area, prompting me to ask, "How many people live here?" Since this is such a remote location, I'm surprised by the town's size.

Shay ponders for a moment before responding, "I'm not exactly sure, maybe around fifty thousand."

Curious, "Do all the mansion staff live there?"

Shay shakes her head, explaining, "No, not everyone. Many of them live locally and commute daily. Living at the mansion, you have to live by the rules of Jenevieve."

The way she says that sends chills down my spine. Even hearing Jenevieve's name makes me sit up straighter and feel tense.

After we finish lunch, we casually walk back to Shay's jeep. The pleasant stroll allows us to enjoy the scenery and continue our easygoing conversation. Shay points out different stores and tells us about the town's history. Then, we make our way back to the mansion.

Shay and I spend time in each other's rooms until Sunday evening, with Lilly and Amber randomly coming to hang out too. Shay and I seem to have developed a strong bond. She shares details with me about her background—attending private school, dropping out of a top-notch law school—and then describes how she fell in love with a stranger in an airport while waiting to fly home. They discover not only are they on the same flight, but they share side-by-side seats. They engage in conversation throughout the flight, parting ways with only the knowledge of each other's names.

However, showcasing her sleuth skills, Shayla managed to find him online, track down his employer, and secure a job as a maid in the very house where he works.

"How exactly does that work for a relationship?" I ask, wondering how they see each other if we aren't allowed to have anyone in the maid's quarters.

She grins at me, "Who's going to stop us? Jenevieve? Jonathan is Mr. Everett's best friend, which I was not aware of when I was worming around to get this job," she quips. "Plus, when he is home, we typically stay in his room since it's way nicer."

"What's Mr. Everett's story?" I ask curiously.

"Well, he comes from money. His family is a bunch of rich tighty whities, he owns a million businesses, he is the head of the mob..." she trails off.

My eyes dart to hers, and she reacts with spontaneous thrill. "Oh my word, your eyes are the size of dinner plates. I was just trying to see if you were paying attention," she continues laughing. "All of that is true except the mob part. I don't really know what he does for work. I know he owns a lot of successful businesses, but I never ask Jonathan, and he never volunteers information."

"How do you like working here?" feeling like this is the most important question.

"Free room and board, good pay, sexy boyfriend. Can't complain," she replies with a smirk.

"Jenevieve seems... interesting," I pause before saying the last word.

"Jenevieve is a bitch," Shay says matter-of-factly. "She loves making people's lives miserable. Just keep your head down and stay out of her way, and you should be fine."

The peaceful weekend ends when the clicking sound of Jenevieve's heels echoes into the maid's quarters.

"Ladies," she announces loudly. "For many of you, tomorrow will mark your first day on the job. I expect well-rested staff in the morning. Don't stay up too late, and we will meet first thing in the morning. You will wear your required uniform," she barks out, glancing around at each of us, and then turns on her heels, retracing her steps back the way she came.

CHAPTER
Three

KALYN

Morning comes too quickly, and I find myself still tired from grappling with a restless night, haunted by the usual nightmares featuring Wyatt. As my groggy mind clears upon waking, I realize it is my first day in my new role.

Climbing out of bed, I quickly get dressed in the required maid uniform—a conventional knee-length black dress with white lace accents along the collar and cuffs. A white apron cinched at the waist completes the ensemble, with matching slip-on shoes.

Stepping into the hallway, I am met by a sea of black and white uniforms worn by the other housekeeping staff. However, one noticeable distinction emerges—each of them has received a perfectly fitted uniform delivered to their rooms the night before, while mine inexplicably seems two sizes too big. I ponder this oddity, wondering if it was a consequence of potentially being a late hire, or perhaps a simple oversight.

Jenevieve methodically strolls up and down the hall, organizing the girls into groups. The anticipation is palpable as the other housekeeping staff eagerly disperses, seamlessly integrating into their newly formed teams. Meanwhile, seven of us remain with Jenevieve, and I unconsciously let out a brief disappointed sigh. "*One year, Kalyn,*" I remind myself, steeling my resolve.

Jenevieve turns her attention to us. "You are all new. Your first day will be with me," she declares sternly. The weight of her expectations hangs in the air, and I brace myself for the challenges that lie ahead under her watchful eye.

"Lucky us," Vanessa, a brunette I recognize from our first day here, whispers conspiratorially to another newcomer, Erica, standing beside her, and a shared chuckle escapes their lips.

Jenevieve, with her sharp instincts, catches wind of the hushed comment. "What was that?" she demands, causing the giggles to cease immediately.

"What did you just say?" Jenevieve directs her attention to me, stomping over and locking eyes with an intensity that could cut through metal.

"I didn't say anything," I respond, maintaining unwavering eye contact.

"I just heard you say something, what did you say?" she repeats through gritted teeth, the tension in the hallway escalating as her stern gaze pierces through the ambiguity. Vanessa and Erica remain silent while Jenevieve glares at me.

"I didn't say any—" Before I can finish the sentence, she backhands me. The force of the blow catches me off guard. Stunned, I cup my cheek, holding it for a moment before regaining my composure and lifting my head back up.

Jenevieve, not satisfied with the initial reprimand, seizes both sides of my face, pinching my cheeks between her long nails. With an intimidating proximity, she brings her face just a couple of inches from mine.

"I do not tolerate disrespectful staff, do you understand?" she utters through gritted teeth. With a final act of dominance, she releases my face, shoving it backward, leaving an unsettling tension in the wake of the encounter.

I contemplate responding by purposely addressing her as "sir" just to test her patience, but I quickly dismiss the thought. "Yes ma'am," I answer instead.

Even this response infuriates her. She stomps back over to me and delivers another backhanded blow to the opposite cheek. The initial strike caught me completely off guard; being subjected to physical assault for the first time in my life left me bewildered, so caught off guard I didn't respond. But this second slap… this slap feels even more devastating than the first. I'm left feeling utterly horrified, degraded, and small.

"Do I look like a ma'am?" she demands, clearly insulted by my attempt at respect. "You will call me Jenevieve. Not ma'am, not miss," she emphasizes with a hiss, establishing her dominance and reinforcing her expectation for a specific form of address.

My mind instantly recalls Gladys calling her 'Miss Jenevieve' and the evident irritation it caused. Opting to avoid further confrontation, I simply nod in acknowledgment of her demand.

We are led out of the house, my cheeks still stinging from her slaps. I catch a glimpse of my reflection in a passing mirror. They're both pink, resembling the aftermath of applying a bit too much blush. With a wry sense of humor, I tell myself, *'Free makeup,'* stifling an inward laugh.

We follow Jenevieve to the horse stables, entering a spacious room filled with an array of supplies. "Everyone grab a pair of boots," she instructs, pointing towards the wall lined with oversized rubber boots. Following her orders, we each select a pair, slipping them on over the shoes we are already wearing. No fashion statements will be made today.

Jenevieve, oddly joyful this time, announces, "You will be cleaning the horse stalls."

The prospect of cleaning out stalls slightly dampens my mood, and I brace myself for the less glamorous aspects of housekeeping duties in the grand mansion.

Claire, the self-identified horse groomer, steps forward to introduce herself as Jenevieve exits the stables. With a confident demeanor, she explains that she'll be demonstrating the proper technique for mucking a horse stall. She guides us in gathering the necessary supplies, then instructs us to follow her lead, wheeling the equipment out to the alleyway nestled between the rows of horse stalls.

In a concise and informative manner, Claire allocates each of us to a specific stall and points out the designated area for depositing horse manure. The practicalities of the task become clearer, and I appreciate Claire's guidance in navigating the unfamiliar but "essential duties" of maintaining the stables.

Once Claire is confident that she has provided all the necessary instructions, she allows us to begin our work. She mentions if we need any assistance, she'll be grooming the horses in the adjacent building.

We spend all morning mucking out the stalls. I'm sweating and glad I threw my hair up in a messy bun before starting work. I continue filling the wheelbarrow with horse manure when I feel someone watching me at the gate. I ignore them at first and after a moment, finally speak up, "Why don't you come in here and help if you have nothing better to do than just stand there," I say, annoyed, without bothering to turn around.

"What will I get in return if I help you?" I hear a joking tone in his voice.

I stop shoveling and turn my head back to look at him, propping my arm on the end of my shovel. "Wow, that's real smooth.

You could keep on walking, or you can get me hurling horse shit at you," I sarcastically smile.

"I don't want either of those options," A grin spreads across his face, "Do you have any other options?" Leaning on the gate to the stall, he rests his chin on his arms, waiting for my response.

"Is she bothering you?" Vanessa's voice reaches me before I see her. She directs the question to the man standing at my gate.

"Not at all," he responds happily. "We were just enjoying each other's company," he tells Vanessa, but his eyes stay fixed on me.

I roll my eyes, unimpressed, and continue shoveling manure, determined to stay focused despite the unwelcomed attention.

"I need to go to the bathroom—can you show me where it is?" Vanessa asks him flirtatiously.

"Uhh, sure," he responds hesitantly, standing up from the gate. "See you around..." he trails off, expecting me to provide my name.

"I'm Vanessa," she cuts in.

"Brad," he introduces himself back, tapping the gate a couple of times. "See you around," he points in my direction, but I pretend not to hear him, disregarding the annoying conversation he was attempting to have with me.

I complete my stall, meticulously laying down fresh hay, and step out, admiring the thoroughly cleaned enclosure. I feel accomplished as I shut the gate behind me. Vanessa returns, casually strolling back into the stables with a devilish glint playing on her face, and her mouth reddened. She nonchalantly wipes both sides of her mouth and attempts to straighten her dark hair. She's smirking at Erica, and I easily fill in the blanks as to why she was absent for an hour, trying not to think about the not-so-subtle escapades that just took place in the bathroom.

Suddenly, the dreaded sound of clicking heels reaches my ears.

"How is it going, ladies?" Jenevieve asks, her presence cutting through the background sounds of the stables.

Nobody says anything, so I respond, "Good," thinking she was looking for a response. However, she ignores my contribution.

"Before we go to lunch, I want to see the progress," she declares, continuing to walk up and down the stalls, inspecting each one. When she reaches Vanessa's stall, she comes to a sudden stop and just stares into it, her face displaying an indecipherable blend of scrutiny and anticipation, leaving her thoughts shrouded in mystery. Each of us stiffens as we wait.

"Kara, come here," Jenevieve commands, her gaze still fixed on the horse stall. The entire group stands frozen, awaiting further instructions. She repeats herself, this time more sternly, "Kara!" The silence persists until she turns her head and starts a deliberate walk toward me. Responding to her approach, I set the wheelbarrow down and straighten.

"Are you all of a sudden deaf?" she questions sharply upon reaching me, grabbing my arm, and digging her nails into my skin. In a forceful move, she drags me across the stable, causing me to almost trip on the oversized boots, before pushing me toward Vanessa's untouched stall. I catch myself on the gate before I face plant into it.

"Why does it look like this hasn't been touched?" she demands, pointing accusingly at the neglected stall. Before I can respond, she orders everyone else to clean up and head to lunch. "You will stay here and get this stall finished," she directs her attention exclusively to me.

"This isn't my stall," I stare in disbelief at what she is saying. The fact she had to walk across the stable to my stall, just to drag me down the alleyway to Vanessa's stall should be enough of a reminder that she is punishing the wrong person.

Our eyes lock as she steps closer. Sneering down at me, she sways her head. "I don't care if you've scrubbed every stall in this stable yourself, you're staying here and cleaning this one."

She is standing so close to me, that the exhale out of her nose is probably tousling my hair.

"What about lunch?" I am overly fatigued from my body being unaccustomed to this type of work. My stomach has been rumbling for the past two hours due to hunger.

"Lunch? *WE* are going to lunch now. I suppose *you* won't have time to eat lunch. Too bad," she remarks in a mocking, feigned sympathy tone, complete with a condescending pout.

As the rest of the group disperses, I hear Vanessa's laughter echoing in the distance as she walks away. Jenevieve follows suit, turning on her heel and departing, leaving me alone to rectify the perceived lapse in my duties.

Sweet, I think to myself, sarcastically acknowledging the irony of the situation. The desire to retaliate against Vanessa's actions crosses my mind, contemplating less diplomatic measures, like knocking her teeth out with my shovel. Maybe she can eat those for lunch. However, I quickly dismiss such thoughts, recognizing their futility and counter-productivity.

Instead, I channel my frustration into action, getting to work on mucking Vanessa's stall.

Brad, who has been observing from behind, unexpectedly comments. "You're a troublemaker," his tone laced with enjoyment.

Regardless of whether he is here or not, it doesn't change the fact that I will spend my entire lunch doing Vanessa's work. "How is that?" curious how he came to that conclusion.

Ignoring my question, he extends half of a sandwich to me, "Here," an unexpected gesture that momentarily catches me off guard.

I roll my eyes. "I don't want your dirty sandwich," I say, annoyed that he's even back from wherever he and Vanessa were doing their nasty deeds. Maybe he should come in here and complete her untouched work because he is precisely the reason she got nothing done.

I try to refocus, determined to ignore his presence with the faint hope that he'll eventually catch on to my disinterest.

However, his persistent cocky behavior suggests he has no intention of leaving.

He takes another bite. "You'd rather starve?" I detect a hint of amusement in his tone.

Growing more irritated at his words and the fact that I am incredibly hungry, I retort, "I would rather finish the failed work YOU caused someone else to not get done than be bothered by you."

Undeterred by my attempt to get him to scram by being an ass to him, he says, "You're already being sassy to me, and we barely know each other," clearly amused by the situation.

"You don't know me, and you are harassing me," I retort.

Isn't there some sort of rule against doing precisely what he is doing right now? He must be lonely out here with the horses to feel the need to bother the new maids... Maids. I am a maid. Why am I out here cleaning horse stalls and not cleaning the house?

His elation remains firmly planted, "Why won't you tell me your name?"

"What will knowing my name change? Will I be able to do my work in peace? Will I be able to do my work faster? Will you quit bothering me?" I fire back with a series of questions. I'm glad he's finding pleasure in this, but I've grown more annoyed with him as time passes.

He lets loose a laugh. "Yes, yes, and no. I'll tell you what, tell me your name, and I will bring you the hay for this stall," he lifts both brows as if he just presented me with the deal of a lifetime.

What an idiot.

My name won't benefit him in any way. "Wanda," my words drip with sarcasm. "My name is Wanda. Now, go get my hay."

He responds with laughter but walks away. Moments later, he returns with a wheelbarrow brimming with hay, wearing a satisfied expression as he places it in front of the stall where I'm diligently working. "Here you go, Wanda," he lets out an exaggerated exhale.

I'm surprised he follows through on his word, even though I know he doesn't actually believe my name is Wanda. I decide to give him a nickname to go with the dumbass games he's playing. "Thank you, Bert," I casually reply, aiming to give the impression that I, too, am oblivious to his real name.

With an unwavering grin, he adds, "I like you, Wanda. You can try and push me away, but I like you." He points his finger at me and walks away.

"Hey, Bert. You have a piece of pepper in your teeth," I call out to him, knowing he doesn't really. But it will force him to take time finding a mirror to check, and wasting his time brings me a sliver of joy.

Now that I have a pretty good hang of how to muck stalls, I finish quickly. After getting everything put back where it belongs, I experience a burning feeling on my arm and remember Jenevieve's talons digging into me. I lift my arm to check where the stinging is coming from and see my skin peeled back and bleeding in four places where her nails dug in. "*Well, that's precious,*" I mutter to myself and put my arm back down.

Exiting the stables, I notice the other girls returning, led by Jenevieve. As we meet in the middle, she sharply questions, "Where do you think you're going?" Her tone is filled with irritation, and without skipping a beat, she commands, "Lunch is over, get back to work!" Pointing her finger, she directs me to turn around and head right back to the stables.

THE WORKDAY COMES TO AN END, AND WE FILE INSIDE. I SPOT JENEvieve stomping down the hall in her characteristic fashion. "Jenevieve," I call out to her.

My voice must be like nails on a chalkboard to her ears, prompting her to halt abruptly. Slowly turning towards me, her eyes widen in what appears to be a mixture of annoyance and disbelief that I am speaking to her.

"I want to thank you for the opportunity to work here—" I begin, but my words are cut short as she instructs me to go away, waving her hand dismissively, turning away to continue her march down the hall.

Unfazed, I remain standing there for a moment before declaring, "I quit." The words hang in the air as the realization of my decision sinks in, marking the end of my tenure under Jenevieve's terrible thumb.

Once again, she stops in her tracks. Swiveling around and slowly stomping towards me, "You can't quit. You signed a year's contract. If you had taken adequate time to read the contract, you would know the only way out of it is to pay your entire year's salary back to Mr. Everett. Since I know you don't have a penny to your name, I'd suggest you take your horse manure-smelling, dirty self back to your room to shower," she sneers.

The weight of her words leaves me standing here, the realization of being trapped in a contractual bind slowly sinking in.

She gives a dismissive chuckle, scanning me from head to toe, then spins around and struts off.

I can't even begin to imagine how awful I must smell. Her hoity toity nose must be so offended. Hurrying back to my room, I strip free of my dirty clothes and step into the shower, washing my hair and body a good four times before feeling clean enough to step out.

The bathroom is filled with the aroma of my high-quality shampoo and body wash, but unfortunately, they mix with the lingering smell of horse manure. *"Yikes,"* I remark, becoming aware I smelled like that as I walked through the mansion.

Dressing in loose-fitting shorts and an oversized T-shirt, I stop at the kitchenette, hoping to find something to satisfy my hunger. Recalling the few items I grabbed during our weekend trip to town, I discover a cup of ramen. This will have to do since Jenevieve seems to be adamantly trying to starve me. I pour hot water into the cup and set it aside to let the noodles soften. Once they reach the desired texture, I eagerly lift the cup, pour out most of the water, and start eating without waiting for it to cool. Unaware of my hunger due to missing both lunch and dinner, my stomach protests with a loud grumble as I quickly devour the meal.

I take a moment to tidy up the aftermath, and my stomach vehemently protests, expressing its displeasure with the food I just ate. The queasiness suggests I might vomit. Trying to ease the discomfort, I reassure myself that lying down will alleviate the pain.

Crawling into my comfy bed, my thoughts shift to my job, realizing it's drastically different from my initial expectations. I didn't expect to make any friends, but I've unexpectedly made three. Shay, in particular, is beyond wonderful. On the flip side, I was hired as a maid, yet I spent my entire day cleaning horse crap. To top it all off, Jenevieve, who seems to harbor a general disdain for humanity, exhibits an intensified aversion to me. I speculate it might have something to do with Gladys being the one to hire me. However, the memory of her scrutinizing me before any introductions are made suggests a more personal animosity that I can't quite fathom.

I'll wisely attempt to follow Shay's advice: *"Keep my head down and do my job."*

THE FOLLOWING DAY UNFOLDS WITH THE SAME REPETITIVE ROUTINE. Jenevieve assigns us the task of cleaning the horse stables, this time in a different location, a bit farther away. We gather our supplies and push them to the next stable. Once inside, we each tackle the initial alley of stalls. Lost in contemplation, I mentally mark the days until I am finished here, when my thoughts are interrupted by Brad.

"Wanda, Wanda, Wanda," he chimes. "I have a feeling you're up to some mischief today. So, I went ahead and packed you lunch. Well, Gladys packed it for me, but I made sure to let her know I'd be twice as hungry," he proudly announces from the other side of my gate.

I stop shoveling, turning to face him. "Bert, I honestly didn't expect you to kick off this glorious day by instantly ruining it. So, if you don't mind, you can just keep on walking," I reply in a jovial manner.

"After that attempt to embarrass me yesterday, I thought you might want to apologize. I wanted to give you the chance," a grin spreads across his face as he bears his teeth. "No peppers today, and none yesterday," he adds, his smile growing even wider.

I feel satisfied knowing my comment bothered him enough to go check his teeth. "You have such a Gaston-like aura, Brad. It's almost too much to handle," I gleefully turn away and continue to scoop.

"So, you do know my name," he remarks.

It's honestly impressive how he manages to fit all his arrogance into these stables. "Yes. Gaston, we just went over this."

"I'll let you call me any name you'd like—" he begins only to be interrupted by Vanessa walking up.

"Hey handsome," she coos approaching him.

His demeanor immediately shifts to one of annoyance.

"You've got work to do," he asserts with a serious tone.

She gently sways, her body moving sweetly back and forth, pretending innocence. "This is a new stable, and I'm completely turned around. I was hoping you could show me to the bathroom again," she adds, biting her lip.

I can't hold back a laugh.

Vanessa shoots me an irritated look. Recognizing Brad isn't moving, she changes her technique. "There's a problem in my stall. Could you come take a look?" she directs the question to Brad, who initially makes no attempt to budge. However, the prospect of a potential issue eventually prompts him to push himself off the gate, giving an exaggerated eye roll before following her away.

CHAPTER
Four

KALYN

The first two weeks of my new job went by, and I survived... barely. Jenevieve, mostly, and one of the new hires, Vanessa, seem to have it out for me. Vanessa has never been the most productive worker to start with, but ever since she hooked up with Brad a couple of times, she seems to lose her composure whenever he's talking to me or anyone else for that matter. She lingers around my stall, and always pulls the damsel in distress card in her best attempt to pull him away and flirt with him, despite his clear disinterest. I feel secondhand embarrassment for her every time, and he makes it painfully obvious he wants nothing to do with her.

I've made several attempts to quit, only to be met each time by Jenevieve reminding me of the year-long contract I was strongarmed into signing—an act that leaves me frustrated at her for not allowing adequate time to thoroughly read it before agreeing.

Over the past two weeks, the team responsible for cleaning horse stalls has dwindled from seven to just four. The three others have been reassigned to inside duties. Vanessa being one of them, and I wonder if Brad made that happen just to get her away from him. I suspect this reduction is also Jenevieve's way of penalizing me, as the workload remains unchanged, expecting the same number of stalls to be cleaned. If they don't get done, I am the one who gets punished.

Almost every day, I find myself without lunch due to someone else's actions, adding to the mounting challenges I seem to face. Fortunately, Brad realizing I am stubborn, started discreetly leaving a brown paper sack lunch on the desk in the supply room that is always labeled "Wanda." I assume this subtle act ensures that no one suspects any preferential treatment toward me, not that anyone would deem it special treatment considering the circumstances of being penalized and regularly missing lunch.

While most days I can't stand him, every day I see it sitting there, it brings comfort that I won't have to starve that entire workday. He even completely disappears around lunch time knowing I would never touch the food if he was around.

It's Monday, the week has just begun, and the day is winding down. I haven't been in trouble at all. I'll pat myself on the back later.

I'm stowing the last of my supplies as Amber enters, audibly releasing a sigh of relief that the job is finally done. Exhaustion is evident on her face as she struggles with the weight of two metal buckets filled with horse feed.

In her attempt to navigate around a carelessly strewn hose on the floor, she stumbles and inadvertently sends one of the buckets airborne, causing horse feed to scatter across the floor. I quickly rush over to check on her, grabbing her arm to help her up as I can hear how hard she lands on her knees.

The room falls silent as Jenevieve enters through the doorway, her scrutinizing gaze sweeping over the chaos before meeting mine. Recognizing the brewing tension, Amber steps forward and begins apologizing to Jenevieve.

"Jenevieve, I'm so sorry. I tripped over the hose, but I'll take care of cleaning up the mess," Amber explains, her earnest tone reflecting genuine remorse and a commitment to rectify the unexpected mishap. The room is tense, waiting for her response to the unforeseen disruption.

Unfazed by Amber's apologies, Jenevieve abruptly seizes the bucket from her grasp. A malevolent expression takes hold of her face as she delivers a swift and forceful swing, cracking the bucket across my face. The impact sends me sprawling to the ground, horse feed scattering in every direction from the second bucket.

"Get this mess cleaned up," she exhales heavily, her command echoing through the room as she storms out. The air is thick with tension, and as the room spins around me, darkness envelops my senses, the echo of my name being called multiple times fading into the void.

I gradually open my eyes, waiting for the haze to dissipate, and discover Shay applying an ice pack to my face. The stark contrast between pain and coldness is so uncomfortable that I want to remove the ice pack, but my brain and arms don't seem to be communicating.

Meanwhile, Brad has me lying in his lap, the back of my head pressed against his chest, while his other arm wraps firmly around my waist. He delicately tends to my lip with a damp washcloth, as Amber, visibly distressed, cries in the arms of the other two new hires. All eyes anxiously focused on me.

"Kalyn, we need to take you to the hospital to get checked out," Shay's words etched with concern.

"I'm fine," I lie, attempting to sit up, only to be hit by a wave of dizziness that sends me falling back into Brad's arms. "Gaston here is making me so nauseous just looking at him." I attempt to joke, and a sympathetic smile crosses his face.

"Well, Kalyn," he emphasizes my name, letting me know he has finally figured it out. "You might have a concussion."

"Please let us take you to the hospital. Brad's truck is right outside, running and ready to go," Shay pleads, her eyes filled with desperation, begging me to agree.

I glance at her, doing my best to reassure her that I'm alright, even though my face is throbbing, and there's a lingering worry about the extent of the damage Jenevieve inflicted. "I'm fine, Shay. Thank you, though," I attempt to reassure her, amidst the discomfort.

Her concerned expression goes unchanged, "You look like Quasimodo," she jokes, and suddenly everyone, including Amber who has been crying non-stop since the incident happened, all begin hysterically laughing.

I remain on the ground a little longer before feeling well enough to try standing. When I sit up this time, the dizziness washes over me, but not as bad.

"Take it slow," Brad advises, steadying me by holding onto my waist more securely. "Think you can stand?" he asks softly, mindful of my headache.

I remain silent while the disorientation begins to fade away.

With Shay and him helping me stand, it becomes apparent that walking back to the mansion is an impossible venture. Brad leans me onto Shay and rushes off, returning moments later with a golf cart. He wraps my arm around his neck, securing his arms around my waist, and guides me to the golf cart. In the darkness of the night, I'm grateful he's in control since I'm utterly disoriented.

Amber and the two other girls take the back seat as he drives us to the back of the mansion, arriving at the door that separates the shared staff area from the maid's quarters.

The cart sits idling as he assists me off. Shay quickly moves to support me on the other side. Feeling a bit uneasy about the attention and assistance, I tell Brad, "We can manage from here," insisting that his help is no longer necessary.

Ignoring my words, Brad replies, "You can walk, but that doesn't mean you should. Let me carry you in. I'll even give you a sponge bath," he smirks.

Looking thoroughly unimpressed, Shay calls out to him, "Go to bed, Brad." She envelops me with her arms, while Amber quickly steps in to take Brad's place. She wraps her arms around my waist on the other side, walking with us until we get to my room.

Shay takes over and helps me, even running a bath for me. "I'm not leaving, so if you're worried about me seeing you naked, you better get over that real quick," she says confidently, beginning to undo my uniform.

I stand there, allowing her to undress me. I wouldn't be able to manage a bath on my own anyway, appreciating her willingness to help me. Settling into the tub, she washes both my hair and body.

"Fuck Jenevieve," she says, seething. "And you've got perfect tits," she adds, eliciting a laugh from me. "Seriously, though, are they real?" her gaze fixed on my chest.

"Yes," I confirm, radiating a sense of mirth.

After my bath, she helps me out and tenderly drapes me in a robe, leading me to the chair at the vanity counter in my bathroom. She disappears into my closet to pick out an outfit for me. Returning, she assists me in putting on my pajamas before brushing my hair and expertly braiding it, allowing it to fall over one shoulder.

She stands behind me, sympathetically smiling at my reflection in the mirror, "Just the way you like it."

I'm taken aback by the swollen and bruised appearance on the left side of my face. But as my eyes land on the carefully braided hair, I express my gratitude, meeting her gaze in the mirror.

She circles around, reaching out both hands to me, helping me up. Wrapping her arm around my waist, she guides me to my bed, pulls back the covers, and lets me crawl in. My lids are heavy, and I don't fight them falling closed. I can hear her moving around in my kitchenette, but I don't pay much attention until she puts an ice pack on my face.

"For the swelling," she explains before climbing into bed beside me.

Throughout the night, Shay woke up every couple of hours to replace my ice pack. By morning, when we get up for work, the swelling has significantly subsided, but the bruising is still glaringly evident.

Jenevieve barks orders at the staff, and her voice, accompanied by my headache first thing in the morning, makes me want to crawl under a rock and hide. She briefly pauses when she sees me, a satisfied smirk appearing on her face before she continues walking.

She's a monster, a complete monster.

It's astonishing how she manages to remain employed among the other wonderful staff without getting fired. The sheer ordeal of dealing with this she-devil will undoubtedly require extra appointments with Maeva.

The four of us are assigned to separate stables today, and Jenevieve, with clear intentions, gives me the largest stable farthest from the mansion and the supply room.

"Hey, Wanda," Brad greets me, while preoccupied with something in his hand. "You have small fingers—can you help me with this?" His brows furrow as he remains focused on whatever he's holding.

I stop shoveling, propping the shovel against the wall. "Sure," I reply, pulling off my gloves and resting them on the gate. I extend my hand, and he places a thin gold chain, knotted up, in my palm.

He sets up a folding chair between the open stall gate and instructs me to sit while I work on the chain.

It's only when he steps inside the stall that I notice he's already wearing rubber boots over his clean jeans, has gloves on, and is picking up my shovel to start cleaning the stall for me.

"As much as I appreciate how quickly you can do that, you really don't have to help me. I can get it done," I assure him.

Undeterred, he continues on, then wheels out the manure, cleaning the entire stall by the time I finish untangling his chain.

"Good as new," I declare, holding up the untangled chain as he starts working on the second stall. "Thank you kindly, sir. I shall take over from here," extending his chain to him. He simply nods in agreement, pulls off his gloves, and tucks the chain into his pocket.

"As you wish," he replies, returning my shovel and stepping out of the stall.

He comes back moments later, sighing, "Blame it on my jeans. It's all knotted again," he holds up the same chain I just untangled, only this time it is knotted ten times more than before.

A burst of laughter escapes me as I stare at the incredibly knotted chain. "You are ridiculous," I exclaim, removing my gloves and taking the chain. He drops the chair with a loud clank in front of this stall and I sit down once again, while he resumes shoveling the manure.

"I know what you're doing," keeping my eyes down on the chain. He knows very well I wouldn't willingly accept his help. Thus, he devised a clever plan to get my assistance, ensuring I have to sit down while doing so, giving him the ability to do my job without me putting up a fight.

"Shoveling horse shit," his usual sarcastic tone is absent.

He tends to two more stalls before I manage to fully untangle the chain again.

"All done." A sense of pride washes over me for the second time. Untangling chains can be quite a challenge. Despite having small fingers, my short nails don't provide much grip. "Should I re-knot it before I give it back to you, or would you like to do the honors?" I tease, holding it out to him.

"C'mon," he says, taking the chain from me and walking toward the golf cart parked outside. "Get in," patting the seat next to him. I stand here, unimpressed.

"Relax, worrywart Wanda, it's lunchtime."

The morning slipped by quickly, and though my first reaction is to protest the ride, I give in, joining him on the golf cart and allowing him to drive us back to the main stable where the large supply room is located. After parking, we both go inside, wash our hands, and take off our rubber boots.

Exiting the supply room, a pair of cooks arrive in a small truck, seemingly delivering lunch. They step out and start opening the doors on the sides of the truck, revealing trays of food. They go through a door of the stable I've never noticed before, disappearing inside with the trays, only to return without them.

"See ya, Brad," they wave before getting back into the truck and driving off back towards the mansion.

I'm confused by their actions. I guess I didn't realize they deliver lunch out here. But the delightful aroma of the food wafts through the air, and my stomach twists with hunger.

"I didn't think you had friends," I nudge his arm.

A subtle twinkle of amusement lights up his face as we approach the door. "I have friends everywhere. I am having lunch with a friend right now," he proudly tells me, stopping at the door the cooks just exited.

"Well, have a good lunch with your imaginary friend," I jest, continuing to walk. He reaches out, grabs my arm, and pulls me back, guiding me into the door.

The mystery room turns out to be a break room designated for the stable hands. It has a rustic vibe that seems fitting for out here. A large kitchenette, with modern appliances, like an oversized refrigerator that seems too big for just the ten or so stable workers' lunches. Adjacent to the kitchenette, there's an L shaped leather couch facing the TV.

In the center of the room is a spacious table with seating for ten, arranged in a circular shape. On the table, rest two trays sitting with hot lunch. The smell permeates the entire area, eliciting another growl from my stomach.

Brad strides over, pulling out a chair. "Wanda," he says, waiting for me to sit.

Unsure of his intentions, I playfully respond, "I'm off to lunch, grasshopper. You and your 'friend' can enjoy alone."

"You are the friend eating lunch with me."

"I'm not your friend," I jokingly roll my eyes at him.

"Okay, enemy, we're frenemies," he grins, extending his hand toward the awaiting food.

"I thought you said you were having lunch with a friend?" I question, hoping one of these trays really is for me because I am hungry and eager to eat.

"I figured if I said we were friends, you would take it as that, and we could be friends, but you are stubborn," he removes his hands from the back of the chair he was holding out for me, pulling out the chair next to it, and sits down. "Let's go, Wanda," he pats the chair next to him. "Time is still ticking away."

I join him at the table and begin eating. I can see out of my peripheral that he keeps staring at me. Growing self-conscious, I pick up my tray and move to the other side of him, keeping one chair between us.

"Damn, do I smell that bad?" he mocks.

"No, but I can feel you staring at the bruises on my face, and I don't like it," I admit. His gaze hasn't wavered. With every bite

I take, I sense his eyes burning into the side of my face, growing even more hyper-aware of my bruises.

He sits quietly for a moment, contemplating his words carefully. "I wasn't staring at the bruises," leaving it at that.

When we finish our meal, I stand. I'm not sure what we should be doing with our trays, and he hasn't said anything else since I moved chairs. "Should I walk these back to the kitchen?"

He hooks his fingers on the edge of my tray, sliding it down the table to where he is, and neatly stacks them. "They will come pick it up," he assures me, heading for the door and holding it open for me to walk through first.

After getting our rubber boots, we return to the golf cart, and he drives us back to the stables where I'm working for the day. After he parks, I step off and resume my duties. Slipping into the rubber boots, I stride toward the open stall. Retrieving my gloves, I pull them on, grab my shovel, and glance down at the fold-out chair. There, I spot the knotted chain in the spot where I had been seated. Brad walks past me, relieving me of the shovel before entering the stall.

Inwardly finding this funny, I pick up the chain and once again begin unknotting it. Crossing my leg, I swing it back and forth while observing him. "You know I'm not going to keel over and die, right?" I comment, continuing to work on the chain.

He finishes shoveling the last pile, propping the shovel against the wall before turning to grab the wheelbarrow. "It would be a sad day in hell for that to happen. They'd send your smart mouth right back," he jokes as he walks away. I stand and follow after him.

Some days, he makes me want to pull out all my hair, and others, he surprises me with his pleasant demeanor. Despite being a womanizer.

"What do you even do around here?" I ask, curious about how he manages his time. He is always out here at the stables, but every once in a while, I see him around the mansion. Usually flirting with one of the staff members that swoon over his attention.

Dumping the manure in a pile, he starts walking back. "A little bit of everything," he replies vaguely.

I contemplate making a joke about him "doing a lot of everyone," and his reputation for being involved with everyone. However, he's unusually helpful today, so I decide against it. I just hope he doesn't expect anything in return from me for his help.

"I think it goes without saying but helping me isn't going to make me have sex with you," I remark.

A suppressed laugh escapes him, "If I were interested, I would have made a move already. You're not my type, Wanda, no offense," he walks back into the stall and immediately resumes shoveling.

I spend the next few moments muling over his words, taking note that all the women he's been involved with here seem to be brunette. A sense of relief washes over me, dispelling the assumption that his actions were all geared toward wanting sex. Now assured that isn't the case, I relax.

After freeing the last knot from the chain, I grab an extra shovel and walk back to the stall he is working away in. Playfully, I drape the chain around his neck, securing it. "So it can't get tangled again," I tease, then join him in shoveling.

Although it's not his job, we make a surprisingly fluid team, working in sync with each other. We finish cleaning all the stalls in the stable, and I'm grateful for his help because I wouldn't have been able to finish even half of them if it weren't for him.

"Thanks for untangling my chain, Wanda," he organizes my supplies and closes the final gate.

Without another word he walks out to the golf cart, climbs in, and leaves, heading in the opposite direction we originally came from. Finding the timing of it slightly contradictory to the way he acted all day, making it a point to cart me around except when work is over. But whatever, I pick up my wheelbarrow and begin wheeling toward the exit.

As I approach, Jenevieve comes screeching up in a golf cart with an older gentleman driving her. I've seen him working in the gardens, so I'm sure he is a random bystander she pulled from his duties to come drive her over here.

"Where do you think you're going?" She snaps. "You're not going anywhere until I see your work," She continues stomping past, eyeing me up and down before inspecting each stall to evaluate my work.

Upon seeing every stall immaculately cleaned, she appears irked. Persistent in her search for an issue, and finding none, she storms out of the stable, clambers into the golf cart, and he promptly speeds away.

Secretly, I entertain the wish that she'd tumble out, suppressing the immense satisfaction I find in the mental image. Heading back to put my supplies away, it occurs to me that Brad likely anticipated Jenevieve's inspection, explaining his abrupt departure and lack of a ride back. He's exasperating and yet, in some perplexing way, considerate.

No, that can't be right.

Womanizer, I remind myself.

CHAPTER
Five

KALYN

Today feels tense. I can't really pinpoint why, and nothing seems to have changed, but there's an undeniable thickness in the air.

It doesn't take long for my suspicions to be confirmed. Vanessa switched places with one of the other new hires just to come clean the stables, obviously wanting to be near Brad. As we gather our supplies in the supply room, I have my wheelbarrow ready with all my stuff inside. While I'm busy grabbing a pair of gloves from one of the closets, Vanessa casually approaches and "accidentally" knocks into it, causing it to topple over. The contents spill out, making a loud clanking noise as they hit the ground. The loud noise catches everyone's attention, and she walks away, a glint of mischief in her eyes, making it clear that she did it on purpose.

"It's hard to know your own circumference sometimes, huh?" I sarcastically remark to her, knowing it will ruffle her feathers.

She abruptly stops laughing, raises her hand, flips me off, and then stomps out.

I clean up the mess she made of my stuff and make my way out of the room. Brad is instructing everyone to stalls. Thanks to Vanessa, I'm the last one to arrive, and I anticipate Brad giving me shit for it.

"Nice of you to join us," he smirks and points towards the stall right across from the supply room. "You seem to be moving at a snail's pace today, so I'll make it easy for you."

Ugh, it just had to be right next to Vanessa's stall.

I open the gate and enter, pretending to be unfazed by the situation. Moments later, Brad leisurely leans on the gate, resting his other arm on a shovel. I turn to look at him, sensing him standing there even before I see him.

"Forget something?" he taunts wryly.

I look down at the shovel and then back to him. "Nope."

Once he's gone, I'll grab one myself. And if he decides to stick around, I'll just use my hands to scoop everything up, just so I don't have to admit that I'm a bit scatterbrained today.

He unlatches the gate and enters the stall, walking over to where I am, and leans against the wall, staring at me.

"What?" I ask, irritation filling my word. It's not even him that I'm annoyed with, it's Vanessa. Yet, I feel like if I'm mean to him, she will hear it and know I'm not after her supposed man.

"I believe the words you're looking for are 'thank you.'"

I keep ignoring him, praying he leaves.

"By the way, good morning," he adds as if we're having a friendly chat.

I can hear by the roughness of Vanessa's cleaning in the next stall that she's not happy with this interaction. He either doesn't notice or doesn't care.

I walk over to him, grab the shovel, and point for him to get out. There is no way he doesn't hear all the commotion she's making.

He shakes his head, seemingly finding this funny, and walks out without a fight.

Once he is out of the stable area, loud banging noises emanate from Vanessa's stall. In a hushed tone, she mutters, "slut."

I don't even need to glance up to know that she's directing it towards me, all because "her man" was talking to me.

It frustrates me how him sticking his dick in any hole he can find puts me in these uncomfortable positions. Though I doubt he intentionally placed us next to each other, he must be aware of her animosity towards me. Yet, here I am, stuck right beside her.

If I finish up quickly, I can move on to the next dirty stall and avoid being beside her. She seems to spend more time creating dramatic scenes and making loud noises than doing her work.

I scoop quickly, dumping the poop into the wheelbarrow, and go back down to shovel the next pile. As I make my way back up with another scoop, hay-covered poop starts raining down on me, flung from Vanessa's stall. I stand there, frozen for a moment, trying to process what just happened. Did I accidentally fling crap in the air? It's only when I hear laughter coming from her stall that it becomes clear she purposely flung it on me.

The realization that I am now covered in horse manure sets in. "Are you fucking kidding me?!" I yell, dropping the shovel and trying to brush it off.

"Sorry, it was an accident," she says condescendingly.

I storm out of my stall, heading straight towards hers, seething with anger when Brad, having heard me yelling, comes rushing into the stable and wraps his arms around my waist before I can get to Vanessa.

"Let go of me!" I scream. "She just threw horse shit on me!" I shout, my fury urging me to march right back in there and slap her across the face with a pile of it.

He lifts me, my feet no longer on the floor, and I frantically kick my legs trying to break free.

"You've just earned yourself cleaning that stall too!" he yells at Vanessa, as he carries me out of the stable while I pull at his arms to release me.

"Calm down," he bites out, setting me on my feet once we are outside the stable.

"I'm covered in horse shit! I'm not going to calm down!" I shout back, still trying to shake it off. I tilt my head forward, attempting to brush the pieces out of my hair when he grabs my arm and pulls me away from where we are. I'm so angry I let him drag me, knowing that if he lets go, I'll go back and maul her.

He leads me to a part of the second stable, down the alleyway, towards a seemingly ordinary wall. However, to the left, there's a staircase that he pulls me up. It leads to a fully furnished apartment above the stable. When we are fully inside, I shut the door behind me and follow him as he walks straight to the bathroom. I am so confused about what we're doing and why there's an apartment up here.

I stand just outside the doorway, watching him move around with ease. He opens a closet, takes out a towel, and drapes it over the shower. Then, he rummages through the cupboards, grabs shampoo and body wash, and sets them inside the glass shower door. As he continues to busy himself in the bathroom, I glance down the short hallway to the bedroom and notice his coat hanging on the bedpost. It's a coat he often wears. I've never really questioned where he lives, but I think I just figured it out...

"Take a shower and wash your hair," he continues, digging in the cabinets.

"My uniform is still going to smell like shit." I'm annoyed, and my crappy mood is making me take it out on him, not realizing that he's being kind by offering me a chance to shower.

"We won't have time to clean it, but I can toss it in the dryer and try to get some of the smell off," he suggests.

Letting out a sigh, I reluctantly agree. He leaves the bathroom and I undress, letting my hair down and turning on the shower. As soon as the water is warm, I step inside and immediately start scrubbing my hair. With every piece of hay I wash out, my anger flares up again. The first round of shampoo is spent picking out hay and debris. The second round is spent making sure I didn't miss anything. By the third wash, I feel confident that I've gotten rid of all the nasty stuff. I scrub my arms, shoulders, and face extra well since they also got covered in crap, and then give the rest of my body a thorough scrub.

As I rinse off, I allow the water to cascade down my back. Glancing out of the glass shower, I notice my clothes are gone. I'm not sure if it's because I'm still furious with Vanessa or because I know he's well-versed in female anatomy, but it doesn't even phase me that he saw me naked.

After turning off the water, I squeeze the excess water out of my hair with my hands and reach for the towel he left hanging over the shower... only to find it missing.

Jackass.

He's standing in the bathroom doorway, leaning casually, probably thinking I'm going to hide and beg him for a towel. But he would be wrong. I push the glass door wide open and confidently step out, extending my hand towards him.

"Give me the towel back," my words and tone unimpressed.

His initial response to me stepping out of the shower nude appears to have caught him off guard. I didn't react to the missing towel the way he expected. Then, an expression crosses his face that I can't quite figure out. If it were anyone else, I might mistake it for desire, but Brad doesn't desire women. He uses them and moves on.

I walk closer to him, still holding my hand out, and rest my other hand on the counter. After a moment, it dawns on me that he has no intention of giving me the towel.

"Fine. Since you want to be an asshole, you can stare at one." While this is less than ladylike, I don't even care. I snatch my hairband from the counter and turn my back to him, bending over and flipping my hair upside down, and again squeeze the excess water to the ground. He's the one that can clean up the mess. I gather my hair in my hands and flip it back upright—the wet strands shower him with droplets of water. I move in front of the mirror, only inches from where he stands, and watch myself as I tie my hair into a bun on the top of my head. I notice that I have lost weight. My breasts are still full but just below them, my ribs slightly show. That's lovely, *'thanks Jenevieve,'* I sarcastically think to myself.

If he would just hand me the towel, I wouldn't be so wet, and I could cover up. I turn and give him a pointed look, my hand extending back towards him, waiting for him to hand it to me. He visibly swallows and stares back at me.

"Am I supposed to air dry?" I question, my hand still patiently waiting for the towel. It's amusing how a naked woman can render him completely speechless. Although he stands frozen in place, I'm convinced he's doing his best not to glance at my wet body. I wish I could read his mind and hear what he's thinking. Did his little plan to take the towel work out how he hoped?

I can see the towel behind his back, so I step closer to him, our eyes locked, and reach around his back, snatching it from his grasp. He doesn't put up a fight with me taking it. I sarcastically smirk at him and begin drying off.

"I need my clothes," I continue to wipe the water off.

He stares, seeming like he can't peel his eyes off me. Then he walks away, and it feels like sweet victory.

I'm mid-drying myself when he returns, but this time he walks right by me and takes a seat on the closed toilet lid. My clothes are resting on his lap. I let the towel fall to my feet and reach over, grabbing my underwear from the pile. I slide them on and then grab my bra, fastening it around me and pulling it up into place. As I reach for my uniform, he clings to it tightly.

"Keep it up and I will strangle you with it," the words fall from my mouth easily. His face reveals the humor he is finding in all of this, but he releases his grip on my uniform anyway.

I slip it on and tie my apron around my waist before exiting the bathroom.

"Where are my socks and shoes?"

He follows me out and walks over to the door, picks them up from the table, and brings them over to where I sit on the couch.

"You know this is your fault, right?" I bite out as I bend down to tie my shoelaces.

"Her actions are not my doing," he plops down on the couch across from me.

"Not entirely, but if you would use better judgment than 'they have something wet I can stick my dick in,' maybe this odd jealousy stuff wouldn't be happening," I bite out.

"That's solid advice. I'll keep that in mind," he replies cockily, propping his arm on the couch's armrest and resting his chin on his middle finger, with his index finger positioned straight alongside his face.

"I get it, you think this is all a big joke, but these women you sleep with are actual human beings with feelings. Women aren't like men. We don't just sleep around and move on. We form attachments, and it hurts like hell when we give ourselves to someone like that, only to be tossed aside like we are trash."

The humor dissipates from his face. "You're right."

"What you do is none of my business, but somehow it always ends up affecting me. I can't even talk to you now without facing the consequences of your flings punishing me. I just need you to leave me alone. Treat me like a past fling and pretend I don't exist. Jenevieve already hates my guts, and every time I try to quit, she throws the stupid contract I signed in my face. I don't need your sexual encounters making my life even more miserable." I rise from my seat.

"I'll talk to Jenevieve," he stands up just as quickly as I do.

"No! Do you honestly think that will solve all these problems? Just leave me alone." I make my way around the couch to the door and jerk it open.

I enter the stable and Jenevieve is already instructing the girls to tidy up and go to lunch. The only reason she ever even comes out here is to catch me or someone else doing something she can punish *me* for, so I'm not surprised when I see her out here.

"YOU!" She hisses as soon as she spots me. "I was just informed that you passed off your work to someone else." She clenches her fist on her hip.

"You mean Vanessa faced consequences for throwing horse manure on me?" My voice is monotone.

"You must not be hungry after taking such a long, self-given break. You'll stay here during lunch to finish both neglected stalls." She points towards my assigned stall and Vanessa's stall. It seems that after Brad and I left, Vanessa decided to do nothing.

"What will starving me accomplish? Why isn't Vanessa missing lunch to clean her stall?" my earlier anger resurfacing.

"Are you questioning my orders?" Her eyes widen.

"Yes. Both my stall and Vanessa's stall are unfinished. I shouldn't have to clean both." Arguing with her will only make things worse for me, but I have to do this alone while missing lunch again, and I'm pissed.

"Missing a few meals will do you some good," she snarls at me.

Vanessa stands at the wide opening to the stables staring at us, I catch a glimpse of her wicked grin as she saunters off.

"Well, I hope you're planning on skipping a few meals as well," I retort, taking two steps back into the stall. I know she wouldn't dare come in here in her heels.

"You've got another thing coming, little girl," she hisses to me before composing herself and stomping off.

Jenevieve is already incredibly thin, almost as if her bones are barely covered by a layer of skin. But I know my remark is going to upset her for days. Especially coming from someone she hates.

I don't know what has gotten into me. Why am I acting unhinged?

Oh, right. I'm hangry.

I can't do anything about it, as she'll punish me even more if I go to lunch without her approval. Tears well up in my eyes, and I scold myself to not let them fall. But once the first tear escapes, the rest follow, tracing a wet path down my face.

I angrily pull my gloves on and grab my manure fork, the closest thing to me right now, and begin scooping piles of hay up. I wipe my tears away with my forearm as Brad enters the stall and begins shoveling alongside me.

"Go away."

Ignoring my words, he continues working.

Tears continue to stream down my face. "GO AWAY!" I yell.

He forcefully pushes the fork handle to the ground and grabs my arm, pulling me into a hug. "I'm sorry, Kalyn," he squeezes me in his embrace.

"Go away!" I repeat, attempting to push him away, but he holds on even tighter. I can't hold back my sobs any longer. The floodgates have opened, and I sob into his chest. My legs give way, and he supports me as we both sit down on the dirty hay. He pulls me onto his lap, holding me tightly.

A whirlwind of emotions overwhelms me, and I release them all through my crying. I'm angry. I'm so angry! I'm annoyed. I'm hungry. I feel alone. I feel mistreated and abused. And it seems like no one else ever faces consequences for anything. It's always just me.

I learned from a young age to keep my problems to myself. No one wants to be burdened with someone else's issues, and they don't want to hear someone with victim mentality complain constantly. I couldn't even burden my therapist with my issues.

He remains silent, allowing me to cry while rubbing my back in a soothing gesture, and this is probably the best kind of comfort someone can give me.

After that cry fest, I am ready for a nap.

I sit up, wiping the tears from my face, and breathe in and out a couple of times, trying to regulate my breathing.

Pushing against his chest, I manage to climb back on my feet. I hold my hands out to him, and he grabs them as I pull, helping him to his feet.

A loud gasp fills the air, causing both of us to look over. Claire stands there, holding a tray of food, before quickly apologizing and rushing away.

"Wait, Claire!" Brad follows after her.

...That reaction from Brad is odd.

Everything happened so fast that I can't even process what's going on. I step out of the stall to see if I can figure it out, only to be met by Vanessa and Erica. They stand there staring at me, mouths agape.

They witnessed Claire running out of here. Brad, coming out of the same stall as me, chasing after her. And now I am looking after them both.

Surely, they don't think that Brad and I were fooling around in a shit-filled stall, right?

Wrong.

A fury burns in Vanessa's eyes as she marches over to me. "Guess that answers the lingering question. He's mentioned you would be the easiest to fuck here. I just figured even sluts have a cap on the amount of dick they'd take. Guess I was wrong, sluts will fuck anyone." With a sneer, she turns and walks past me.

Erica follows suit, shooting me a dirty look as she passes.

I remove my gloves and head to the bathroom. My face is still red and swollen from crying. Do they honestly think I would be having sex while crying?

I splash cold water on my face before heading back to the stalls we're cleaning.

"Sorry about that," Brad catches up with me and falls into stride alongside me.

I ignore him and keep walking.

"Can you come with me to the office?" not so much a demand as I would expect if I were about to get in trouble. But it still makes my stomach sink.

He instructs me to take a seat at the desk while he rummages through the fridge. I keep my eyes on my hands and hear the fridge door closing, looking up when he places a brown paper bag in front of me.

"I'll be back in fifteen minutes," he informs me before walking out and shutting the door behind him.

I turn to look at the door he just exited and then shift my attention back to the bag. As I open it up, I discover that it's a packed lunch. I already had a feeling that's what it would be. But why is he giving it to me? I'm assuming this was his packed lunch and the tray of food Claire had was meant for him, and he's feeling guilty, so he's trying to feed me. Or does he know he can always grab food from the mansion whenever he wants and I can't? Also, is this his office? He never really mentions what he does around here, but he keeps his food in the office fridge instead of the lounge fridge like the other stable workers.

He is so weird. What is he doing?

This is one of those times where I want to call Maeva and ask her what the actual fuck is wrong with me? I know I need to eat something, but I can't bring myself to accept anything he is offering. I'd rather go hungry.

I get up from his desk like the big giant baby that I am and leave.

I notice Brad holding a clipboard and having a conversation with a delivery guy who's dropping off horse feed. He seems focused on what the guy is saying but glances up at me and watches me go.

I don't have the energy by the end of the day to move very fast. The other girls have already finished cleaning and are long gone while I'm still here tidying up my things.

"Not feeling good huh?" Brad asks from the doorway. "Maybe you wouldn't feel fatigued if you ate the lunch that was provided to you," he says, sounding annoyed.

I continue cleaning my stuff and ignore him. I don't think I could even muster up enough energy to speak. I am saving the last shred of energy I have right now just to get me back to my room.

"Do you think you're proving a point by not eating?" he persists.

I scrub the soap onto my hands, rinse them off, and turn off the water. Grabbing some paper towels, I dry my hands and toss them into the trash as I walk past the bin. As I pass by him in the doorway, I half expect him to block my way, but he lets me pass. He then turns and follows me.

"You're only hurting yourself," he calls after me.

But I just continue walking back to the mansion.

As lunchtime approaches on Wednesday, we store our supplies before heading inside. Gladys, with a friendly presence, greets all the girls as she passes by. When she sees me, she does a double-take, and a look of horror quickly crosses her face. Without hesitation, she delicately takes hold of my arm and guides me aside for a private conversation.

"Kalyn," her eyes widen in surprise. "What happened to your face?!" she exclaims, genuine shock evident in her voice, reaching out to my bruised face.

Aware of the less-than-ideal state of my face, even though the swelling has subsided, the bruising remains quite prominent. Shay has diligently applied ice to my face after work, yet the bruised appearance persists.

With a touch of humor, I playfully remark, "Gladys, some might find it disrespectful to come right out and ask that without buttering me up first."

"Beautiful girl," she says in a soft voice while tenderly caressing my cheek with the back of her hand. Her eyes scan my face as if trying to capture every detail, before enveloping me in a warm embrace. I hug her back because this hug feels like it's one she needs, not me. When she finally lets go, a sympathetic curve of her lips takes over as she gently squeezes my hands. "Alright sweetie, go eat," releasing my hands, patting my back before she begins walking away down the corridor. I notice her hands reaching up to her face as if she were brushing away tears, and then she rounds the corner out of sight.

The rest of the day seems to drag on endlessly. On our way back from the stables after work, I notice Gladys and Jenevieve engaged in what appears to be a heated discussion, instantly making me anxious as if it might be related to me somehow.

The unsettling sensation lingers with me throughout the remainder of the evening. After dinner, I promptly retreat to my room. Shay joins me, wordlessly settling into my bed, absentmindedly playing with my hair while scrolling through social media on her phone.

Eventually, I succumbed to sleep, only to awaken in the morning with the same sinking feeling that had plagued me the night before. I experience the familiar cold sweats that accompany my mornings, yet a sense of relief washes over me as I realize I am still within the confines of the mansion.

It's quite disheartening that finding comfort here serves as a stark contrast to the nightmare that was Wyatt's presence.

I rise from my bed and prepare for the day, autopilot instantly kicking in as I make my way through my room. I toss my hair into a large messy bun atop my head, then opt to apply an additional layer of cover-up in the hope that it might divert attention away from the noticeable bruising on my face. Satisfied with my efforts to conceal the marks, I dress myself in the familiar baggy work uniform and join the line, ready to embark on my usual journey toward the horse stables.

"Actually," Jenevieve says as she yanks my arm and squeezes it, tugging me out of the line I was in. "You're on dusting duties," she declares, shoving me toward a different line and then motions for me to get in the line that Shay is in. She and I exchange puzzled glances, and then I excitedly squeeze in line behind her.

Cleaning the mansion is more my speed. Although I appreciate the constant physical activity and workout I receive from cleaning horse stalls for eight hours straight, the relief of not having to continuously bend over and back up feels much gentler on my sore back.

Shay and I discuss how weird it is that Jenevieve randomly decided to pull me from mucking stalls today. But I think I might have Gladys to thank for that.

Shay and I join forces, collaborating to clean our assigned rooms side by side.

About an hour into our cleaning, Shay's phone chimes, and a radiant smile lights up her face. She mouths "Jonathan" to me, holding her phone up before excusing herself from the room to take the call from her boyfriend.

When she returns, I immediately notice a change in her attitude. There is a hint of nervousness and unease that seems to linger. I refrain from prying, assuming it might be a typical disagreement between couples. I give her space, thinking she would share if she wanted to talk about what's bothering her.

Continuing to clean, Shay seems lost in thought, making it difficult to engage her in conversation. Every attempt to start a discussion is met with moments of silence, only for her to respond with a distracted "What?" or "Did you say something?"

My heart goes out to her, and I want to help ease whatever is troubling her. It frustrates me, and I can't shake the urge to give Jonathan a knuckle sandwich for obviously being the one who upset her.

OUR LUNCH TODAY IS DELAYED BECAUSE JENEVIEVE INFORMED US WE weren't productive enough, ensuring to shoot me a disapproving glare as she voices her dissatisfaction. Once she permits us to go for lunch, we return our cleaning supplies to the storage room, wash our hands, and head back out to where Jenevieve impatiently sits in a chair in the living room, crossing her legs and displaying signs of annoyance by absentmindedly plucking her thumbnail under her ring fingernail. It's evident she feels we took too long.

As soon as she sees us, she lets out an exaggerated sigh, stands up, and angrily instructs us to move along.

"I don't know what we're having for lunch today, but it smells amazing," Shay whispers back to me in line.

My stomach grumbles in response. "There you have it. My stomach agrees."

In single file, we walk down the corridor, forming a line with Jenevieve at the front, a single step over to walk alongside the line.

The sound of large footsteps on marble has Jenevieve halting the line just before reaching the dining hall.

"Mr. Everett!" Jenevieve exclaims with a rising tone, almost turning her words into a melodic cadence. "I didn't realize you were back." Her words cease abruptly as the gentleman she addresses comes to an unexpected stop beside me. Even without turning to look at him, I can sense his commanding presence. He towers over me. Though I can't see what is happening and I keep my eyes on the back of Shay's head, I feel some sort of interaction taking place between the man standing next to me and Jenevieve.

"Ladies," she addresses us, attempting to infuse cheer into her tone, but I detect an underlying annoyance as if we somehow forgot to read her mind on what she is expecting us to do. I follow the lead of the others and shift my body towards the opposite wall. The distinction for me is that, upon turning, I discover myself face to chest with the man Jenevieve referred to as Mr. Everett, while the other girls have the privilege of staring at the wall opposite the expansive hallway. I keep my gaze deliberately unfocused, fixed on his chest, hoping he will simply continue down the hall. However, he remains, standing and scrutinizing me.

"How long has she been here?" he inquires, irritation lacing his seductive voice.

Jenevieve pauses momentarily, recovering from her surprise at the question, and responds, "You mentioned hiring additional help. She applied, and given our need for assistance, she was hired. Not by me of course. I didn't want to hire her. In fact, I vehemently pushed back." Her words, though delivered with a smile, hold a subtle undertone of apprehension, like she fears repercussions for a decision she had no part in.

"What happened to her face?" his attention remains fixed on me. I can sense the intensity of his stare burning into my face, my bruises and split lip causing a surge of self-consciousness. His scrutinizing gaze compels me to maintain my focus resolutely on his chest.

I can see his hands tightly balling before releasing. I suck my lower lip into my mouth hoping to hide the split, and I curse myself for wearing my hair in a messy bun on top of my head as it gives a full view of the bruising on my face aside from the shorter pieces of hair that fell throughout the day framing my face.

Jenevieve takes a step forward, moving in our direction as if she has thought up an explanation for what had happened. "She is a bit clumsy, she—" her words abruptly cease as Mr. Everett snaps his head toward her. Still composed, he turns his body and advances in her direction. She stands frozen as the large man approaches.

"I suppose the same could be said about you," he remarks calmly, raising his hand as if to backhand her. While the prospect of Jenevieve facing consequences is something I secretly welcome, my body betrays me, instinctively stepping forward out of line before my brain can intervene.

"She's telling the truth," the words start vomiting out of my mouth before I can reel them in. "I wasn't paying attention, I tripped, and a bucket of horse feed fell on me. I'm sorry, I will be more careful from now on, it won't happen again," the words come out so fast his hand remains suspended mid-air, and Jenevieve's face retains a frozen expression tinged with slight fear.

"Is that so?" He turns his head to the side and looks back at me. His hand lowers and he slowly turns, walking back towards me. My gaze meets his briefly before I lower my eyes. I start cursing at myself for the perceived foolishness of defending the person responsible for the bruises on my face. Too late now, he stands towering before me once again.

I can't pry my eyes from his chest. I am utterly gripped by fear. "Do you know who I am?" he questions with a sincere curiosity lacing his angelic tone.

I stand rooted in place, my thoughts racing as I grapple with how to respond. In all honesty, I'm clueless about his identity. I can only surmise that he's the elusive owner everyone murmurs about. His name was spoken just moments ago when Jenevieve said it. Before this encounter, I never had a man to put to the name.

"Mr. Everett, sir," I cautiously reply, stealing a glance at Jenevieve. My eyes plead for her to rescue me from the predicament I had just helped her evade.

A wry laugh ripples through him in response. "*You* will know me soon enough," he emphasizes the word 'you,' while he stares at me. After a brief pause, he turns around and begins to walk away.

"I hope not," I mutter under my breath. And in a split second, I find myself lying on my back on the hall table across from where we were just standing. He is positioned firmly between my thighs with both of my hands pinned above my head with just one of his. His fingers laced between mine, and I can feel his manhood pressed between the inside of my legs.

Confusion is apparent on my face as I struggle to comprehend how he got me from my previous spot in the hallway to this vulnerable position in seconds without causing harm.

The hallway is silent.

Our eyes lock and my breathing hitches. The world seems to blur into insignificance. His presence is a magnetic force drawing me in. It feels as though I have been drowning for years, struggling against every current that kept me submerged. Then, in an instant, I finally broke through the surface, gasping for air after an eternity underwater.

In a low voice, his lips merely an inch from mine, he speaks. "My name will moan from your lips and echo off every wall in this place. *YOU* are mine. Welcome home, baby," he states, matter-of-factly, his hand squeezing my thigh, revealing a semblance of restraint as his body resists surrender.

My hands unintentionally grip his hand tightly, as if trying to hold him in place, and I don't know why.

I find a faint echo of my voice and summon the strength to murmur, "You have me confused with someone else," I assert truthfully.

The awareness that an impending realization of mistaken identity is going to leave us both feeling embarrassed. My eyes are apprehensive to roam his face, so they remain fixed on his intense gaze.

He seems familiar to me… to my soul.

I feel every breath he takes, his body unyieldingly pressing against mine.

A mischievous grin spreads across his face. "Someone else?" his expression lingers for a moment, then gradually fades away. "Three years. Eleven months. And fourteen days," he says each word slowly, pausing, and then reiterates the same words with a hiss. "Three years. Eleven months. And fourteen days. I haven't been able to be with another woman for three years, eleven months, and fourteen days." Frustration seeps into his voice as he decisively tightens his grip on my thigh.

Caught off guard, I instinctively hold my breath. My mind races with the words he is saying, but I am unable to comprehend his meaning.

"I have been deprived of any form of release for almost four years because of you," he grits his teeth together. "No, I don't just think I have you confused with someone else," he glances from one eye to the other, down to my lips, and then back up to my eyes.

"I had nothing to do with that," I reply truthfully.

A look of astonishment washes over him. Removing his grip on my thigh, he swipes his fingers down both sides of the stubble on his face. Our eyes lock once more, his composure restored.

"Do you feel that?" he presses his member more firmly into me.

What I feel is my body betraying me as the moisture between my legs seeps through my panties. I'm aware that even my nipples have hardened, and I attempt to control my breathing to conceal audible signs of arousal in the presence of this captivating man above me. Nobody has touched me in so long that I have forgotten how good it could feel. My body aches to glide up and down his shaft, knowing even between our clothes, the wetness coming from me would allow me to easily move up and down his length.

"Blood has not circulated through my penis in a very long time. Can you confidently tell me that I couldn't tear through the thin fabric of your panties and penetrate you right now?" he mutters, his voice steeped in arousal, suggesting that he too is struggling to maintain his composure in the face of our closeness.

A lengthy silence ensues, and he continues, "If I have you confused with someone else, then you surely do not possess the power to turn me on," he says, even though we are both highly aware of just how turned on he is.

We pant while staring into each other's eyes. Neither of us seem to harbor any desire to resist, succumbing to the unspoken connection that intensifies with each passing moment.

He's the one to break the silence, "Regardless, if I weren't so busy, you would be sprawled out naked on my bed right now while I fuck you raw," he asserts as he presses himself into me harder, hitting my sweet spot, causing my body to tighten around him, and then he straightens up. "But duty beckons."

Then, as though he tugs at the thread binding our souls, unraveling the delicate stitching that had been forming, he lifts me off the table by my waist and sets me down gently until my feet are planted on the floor. The room sharpens into focus, and the return to reality unfolds once more.

Running his hands down the front of his flawlessly ironed button-up shirt, he strides away down the expansive hallway, leaving all of us standing there in astonishment and bewilderment.

Shay catches my attention by softly calling my name and gesturing for me to join her in line.

As if on cue, Jenevieve blinks back into reality. "Carry on, ladies. Eat your lunch and take the rest of the day off. Head back to the maid's quarters when you're finished. I shall see you all first thing in the morning," she says, her eyes welling with tears. With her usual confidence, she turns and strides away, the only sound being the click of her heels on the marble floor as she leaves down the hall in the same direction Mr. Everett went.

Throughout lunch, I grapple with confusion, attempting to make sense of the events in the hallway. My entire body was ignited in arousal by that man. Even more perplexing was Jenevieve's subsequent demeanor. She had never displayed any emotion other than the authoritative control she exerted over the staff every day, but now she seems genuinely affected. It left me questioning how that could possibly be. Everyone had talked about Mr. Everett being harsh, with some staff even describing him as a heartless monster. I had even overheard the kitchen staff making jokes about how he could eat without teeth, given that nobody had ever witnessed him smile.

Based on all the hushed conversations, I assumed he was a wealthy, old man simply tired of everyone's bullshit. And Jenevieve's reaction to him has me convinced she likes him. Really likes him. I can see the attractive appeal as he is remarkably handsome... Devastatingly handsome. He's also possibly the biggest man I have ever seen. When he stood next to me, I expected to see where he ended, but even my peripheral couldn't reach that height without shifting my eyes. Beneath his clothing, he looked well defined, and I could feel the solidity of his body, leaving me almost salivating. And his blue eyes, the bluest eyes I have ever seen.

Now, I have to worry the interaction between him and I will have Jenevieve gunning for my throat again at every corner.

We all gather in the large dining hall, and conversations amongst the staff resume as usual. Shay, Amber, and Lilly are engaged in a lively discussion, but my mind is still on him, and I struggle to focus on their conversation. Shay is the only one present from our group who witnessed the hallway incident, but she has made no mention of it. Strangely, there is no gossip circulating about the event, which strikes me as somewhat peculiar. I had expected that every girl who saw what transpired would be sharing the details during lunch, leading to curious glances and a game of telephone circulating through the staff. I half-anticipated the story evolving into a sensationalized account of Mr. Everett and me engaging in public intimacy with an audience of other maids. But it doesn't happen. Everyone carries on as if nothing interesting happened.

Had I hallucinated the entire incident?

CHAPTER

Six

JONAH

Hours pass, and nightfall arrives. I still can't gather my thoughts. "How can I be gone for a month and come back to this shitshow?" I pace back and forth in my office. "She has been working in the very place I planned on bringing her home to!" My anger builds more rapidly. "And her face! someone put their hands on my girl," I say through gritted teeth.

"What has Shay said about it?" I question.

Jonathan thinks for a second. "Nothing really, Shay just said she had an accident, and her face is pretty beat up." He doesn't look like he's lying but I still don't buy that's the whole story. I'll need to look at the security footage and find out what Gladys knows. Maybe she can do some digging.

"She's lost weight. Does she look like she's lost weight?" I turn to Jonathan seeking confirmation but not wanting a response. I know she has lost weight. Is she refusing to eat? Does she not like the food that is prepared here? Maybe Gladys needs to switch the menu.

"What can I do, sir?" Giles, my loyal butler, asks.

"There is nothing that can be done now, Giles. This should never have happened. How am I supposed to get anything done with this?" I gesture to my still-hard cock, which is on the verge of tearing through the seams of my dress pants.

"Well, the woman responsible for that just so happens to be under the same roof as you… right now," Jonathan nods his head towards my dick, "I am going to see Shay, want me to send Kalyn here to come see you?" he asks, offering a solution to my current predicament.

"No!" I bark out, a little more aggressively than I intended.

"Okay, okay," Jonathan puts his hands up in a conceding manner.

"Have you considered trying to relieve yourself, sir?" Giles offers sincerely.

"Thank you, Giles, that will be all for the night. Close the door on your way out. Both of you," I say dismissively. He hesitates, contemplating whether to stay or go, but eventually gives in and walks toward the door. As soon as the door clicks shut behind Giles, I run my fingers through my hair, "FUCK!" I yell as I sweep the contents of my desk onto the floor. The sound of breaking glass and other items hitting the floor reverberates throughout the room.

I can't stop pacing, my mind completely consumed by thoughts of her. It's been four excruciatingly long years and I've been utterly captivated by her. I've spent countless hours devising strategies to approach her, earn her trust, and ultimately make her fall in love with me. All I want is to have her in my life and shower her with my love, to prove that I am the only man she'll ever need. But now, what do I do? I can't just confess that I witnessed her break-up the very first night I laid eyes on her. Nor can I reveal that I've secretly watched her at work… watched her at home.

My desire for her is undeniable, evident in the way my body responds whenever I lay eyes on her. A couple of times, I found myself so turned on watching her, I would send Jonathan away for a walk, hoping to relieve myself, only to be left more pissed off with even worse blue balls because I couldn't climax.

I've never felt the need for a committed relationship before. I relish the freedom of being with different women whenever I please, without anyone questioning my choices. I answer to no one.

My employees appear to fear me, likely due to the perpetual scowl on my face, probably why nobody ever approaches me. Yet, this woman has the power to reduce me to my knees, begging for her acceptance in any manner she feels appropriate.

Gone are the thoughts of casual encounters and fleeting moments. She has replaced them all. I crave her in every sense of the word. I want to experience every possible way of being with her, and I'll take her all the ways she'll allow me.

I want the world to hear her scream my name, knowing that I am the one responsible for her pleasure.

What has she done to me?

I can vaguely recall moments in my early life of complete relaxation. Now, my body is riddled with knots, and I constantly feel tense and unable to unwind.

In the past, I could find temporary relief after I'd fuck. Releasing my pent-up aggression on women that begged to be fucked by me. Now, I just feel like half of me has been missing and is walking around inside of this woman. I have been more uptight with a short fuse for the last four years.

Fuck! I need her.

I abruptly stop at the expansive windows that provide a glimpse of the boundless courtyard behind the house. Observing intently, my heart quickens its pace once more, and my erect and throbbing member flexes excitedly upon catching sight of her. "Kalyn," I murmur, as I see her descending the stairs towards the courtyard.

CHAPTER
Seven

KALYN

I'm convinced I'm losing my mind.

I find myself on an unexpected rollercoaster ride that just won't seem to end. It all started with losing my job and being evicted from my apartment, but then things took a turn for the better. I managed to find a new job that not only provides me with a beautiful mansion to live in but also offers a well-paying position. However, this rollercoaster ride quickly took a downward spiral when I had to face Jenevieve's wrath on multiple occasions: she slapped me, dug her talons into my arm, kept me from having lunch almost every day, some days keeping me late at work where I had to miss dinner too, knocked me out with a bucket of horse feed, and talks down to all of us on a daily basis. She is a fucking monster.

Just when I thought things couldn't get any crazier, the roller-coaster unexpectedly climbed to its highest point and took a freefall when I encountered the most attractive man I'd ever seen. To make matters even more complicated, he happens to be my boss and the owner of the mansion. Contrary to my expectation of an old, irritable man, Mr. Everett turned out to be quite the opposite. He has the deepest blue eyes, and his wavy light brown hair is just long enough to run my fingers through on the sides and a couple of inches on top that swoops off to the side, both thick and lustrous. A shaved face revealing perfectly chiseled features, although the first day I met him, he had slight scruff on his face that was so sexy. Every detail, from his piercing gaze, his intoxicating scent, to his authoritative disposition, is utterly mesmerizing. I'm captivated by him, and I don't quite understand how it is possible after just meeting. And to top it all off, he had me sprawled out on a hallway table filling me up in front of the other maids. I was all but panting and drooling all over myself, feeling his arousal between my legs.

Hours after that incident I still can't shake it. His touch lingers and I only want to feel it again.

Am I in the Twilight Zone?

After the eventful day I've had, a breath of fresh air beckons. Everyone in the maid's quarters has already retired to their rooms for the evening, and Shay is with Jonathan in his room, so I decide to slip out to clear my head.

Navigating through the expansive interior, I reach the imposing doors leading to the back patio. A majestic staircase unfolds, guiding me to an enchanting courtyard below. The steps widen as I descend, and an unmistakable princess-like feeling envelops me in the magical atmosphere. Meticulously laid paths wind through a vibrant tapestry of flowers and potted plants, their sweet fragrance lingering in the air.

In the darkness, the mansion being in the middle of nowhere allows the stars and moon to illuminate the courtyard. Lamp posts dot the pathways, with smaller lights nestled just off the path making it easy to see where I'm walking.

Seated on a bench, I marvel at the breathtaking surroundings, a tender breeze tousling my hair, my legs swinging back and forth. Glancing back at the mansion, I'm captivated by its beauty and sheer size.

Then, my eyes lock onto his. A surge of earlier emotions floods back, causing my breath to catch, and my feet immediately stop swinging. Chills sweep over my entire body, rendering me immobile, unable to break the intense eye contact.

He stands in a room with large windows, his back pressed against the wall as he gazes out at me. There's an undeniable hold he seems to have over me—a profound awareness that he's watching me instantly hardens my nipples.

Can he see that?

Can he feel what he's doing to me?

Our gazes remain locked, neither of us willing to take our eyes off the other. I am filled with a longing for his touch again, for him to walk out here and sit beside me, or climb on top of me…

The spell is broken when Gladys quietly walks up.

"Kalyn, sweetie," she smiles warmly. "It's late. Why don't you come back inside?" She extends her hand toward me. My gaze briefly returns to the mansion window, where he had been standing, only to find it empty. Smiling at Gladys, I accept her hand, allowing her to guide me back inside.

CHAPTER

Eight

KALYN

Two days have passed since our chance encounter in the courtyard. I am certain he is somewhere in this huge mansion, yet our paths have not crossed again. During this time, Mr. Everett has remained elusive, and my thoughts are incessantly drawn to him. Despite my struggle to think of anything other than him, the fascination the new ladies have for him only adds to the difficulty of diverting my attention elsewhere.

Initially, I think we all were under the impression that the scary, big bad wolf, Mr. Everett, was the Crypt Keeper, with both feet basically in the grave already. Perhaps, the notion was subtly implanted by the more seasoned staff. After all, why would they never comment on how gorgeous he is? However, it has become abundantly clear that this perception is far from the truth. Instead, he emerges as the most divine man any of us have ever laid eyes on.

Among the new staff, hushed conversations circulate, acknowledging both the intimidating aura he exudes and the more daring description of "fucking sexy"—and these are the comments deemed appropriate. In his absence, these murmurs evolve into desires of him "having his way with them." A sense of possessiveness starts to emerge within me as if I want to claim him as my own. However, I acknowledge the foolishness of these sentiments and recognize that there is no valid basis for such feelings.

The morning brings subtle rain, a serene spectacle we observe throughout the day, the clouds veiling any attempt by the sun to break through. As the hours pass, the rain intensifies, turning into a steady downpour by the afternoon. A sluggish gloom settles over the staff as everyone meanders about, attending to their chores.

Peering through the window, my gaze fixates on the rain as it descends, gracefully forming intricate patterns on the windows and creating puddles below.

"Do you think it will cause road flooding?" Amber inquires, standing beside me, peering out of the expansive window into the courtyard.

Captivated by the downpour, I remark, "I'm sure it will if it keeps up like this. I love rainstorms."

"I'm just relieved we're in here and not caught out in that," she mentions before stepping away from the window.

Mesmerized by the scene, I remain fixated on it. "I love the smell of rain when it first begins," I recall, inhaling and savoring the memory.

"I'm not particularly fond of anything related to the rain," Amber remarks, pausing before she continues as she moves around the room, tidying up. "Except for the fact that it provides a drink for plant life."

I laugh softly. "Well, you'll find joy in knowing that everything outside is currently enjoying a drink and a swim at the same time," blades of grass peaking above the pooled water.

Enveloped in my fascination with the rain, I was oblivious to Jenevieve's approach. Her sharp voice breaks through my trance, "If you keep staring out the window, you'll be working until night-fall. You're not here to gaze at the rain—you're here to work. Take your eyes off the window and get back to work," she scolds. Her words make me flinch, prompting an immediate retreat from the window. She stands, sneering at me, even as I resume working, remaining in place for a few moments before finally stomping off.

As the evening unfolds, the weather transforms into a full-fledged thunderstorm, its echoes reverberating beyond the walls of the mansion. The ominous thunder sends a ripple of anxiety through everyone, exacerbated by alerts on all devices warning of a potential power outage.

Jenevieve instructs us to persist in our job duties until the end of our shift at five, emphasizing the importance of thorough cleaning and urging us to be both meticulous and swift. Her concern stems from a lack of trust in our ability to work in the dark, fearing that any mishap might lead to the irreplaceable damage of items within the mansion, for which she says we would never have the funds to replace anything we carelessly break. Whenever she reprimands us, I find myself laughing inwardly and sarcastically noting her inspiring and poetic words as she lashes out at us.

Sam and I used to find amusement in the TikTok videos creators would post featuring sweet songs playing over their video, often captioned with phrases like 'uplifting words my family/mom/dad say to me daily.' The twist would come when the captions revealed more sarcastic or humorously critical remarks like "Did you purposely choose to wear that? Have you had a chance to look at it in the mirror?" or "Get your hair off your face like that, you look like a greasy emo"—intended for humor and garnering likes.

Every time these videos came on Sam's FYP we would fall into fits of laughter. This trend turned into an inside joke between Sam and me. Whenever either of us teased with a sarcastic remark, we'd playfully act out the scenario of retrieving our folded hand out of our pocket, opening it up like a notepad, then retrieving an invisible pen from behind our ear, and whimsically pretending to write down the insult on an unseen notepad. This became a humorous ritual, alluding to our in-depth compilation for the "uplifting TikTok" we knew we would never actually create.

In the last half-hour of our shift, the lights begin to flicker intermittently. Amber and I exchange glances each time, my silent plea hoping they will stay on just long enough for a quick after-work shower to wash away the dirt and sweat.

With every flicker, a quiet curse echoes in my thoughts. As the clock counts down to the last few minutes of our shift, we quickly stow away our cleaning supplies, hurrying toward the maid's quarters.

I rush through the quickest shower, meticulously scrubbing my body twice with body wash and thoroughly washing my hair. Each flicker of the lights causes a momentary pause in my movements, a fleeting concern that this might be the moment the power finally gives out. When the lights hold steady, relief surges, and I resume my brisk cleansing, determined to finish before any potential outage could interrupt my rinsing. Turning off the water, I squeeze the excess moisture from my hair and secure it atop my head with a towel. Wrapping another towel around my body, I step out of the shower, wiping my feet on the mat before darting to my closet in search of an outfit. I dress myself in cream-colored silk shorts paired with a matching silk tank top. Completing the ensemble, I affectionately drape what I term my "silk house coat" over my shoulders, although it's simply a robe. Towel-drying my hair to the best of my ability, I brush through it, unraveling any knots before loosely braiding my thick locks, letting them cascade gracefully over one shoulder.

As I emerge from my room, I notice everyone has retreated to their rooms. Despite Jenevieve's repeated reminders that snooping around the mansion is strictly prohibited, especially after work hours. Yet, I catch myself engaging in precisely that forbidden activity. With everyone seemingly confined to their rooms, the entire house appears empty. Aimlessly roaming, I tread barefoot through the mansion, the distant rumbling of thunder echoing in the background.

Navigating the extensive, winding hallways, I pass by muted laughter and whispered conversations. Eager not to intrude, I briskly walk past, stealing a glance down the hall to identify the source. There, one of the housekeeping staff leans against the wall, with Brad hovering over her. His hand groping the contours of her body, and he leans in to kiss her neck, her hands entangling in his hair.

A surge of adrenaline rocks through me, and I awkwardly hope they haven't noticed my presence. Continuing my stride, my thoughts shift to the disgust I feel towards him. Especially after calling him out in his apartment for being a man whore. And I haven't seen him since that day of work. What kind of man purposely has sex with the entire staff? He must be aware of the potential issues it could cause among the women he's involved with. Vanessa convinced herself that she and Brad are meant to be together and would undoubtedly be pissed to find out he was sleeping with other staff members. Despite warnings about his behavior, he remains a smooth talker, capable of charming the staff. A single smile from him seems enough to make them swoon, and their panties drop.

My irritation bubbles more than it should. The workplace tension is already palpable, exacerbated by Jenevieve's unpleasant demeanor towards all of us. Brad's inability to keep his penis in his pants only contributes further to our problems. To MY problems.

Lost in contemplation, I realize I've inadvertently wandered into an unfamiliar section of the house, evidence of how preoccupied I am with the impending issues he is going to cause.

I find myself passing by a dark room. The door is slightly ajar, and as if being pulled to it, I peek through the crack in the door, noticing the towering windows that allow the moonlight to pour inside, illuminating the room, cascading window shadows on the floor.

I see him leaning his back against the tall window frame at the end of the room. He is just standing there with his arms folded across his chest looking out the window at the rain coming down, completely lost in thought, in the same spot I saw him a few nights ago from the courtyard.

I debate whether I should disturb him. I'm not supposed to be wandering around his house after all. Not even allowing myself a full moment to contemplate the pros and cons of interrupting him, I open the door wide enough to squeeze through and quietly walk toward him. Though I can't be heard walking across the cold floor, I see my reflection in the windows as I approach him, noticing his breathing hitches when he sees me. Coming to a halt once we are merely a foot apart.

We stand in silence, observing the rhythmic dance of raindrops. My heartbeat races as I feel my skin tingle from the closeness to him. Ten minutes slip by, a tranquil period where not a single word is exchanged. Oddly enough, it's during this moment that I realize an overwhelming sense of peace settling within me, a feeling that has been absent from me for quite some time.

By the window, wearing only my silk pajamas, a shiver runs down my spine, causing goosebumps to prickle across my skin. In the window's reflection, my hardened nipples are distinctly visible. I encircle myself with my arms, unintentionally pressing my breasts together, creating two peaks beneath the open neckline of my silk top.

Noticing his eyes look at my reflection in the window, he silently pushes himself off the wall and walks away. I watch him slowly fade into darkness. There is emptiness in the reflection, but then, from the depths of the darkness, he emerges once more, his silhouette gradually materializing. With each passing second, he regains his form, as he walks up behind me and wraps a soft blanket around my shoulders, holding both ends around me until I grab the bunched-up material. His arms continue encircling me briefly, his face turning towards mine. I hear him inhale, and shivers course through me.

The blanket is plenty warm, yet it's his comforting warmth that I am reluctant to have leave.

He strides toward the leather bench strategically positioned between the windows, providing an optimal vantage point. With purpose, he lowers himself onto the seat, settling in with a deliberate yet composed demeanor. Peering through the window, I notice his eyes fixed on me, a gaze both intense and enigmatic. His expression offers no discernible emotions, leaving me to ponder the thoughts that may be taking place in his mind. For a brief moment, I remain rooted in the same spot, capturing his flawless figure in the reflective glass.

"He is utterly gorgeous," I acknowledge inwardly, and a growing sense of nervousness creeps over me beneath the weight of his attentive scrutiny.

Turning my head back casting a glance over my shoulder in his direction, our gazes meeting in a magnetic lock. The air in the room seems to thin as our eyes connect, creating a breathless moment. Does he want me to come sit next to him? Would he mind if I did?

Urging my legs to move, I turn toward him and slowly walk over to where he is seated. Lowering myself onto the bench beside him, I draw the blanket down around my waist and settle on it. My robe slips off my shoulder, and our arms make a gentle connection. His arms are solid, and the muscles, even as he just sits here bulge, flexing further when our arms touch. The mere simplicity of this sets off sparks that ignite throughout my body.

Moments drift by, hyper-aware of the subtle sensation of our skin gently brushing.

Is he feeling this too?

We both appear to be captivated by the storm's spectacle outside the window. However, my attention isn't on the storm—it's fixated on his reflection. I even see when his gaze shifts from the window toward me, his eyes study my face before descending to my shoulder, seemingly contemplating whether to make contact. Slowly, his finger glides along the bare skin where the robe has shifted, delicately slipping inside the edge, tracing his finger back and forth against my skin and the robe, then gradually pulling it up on my shoulder. A wave of goosebumps follows the trail of his soft touch. Once my robe is securely in place on my shoulder, he leisurely trails his fingers down my back, and my eyes close as I savor the feeling. Eventually, resting his hand on the back of the bench opposite where I am seated, his arm exerting a gentle pressure against my back.

Silence hangs between us, yet the sexual tension is palpable. My fingers fidget nervously, awkwardly intertwining with each other, their path guided by uncertainty as I ponder where they should settle—an action I'm unconsciously engaged in. In response, he gracefully positions his right arm on his thigh, palm up, extending an unspoken invitation for me to put my hand in his.

I divert my gaze to his open hand, studying it briefly before looking back at him. Our eyes lock, and a burning intensity ensues. Navigating my hand toward his, I place it in his outstretched palm, feeling his grasp enveloping mine—a large, comforting gesture that makes my hand feel small in comparison. My heart begins thudding in my chest, my lips subtly curve upward at this interaction. He adjusts our hands, shifting them to my lap, a maneuver to prevent any discomfort caused by my arm extending too far toward his lap. His longer arm makes the adjustment more convenient for both of us. I notice a faint smile playing at the corner of his mouth as the back of his hand rests on my bare leg. Redirecting my attention to the storm outside, I sense a growing connection unfolding.

A sense of time suspension envelops us, trapping us in this remarkable moment for an entire hour. His thumb traces my skin, and his gaze alternates between our hands, me, and the storm outside. Each time his eyes focus on our joined hands, mine instinctively follows suit, almost as if I seek confirmation that the perfection of how my hand feels in his matches how it looks. I wonder if he experiences the same sensation.

The moment dissipates by a knock on the door. Both of us turn our heads toward the sound, where the flickering silhouette of Giles holding a candle approaches.

"Mr. Everett. Kalyn," Giles greets us with a soothing tone that reflects happiness in his eyes. "Sir," he continues, "The power has gone out, as I'm sure you're aware," he surveys the darkened room. Although Mr. Everett had chosen to sit in the dark long before the power outage, we remained oblivious to the situation. "Most everybody has retired for the night, and candles have been provided for those still awake. We've also started a fire in the grand room. I'd offer for you both to join, although I suspect you're perfectly warm in here."

Mr. Everett maintains his gaze on Giles, "Thank you, Giles," his voice is irresistibly sexy.

"Of course, sir," Giles responds warmly. "Can I get either of you anything?" he asks in a soft tone. A subtle exchange of glances between Mr. Everett and me follows.

Giles is such a kind man, displaying a genuine care that highlights his unwavering loyalty to Mr. Everett. His eyes, always devoid of judgment, emit honesty and kindness, solely focused on seeking Mr. Everett's best interest.

"I'm fine, thank you, Giles," I smile up at him.

Mr. Everett fixes his gaze on me briefly before redirecting it to Giles. "We're fine for now, Giles. Thank you."

Giles face lights up as he glances between us. "Let me know if you need anything, absolutely anything," offering a nod to both of us before quietly exiting.

The storm is intensifying with time, the rain crashing down louder, and thunder resonating throughout the room. Despite the storm's uproar, a soothing drowsiness envelops me. My eyes slowly grow heavy, and I find myself resting my head on his broad shoulder. His head leans back against mine, and his other hand, initially resting on the opposite side of the bench, delicately wraps around my waist.

A sudden jolt awakens me, propelled by the piercing scream that echoes through the mansion.

"What was that?" My heart is racing so fast my hands begin to tremble from adrenaline, turning my attention to Mr. Everett, who shares my wide-eyed alertness. He rises swiftly, and I follow suit. Observing him as he strides towards his desk, keeping his eyes on the office door, he pulls open a drawer, enters a code, and unlocks a safe, retrieving a gun with practiced efficiency.

The room holds a tense stillness as our senses sharpen in response to the unexpected disturbance. He glances down as his fingers deftly slide the magazine out, each metallic click echoing in the charged atmosphere. Satisfied with the loaded clip, he smoothly slides it back into place and chambers the gun with a confident cock.

"What's going on?" my voice trembles like the rest of my body.

"Come with me," he says, extending his hand for me to take. I quickly move across the room and interlock my fingers with his, as he walks us to the office door, peering out the slightly ajar opening.

My gaze remains steadfast on him, carefully noting each move. He glances out, scanning in every direction before turning back to me. In a hushed tone, he whispers, "Come on," and gradually widens the door with his foot, allowing us to slip through. As he gauges the safety of the surroundings, we step out cautiously, hugging the wall. His vigilant eyes sweep across the expansive room before approaching a hallway. His pace slows, and he discreetly peeks around the corner. Shielded behind his towering frame, I'm unable to see what he observes. He lets out a low whistle, followed by a quiet "Dame" addressed to a man who materializes seconds later, accompanied by Giles, Brad, and a couple of unfamiliar faces.

Dame, the man he had called upon, quickly updates him on the unfolding situation. "One of the cooks spotted two armed men entering through the cook entrance. They bolted further inside the house after she screamed," Dame elaborates. All eyes fixate on Mr. Everett as Dame continues, "How do you want to sweep the house, sir?" The men, all fully alert, await Mr. Everett's instructions.

I observe Brad's initial response, noting a moment of surprise upon unexpectedly seeing me. His eyes roam up and down my body, prompting a self-conscious feeling about my revealing attire. Regret sets in for leaving the blanket behind, leading me to grab both sides of my robe with my free hand, attempting to cover up.

His gaze descends once again, this time freezing on the intertwined hands of Mr. Everett and me. A fleeting shadow of anger or jealousy crosses his face. The subtle shift in Brad's features hints at underlying emotions, leaving me completely unsure about the reason for his reaction. Ironically, he seems to be judging me, even though he was just balls deep in someone just a couple of hours ago.

Giles, composed, suggests, "Kalyn, why don't you come with me, and we can get you somewhere safe," gesturing an open hand toward me. Immediately I make a move to walk to him, liking the idea of going to hide.

Mr. Everett tightens his grip on my hand, "She stays with me," leaving no room for discussion. This also prompts a noticeable tightening of Brad's jaw. Why does he seem so irritated? Does he somehow believe that Mr. Everett is jeopardizing my safety by not sending me with Giles for protection, or is it simply the fact that Mr. Everett and I are holding hands?

Brad might not be displaying these odd jealousy behaviors if he knew how bad my palms were sweating. The only thing preventing my hand from slipping right out of Mr. Everett's is the secure grip he has on it.

"We might cover more ground if just the five of us sweep, sir," Dame offers, gesturing towards Mr. Everett, Brad, and the three-armed security guards. Dame concurs with the notion that I shouldn't accompany any of them. I also find that I agree with him, I should be hiding in a cupboard somewhere or better yet, sleeping like the rest of the staff. Damn thunderstorms. I've always loved them and will try my hardest to stay awake anytime one grumbles in the sky. Yet now, I find myself in a dangerous situation because I went exploring instead of sleeping like everyone else.

Irritation clouds Mr. Everett's eyes. "She is safest with me." Despite the tension, he remains resolute in his decision.

Appearing torn, as though an impulse to protest lingers, Dame deliberates on whether he should continue voicing his concern. Ultimately, he concedes with a simple, "Yes, sir," leaving the matter unresolved.

Swiftly issuing sweeping orders, Mr. Everett orchestrates the dispersal of everyone. However, Brad, assigned to a different location, persuasively convinces Mr. Everett to join our wing, citing the proximity to the kitchen where the intruders entered and his familiarity with this side of the house would be more beneficial to have them both sweeping this area. Mr. Everett, with a single nod of agreement, promptly rearranges Brad and another man's designated areas. He maintains a firm grip on my hand as he navigates us to the west wing of the house skillfully with Brad right behind us.

Upon reaching a section of the house where the path diverges, Mr. Everett signals with two fingers, indicating the direction for Brad to take one side, while he steers me down the opposite corridor. There's a fleeting moment where Brad's gaze remains fixed on me before reluctantly moving in the opposite direction, adhering to Mr. Everett's directive.

Detecting movement ahead, we abruptly stop, Mr. Everett instantly positions me fully behind him. "We have eyes on the sky," he says, awaiting a response.

A tremulous voice responds, "The blue moon rises, sir," Mr. Everett exhales with relief, his body relaxing, tugging on my hand as we move toward the source of the sound. Whatever that code phrase was they exchanged, let him know it was his staff that made the noise. What if that was me? Nobody told me anything about a code phrase.

An unfamiliar worker, seated on the ground in a recess of the wall, comes into view. Rushing toward her, he swiftly pulls me along, releasing my hand when we get to her as he kneels in front of her, quietly asking, "Are you injured?" The woman, visibly frightened, scoots further into the dip in the wall.

"No, sir," she replies, her voice shaky, and tears well at the edge of her eyes. Mr. Everett holds his hands out to her, assisting her to her feet. Her eyes dart to mine, and I instinctively take her hand. He immediately interlocks our fingers once more as she follows behind me down the hall. Mr. Everett takes us into the first room adjacent to the hall. As we enter, the only light comes from the moonlight streaming through the windows, casting a soft glow within. Like every other room in the mansion, this one is spacious. Even in the darkness, I can discern the room is beautifully decorated.

Positioned by the door, we wait as Mr. Everett meticulously sweeps the entire room before gesturing for us to join him at the opposite end. He instructs, "Stay in here, on this side of the bed. I'll lock the door on my way out and come get you when it's safe." The woman quickly nods in acknowledgment as she stays crouched down on the side of the bed farthest from the door.

He stands, extending his hand out to me to take.

"I'll stay here with her," I offer, my voice likely trembling more than her body is.

"No," he responds sternly, and I promptly stand, taking his hand once again as he guides us back to the door. Before we exit, I peer back at the woman we are leaving behind and feel slightly relieved when she remains unseen. Opening the door, he clicks the lock into place and quietly shuts the door behind us.

Proceeding down the hall, a single beep emits from Mr. Everett's phone. Retrieving it from his pocket, he glances at the message, choosing to keep its contents to himself. After reading, he smoothly places the phone back in his pocket and directs me into a nearby closet, leaving the door open just a crack as he awaits additional information. The abrupt transition into a closet has me both frightened and instantly turned on, a mixture of emotions I can't quite comprehend.

He stands tall by the door, peering into the dark hallway. Positioned directly behind him, I lean around to glance through the crack in the door, my hands gently resting on either side of his hips, ensuring he is aware of me standing right behind him, trying to see what he is looking for.

Sensing a shift in his body, I take a step back and observe him placing his gun in the waistband of his pants. He turns toward me taking a wide stance, and leans his back against the wall, his gaze fixed on me. His hands reach out to my waist, pulling me closer—a gesture I readily accept, taking a single step toward him. Standing between his legs, our bodies so close they subtly touch. In the stillness of the closet, he whispers, "Are you okay?"

I nod, maintaining eye contact.

"I won't let anything happen to you," he reassures me.

I have absolute certainty that his words ring true. "I know," I respond with a smile, wholeheartedly embracing the veracity of his statement.

His touch glides across my cheek, the back of his fingers tracing a delicate path, and then they smoothly descend along my jawline. Lifting my chin with a single finger, he tilts it up towards him, his gaze shifting between mine. Leaning in, drawing his mouth nearer to mine. My hands instinctively rise, settling on each of his hip bones. My heart picks up speed, and I eagerly await our lips to finally touch.

A single beep from his phone interrupts the moment, signaling a new message.

Letting out a pronounced exhale, he leans his head back against the wall momentarily, displaying a gesture of defeat. Retrieving his phone from his pocket, he reads the message before returning it to its place. His disappointment mirrors my own, and I almost want to take his phone and stomp on it until it's a pile of pieces beneath our feet.

He offers a tight-lipped smile and inquires, "Are you ready?" as he grabs me by my waist with both large hands and pushes himself up from the wall. I nod, despite my profound disappointment over the interrupted kiss.

Silently, we leave the closet and navigate down the hall. While passing a spiral staircase, the sound of someone bumping into something from above grabs both of our attention. He glances in my direction and motions towards the staircase. We make our way up, pressing ourselves against the wall. Mr. Everett raises his gun, aiming it toward the balcony above, as I tightly grip his hand, while my other arm wraps around his arm. As we reach the top, he scans both directions and once again, the sound of a noise reverberates down the hallway.

In the shadows ahead, a table is bumped, prompting Mr. Everett to stop and once again say, "We have eyes on the sky," yet this time, silence follows. He releases my hand, positioning himself between me and the source of the noise. "Put your weapon down and slowly come out with your hands up," he commands, his voice so dominant it has me feeling like I need to put my hands up.

Still met with silence, he motions one hand behind his back for me to stay put as he proceeds down the hall, both hands on the gun now.

Paralyzed with fear, I watch him advancing down the hall. Suddenly, a smaller but bold figure lunges at him, wielding an unknown object. In the darkness, two silhouettes grapple, yet it's evident the intruder is no match for Mr. Everett. Skillfully evading the assailant's strike, he seizes the intruder's arm, twists him around, and forces him face down on the floor, ultimately sitting on his back to restrain him.

"Babe, get my phone from my pocket and dial 6," he instructs urgently. My feet instinctively move quickly toward him, my hands tremble as I reach into his back pocket, retrieving the phone. I dial 6 as he directs, "Put it on speaker," he orders, while the subdued intruder yells in pain beneath him. As Mr. Everett sternly communicates with Dame, holding the intruder in check, I struggle to focus on anything beyond quelling the tremors in my hands.

Dame and Brad swiftly approach. Brad immediately steps toward me, wrapping his arm around my back protectively and guiding me a couple of steps away from the intruder. Meanwhile, Dame efficiently secures the intruder's hands behind his back with handcuffs. They elevate him to a standing position, and Dame begins to escort him away.

Mr. Everett returns to me, extending his hand. Shakily, I move towards him, placing my trembling hand in his and handing back his phone. As they walk away, the intruder makes eye contact with me, licks his lips, and utters, "Damn, had I known you were here, I would have destroyed your pussy before—"

In an instant, Mr. Everett lands a powerful punch on the intruder's nose, accompanied by a resounding crack. Blood gushes from the injured nose as the guy screams, "You broke my nose!"

"If you ever talk to her again, I will cut your fucking tongue out," Mr. Everett declares, his words seething with intensity.

As Dame and the intruder move past, I subtly maneuver myself, positioning farther behind Mr. Everett's back to use him as a protective barrier. I hold tightly onto his arm, even though I'm aware that the intruder currently poses no direct threat to me. Mr. Everett's breathing is audible, not from the recent struggle but due to the intruder's unsettling words directed at me. His gaze follows Dame leading the restrained man down the hall.

As soon as they disappear from sight, Mr. Everett shifts his focus to me, his eyes scanning my face, possibly searching for any signs of hesitation or fear. Satisfied I appear fine, he encourages me to proceed down the corridor. I remain vigilant, attuned to every sound and movement, or the absence thereof. As we pass by expansive windows adorned with thick floor-length curtains, Mr. Everett steals a glance outside, and my eyes follow suit. He surveys the remarkable scene beyond. The rain has now transformed into a gentle drizzle, a stark contrast to the furious storm that previously raged.

CHAPTER
Nine

JONAH

Her hand initially trembled uncontrollably when we left my office. The tremors subsided during our time in the closet, and she visibly relaxed. Seizing the moment, I made my move to kiss her, my gaze fixated on her plump, pink lips. I felt consumed to kiss her and lash my tongue against hers.

The interruption came when Brandt, another one of my security men, alerted us that it was safe enough to continue our sweep. I thought I detected a glint of disappointment in her expression, mirroring my feelings about our interrupted kiss. Yet, in hindsight, perhaps it was for the best. Her vulnerability in the face of fear made me hesitant to act on my impulses. I can't shake the feeling that taking advantage of her fear by kissing her would be unfair. I knew that once I tasted her, my self-control would be tested, and in the heat of the moment, a mere kiss might lead to forgetting my current responsibilities in the pursuit of the intruders.

Anger simmers within me as I ponder the stolen moment in my office, the interrupted kiss, and the audacity of the two armed men who exploited the power outage to breach my property's secure gates and infiltrate my home. Their knowledge of my house layout indicates a calculated intrusion. Once both intruders are apprehended, I am resolved to uncover the motives behind their actions and what they sought for invading my sanctuary.

As her fear resurfaces after the recent scuffle, I respond by tightening my grip on her hand—a vow that I will shield her from harm.

The rain outside has dwindled to a mere drizzle. Scanning the perimeter of the house for any signs of disturbance, I find only darkness illuminated by the faint light of the moon. Satisfied that all is well outside, I tear my gaze away from the window and guide her down the hall with Brad following behind. While the reassurance of having someone protect her from both the front and back brings slight relief, I find discomfort in his proximity to her. A flicker of anger crossed his eyes when he saw her hand in mine, and I can see the realization on his face as he processes that she is mine. His lingering looks, however, are starting to piss me off, though I'm confident he won't be foolish enough to risk jeopardizing his position, especially given the substantial compensation.

Straight ahead, the hall unfolds into a capacious room, ideal for a large group of people. At the room's far end stands another grand staircase, spiraling upward. At the halfway point, it diverges into two separate sets of stairs, each leading to different sections of the house. Navigating swiftly through the room, we ascend the stairs, and I silently signal Brad to take the left staircase while Kalyn and I take the right. After a moment of hesitation, he nods in comprehension and heads to the left.

With my gun pointed towards the top of the stairs, we ascend cautiously. My vigilant gaze sweeps across the landing, ensuring no signs of danger. Reaching the top, I cautiously peer around the corner, confirming the emptiness of the left-wing hall. Our eyes lock, and I nod to signal it's clear, guiding her off the final step as we proceed down the hall. The surroundings evoke a luxury hotel ambiance, with alcoves in the walls adorned with decorated tables, unlit sconces, and neatly hung mirrors and pictures. Five doors on either side are generously spaced, none of them locked—an opportune hiding spot for an intruder that I am determined to expose.

The first door opens to an undisturbed room, the carpet still showcasing smooth vacuum lines, a clear indicator that nobody has stepped foot in here since the last time a maid was in here. Moving down the hall, I methodically check each room, opening the doors one by one and inspecting the vacuum lines on the carpet. With every door I open, she tightens her grip on my hand, a gesture that I savor each time. Some rooms lack windows, relying on my phone's flashlight to reveal their untouched state. Each room appears undisturbed as my eyes meticulously scour wall to wall for signs someone has entered, vowing to tear apart my own house in pursuit of the unwelcome intruder. Approaching the final door, I almost wish there were a hundred more doors to check in this hall. The thought arises from an unwillingness for our time up here to end, yearning to prolong the moments I'm with her.

Coincidentally, just as I complete a thorough scan of the last room, assured of its emptiness, my phone emits a single beep. Pulling it from my back pocket, a message from Brandt appears on the screen, as if the timing couldn't be more precise.

Second intruder has been apprehended.

**No injuries. Taking him to the holding room.
Waiting for your instructions.**
-Brandt

Reading the message, a sigh of relief escapes me. We stand at the end of the hall, bathed in the moonlight pouring through a large window decorated with thick curtains to the floor that are drawn open. Glancing down at her face, etched with concern, I'm captivated by her beauty—a sight that leaves me breathless. I have longed for this woman for so long, it feels surreal that she is standing here with me. Gently brushing my hand on her cheek, I share the news, "The second intruder has been apprehended."

An audible exhale of relief brushes passed her perfect mouth, and her entire body relaxes as she leans into my touch.

As if he runs on the worst timing, Brad confidently strides down the hallway, informing us, "The final intruder has been apprehended." Irritation surges within me. I had already received the same message, which he knows. His unnecessary update pisses me off. Putting my frustration aside, I manage to muster a curt nod.

"Mr. Everett just received the text as well," she innocently remarks, seemingly unaffected by the repetitive information. Her lack of annoyance serves as a stark contrast to my own, reminding me of how much this intrusion has tested my patience.

As Brad approaches, he stands his ground, seemingly oblivious to the daggers I shoot his way—or he's choosing to ignore them—because he remains in place, patiently waiting for our next move. Suppressing my growing annoyance, I take the initiative to step forward, unwilling to unleash my frustration on him when two unwelcome individuals in my house truly deserve the full force of my anger.

"Let's go," I prompt us to move, giving her hand a reassuring squeeze.

Without a moment's hesitation, she confesses, "I want ice cream," casting a glance at me.

Her unexpected response catches me off guard, and a small laugh escapes my throat. "We'll get you some ice cream," I assure her, "We just need to stop and get Alice," acknowledging the likelihood that she's still frozen on the floor near the bed where I left her.

"Why don't I take Kal to the kitchen while you go get Alice? I'll make sure she gets her ice cream," Brad suggests as if he assumes I would entertain such an idea.

A condescending laugh escapes me. "Probably not," I remark, walking past Brad, pulling her along as we continue down the lengthy hallway. The absurdity of his suggestion doesn't go unnoticed, and I have no intention of relinquishing control over knowing where *my* girl is.

Descending the stairs, we navigate through the mansion's corridors, retracing our steps to the room where I had left one of my chefs trembling, seeking refuge from the chaos. Guilt tugs at me for leaving her alone, but my priority is ensuring my girl's safety—I can't afford to be distracted by anything else.

Approaching the door, mindful of the anxious woman on the other side and the absence of the intruder threat, I speak with a steady voice so as not to startle her further. "Alice, it's Mr. Everett. Can you unlock the door?" While I could easily break it open, I know this would only intensify her fear, and I intend to reassure her it's safe.

Rustling sounds emanate from the other side, accompanied by the frantic jiggling of the door handle as she works to unlock it. With a swift motion, the door swings open, and Alice practically flies into Kalyn's arms. It's an embrace that Kalyn welcomes as she hugs Alice back.

"It's alright," Kalyn offers reassurance to the trembling woman. "Mr. Everett promised me ice cream—would you like to join?" Her smile, radiant even in the dim light, reveals perfect, straight white teeth as she tilts her head back, gazing at Alice. The invitation seems to alleviate some of the lingering nervousness.

Alice responds with a subtle nod, and I guide them forward, urging them to continue toward the kitchen. In the background,

I hear rapid footsteps, and when I glance behind, I see Brad taking long strides to catch up… with Kalyn. Positioning himself to walk alongside her. This sight irritates me, only adding to my frustration.

When she quickens her pace to move away from him and walk beside me, I feel elated but realize there is tension between them. What did he do to upset her?

As we continue toward the kitchen, we pass by Gladys, seated in a recliner near the window, flipping through a magazine. As she spots us, she stands up from her chair and walks over, pausing briefly. "Mr. Everett, is everything taken care of?" Her gaze shifts between each of us.

I nod and offer a curt, "Yes," ensuring she knows the imminent danger has been handled. Though the full details of why my house was targeted is still a mystery, I anticipate I will have clarity in the next few hours.

I shift my attention away from her and turn toward the gorgeous woman beside me. Her face lights up as she mentions, "We were heading to get some ice cream." Her smile never fails to captivate me, making me want to press my mouth to hers—a craving I am desperately attempting to suppress. She has awakened a beast in me, and restraining it is proving to be much more difficult than I initially expected.

Gladys lights up at the prospect of ice cream. "Oh, honey, I knew I liked you," she remarks to Kalyn, attempting to take her hand from mine. I tighten my grip, reluctant to release her hand. This prompts Gladys to playfully slap my hand. "Oh, stop, she's safe with me." She winks at Kalyn, then takes her hand and leads her toward the kitchen, with Alice following. Brad also walks past me and joins them.

Alice and Kalyn settle at the metal table, and I position myself behind Kalyn, standing guard as Gladys prepares two bowls of chocolate ice cream. Placing the bowls in front of Kalyn and

Alice, Kalyn eagerly takes a spoonful, savoring the taste. "Thank you. It's my favorite."

A single beep from my phone reminds me that I need to get downstairs to where the two men are being held. Shifting around Kalyn, I position myself between her and Alice. "I need to go take care of some things. Stay here with Gladys until I return." The directive is clear, emphasizing that I don't want her leaving the kitchen in my absence.

"Yes, sir," she responds, her mouth still filled with the ice cream. Her reply, coupled with the use of "Sir," stirs a primal response in me. The desire to spread her out on the table right now and lick her pussy the same way she has been licking her ice cream.

"I'll be back soon," I assure her, cutting through the inappropriate thought, maintaining my gaze on her and then turning to Gladys and then to Brad. "Let's go," I say sternly, as I exit the room, Brad following suit. The urgency of the situation propelling me forward, leaving behind the lingering desire that threatens to disrupt my focus.

CHAPTER

Ten

KALYN

The room descends into silence as Mr. Everett's fading footsteps retreat down the corridor, leaving an absence that's intensely felt. I miss his presence already. Breaking the quiet, Gladys interjects, "Hardly a month of you being here, and we get excitement." She takes a seat across the table, resting her hands on the surface.

"I was shaking like a leaf," I confess, my admission accompanied by a sidelong glance at the woman beside me, who quietly eats her ice cream. I'm not sure why I share my vulnerability. Perhaps I'm hoping it will provide some solace to her, yet she shows no sign of acknowledging my words.

Gladys lightheartedly teases, "With that human shield, you were the safest one in this place," her voice laced with amusement as she alludes to Mr. Everett's towering stature. My mind wanders briefly, contemplating his physique and how he manages to stay so fit despite his busy schedule. This leads me to envision him in a more intimate setting, completely nude, and spreading me out on this table while he fucks me. An inappropriate and intrusive thought that brings a sly grin to my lips.

"Here, honey," Gladys interrupts my musings, handing me a napkin just as I realize I have a bite of ice cream waiting at my lips. My fleeting, inappropriate thoughts had distracted me, as I lazily swiped the spoonful of melting ice cream over my lips, allowing it to drip onto my lap.

Embarrassment colors my cheeks. "Oh my gosh, I'm sorry," I stammer, putting my spoon back in the bowl. I take the napkin from Gladys and begin dabbing at the ice cream on my lap, attempting to salvage some semblance of composure.

Gladys maintains a serene smile as I finish my attempt to clean the dripped ice cream off my lap. A nagging suspicion creeps in, making me wonder if she could somehow hear my inappropriate thoughts, her smile perhaps a subtle acknowledgment of my momentary lapse.

I really need to get laid. My lack of sex has my mind wandering to places it shouldn't, and an insatiable craving for a man's touch… Mr. Everett's touch. A sensation I thought I had left behind when Wyatt destroyed my heart.

"So um, do we know what they wanted?" I redirect the conversation, steering my thoughts away from the gutter and to dispel the feeling that Gladys possibly regards me as an idiot. Although I know she doesn't, I can't help but project my own sense of foolishness onto her.

Rising from the table, she gathers our empty bowls and walks towards the sink. "Probably just seeking shelter from the rain," she remarks, placing the bowls in the sink, the only audible sound being the clinking of the bowl and spoons against the metal. She then returns to the table, reseating herself across from me.

"Yeah," I agree, knowing it wasn't the real reason. I interpret Gladys's statement as an attempt to steer the conversation away, especially since the woman beside me still appears frightened. So, I don't press the subject.

Giles enters the room to check on our well-being, and I wonder whether he has been with Mr. Everett. His presence is fleeting because Gladys asks him to accompany the frightened woman back to her room. Giles readily agrees, and the woman relaxes, looking like all she wants to do right now is go to sleep.

Once they depart, Gladys reaches across the table, taking my hands in hers. "Mr. Everett is fine, sweetie," she reassures me as if sensing my concern about his whereabouts. While I assume he may be with the intruders, attempting to discern their motives, the potential issues of him being with dangerous men, and the entire situation looms in my mind. Even with me witnessing firsthand Mr. Everett's capabilities and knowing he can absolutely take care of himself; I worry for his safety. I would feel more at ease if I were still with him.

Not entirely sure how to articulate my feelings, I respond with a simple, "I know," and offer a smile that doesn't quite reach my eyes.

Gladys, ever perceptive even when I think she isn't, senses my unease. "He won't let anything happen to you either," she reassures.

I project a warm disposition and affirm, "I know. He cares about his staff," acknowledging Mr. Everett's apparent concern for the well-being of those under his employment. He rushed right to Alice to make sure she wasn't injured and took her to a safe room to hide while he looked for the men who broke in.

Though Gladys's expression suggests that wasn't what she meant, she responds with a gentle, "he does," while tenderly squeezing my hand.

The room descends into a brief quietness before Gladys breaks the silence, making a concerted effort to divert my thoughts from Mr. Everett. "I do love thunderstorms," she says, the corners of her eyes crinkling.

Finding common ground, I agree. "Me too. This one put me to sleep," reminiscing about resting my head on Mr. Everett's shoulder.

Gladys responds with a reassuring squeeze of my hand.

Curious about how long the power might be out for, I shift the conversation. "How long do the lights usually stay out?" gazing at the candles flickering around the kitchen area.

She follows my gaze and scans the kitchen. "They'll be back on by morning. Mr. Everett has backup generators in case he needs to restore power," she explains. "Although, he likes the dark," she adds with a smile, and this admission feels like another connection between him and me. I, too, appreciate the darkness.

"Will he get in trouble for breaking that guy's nose?" The memory of the audible crunch when Mr. Everett struck the man in the hall flashes in my mind. It was an unparalleled display of strength, making me shudder at the power behind that punch.

She appears slightly startled. "He broke someone's nose?" she questions, surprised. This seems to be an unusual occurrence for Mr. Everett, leaving Gladys momentarily stunned by this revelation.

"Yes," I confirm the unexpected turn of events.

"Was it during a fight?" she queries, still seemingly skeptical about what I'm recounting.

I shake my head, vividly recalling the intensity in Mr. Everett's eyes and the creepy smirk that had stretched across the intruder's face as he looked me up and down. "No, the guy said if he knew I was here, he would have destroyed my... you know," I gesture discreetly to indicate my vagina.

A knowing smile crosses her face. "Ahhh, that makes sense," she remarks as if she finally understands. "Not about his disgusting words, but about Mr. Everett's reaction."

Although I don't know Mr. Everett well, I get a feeling he is a man who would stand up against sexual assault or harassment for anyone. "What's going to happen to them?" I ask, referring to the intruders.

"They will be arrested," she assures me.

CHAPTER

Eleven

JONAH

Beneath the unassuming exterior of my home lies the staff parking garage, along with additional hangout areas. At first glance, one might assume there's nothing noteworthy down here. However, past the lounge room equipped with a pool table, bar, and various other amenities, there's a door that, once opened, reveals what appears to be a simple closet. Beyond the door lies a secret domain: a high-end underground space with cutting-edge technology, accessible only to those who need to know it's here. Despite the power outage in the main house, the backup generators are set to instantly activate down here. This is also where my security staff monitors my property and house.

The sleek, dimly lit corridors reveal a maze of interconnected rooms, with surveillance and security systems. The walls are adorned with muted, modern aesthetics. Biometric scanners and retina recognition devices safeguard entry points, ensuring only those authorized can proceed.

My security team has undergone thorough vetting before hired.

High-tech monitoring stations line the periphery, displaying real-time data and providing control over the cameras and security measures.

Entering a room with a large desk that accommodates a pair of computers, I face a two-way mirrored wall that spans the entirety of the far end of this area. In two isolated rooms, shrouded in soundproofed walls side by side, emanating an unsettling feeling purposely built this way, sits both men restrained in uncomfortable chairs, their gaze uneasy as they scan the entirely white surroundings.

Guarding each room, two security personnel sit in front of their respective computers. There's a walkable space between the computers and the windows, allowing me to pace back and forth as I observe the detainees.

"Have either of them said anything?" I ask, halting in front of the glass to glimpse into both rooms, folding my arms as I maintain a vigilant gaze on both men.

"No, sir," Dame responds.

Releasing a sigh, I turn and stride towards the opposite wall, using the door in the corner next to the two-way mirror to exit. The hallway unfolds as I step outside the room, and the door immediately to the left leads to the furthest interrogation chamber, housing the man I have yet to encounter.

Grabbing a metal chair positioned nearby, I shove the door open and walk inside, startling the man whose eyes widen with fear upon my entrance. I get this reaction a lot. Placing the chair in front of him, I straddle it, resting my elbows on the back as I position my chin on my fists, staring at him.

"Sir, our car broke down a mile down the road, we were just trying to get out of the rain," he says with panic in his voice.

"Hmm," I nod, skeptical of every word he utters. Experience has taught me that silence is a powerful tool for coaxing out information.

"We didn't mean any harm. We thought the house was abandoned, and we could just get out of the rain for a little while," he starts. "We weren't going to take anything."

"You thought my house was abandoned?" I lift an eyebrow.

"Yes, sir," he appears to subtly relax as if he believes I am buying into his bullshit story.

"And you weren't going to take anything?"

"No, sir, I would never," he adds, pleading in his tone.

"Yet you brought weapons into my house?" his eyes widen as he falls silent. "And you ran into my house, startling one of my chefs," I continue. "Let's not go down this path. Let's not start off lying. You broke into my home and scared my staff, and I want to know why."

"I already told you," he pleads.

"I said let's not do that," my patience is wearing thin.

His voice quivers while mine rises, just below a shout. "Please," he implores.

I merely arch an eyebrow, signaling for him to continue. What could he be pleading for? It's evident he wants to fabricate a story about why he broke into my house, and I am determined to unearth the truth.

"We were just looking," he stammers.

"Looking?" I press.

"Yes, your house is so big we wanted to see what it looked like on the inside," he makes his best attempt at trying to convince me this story is the truth.

"I'm tired. You know the layout of my home, knew where you were going, and where to enter. I'm done with the deception. Here's what's going to happen," I lower both fists, resting my forearms on the back of the chair. "You're going to tell me the truth, or things are going to get painful for you until you inevitably succumb to the pain and reveal the truth anyway."

"I have alre—"

I rise from my chair, seizing his middle finger and wrenching it backward until it touches the bound wrist on the chair. A resounding crack of bones breaking pierces the air, and his eyes widen in shock as he screams out in agony.

"You see, I know it's more than just a broken-down car or wanting to get out of the rain or intending to look around," I hold his finger folded back as he continues his blood-curdling yell. "I am going to give you one last chance to tell me before I leave and I send in someone... not quite as nice as me. Your friend made a disgusting comment to my girl, and I want some alone time with him," I smirk.

"Okay, okay," he concedes. "We were here trying to find valuables that we could try to get some money for," tears leak from his eyes.

Releasing his finger, I stride toward the door, a click of it being unlocked emanates, and I open it. Turning back to him, I tap on the door with a single finger. "Completely soundproof in here," I grin, and walk out, slamming the door behind me. I see him wriggling in his chair as I reenter the main room once again.

"All yours, Brad," I say as I stroll over to the door opposite that one, eager to confront the other guy who spoke to Kalyn in a derogatory way.

"Fuck yeah," Brad exclaims as he begins walking toward the door I just came through.

I met Brad during tactical training; he used to be in special ops, interrogating criminals using less-than-ideal tactics to extract information. He retired from the job and sought me out for a position where he could lay low, away from "the scum of the earth," living his life in the middle of nowhere with a house on the other side of town and a couple acres of property. He lived in one of the apartments above the stables when he first moved here, and still stays out there sometimes, most likely when he's hooking up with someone here. Then goes home when he hooks up with someone from town.

He was married years ago and came home from a mission to find his wife in bed with another man. Although I discovered that she is now married to the guy she was having an affair with and they have two kids, I've never revealed this information to Brad, unsure if he keeps tabs on her. He's a good guy but known for hooking up with any woman who will sleep with him. Which is anyone he tries to sleep with. He's a good-looking dude and women love him. He was loyal to his ex, but compliments to her fucking him over, he refuses to get serious with anyone. He almost acts like he hates women now.

We implemented a "no sleeping with other employees" rule for a while, but it proved ineffective. I realized that only adults are hired, and they know what they're getting into when they sleep with him. I don't think he will ever allow himself to actually get close to another woman for fear of his heart being crushed again. And I have more pressing matters to attend to than dealing with the consequences of him sticking his dick in willing women.

Entering the room, I find my new bloodied friend with a swollen broken nose and bruised eyes. Fear flickers in his eyes as he notices my presence and just as quickly, he puts on his tough-guy facade.

"I'll get straight to the point. What were you looking for?" I question.

"Fuck you," he spits defiantly.

Realizing that torture techniques won't be effective with him, a sinister grin spreads across my face and I spit into my hand, maintaining eye contact with him. His gaze remains unwavering, anticipating harm.

Holding the spit in my hand, I begin undoing my belt. As I start unbuttoning and unzipping my pants, his panic resurfaces.

"Whoa, what are you doing, man?!" he exclaims, eyes widening as he watches me.

Smirking, I reply, "I am so goddamn horny, and you're keeping me from my girl, so I'm going to get it from you." I pull my dick out and wipe the spit on the tip as I slowly approach him.

His eyes bulge at the sight of my size. "It's not your first time, is it?"

"Whoa, whoa, we can talk about this," he begs.

"Talk," I stand in front of him, my dick barely a foot from his face.

"We got caught out in the rain…"

I stroke my cock, "Your friend already tried that one, let's get to it." I release my dick and grab a tight grip of his hair.

"Okay, okay," he pleads, breathing heavily. "Mr. Walters sent us. He says you stole a client from him, costing him millions, and he paid us to break into your house. He told us to go through the kitchen—the old woman there could show us to your office, where we could get your computer and files of your top clients. We were just trying to get paid, man, come on, nobody got hurt," He speaks rapidly, spitting as he talks.

"Your mouth seems awfully wet, 'man.' My dick should slide in your mouth easily."

"NO! Please no," he turns his head away as I approach.

See. Now that is believable. Mr. Walters is a piece of shit pig that is known for forcing clients staff and receptionists to have sex with him in order to close deals with them. The client in question practically begged me to have their business.

As he averts his gaze, I put my dick away and zip up my pants. His body trembles, and he makes his best attempt at keeping his head facing the opposite direction. He is acting like I am going to shove my dick down his throat when he turns back toward me.

Funny thing is, if I wanted to, I could effortlessly force him, but that's not the type of shit I'm into. Yet, I allow him to struggle, albeit briefly, letting him believe he possesses the strength to prevent any unwanted advances.

Relief washes over him when he sees my pants are fastened back up. "Your nose looks a little crooked," I sneer, delivering another punch to his nose in the opposite direction, prompting another agonizing scream.

I leave and walk back into the main room, banging twice on the window to get Brad's attention.

He reemerges with traces of blood on his shirt. "Already?" he looks disappointed.

"Yeah," I reply, instructing Dame to call the sheriff in the morning. We can let them stay tied up and sweat all night. "I gotta get back," I say to them as I exit.

CHAPTER

Twelve

KALYN

"Thank you, Gladys," Mr. Everett expresses his gratitude upon reentering the kitchen. The mere sound of his voice has my heart skipping beats, and I turn toward the doorway where he came through. His size is scary in the darkness, a large looming shadow that walks purposefully into the room. Mr. Everett extends his hand toward me. "Come, I'm going to get you to bed."

"Thank you for everything, Gladys. Not just for this, but for being so kind to me," I say, and then take Mr. Everett's outstretched hand.

As he guides me off the tall stool I am sitting on, I offer a final wave to Gladys before disappearing from the room.

"I can carry you if you'd like. It's dark, and you're barefoot," he says just outside the kitchen.

"I'm okay," my voice is soft. I would love the feel of his arms around me, but I don't want him to have to awkwardly carry me.

"I don't mind," he offers again.

"I'll stay close," I assure him as I grab his forearm with my other hand. This must do the trick because he begins walking.

Guiding me through the impenetrable darkness of the house, he leads us easily. Every step, whether climbing or descending, he anticipates and forewarns me just before we approach it.

Upon reaching the maid's quarters, I mention that I can find my way to my room. However, he opens the door and accompanies me. I'm taken aback when he guides me directly to my room, a detail I wasn't aware he knew. He extends his hand, opening the door and holding it ajar for me to enter first. A surge of anticipation rushes through me, thinking we might be on the verge of having sex. Though I feel nervous, I'm thankful I took a shower after work.

Turning to face him, I expected him to be right there, but he is still at the door. He watches me before abruptly saying, "Good night, Kalyn," keeping his hand on the bedroom doorknob.

Momentarily bewildered by the suddenness of his entrance and exit, I reply, "Good night, Mr. Everett."

"Jonah," he corrects, "Call me Jonah." He stares at me for a moment longer and then locks the door before leaving, closing it behind him. The air feels charged and then immediately fills with disappointment.

CHAPTER
Thirteen

KALYN

I spend the night lying in bed, seemingly awake for an eternity. Uncertain if sleep ever claimed me, my mind replays the events of the evening—from the moments shared with Mr. Everett in his office to the encounter with the intruder. I marvel at how skillfully and impressively Mr. Everett handled the situation, finding that I was scared and incredibly turned on watching him during the struggle. Recollections of him escorting me back to my room and how I had anticipated we were going to have sex, and then his abrupt exit left me with a nagging feeling that perhaps I have upset him.

Morning arrives, and it appears I must have slipped into sleep at some point, yet the persistent feeling of having done something wrong lingers, or maybe it's a feeling of complete disappointment at how the night eventually concluded. Glancing at the clock on my nightstand, the time just flashes but at least the power has been restored. Looking at my wall clock, I see its 7 AM. The events of the last night almost seem like a dream, and with each moment of awakening, they become increasingly surreal.

Taking my time getting ready for the workday, I casually tie my hair into its customary messy bun atop my head, slip into my oversized maid uniform, and exit my bathroom. Stepping out of my room, a murmur of hushed whispers permeates the air, circulating news about the intruders from last night. The hall is filled with a mix of curiosity and concern.

"Kalyn," Lilly exclaims, grabbing my arm and leading me over to where she, Amber, and Shay are gathered. "Two armed intruders broke in last night!" she shares, eager to bring me up to speed. "Mr. Everett fought them off and subdued them," she adds enthusiastically.

"I miss all the action," Shay comments, sounding disappointed.

"I'm glad I was sleeping," Amber remarks.

Lilly appears impressed. "Can you imagine Mr. Everett in a fight? I bet he looked so sexy," she smiles, and then fans her face in a swooning motion.

"You need to get laid," Shay injects a dose of humor into the conversation.

"Have you ever noticed the size of Mr. Everett's hands?" Lilly asks, holding her hands up and examining them. "If what they say is true," her eyes widen, "He has a MASSIVE penis," she gazes at each of us, her mouth hanging open wide.

"That's for him to know and you to never find out," Shay teases.

"Is there such a thing as too big?" Lilly questions, looking at Shay.

"The bigger, the better," Shay responds. "For me, anyway. Jonathan works every single inch of his thick dick," she dreamily sighs.

Realizing I never actually saw Jonathan last night, he must have been with Shay, "Was he with you last night?" even though I already worked out the answer in my head.

"Yes, he's so mad nobody woke him up," she laughs.

Jenevieve interrupts the conversation abruptly. "Last night, a serious incident occurred. I'm sure you've all heard bits and pieces about it. *Some of us* couldn't resist getting directly involved," she remarks, giving me an eye lashing with her evil stare. "In the future, when the power goes out, all of you will immediately return to your own rooms," she emphasizes, keeping her eyes on me. "The situation has been handled, but there's no reason for any of the staff to be out during the night. If you get a thought you can be of use, just know you will only be in the way. Going forward, there will be consequences for being outside of the maid's quarters after dark," she warns, fixing her gaze on me once again.

Jenevieve proceeds to give instructions for the girls and then singles me and two others out, stating, "The three of you will be washing and folding the linens today."

We are led to the laundry room. I find it to be unlike any I have ever encountered. Rows of multiple washers and dryers create a harmonious hum that reverberates within the high ceilings. The space is meticulously organized, even including labeled bins and shelves abundantly stocked with an array of detergents and fabric softeners. Large folding tables provide plenty of space for sorting and folding laundry, and the air carries a refreshing, clean scent.

Throughout the day, the three of us work side by side. I discover that the two girls, Katy and Jess, who also started on the same day as me, are rather reserved and don't engage in much conversation. It makes it easy to get a lot done, but I can only be alone with my thoughts for so long. Repeatedly, I find my mind drifting back to him, dominating every train of thought.

"You have to stop this," I scold myself, *"Get over it."* Even with my inner scolding, the persistent pull of him weaves its way back in throughout the day.

After lunch, Jenevieve gathers us in a line. "We've all heard about last night's incident, and while it may seem thrilling, it's a serious matter. As I mentioned on your first day, gossip is not ladylike, so refrain from speculating further on the events from last night," she declares sternly. Although there was no mention of last night in the laundry room with the two silent girls, I deduce that discussions about the events must have persisted among the other girls; otherwise, she wouldn't have felt the need to bring it up again if it hadn't. "You will proceed with the chores assigned this morning," she adds, standing firm. "Move!" she barks at us.

We start walking and come to a halt as security and police officers pass by with the intruders in cuffs. The man from the previous night in the hallway glances our way, his face twisted with anger until his eyes meet mine. That creepy stare from last night returns to his face, and he blows a kiss in my direction. Caught off guard, I blink rapidly, quickly regaining my composure, praying that nobody else noticed.

"Eww, did he just blow you a kiss?" Lilly asks disgusted.

Jenevieve, also witnessing the scene, displays her annoyance although she attempts to conceal it. "You're not being paid to gawk! Get to work."

Quickly, we all hurry off to our jobs. Arriving back to the laundry room, I immediately start pulling warm linens out of the dryer, and fold them, and cringe when I hear the distinct sound of Jenevieve's heels entering. The room grows tense, with the lingering discomfort of the newest encounter with the intruder.

Advancing towards me with an assertive stride, I can sense her piercing gaze burning into the back of my head as she nears. "Why weren't you in bed last night?" she questions, coming to a halt beside me, hand confidently on her hip, asserting dominance.

"Was I supposed to be?" I inquire, maintaining focus on my folding.

Her anger escalates. "You had no business being in that part of the house," she hisses.

"Okay," I reply calmly. The tension in the air growing thicker.

She stands there momentarily, processing that I'm not engaging in an argument.

"In the future, stay in your room," she instructs, her anger palpable. "You could have gotten people injured."

Growing weary of her accusations, I stop folding the linens and turn directly to her, "Who?" I anticipate her mentioning Mr. Everett, but I can sense her hesitation to acknowledge that he and I were together.

"Don't play coy with me, little girl," she hisses.

"I'm not. I was simply asking who I could have gotten injured. You're throwing accusations at me, and I'm seeking clarification," I assert, refusing to back down from her confrontational stance.

A look of complete disbelief and animosity paints her face as she advances toward me, her teeth clenching together, and her eyes ablaze with fury. She resembles a fire-breathing dragon, ready to attack, smoke billowing from her flared nostrils.

"How is everything going in here?" Gladys interjects from the doorway.

Jenevieve blinks as if Gladys pulled her back from her seething rage. "Fine," she replies sarcastically, giving me a once-over before making her exit, leaving an uneasy feeling in her wake.

Now, I'm certain that Jenevieve holds a grudge against me, and I feel more annoyed than anything. The reasons for her animosity remain a mystery. She never provides an explanation and constantly treats me poorly. I suspect it has everything to do with Mr. Everett, but I haven't figured out why. Does she have romantic feelings for him? Or does she think I am unworthy of him being interested in me?

Katy excuses herself to the bathroom, leaving Jess and me alone. "I was still awake last night," Jess says out of the blue.

I'm momentarily taken aback because she is speaking, and it's surprising to learn that she, too, was awake last night. "During the intruder incident?" I inquire.

"Yes," she replies, continuing to fold. "I wasn't the only one," as if her words carry some significant meaning.

"I'm glad you're safe," I smile.

"Somebody else saw you two," she reveals. "That's why Jenevieve is upset. She knows who you were with."

"We weren't doing anything inappropriate," I clarify, conscious of the potential misconceptions that might have arisen from seeing Mr. Everett and me together.

"It's not my place to judge, and I won't say anything to anyone," Jess reassures me. "You should know, Jenevieve has eyes everywhere in this house; nothing gets passed her."

"Thanks, Jess," unsure of what else to say or why she is even telling me this.

I also find it frustrating that other people were awake in 'off-limit' parts of the mansion, and it seems like I am the only one who got in trouble for it. What was Jess doing out and about? Was the woman Brad hooked up with the one who told Jenevieve?

As I walk myself through that conversation we just had, it dawns on me that Jess was awake somewhere in the house and witnessed me and Mr. Everett holding hands. Someone else, concealed in a hidden spot, also observed us, and chose to inform Jenevieve. However, it appears that the events were narrated differently than they actually occurred. It sounds as if it is being told like I was allowing Mr. Everett to finger-bang me in front of anyone who was still awake. At least, that's the narrative Jenevieve decided to adopt.

Finishing folding the freshly dried load of linens, I glance at the clock, noting it's 4:50, the designated time to head back and stow away cleaning supplies. As we've been on laundry duty, all the necessary cleaning materials are already in the room, streamlining our departure to join the rest of the housekeeping staff. It's the moment when Jenevieve tells us all the things we did wrong throughout the day.

Exiting, we head back through the mansion. My thumbs rest inside the pockets of my uniform on either side. Upon reaching a spacious area with a sitting room, we spot Mr. Everett, Jonathan, and two other individuals engrossed in conversation. One of them presents information on a tablet to Mr. Everett, who briefly glances up and then does a double take when he sees me, prompting the other men to also turn their attention in my direction. With only my pinky, I discreetly offer a wave as I proceed to follow the other two. Looking back one more time, I observe a smile forming at the corner of Mr. Everett's lips.

We enter as Jenevieve is already delivering a barrage of insults. "It seems you all forget that you're being paid to be here. Judging by the work I'm witnessing, I'm tempted to fire all of you and start new. Cleaning isn't that hard, yet some of you seem to lack the basic ability to complete simple tasks. And some more than others," she asserts, shooting a glare in my direction as Katy, Jess, and I approach. "Go get cleaned up and head to dinner. Let's aim to start tomorrow on a better note than today. Today, unfortunately, was an utter failure," she concludes, wearing a look of disgust as she walks away from us.

"Her speeches are so motivational," Shay teases as she approaches me, watching as Jenevieve exits the room.

"I was wondering how she hasn't landed a TED Talk for her motivational skills," I jokingly add, exchanging giggles with her as we make our way back to the maid's quarters.

"I won't be at dinner, Jonathan is taking me on a date tonight," she shares as she wraps her arm around mine.

"Ooo, where are *we* going? Or are we not going to be a throuple tonight?" I tease pretending they would be taking me as a third wheel.

"He won't tell me—it's a surprise," she says, air-quoting "surprise," her entire demeanor radiating joy.

"Well, I'd say let me know when you get home, but I'll know when your bed sounds like it's about to break through my wall," alluding to the audible moans, screams, and thumps coming from her room every time she and Jonathan are having sex. While the rooms are decently soundproof, they are by no means foolproof, and it's clear they make no effort to keep things quiet.

She grins widely. "What can I say? He rocks my world," she breathes out a sigh, her radiant smile beaming pure happiness.

CHAPTER
Fourteen

KALYN

I woke up today with a sense of anticipation, feeling that it was destined to be a positive day. I fell asleep before Shay returned home last night. So I was excited to see her and find out how her date went. She is so head over heels in love with Jonathan, he could take her on a date where they sift through dog turds, and she would be thrilled because it was with him.

I have been mindful about manifesting positivity, a conversation Shay and I had. Regardless of the job Jenevieve gives me, I made a conscious decision to maintain a positive outlook.

As we assemble in line, Jenevieve conveys a change in our usual routine. "Today, our focus is on the finer details," she announces. "You'll be paired up and assigned specific rooms. If you finish cleaning and the room doesn't look impeccable, you haven't done it well enough," she emphasizes sternly. "Every surface—walls, ceiling, lamps, tables, chairs, and decor—should be spotless.

Approach for a card that outlines your assigned room, a map for navigation, and a detailed list of cleaning duties. If you doubt your ability to handle this task, speak up now, and you can head to the stables," she adds with an inquisitive raise of her eyebrows.

"You'll be responsible for distributing the cards," she casually designates a random girl to distribute the cards. "I have pressing matters to attend to, and I'll return in a couple of hours," she declares glaring down at each of us before exiting the room with a determined stride.

Shay and I share knowing smiles as we decide to retrieve a card together, having already mentally arranged to be partners for the day. It's the perfect opportunity to catch up on all the details of her mystery date with Jonathan last night.

"What room did we get?" I reach for the card and pluck it from her hand, glancing down at it as we make our way out of the maid's quarters.

She grins mischievously. "The one conveniently located near Jonathan's office," she reveals, her excitement radiating out of her. It's clear she intentionally picked that card to work close to him. While she's thrilled, I note that Jonathan's office is near Mr. Everett's office. A sense of uneasiness engulfs me, uncertain if we are still on speaking terms. It seems irrational to feel this way, but a part of me senses a form of rejection, especially after he didn't take me to bed the other night.

Arriving at the room listed on the card, I take in the spacious surroundings. "Did you accidentally select the largest room in the entire house as well?" I find some amusement in the situation. She wanted to be near Jonathan so badly, she purposely took the card that possibly has the biggest area to clean.

"Maybe, but hey, we are right by Jonathan," her face brightens at the mere mention of his name.

I watch as she pulls her phone from her pocket and sends off a text. "Had to let him know that we're right here," her enthusiasm is contagious.

"You're such a dork," I playfully remark, smiling as I take our card to peruse its contents. "Why does Mr. Everett employ so many housekeepers? We're always cleaning, but I can't recall ever seeing any dust in any part of the house," I comment, noticing that the room already appears to be in pristine condition.

"It's all about the ventilation, baby," she teases. "Maybe he just doesn't know what to do with all his money, so he overpays people to endure Jenevieve," she sifts through our cleaning supplies, pulling out a couple of different items and a towel.

"That makes sense," I admit. "But seriously, why does Mr. Everett keep her employed? Is he aware of how awful she is?" I ask, realizing I haven't questioned this before. A sudden realization hits me. Could there be an intimate relationship between him and Jenevieve? Maybe that's why he retains her employment and why she seems to harbor resentment towards me. I wonder if I unintentionally stepped on her toes without realizing it.

"Mr. Everett is up to his eyeballs in his work. Jenevieve acts as sweet as pie when he is around. The rest of the staff is too intimidated to approach him, let alone report her for her behavior. She's never had an issue with me because she knows Jonathan wouldn't tolerate it, and I would sing like a canary if she tried bullying me," Shay explains matter-of-factly.

"She'd slit my throat if I dared open my canary mouth," I joke, and she bursts into laughter. However, there's an undeniable truth to it. I understand why everyone finds her intimidating. She consistently reinforces the notion that we're all beneath her, creating an atmosphere where you instinctively sense it's safer to stay in your lane, to avert the world turning against you.

Our cleaning grinds to a halt as a flurry of commotion erupts from inside Mr. Everett's office. Shay and I exchange glances, our attention fully captured by the unfolding events behind those closed doors. The noise suggests cursing and perhaps something being dropped, accompanied by more yelling.

"Suit yourself," Jonathan calls from inside Mr. Everett's office, closing the door behind him as he joins us. "He is chipper as ever," Jonathan remarks in a teasing manner, approaching Shay and kissing her. "Kal, Mr. Happy Pants needs coffee cleaned off his desk. Don't worry, he's not in there—he already stormed off to go change his diaper," he teases.

Shay and I glance at each other for a moment, then we both giggle as she begins to gather cleaning supplies. "I'll do it, hun," she says to Jonathan, still amused by his comment.

I step forward and take the towel and cleaning bottle from her hand. "I'll do it. Though I know I am awesome company, I'm pretty sure Jonathan here isn't yearning for mid-day alone time with me," I joke as I start walking toward Mr. Everett's office.

Shay walks over and perches on Jonathan's lap, who is sitting on the arm of one of the chairs. "Thank you for understanding," he teases, planting a kiss on Shay's lips.

"Be good, you two," I call back to them.

I felt confident when I spoke up to take over this mission, but now, as I reach Mr. Everett's office door, I almost regret not staying silent and letting Shay do it. My nerves are in disarray. I can hear Shay and Jonathan's banter and heavy flirting. My smile fades as I knock on the office door, even though I know he isn't in there, as Jonathan had mentioned. Nervousness creeps over me, and after a brief pause, I knock again.

No response.

I twist the door handle until I hear the satisfying click, indicating I can push it open. Stepping inside, I find the expansive office bathed in daylight, affording me a clear view of the entire room. It looks a lot bigger in the daytime, now that I can see every inch of the room. Windows stretch from floor to ceiling along the entire west wall, while towering bookshelves adorned with a diverse array of books line the remaining walls. There are two tiers of bookcases, and each level has a ladder that moves effortlessly, providing easy access to the highest shelves. Towards the back of the office sits an oversized L-shaped desk, and across from it, two chairs are arranged facing forward.

Walking towards the desk, I spot the spill Jonathan mentioned. I make my way around his desk, so I stand directly in front of it, grabbing a stack of papers, allowing the coffee to run off, and then dab them dry with my towel. The desk, I notice, is impeccably organized, facilitating an easy cleanup. Mr. Everett is a very clean man.

I initially thought his house was immaculate due to the cleaning staff he employs, and that may contribute to it to some extent. However, even if he didn't have help, I believe his personality compels him to maintain order and a clutter-free environment. I took note of this on my first night in here, but in the daylight, it's even more apparent that he meticulously ensures everything is in its designated spot. As I work on the spill, I hear the creak of his chair as he settles in directly behind me.

"For such a big man, you sure know how to walk quietly," I continue wiping up the desk not turning around. I glance down at his dress shoes positioned wide on either side of where I am standing as he leisurely swivels in his chair. I notice a puddle of coffee at my feet. Hesitating momentarily trying to contemplate whether I should act like I didn't see it but decide against it.

"I need to clean the floor," I mention, anticipating that he will scoot his chair back. However, he remains unmoved. Turning to meet his gaze, my belly erupts in flutters. Regaining my composure I gradually extend my foot between his legs. Placing it on the chair wheel, exerting pressure to push him back, but to my surprise, the chair doesn't budge even an inch. I hadn't anticipated it being so hard to move. His facial expression unchanged. He keeps his gaze locked on mine. Giving no indication as to what he is thinking.

"Thank you," I tell him as if he did something to be helpful. Turning back toward the desk, I lower myself onto my knees with my backside facing him. I am on all fours wiping up the coffee and I can feel his gaze on me the whole time. I go over the spot multiple times to make sure I wipe every bit of coffee up.

Sitting back on my heels, I glance around the floor, making sure I didn't miss anything. I swivel myself toward him, locking my eyes on his. "What about you?"

"What about me?" He looks down at my lips as I speak and back up to my eyes.

His voice is so sexy it elicits another flutter in my stomach, igniting a fiery surge of arousal that courses through every inch of me. "Did your slippery fingers spill coffee on you?" I tease as I raise the cleaning towel stained with coffee, hoping my nerves don't give away the tremor in my hands. Fortunately, as I look from my hand to him, I find that it remains confidently steady while I hold the towel up for him to see.

"If they did, are you going to use that dirty towel to clean me up with?" He questions lifting an eyebrow.

"Obviously," I playfully retort, "This is the coffee towel," casting a glance at the heavily stained cloth. It's comically dirty, and the idea of using this dirty towel to clean up this impeccably groomed man amuses me. "It would make sense if I use the same towel to clean the same coffee mess off you." I offer an innocent look.

"Obviously," he concurs, bringing his swiveling chair to a halt. Leaning forward deliberately, he inches his face closer to mine, keeping our eyes locked. With a casual motion, he reaches around my back, deftly untying my white apron and smoothly bringing it back around in front of me. "This," he holds it up delicately between his pointer and middle finger, "seems cleaner than that towel," his gaze shifts from my apron to the towel in my hand and then back to my eyes. A subtle glint of amusement sparkles in his eyes.

"I'd prefer not to use my uniform to clean coffee spills. I don't like the smell of coffee, that sounds miserable to have to smell like it all day," I muse back, reclaiming my apron from his hand. "However, if it means you will be coffee-free Mr. Everett, then I suppose I would do it," I add with casual ease.

"Why would you do that for me?"

"Because," I say, placing my hand on his knee to assist myself up, "You sir, sign my paychecks." My upbeat response appears to not sit well with him as his eyebrows shift together.

"Well," I say, bunching my apron between my hands, "coffee is all cleaned up." I exhale, turning to exit. He yanks my apron out of my hand, rises from his seat, and wraps it around my waist, deftly tying it from behind, his fingers gently trailing down the ends of the bow he crafted.

"Thank you," I respond softly, glancing back at him before grabbing the spray bottle from his desk and making my way toward the door. He remains standing there as I exit the room.

The next day feels like déjà vu all over again. Once again, I find myself in Mr. Everett's office cleaning up a spill—this time, it's tea. However, as I enter, the room isn't vacant. He is seated, reclined in his chair, with both hands casually positioned on either side of the armrest. My gaze is drawn to a visible wet spot on his light grey dress pants.

"We really have to stop meeting like this," I jest, sauntering up to the desk, balancing the cleaning bottle on my hip.

"These are to blame," he says innocently, holding up his hands. "Slippery fingers, remember?"

"I do remember. I feel like I was just in here doing this exact same thing," I tease, making my way around his desk. Before I can fully reach the same side as him, he extends both legs and moves a foot closer to his desk, keeping his gaze fixed on me. I come to a stop, realizing this little stunt makes it almost impossible for me to reach the spill. Weighing my options, it's clear I can't move the chair with him in it, having attempted that yesterday with absolutely no success. In this situation, professionalism seems to have gone out the window. Despite his attempt to be difficult, I won't let it deter me from doing my job. I smile at him, noting his unwavering stare since I entered the room.

Lifting one leg over his, I place my foot on the ground directly between his spread legs, then raise the other, positioning both of my legs between his. I'm proud that the maneuver went smoothly. I begin carefully wiping up the spill on his desk, feeling his gaze on my every move, causing a tingling sensation in my body. As I finish, I notice a spill at our feet, but there's no room for me to bend down and clean it up.

"You will need to move your chair back if you want me to clean the floor," I declare, aware that he has no intention of moving. As my prediction proves accurate and his only response is to close the space between our legs a bit more, I decide to drop the towel on the floor in a last-ditch effort to see if this action will prompt him to scoot his chair back, but once again, he remains still. In a spontaneous decision, I confidently seat myself on his lap, directly over the tea spill on his crotch. I half expect him to push me away, react with surprise, or question my actions, but all he does is tighten his grip on the chair's arms and inhale deeply.

I part my legs open slightly, leaning forward, allowing enough space for me to look down at the floor between them, and position my foot on the towel. At this moment, I become acutely aware of his arousal, situated prominently between my cheeks. I remain seated, unmoving, my body responding to this playful attempt to clean the floor, yet realizing I've inadvertently placed myself in an unexpectedly intimate position with him. My mind races a million miles a minute.

"Clean the floor," I tell myself.

My hands encircle behind me, finding stability on his hips. His breath catches at the initial touch of my hands, and soon, he starts breathing more heavily. Gradually, I begin wiping the floor with my foot. What started as innocent intentions now takes on a more sensual and pleasurable tone.

Each circular movement of my leg causes my entire body to shift over his thick member. I persist in the deliberate motion of circling the towel on the floor to clean up the tea. Or so the original plan went. My fingers grip the fabric where his shirt is tucked into his pants, and I press my hands into his hips. With closed eyes, I continue the slow, circular motion of the towel on the floor.

"I think I got it all cleaned up," a breathless whisper passes my lips.

"Not even close," his voice heavy with desire.

Unable to speak for a moment, I manage to find a faintness in my voice to respond, "You're right," agreeing in a hushed whisper. "It still feels wet."

"So wet," he responds, resting his head on my back.

I continue my slow circles on the floor, knowing damn well all I am doing at this point is shining his floor, or rubbing all the wax off, either way, the spot I was circling is going to be noticeable.

I ache to move my hips on him intentionally in the same circular motion my foot is moving. Testing the waters, I subtly shift my hips backward along his shaft and then return, as if adjusting myself innocently. Glancing back at him, I observe his gaze fixed on my bottom. A shaky exhale escapes him, confirming his approval.

After a brief pause, I repeat the movement, and this time, both his hands steadily grip each side of my hips, either guiding me or ensuring I don't stop. Adjusting my position, I release my hold on his hips, leaning forward, I place my hands on his knees, and shift my bottom back toward him.

Sitting upright again, this positions his erection atop my slit, providing more direct pleasure to my sweet spot. He firmly squeezes both sides of my round bottom. Reaching my hands behind me, I set them on each side of his solid abs. Slowly rocking my hips back up his shaft and descending even more leisurely.

Tilting my head backward, it comes to a rest on top of his, his face pressing into my back. His large right hand slides around to my inner thigh, squeezing it firmly, causing my belly to flutter. He grabs my leg positioning it over his leg as his hand inches higher up my thigh, squeezing again. A moan escapes my throat as I place my hand on his, slowly guiding it with my own to exactly where I need his touch.

Meanwhile, his other hand squeezes the side of my bottom and gradually moves toward my inner thigh, grabbing hold and repeating the same movement, pulling it to the other side of his leg, causing my legs to spread. He widens his knees, spreading my legs even more. The tips of his fingers graze the edge of my panties, our breathing becoming heavy, and I feel the warmth of his breath on my back.

With the softest brush, his fingers trace the outside of my panties, down my slit. My breathing is ragged as he moves closer to my center. We are both completely lost in the moment.

"Oh hush," Gladys says to Jenevieve during their arguing. Jenevieve takes the lead as she storms into Mr. Everett's office.

"YOU hush," Jenevieve fires back.

I am off his lap, pulling my skirt down and grabbing my cleaning bottle before either of them notices what was just happening.

Jenevieve halts when she notices only Mr. Everett and me in the room. He stays seated, his arousal visible only from my vantage point on this side of the desk. Leaning slightly toward me, his elbow propped on the armrest as he runs his finger along his teeth. He glances up at me before shifting his attention to them.

"I was cleaning spilled tea," I offer to Jenevieve abruptly.

She just blinks at me, as if whatever brought her and Gladys in here completely slipped her mind.

"Lunch is ready, sweetie," Gladys fills the silence with her pleasant tone.

"Thank you, Gladys," I use this as the perfect opportunity to hurry out. My nerves are on high alert.

I quickly walk to the nearest bathroom, shove the door open, and lock it once inside. Grabbing a pile of tissue paper, I lower my panties, needing to clean myself up. Thoughts race through my mind about the insane effect he has on my body. I swipe tissue paper over my vagina repeatedly, seemingly unable to achieve dryness.

Now away from the situation, my nerves seem to ignite, and I begin pacing the length of the room. *'What were you thinking?!'* I scold myself. *'He's your boss, and you have a year-long contract here.'* I repeatedly remind myself to distance myself from this situation. Did Jenevieve see anything? What if she saw me not-so-dry humping him? If they had waited just ten more minutes, we might have been caught in a more compromising position that we wouldn't have been able to get out of so easily. The thought of them walking in on us having sex mortifies me. *'Gladys!'* I mentally chastise myself. *'She's going to think I'm so trashy.'* *'Ugh,'* I exclaim in frustration.

A knock on the door interrupts my self-scolding. "One minute," I call out, quickly checking my face in the mirror for any visible signs of embarrassment. *Nope*, I note as I examine every inch of my face—I'm as pale as ever.

I unlock the door and pull it open.

"Kalyn," Brad says, leaning against the door frame. "Everything alright?" He smirks mischievously at me.

He's likely the fourth-to-last person I expect to find standing here, with Jenevieve, Gladys, and Mr. Everett occupying the first, second, and third spots. "Why wouldn't it be?" I reply, stepping out of the bathroom and walking past him.

"You were in there for a long time," he matches his pace with mine.

In addition to feeling intensely embarrassed, I find his presence at this moment only adds to my irritation. "Were you timing me?" I ask, annoyed.

"No, but it sounded like you were going to wear down the marble in there pacing back and forth," he says with a hint of humor in his tone.

"Go away, Brad," is my only reply as I attempt to quicken my pace. I can't fathom why he insists on bothering me when there are numerous other staff members he could engage with, perhaps he could even be getting his dick wet with them.

"Are you still upset with me over the food thing?" He questions, his tone suggesting genuine concern by the thought of me being upset with him.

"I have no ill feelings toward you," I reply honestly. "I would just prefer you leave me alone," hoping this straightforward statement will encourage him to leave me in peace. Unfortunately, it doesn't work. He continues walking beside me for a minute. The silence almost allows me enough time to forget he is even here, only to be abruptly reminded of the humiliation back in Mr. Everett's office, where I nearly guided his fingers to my incredibly wet pussy.

Breaking the silence, he comments, "Lasagna is for lunch today."

Approaching the dining hall, the delightful aroma of lasagna greets us before we even set eyes on the food. The room is already filled with staff enjoying their lunch.

"Told you," he says proudly, pleased with himself for predicting the lunch menu, though I doubt it was a prediction at all. He must have already known what was for lunch.

I roll my eyes, grab a plate of food, and walk toward the row of bottled beverages to get water, with Brad still trailing behind me. Vanessa steps between us, twirling her hair between her fingers.

"Hi, Brad," she greets with her most flirtatious tone.

He steps around her, mimicking my earlier actions at the bathroom. We probably appear quite comical as he follows behind me, attempting to converse with me, while she trails after him, desperate for his attention. I come to a halt before reaching the table where Amber sits and turn towards them.

"Can I please eat in peace?" I request, addressing him.

He appears noticeably irritated, and I can tell it's because of Vanessa, but he doesn't try to leave. "I don't want *her* anywhere near me." I pointedly look at her and then back at him. "So please go so she will get away from me."

He turns to her, "You heard her. Leave," he says to Vanessa.

"I'm not going anywhere until you talk to me," she says, showing no signs of leaving without him.

"Brad. Go," I say, growing increasingly more annoyed.

He either notices how mad I'm getting or decides to leave so he can rip Vanessa a new asshole, but either way, he goes.

"See you around, Kal," he mutters, clearly agitated, with Vanessa trailing behind him.

"What was that all about?" Amber inquires, taking a bite of lasagna.

I turn toward the doors through which they exited and spot them in the hall, engaged in a heated discussion. She's grabbing at his arm, and he's shrugging her off. It dawns on me that the way to get Brad to go away might be to give in and act interested. Or sleep with him. I know Vanessa did merely seconds after meeting him, and he wants nothing to do with her. The part that I find so odd is that all the women he sleeps with are gorgeous. I know Vanessa is a problematic person who has gotten me in trouble more times than I can count, but she is undeniably pretty. However, looks must not mean anything to him. He is either just after women for the chase, or he isn't looking to settle down at all and doesn't like the idea of sleeping with the same woman over and over.

"Are they like an item?" Amber asks, continuing to eat.

"Who knows," I reply honestly.

"Is there something going on between you and Brad?" She asks quizzically.

I nearly choke on the first bite I take, "Heavens no," I say, wiping my mouth with my napkin. "Why would you ask that?" I wonder if he has said something to give her that impression.

"It was just a question, I'm not judging you," she says, scooping the remaining food on her plate into one spoonful and shoving it all in her mouth.

"Nothing to judge," I remark. "We aren't anything." Annoyance lingers as I consider why she would even ask such a question. If she's thinking that, could others be as well? What if this information reaches Mr. Everett? He might not want anything to do with me if he thinks I am involved with other staff members, especially Brad, as I'm sure Mr. Everett is aware of the number of staff Brad hooks up with.

After lunch, I walk down the hall with my duster, still processing the earlier events. I'm curious about what Gladys and Jenevieve were arguing about. It was obviously serious enough, it prompted them to bring the issue to Mr. Everett. As I continue walking, I realize I must pass Mr. Everett's office to return to the part of the mansion I am cleaning. The door is ajar, so I quickly and quietly walk past, knowing that he is working at his desk without needing to glance in.

"Kalyn," he calls out, as if he was waiting for me to pass, but I ignore him and keep walking. "Kalyn," I hear him say again. I pick up speed, hoping he doesn't decide to follow me. Glancing back to ensure he isn't behind me; I feel relieved when I confirm he's not there. When I'm confident I'm in the clear, I turn back around, only to collide right into him.

"Sorry," I quickly say as it feels like my face just ricocheted off a boulder.

Confused by how he is now in front of me when he should have been behind, I turn to glance down the hall in the direction I just came from and then back at him.

"What kind of witchcraft is this?" I ask, confused and rubbing my forehead.

He points to the opening in the wall he just came out of. "Secret entrance to my office," he explains.

"Sorry again," I say and step around him.

He seizes me by my waist and draws me towards the door that he just exited. "Are you okay?" confusion written all over his face.

"I might have a headache later but other than that I'm okay," I admit.

"I can get you medicine for that. Come with me."

"No, I'll be fine. My face already feels much better," I lie. Then accidentally glance down at his pants, and my face instantly flushes, thinking about what we were doing an hour ago.

"Is everything else okay?"

"Yeah, fine. I need to get back to work," I say dismissively, eager to leave the vicinity with him. Primarily because embarrassment sets in, but also because I can already sense my body betraying me again, feeling the increasing wetness between my legs.

"I sign your paychecks, remember," he says repeating the same words I said to him only yesterday.

"Mr. Everett, sir." Gag, I think to myself as those words come out of my mouth. I sound lame. "I am just trying to get back on my feet. I crossed a line earlier, and I am disappointed in myself for doing so. I apologize for putting you in an inappropriate position. It won't happen again."

"Disappointed?" The words come out as if I have offended him, and his face mirrors a sense of offense.

"Again, I apologize and would like to remain professional," I assert firmly. He stands there, visibly stunned. Seizing the moment, I make my exit. "Good day, sir," I say, walking out through the door opening in the wall, and continuing down the hall toward my assigned duty.

Although relieved that he doesn't follow me, an unsettling pit in my stomach lingers, questioning the odd sensation it feels like we just ended our nonexistent relationship.

I AM WALKING OUT OF MY BATHROOM, TOWEL DRYING MY HAIR AFTER a nice long hot shower after work. To my surprise, Shay is lounging on my bed. "Well, aren't you a sight for sore eyes," I greet her cheerfully, curious about how long she's been waiting since my shower took a good forty-five minutes. Nonetheless, I appreciate the company. I just would have been mindful to not take so long had I known she was out here.

"I'm a sight with sad eyes," she responds, as she overdramatically pouts her bottom lip out.

"I just got clean, but I will get dirty again, who are we fighting?" I walk to the bed and rest my knee against the side of my soft bedding.

She continues with a pitiful blink, "Jonathan left for who knows how long," appearing genuinely sad.

This news is unwelcome to me as well, knowing it likely meant Mr. Everett was gone too. "Did he say where he was going?" I ask, attempting not to sound too interested.

"Last-minute work stuff," she sighs, providing no additional details as she reclines on my pillows and theatrically flops her hands above her head onto the soft surface.

"Perfect," I reply, picking up the remote from my nightstand. Stepping onto the bed and over her, I lie down next to her, trying to act like the pit in my stomach doesn't exist. "We're gonna watch *Tangled*," I excitedly wag my eyebrows at her.

"You're such a goober," Shay nudges me, "Come, come," holding her arms out and gesturing for me to join her. "Give me boobie pillows." I lay down beside her, and she wraps her arms around my waist, rubbing her cheeks into my chest like a cat.

"Why do you always get boobie pillows? I thought it was my turn," I say, wrapping my arms around her shoulders and smiling.

"I'm the sad one, plus, yours are bigger than mine," she says, cozying up even more.

We make it halfway through the movie when Amber and Lilly walk in.

"Screw you both. Where was my invite?" Lilly questions, climbing onto the bed.

"You got the same invite I did," Shay retorts with a pouty tone. "I invited myself."

"What was happening at lunch today?" Lilly asks, intrigued, looking at me.

"Nothing I don't think," confused by what she is talking about, for a brief second, I wonder if this has something to do with what Mr. Everett and I were doing in his office. My palms instantly feel clammy.

She casts a glance between Shay and me, trying to discern if we're keeping something from her, then adds, "Amber mentioned Vanessa and Brad were in the hall big arguing," she says, digging for details.

"Vanessa slept with Brad the first day on the job, and in typical Brad fashion, he hit it and quit it. Vanessa thought he was her prince charming, but Brad is Brad's prince charming. Vanessa will cry about it until she moves on to the next person who shows her an ounce of attention. Brad is probably balls-deep in another maid as we speak. Now can we watch the movie?" Shay says in the most monotone voice I have ever heard.

"That's not fair," Amber says defensively. "Everyone makes Brad out to be the bad guy." She appears genuinely upset that people discuss Brad in a negative light as if she's oblivious to his womanizing behavior.

"If it walks like a duck, and quacks like a duck, it's probably a duck," Shay responds. "Brad is a duck."

We fall silent and continue watching the movie. My eyes drift toward Amber. She has sure been asking about Brad a lot. She even questioned my feelings for him. I think she might have a thing for him. No, not possible. I end that thought before I can even finish it because there is no way she would have a thing for someone like him. Though he is attractive, everyone knows he sleeps with all the housekeepers. She couldn't possibly be interested in a playboy like that… Right?

We finish the movie and then put on *Encanto*. I am the only one still awake at the end of the movie. I slide out from under Shay, slip on my slippers, and quietly open my door, careful not to wake anyone. I walk around the halls in this part of the mansion thinking about Brad and Amber, Shayla, and even Mr. Everett. I make a couple more laps and change up the halls each time when I hear muffled noises coming from down the hall in the shared staff space. I walk quietly down the dimly lit hall into the shared living room and peek around the corner.

Erica, Vanessa's shadow and "best friend," is fully nude, riding on top of someone's lap. Her muffled moans are now more audible as I am standing in the doorway. I linger for a moment, attempting to discern the identity of the person she's with. As she tilts her head back, it becomes unmistakably clear. It's Brad!

I can't pull my eyes away. I think for sure I am seeing things. But absolutely not, that is Brad and that is most definitely Erica. Carefully, I take a step backward, retreating around the corner, and hastily make my way down the hallway.

'*Nope, don't like that,*' I whisper to myself as I make it back to the maid's quarters in record time. By the time I am back in my bed with the three sleeping beauties, my heart is thundering in my chest. I still feel the adrenaline from seeing them, anger that he is sleeping with yet another maid, but my anger only rises when I think how he is sleeping with Vanessa's friend. I know it takes two to tango, but Vanessa is only a couple of steps down on the evil scale below Jenevieve. If Vanessa finds out about this, it's going to make an uncomfortable situation for all of us.

CHAPTER
Fifteen

KALYN

"We need a volunteer to work in the stables today. We have three girls that aren't feeling well," Jenevieve says, glancing at the other girls and then turning her attention to me. "Well?" she says pointedly, staring at me.

I stay quiet as the last place I want to be today is anywhere near Brad, and she has trained me to just keep my lips sealed.

"Kalyn," she says, "You can go," then promptly dismisses me to leave now.

I don't mind mucking horse stalls for a day. It changes my typical daily routine. What I do mind is that upon entering the stable, I find I am the only one of the housekeeping staff here. Which I realize must have been her plan. Maybe she did know something happened between Mr. Everett and me. '*I really screwed the pooch on this one,*' I think to myself.

"Someone's been an awfully bad girl," Brad says, walking into the stables as if right on cue.

"Excuse me?" I look in his direction, annoyed.

"I don't see anybody else coming to muck stalls." He looks around, holding his arms out to show me.

"Do you need something?" I roll my eyes.

"Actually, now that you ask, I do indeed need something," he begins to walk toward me.

"No," I cut him off. "You can go now," I don't even care what he wants to say right now. I don't want to hear anything. I want to yell at him and even spit on him, but somehow, I feel he would enjoy both of those.

"You didn't even hear what I was going to say," he grabs at his chest, pretending to be hurt.

"And I don't want to hear anything you have to say. Just go," I open the gate to the first stall and step inside. To my surprise, he walks away. I begin shoveling manure when a fork scoops a pile up right next to me. Startled, I look over and see Brad, rubber boots, gloves, and a manure fork in hand, picking the pile up, and then looking over at me.

"Get to work Wanda, I'm not doing this myself, lazy bones," he teases as he continues scooping.

Without another word, we work. I'm not going to argue with him—I don't have the energy. I find that if I just keep my mouth shut, I get free help from him, which in turn helps me.

We get nine stalls done before lunch. Side by side, we go to each one. Every time the wheelbarrow is full, he brings an empty one in and takes off with the full one before I can take it.

When we take a break to get some water, I wipe my arm across my forehead to remove the sweat. "I've never ridden a horse," I say, glancing around the stable.

He looks as if he might choke on his water from me initiating a conversation for the first time ever with him. "What about a stallion?" he grins, his joke not being lost on me. "Are you scared or never had the opportunity?" he continues curiously.

"Both, I suppose. They are so big, but I also don't want to hurt their back," I say honestly.

He lets out a laugh. "Are you saying you think all one hundred and thirty pounds of you might break a horse's back if you got on?" he asks in disbelief.

"That's not what I meant at all. I simply don't want to ride around on their backs because I don't know if it hurts them," I add. While I'm aware that riding a horse won't necessarily hurt them, they lack the ability to let us know if it did. For some reason, this conversation and Brad mentioning stallions make Mr. Everett pop into my mind. I would love to ride that stallion. I bet he's been with just as many women, if not more, than Brad. But I don't think he'd ever approach things the way Brad does. Brad makes you feel like you're the most important woman in the world and that he wants to be with you forever, charming his way into any woman's heart. On the other hand, Mr. Everett seems like he'd be more reserved, not leaving much room for daydreaming or uncertainty about a potential relationship with him.

"I can vocalize how it feels. Here, get on my back," he says, playfully pretending to get down on all fours to imitate a horse.

"I dare you," I say, hoping he really will.

"I will get down on my knees right now if you ride me," he grins.

"I think you have enough people riding you around here," I say jokingly, but his demeanor changes, and he looks as if I almost hurt his feelings. "There's no way that upsets you when you have sex with different people every day. Especially in public areas where other people can accidentally walk in and see," I say candidly, then hope he doesn't ask if I saw him having sex with Erica. Then again, who knows how many women he has slept with since he slept with her that someone could have accidentally seen.

"We should finish up. Only an hour left of work," he says, tossing his paper cup in the trash and setting off toward the next stall.

"Wow, you're awfully sensitive today," I remark. For someone who is always dishing out inappropriate comments and sleeping with a different woman every day, he sure is bothered by my comment. He always comes off as so cocky and arrogant that I forget he is a person with feelings too. It just confuses me that he would be bothered by my words when he has slept with half the staff, and judging by last night, and the way Vanessa is with him, I'd say there must be a reason they keep coming back.

We finish cleaning the last stall without saying another word. He takes the wheelbarrow out to dump it, and I go start putting supplies away. While he is out rinsing the wheelbarrow, I can hear talking. Chalking it up to most likely being Vanessa, I just ignore it.

When he walks in, I see Erica following behind. "Hey, Kalyn," she says, offering a wave. This is the first time she has ever acknowledged me in a decent manner, and it feels… odd.

Brad starts putting supplies away, "We need to finish up here," he tells her, giving the impression he doesn't want her here.

"I can help," she offers willingly, "What needs to be done?"

"We have it under control," he says in a dismissive tone, continuing to clean.

"I want to help," she says, looking at him in a pleading manner.

He seems irritated that she is even out here. "It won't take three of us."

"Actually, Erica, if you don't mind, I would love to go shower," I tell her, hopeful she will agree to stay and finish cleaning and I can get back a little early.

Erica's eyes sparkle, "Yes, please. Brad and I can finish up," she says happily.

I wink at Brad before I leave. "Thanks, Erica," I wave, while Brad shoots daggers in my direction.

I barely make it out of the stable before I hear Brad angrily stomping after me, whispering my name, "Kalyn!"

I casually turn around to see him approaching. I offer a pleasant smile, pretending not to notice his anger.

"What are you doing?!" He demands in a hushed tone.

"Going to shower," I feign ignorance.

"Did you not get the hint, I don't want her here," he emphasizes.

"Then you need to learn to keep your stupid penis in your stupid pants," my demeanor changes, and I whisper-argue back at him, pointing to his pants as I say it.

"Okay, I admit, I fucked up. Again!" he whispers back, raising his hands in a surrendering gesture. "Please come back, Kalyn," his eyes plead.

"No thanks. YOU did this to yourself. Go face your consequences," I bite back, pointing toward the stables.

"You have a job to do," he grabs me by my arm and starts pulling me back.

"No, she offered to finish for me. Go spend time with your girlfriend," I forcefully tug my arm in his grip.

He pulls me in closer to him, angrily whispering, "Don't ever call her that again." His grip still firm but not hurting me.

He wins in this battle. He's too strong for me to pull away.

When we reach the supply room, Erica's face lights up when Brad enters, and then it slowly fades when she sees me.

He releases his grip on my arm, and I contemplate trying to make a run for it. However, he looks like he could run fast and would catch me before I fully make it out of the stable. So, I stand here and give Erica a polite nod.

"I just realized I needed to finish cleaning in here." I brush my hands down my uniform and walk in further.

Erika looks disappointed.

"But this doesn't take two people, you two go ahead and go, I've got it from here," I encourage.

Brad's face reddens with rage. "Goddamnit, Kalyn," he snaps, then turns to Erica. "Can I speak with you out here?" as he leaves the supply room.

I don't have to listen hard because he all but starts yelling at her.

"This is work. If you don't need anything, don't come back out here again. I don't want to see you," he barks out at her.

"You don't want to see me?" her voice cracks as she says the words.

"Not even a little bit," he replies coldly.

"But…" her words trail off as she seems to be lost in what he is saying.

Even without being out there, I can tell she starts crying.

"No. There's no 'but.' We had sex. That's all it was. One and done. I need to get back. Don't come back out here again," he says sternly and then walks back in here and slams the door so hard the rakes on the wall shake.

I decide at this moment I should keep my smart mouth shut. I just continue sweeping quietly as he stomps around the room putting supplies away.

When I walk my shovel over to where he is, he takes it out of my hand softly. It catches me by surprise because I expected him to yank it away forcefully, possibly even jerking my arm out of its socket. But he doesn't.

When we finish, we leave the stable, and I go right, back to the mansion, while his apartment is to the left.

"Good work today, Wanda," he calls after me, no hint of sarcasm in his words.

"Thank you for your help, Bert," I respond back.

As I approach the mansion, I see Erica sitting outside on a bench. Catching sight of me, she rises and strides in my direction, obviously having been waiting for me. Her troubled look and tears cascading down her face reveal her distress.

"Why?" she asks, her voice trembling.

"Why what?" I ask, confused, stopping in my tracks.

"Why does he still talk to you after you two slept together? What did you do that is different than everybody else?" She searches my face trying to figure out some secret I seem to have.

"Brad and I have never slept together," I say honestly and slightly confused as to why she would even assume we have.

She laughs condescendingly, "Yeah right."

"I'm not joking. We haven't," I tell her, remaining serious. "It's also disrespectful to accuse someone of something like that when you don't even know what you're talking about. And this is obviously something that more people than just you seem to think has happened."

"Vanessa is the one who told me you and him have sex? He has sex with her over again because she will screw him anywhere. And she said he likes to watch you while he fucks her. But when does he find time to have you too?" she questions.

I'm caught off guard by her words. "What are you talking about, Erica?" I manage to ask after a moment of stunned silence. "What do you mean he watches me? Where would he watch me?"

"Brad sleeps with Vanessa in the horse stalls next to yours while you're working, and they watch you."

My skin prickles as her words sink in, and I don't know how to process the information. I am busting my ass working hard, while they are getting their rocks off watching me. I feel violated.

She stares at me like I'm an idiot for not noticing, or like I somehow played a role in their sneaking around. Does she think I just stood there knowingly letting them fuck while they watched me? What the fuck?

She stares at me, then laughs as if she's finally figured it out. "He's in love with you," her snickering becomes louder.

"Erica, you aren't making sense. I think you should go inside and try to get some sleep."

"Have you really not had sex with him?" her eyes become round with a hint of excitement.

"No, Erica. But even if I had, it would be none of yours or anybody else's business," I respond.

"You have to sleep with him. He must think you are unattainable, so he's infatuated. But if you sleep with him, he will get over that and move on, and we can be together," she says, a crazed look glazing over her eyes.

"No, Erica, you need to calm down. Go inside and try to sleep whatever this is off," I say to her, starting to become worried about her mental state.

"Please, Kalyn! I'm begging," she whimpers.

"Sleeping with him will do nothing. He doesn't love me. He doesn't love anybody, Erica, that's why he's called a womanizer," I tell her, frustrated.

"Well damn. This hurts like hell," tears stream down her face. "All I heard is how great he was in bed. He is as great as the rumors claim. I love him, Kalyn."

Exhaling deeply, I feel sad for her. She fell into his web and finds herself to be yet another heartbroken woman due to his ways.

"You don't love him, Erica. You lust him at best," I know it comes out harsher than I anticipated but maybe that's what she needs. Someone to not pussyfoot around the elephant in the room. Brad doesn't love her. He doesn't love Vanessa and he doesn't love me.

"I truly love him, Kalyn. I really do," she sounds as though she's trying to convince both of us.

"What do you think is going to happen when Vanessa finds out you slept with him? She also believes she loves him. Did you ever think about that?" I ask, my chest rising and falling rapidly, really hating this conversation. "I know he didn't think about that.

You see how she treats me and everyone else. How do you think she will treat you when she finds out?"

"I don't care what she thinks. I'm not scared of her," she argues.

"Well, I'm glad for you then. Because all Brad is doing is causing issues and tension between the staff. Yet you all are too smitten by his pretty words to realize all he wants is sex."

"You're a real bitch. No wonder Jenevieve hates you," she spits, turning and leaving back toward the mansion.

ALL THE STAFF IS BACK AT WORK TODAY. THIS MEANS I AM BACK ON dusting duties, partnered with Jess and Katy. While I like them both, I'm slightly disappointed because neither of them talk. So I will spend the next eight hours in complete silence. At times, my brain becomes so loud I wonder if they can hear my thoughts. Numerous times throughout the day, I imagine Mr. Everett and I in various sexual positions, and I always wonder if they can somehow hear how inappropriate I am being.

Giles enters around the last three hours of our shift, and with a cheerful tone, announces a new assignment for us. "I have a job for you ladies to do," he seems to be in high spirits.

"Of course, Giles. What do you need us to do?" I ask, ready to begin whatever he needs from us.

"Come with me," he smiles, waiting for us to gather our cleaning totes.

He walks us to Mr. Everett's office. I stand frozen, not sure what we are supposed to be doing. My stomach twists in knots in anticipation that he might be in there. Maybe he spilled something again.

"Mr. Everett has been gone, and his office is collecting dust," Giles opens the door wide and walks in.

To my disappointment, the room is empty and cold. I can sense that Mr. Everett hasn't been here recently, and I hate that.

"I'll have you ladies' dust in here while he is away," he says, swiping his finger along a bookshelf and rubbing the nonexistent dust between his digits. "If you need anything just let me know," he adds before exiting.

"I'll take this wall," the taller girl, Katy says, pointing at the south wall.

"I'll start this one," Jess says, walking over to the East wall, which is also the wall lined with the most amount of books. Who needs this many books?

While we clean, there is hardly any dust, making this project seem almost pointless, which inevitably has my thoughts trailing right back to Mr. Everett. About his voice, his body, his face, his big hands, the way he touched me. *'And it won't happen again,'* I interrupt my own thoughts. *'You have a year here Kalyn,'* I tell myself. *'Quit trying to fuck it up,'* I scold myself.

I wish we had music or something to listen to so I could distract my thoughts. They need to be put in time out for the amount of naughty thoughts that keep creeping in.

It's so quiet in here. The numerous times I have tried to carry on a conversation with them, it just goes flat immediately. So, I get to spend quality time with myself and my dirty thoughts. Which gets really annoying after a while.

I find myself wishing at this moment I could smell coffee. Yes, coffee. That smell I dislike but reminds me of the first interaction he and I had in here.

I saunter over to his desk, running my fingers along the dark wood. His desk is perfectly organized as usual. He has a glass of water sitting on a coaster, and his chair is pulled out as if he stood up from it and left without knowing he wouldn't return that same day. I run my fingers across the spot where I cleaned up spilled coffee and tea and smile to myself. All remnants of it are now gone, but the memory remains.

He has been gone for two and a half weeks. Each day feels like an entire month. Despite my attempts not to care or notice, his absence bothers me. He has consumed me. It doesn't help that even while he is gone, everything around me seems to remind me of him—every step I take, I am reminded that he too has walked these very halls. All the different scents, whether it be food, cleaning products, or just the smell of his house, he too experiences them. Everything surrounding me—each art piece, decoration, furniture piece, the ceilings, walls, doors, and floors—are all here because of him. He is a constant presence.

I glance down. Maybe I really did rub a noticeable spot on the floor from our last encounter but am startled when I see two dress shoes planted on either side of where I stand. My heart races, and I turn around to find Mr. Everett slowly swiveling back and forth in his chair.

"Hi," he says, tilting his head partially to one side.

"Mr. Everett," the words come out more shocked than I had hoped.

Katy and Jess stop dusting and look over. Apparently, none of us heard him come in.

"When did you get back?" I ask, trying to steady my words.

"Why, did you miss me?" he asks, an intensity in his tone as he stands from his chair, inching toward me, maintaining eye contact.

"I... uh..." I mumble, not even sure what to say.

He leans forward toward me and wraps his arm around my waist, effortlessly lifting me off the floor and settling me onto his desk. Leaning in, he positions his body between my legs, bringing his face just inches from mine.

"You can put distance between us, you can say you are just here to work, but I already told you, Kalyn, you are mine," his voice so laced with arousal I wonder if the drool inside my lips managed to leak out.

"Mr. Everett," I whisper, closing my eyes.

"I told you to call me Jonah," he says sternly.

My eyes open, and I meet his gaze with a nod, "Jonah," is all I can get out, knowing we can't do this. We can't do any of this. I need the job. I don't want to deal with Jenevieve trying to murder me every day. I don't have anywhere to go if things go south between us. We just need to remain professional.

His eyes close, and he leans his forehead against mine. "Baby, stop," he whispers back.

Neither of us speaks—we just keep our foreheads pressed together.

"I need to get back to work," I whisper, breaking the silence.

I feel his hand move and then hear the glass on his desk get knocked over.

I look over, and a playful smile tugs at my lips at the fact he intentionally knocked it over.

"Oops," his gaze stays resolutely planted on me.

"Smooth. I need to go get a towel so I can clean that up," glancing down at him between my legs.

"I can give you my shirt," he suggests, gazing at me.

"You can move so I can go get a towel," I scoot myself toward the edge of his desk, but he stands securely in place, causing my spread legs to be pressed right up against him when I do this.

"I can give you my pants," his voice lowered, moving his face closer to mine. "I can give you my boxers," he slides his hand from my waist down to my thigh. "We can use your dress," biting his lip, glancing down at my dress hiked up to the top of my spread legs, my black silk panties visibly showing. "I like that idea best," he slides his hand up to my hip, his thumb gently grazing the front of my panties.

"You, sir, are making cleaning this water up… interesting," arousal laces my whispered words. "I'll be right back." I sit up straighter and push on his chest.

He takes a step back, and I climb down from his desk and go retrieve a clean towel. I can feel Jess and Katy still staring between Jonah and me, but I pretend there is nothing to see here. I walk back over to his desk—he is sitting on the shorter part of the L shape with his legs crossed out in front of him, his hands gripping the edge of the desk.

I wipe the water that somehow managed to spill only on his desk. He leans over, sliding two fingers into the back side of my apron, and pulls me toward him. I walk backward two steps, finding my back pressed against him. He wraps his arms around my waist and whispers in my ear, "My name will moan from your lips and echo off every wall in this place." He says the same thing he said the first day I met him, and my body reacts the same way, only this time I contemplate turning around and jumping into his arms, knowing if I did, he would catch me and probably spread me out on his desk.

Taking a step forward, he releases me. "You," I turn to face him and gently poke his chest.

He reaches up grabbing hold of my hand, lacing his fingers in mine, and placing a soft kiss on my knuckle before pulling me back to him.

Giles walks into the office through the doors he left open, clearing his throat to make his presence known. I pull my hand from Jonah, bringing them to my sides, turning to face Giles. I watch out of my peripheral as Jonah moves off the desk to sit back in his chair.

"Hi, Giles," I greet him warmly as he walks up.

"Hello again, Miss Kalyn," his eyes brighten.

I stand just next to Mr. Everett's chair and feel his hand slide up the back of my dress and loop around my thigh closest to him.

"How was your flight, Mr. Everett?" Giles asks.

"It was long," he admits, rubbing his thumb back and forth where his hand is resting. Each stroke leaving a delightful trail in its wake. As my heartbeat accelerates, a yearning intensifies, aching for his touch to move higher between my legs.

"Sir, the South wing needs to be prepared. With your permission, I'd like to take these two ladies?" Giles asks politely.

"Of course," Mr. Everett responds, his thumb still rubbing my leg.

I can already tell the effect he is having on me, and it always ends with my poor panties being left completely wet with my arousal.

With hesitation, Giles adds, "Your mother called, for the nineteenth time today, sir. She wanted me to let you know since you don't want to return her calls, they will be leaving a couple of days early and will be arriving tomorrow instead of Monday." His nervousness appears to intensify once he finishes speaking.

Jonah's thumb stops moving, and he lets out a long sigh before dropping his hand. "Of course they are," his frustration is palpable.

"I'm sorry sir, is there anything I can do?" he asks, concerned.

"No, Giles, thank you." Giles nods and turns to exit, bringing Katy and Jess with him.

Standing from his chair, he leans over and kisses my cheek. "Come with me," he says, taking me by the hand and leading us toward the bookshelves along the far wall. He touches a spot inside one of them, triggering a click. The bookshelf opens an inch, which he pushes open the rest of the way, revealing a dimly lit hallway. Pulling my hand, he guides me inside.

Beyond the door is a corridor, and at the end, I can see closed double doors emitting a soft glow underneath. Five steps in, there is another hallway branching off to the left.

"Is that..." I begin, nodding towards the door.

"My secret door?" He finishes my sentence. "Yes," he confirms.

We continue down the hall, heading toward the double doors. Reaching out, he unlatches the door and pushes it open. The spacious room is luxurious. It is bathed in soft, ambient lighting that accentuates the muted tones of cream and gold.

At the center of the room is a sitting area, with plush, tufted sofas and armchairs upholstered in rich, velvety fabrics. Intricately carved wooden tables with polished surfaces and a glistening crystal chandelier hang from the ceiling, casting a warm glow over the seating area.

In one corner of the room is a majestic spiral staircase, its black wrought iron railings curving gracefully upward.

At the farthest end, a large, elegant bed with a lavish canopy and posh bedding sits, perfectly done up. Cascading drapes in rich fabrics frame the bed. Throughout the space, carefully curated artworks and decorative accents adorn the walls.

"Woow," I say, entranced by the room, trying to take it all in. "Is this your sex cave?" I jokingly ask, still looking around.

"You're the first woman I've brought in here," he says, watching me.

"I see," I respond, growing slightly nervous as my eyes land on the bed, realizing he might have brought me in here to have sex… now. Growing self-conscious, my cheeks flush, trying to figure out how I can excuse myself to a bathroom to try and freshen up.

He must notice my mind is racing because he starts pulling us around the room. When I think we are headed to the bed, he continues toward the staircase. This throws me off as I don't know why he would have brought me in here if he didn't plan on taking me to bed.

We make our way up, winding to the top of the grand staircase. A light emanating under a closed door beckons from down the hall. As we approach, the glow intensifies, revealing a doorway leading into an observatory. A magnificent telescope stands in the center. Greenery and flowers are planted throughout the room. An expansive covered balcony at the farthest end awaits. We walk through the wide-open doors and toward the edge. From this elevated vantage point, the view is nothing short of extraordinary. Looking out at the vast endless landscape, stretching far beyond the confines of the mansion. The courtyard below with its manicured gardens appears even more pristine from this viewpoint. The distant horizon appears to expand forever.

"This is the highest point of the mansion," he states, a look of happiness covering his face as he leans his arms on the railing.

"It's breathtaking," I sigh, trying to take it all in.

"Yes," he utters, fixing his gaze on me.

"Wow," amusement fills my words. "You must be such a treat to women," I playfully tease, assuming he is trying to flirt with me.

"I don't care about other women," he states bluntly, his gaze unwavering.

"That can't be entirely true," I respond, leaning my arms next to his on the railing. "Your mother will be here tomorrow."

The reminder evidently doesn't sit well with him, as his demeanor shifts noticeably. There is a hint of irritation in his expression, perhaps triggered by the thought that his family would be arriving.

Rising from his leaning position, he moves behind me and wraps his arms around my waist. As he draws near, his scent washes over me, engulfing my senses in the most exquisite smell I have ever experienced in my life. I would expect his cologne to smell pricey, but it mixing with his own natural pheromones is intoxicating. "I'd rather not talk about my family right now," he murmurs, burying his face in the crook of my neck and inhaling deeply.

"Okay," unsure if he's avoiding conversation altogether or just conversation related to his family. "Do you ever feel scared up here?" I ask, staring out at all the land. Though a lot of the property has perfectly manicured paths and ponds and sitting areas, there are large amounts of forest that surround us.

He gently brushes his teeth against my neck. My skin comes alive by his electrifying touch, and I lean into it. "Scared?" he questions with a lighthearted tone. "Of what?" He presses his lips to my neck.

A shiver courses through my entire body, momentarily causing me to lose track of our conversation. The sensation of his kiss lingers warmly on my skin even after his lips move away. I lean my head back on his shoulder, loving how this feels. Regaining my voice, "I'm not sure—falling... or monsters," I add playfully.

He plants another kiss on my neck, just a bit higher than where he left the first one. "No, the idea of falling doesn't scare me, and I couldn't possibly be scared of monsters when everyone whispers about me being one," he muses aloud.

I am aware that he is right. People do whisper about him being a monster, but just as much, about wanting him to fuck them.

"That's not all they say," I tease.

"Oh? Perhaps monster is the most fitting," he says in a seductive tone as he presses a kiss to my neck once more, this one right below my ear.

"Is that so?" I respond flirtatiously, turning my head to meet his gaze.

"I couldn't care less what anyone thinks of me... except for you," he confesses sincerely, his eyes scanning every inch of my face.

"Oh really?" A sparkle ignites in my eyes.

"Mmhmm," he shifts from behind me, leaning against the balcony, taking a wide stance, delicately wrapping an arm around my waist. When he pulls me toward him, I willingly comply, positioning myself between his legs until the front of my body is snugly against his solid chest.

His hand comes up, softly tracing the outer edges of his fingers across my cheeks before cupping my chin. I am transported to the night in the closet with him, and I swear if anyone interrupts our kiss this time, I will hurl them off the balcony.

A flurry of butterflies erupts in my stomach as he brings our faces together and presses his full lips against mine. They are the softest I have ever felt.

Time stands still.

He places his hand on the small of my back, drawing me closer. At the same time, his other hand tenderly finds the nape of my neck, cradling me with the gentlest touch. I rest my hands on his hips, as our lips gently part, our tongues intertwine for the first time, initiating an electrifying moment. The slow, rhythmic dance of our tongues begins—an intimate exploration involving caressing, sliding, and rubbing against each other.

My fingers trace up his chest to his neck, one hand delicately resting at his nape, while the other glides through his hair, pulling him closer into our deepening embrace. Our tongues continue their synchronized dance, and I feel a growing wetness between my legs as his arm tightens around my waist, pulling my face closer to his, mirroring my own movements.

Our mouths move in harmony, and I find myself squeezing my hand in his hair to release the building tension. The grip on his hair elicits a moan from him, resonating with the passionate intensity of our kiss. The sultry sound of his moan ignites a desire to pant in response, as I've never heard something so seductive. I entertain the fantasy of climbing up, propping my knees on either side of the balcony rail, and riding him right here.

His tongue remains soft and delicate. The fervor of our kiss intensifies, even as we suck the souls out of each other, his mouth is eager but soft. The countless moments of separation and interrupted closeness have propelled us to seize this opportunity fully.

Never have I experienced a kiss of this caliber, nor have I desired a kiss to linger eternally as fervently as I do now.

Our tongues gradually slow, and with a deliberate pace, our mouths part as he draws his head back. A smile gracefully spreads across his face, a sight that is entirely new to me and utterly captivating. I am rendered speechless, my gaze fixed on him—a sight I could cherish indefinitely. Unable to contain my joy, I mirror the same look in return.

"Glad to see you have teeth," I joke, alluding to the whispers that hinted at him not having teeth because nobody ever sees him smile.

He bursts into laughter, then affectionately presses a kiss on my lips before resuming his gaze upon me. "Yes, I have teeth," he confirms, maintaining that incredible smile. "I wouldn't care if you didn't have teeth, however," he adds, his eyes dancing with warmth as he stares down at me.

"Is that so?" I jest, engaging in a flirtatious banter. "And why is that?"

A mischievous glint sparkles in his eyes as he flirts back, wagging his eyebrows. "I can think of a scenario where no teeth would feel incredibly good."

"Okay, okay. So, if I understand correctly, you're perfectly fine with a toothless wonder as long as your penis gets sucked on," I quip back.

"You get me," he retorts jokingly.

I am utterly captivated by this man. My mind can't even grasp how such a perfect man was even created.

Time slips away while we stand on the balcony, engulfed in lighthearted conversation. It only registers the shift in the day when I glance away from him and see the sun beginning to set.

"What time is it?" I ask, shocked that it seems to be evening.

"Uh, just after seven," glancing down at his watch and then back to me.

"Seven? I need to go. I haven't finished my work, and I missed dinner," I try to sound unfazed but full panic is already settling in.

"I will have dinner brought to us, and if I recall, you were cleaning your boss's office. He is pleased with your impeccable work," he reassures, attempting to alleviate the concern I am trying so hard to hide.

"I do need to go," I insist, feeling a bit calmer this time. Even if Jenevieve were to attempt the impossible in this very moment, like tearing out all my hair, I would likely hardly feel it, given how incredible I feel after our kiss.

"Okay, Cinderella," he muses, "Only if you promise me something."

I raise an eyebrow, "Okay," I say intrigued.

"Miss me," he grins, bringing his face to mine and placing another delicate kiss on my lips. Without waiting for a response, he gracefully rises from the balcony railing, taking my hand and leading me back through the doors we had ventured from.

"I suppose you aren't going to let me walk you back to your room," he remarks as we reach his office doors.

"You would suppose right," I playfully respond.

Leaning forward to grab the door handle, he brings his face close to mine once more, placing another one of his remarkably gentle kisses on my lips.

"Good night, Kalyn," he says, locking eyes with me before opening the door.

"Good night, Mr. Everett," I respond, smiling back at him, and begin to walk away. But just like earlier, he slides two fingers into the back of my apron and pulls me to him until my back is to his chest.

He envelops his arms around my waist and whispers in my ear, "Jonah. Or I will have to spank you next time," he says, softly nibbling my earlobe.

"I just might like that… Mr. Everett," I flirtatiously tease back looking up at him.

A flicker of arousal gleams in his eyes as I push off him and move toward the door. He extends his hand, playfully slapping my butt. "Next time, there won't be clothes to dull the sting."

"Don't make empty threats," I cheerfully retort as I walk out.

I make my way back toward the maid's quarters when Giles emerges from around the corner.

"Miss Kalyn, I just put dinner in your room," he informs me.

Giles's kindness never fails to surprise me. "Thank you, Giles," letting my joy show on my face. "I'm starving," I admit.

"You won't starve as long as you're here," he replies mirthfully.

"You are too good to me."

A genuine look of happiness crosses his face as he remarks, "You are good for him," referring to Jonah.

"You!" Jenevieve's screech echoes down the hall. "Where have you been!" she demands as she stomps toward me.

Giles immediately intervenes. "I was given direct orders for some of the staff to get things ready for tomorrow," he responds to Jenevieve's accusatory tone.

"Tomorrow? What about tomorrow?" she hisses at him.

"Mr. Everett's family arrives tomorrow, ma'am," he explains, appearing completely unfazed by her frenzied look.

A glimmer of anticipation rushes into her eyes. "Well," she says, smoothing her dress, "Thank you for letting me know at the last minute. Have a good night," walking off with a wave and her fingers wiggling in a cheerful goodbye. This news makes her so happy she forgot she was in the middle of scolding me.

Giles and I exchange a puzzled glance.

"Have a good rest of your evening, Miss Kalyn," he nods his head to me before turning to walk away.

CHAPTER
Sixteen

KALYN

Chaos reigns throughout the house in the morning as everyone scurries around, preparing for the impending arrival of Mr. Everett's family. The exact arrival time is unknown, but the atmosphere is charged with tension. We're instructed to ensure everything is spotless and then effectively disappear by retreating to the maid's quarters.

Curious about the commotion, I turn to Shay, "Why is everyone so worked up about Mr. and Mrs. Everett coming?" I don't understand what can be so intimidating. Mr. Everett is wealthy like his family, and he isn't frightening. Quite the opposite, he is magnificent. This thought brings me back to our incredible kiss. A kiss I crave to feel again.

Shay seems completely unimpressed, "You mean, aside from the fact that they're snobs?" she replies with unfiltered candor.

"Like, from being rich?" I ask, a bit perplexed.

"Possibly. They certainly let something get to their big heads," she remarks. "When I am filthy rich like this, slap me across the face as hard as you can if I ever turn into a douche," she playfully adds.

Shay has been employed here for a couple of years, so I imagine she has a lot of inside information about Jonah and his family. "Mr. Everett doesn't seem snobby," I mention, making sure to refer to him as Mr. Everett so she doesn't get suspicious. Inside, I feel a bit naughty and almost wish he heard me refer to him so formally, so he could make good on his promise to spank me.

"Probably why he and his family don't get along. You know, his mother calls him like one hundred times a day. Then shows up unannounced when he ignores her calls," she says, a hint of mirth in her voice.

"You both might accomplish something if you quit yacking," Jenevieve snaps from a distance, her voice resonating down the hallway. "On second thought, split up. I don't trust that you two will be of any use working so closely," she commands, striding away. Glancing back at her, I notice she really went the extra mile getting ready today from her usual appearance—her hair cascades down in loose curls, a stark contrast to the usual tight bun. While she's donned her typical form-fitting dress, today she sparkles with what seems to be genuine diamonds adorning her wrist, neck, and ears. Not to mention the additional layers of makeup, which doesn't go unnoticed.

"How rude," Shay remarks, feigning offense at Jenevieve's words, though it's clear that she remains unruffled. "I'll just head this way," she says with a carefree attitude as she strolls away, whimsically waving her duster and swaying her hips with elegance.

"I guess I will go this way," I mutter to myself, walking in the opposite direction.

I am still pondering Jenevieve's extravagant attire. Why does she feel she needs to impress them that badly? Is she trying to convince herself she is 'one of them?' These thoughts of her dissipate when I wander down a grand hallway, becoming entranced by the art pieces and sculptures on the walls. I admire each masterpiece as I walk along the red and gold carpet at the center of the white-marbled floor. Everything appears quite pricey. There are even mid-sized pillars adorned with sculptures on top of them, accompanied by elegant tables lining the walls, showcasing more art. Knowing my luck, I'll probably trip over something, causing the sculptures to topple like dominos and crash to the ground.

"Hi baby," Jonah whispers in my ear, wrapping his arms around my waist. I notice Giles must have been walking with him as he continues walking down the hallway and disappears around the corner.

Jonah pushes us toward a dimly lit dip in the wall, merely big enough for us to not be noticed if someone were to pass the hallway.

"Did you keep your promise?" he inquires, his voice tinged with desire.

Confused, I ask, "Promise?" as all my senses seem to be sparking all at once, just being near him. My lips ache to be against his again.

He responds, "To miss me," as he pins me against the wall and presses his lips to mine.

"Always," I breathe as we part momentarily. "I am supposed to be getting things ready for your parents."

"Mmhmm," he moans, and his lips reclaim mine. We are behaving like two horny teenagers, yet I can't find it in me to care.

"Jonah, someone might see us." My body aches for him, but I would probably die of embarrassment if someone saw us.

Unperturbed, he assures me, "I guarantee they will pretend they didn't see anything. They think I'm a monster, remember?" A grin spreads across his face as he presses his lips to mine once more.

His hands slide down my back, eventually resting on each cheek. "Incredible," he squeezes gently. "You have an amazing ass," he breathes out an aroused groan.

"I have other things you might find amazing too," I breathe back.

"Oh really," he replies, sounding intrigued, and reclaiming my lips.

"Mmhmm," I moan softly.

Our tongues delicately intertwine, caressing each other. He leans to the side, sliding a hand around my thigh, lifting it towards him. With my leg raised, pressed against him and the full-length mirror on the wall, my dress rides up. Heat dances across his eyes in response and our kiss intensifies. His fingers trace up my thigh, sending shivers throughout my entire body. Our tongues continue their rhythmic dance, accompanied by small moans escaping our throats. His hand pauses where my leg is bent, meeting my hip. Lowering my hand from his neck, it finds its place on top of his hand.

Our eyes lock, and I bite my bottom lip, craving his touch, as I guide his hand toward the warmth between my thighs. An aroused glimmer flashes in his eyes as he becomes aware of my desires and his lips reclaim mine.

He brushes his fingers along the outside of my panties, tracing a path toward my center, causing my hips to arch toward him. Upon reaching the dampness, he runs his middle finger over it, smoothly sliding between my folds, trailing the moisture along the silk material to my swollen clit. There, he begins to rub deliberate circles.

We both stare down at the wonderful work of his skilled finger. My lips part slightly as my breath quickens, stirred by the exquisite sensations he's coaxing out of me. With a steady hand, I release my grip from the mirror, tracing the buttons of his shirt, one by one, undoing them until his neck and chest are exposed. His scent is intoxicating—I want to suck on every inch of him. Pressing my mouth against his bare chest, I savor the taste of his skin as he leans closer to me. I comb my fingers through his hair, drawing him closer, and he willingly complies. My tongue finds its way back to his neck, kissing and sucking on the soft flesh.

While my mouth is busy, he slides my panties to the side, his fingers slipping into my wet slit. Slowly circling my sweet spot with the perfect amount of pressure.

"Jonah," I moan into his chest, taking a handful of his thick hair with one hand and squeezing.

After what felt like an eternity without a man's touch, his fingertips against my skin awaken dormant desires, and I have to remind myself to calm down and enjoy the slowness of his movements.

I can vividly recall the feeling of the few men who came before him, who have touched me. Yet, none of them compare to the potency of Jonah's powerful touch. Even memories with Wyatt, and numerous times he would grope me, felt so wrong it made my skin crawl with discomfort, and I pushed those feelings aside and allowed him to continue until I would fake an orgasm, and later listen to him brag about his magical skills to our friends. But with Jonah, it's different—I can't imagine a single woman that he has been with ever feeling anything other than pure ecstasy and total satisfaction afterward. He has a touch that will leave women craving it.

A low moan vibrates up his throat, and he continues circling my swollen bud before slowly inching his fingers down toward my center.

"Yes," I say shakily, needing him to penetrate me. It's been far too long, and I need release any way he will give.

Without another word, he stretches his middle finger inside me. I let out a moan and tilt my head back, drawing my hips down on his finger.

"Fuck baby, you're so tight," he whispers, slowly moving his finger in and out of me, ensuring every inch is coated before sliding it deep inside and skillfully rocking it back and forth. He persists in this same rhythm, then withdraws his finger, eliciting a protestive moan from me.

He seals his lips against mine, and then skillfully inserts two fingers back in, igniting an impatient response in me. I instinctively start rocking my hips in sync with his movements, my breath quickening. His fingers exhibit a seasoned touch, finding my G-spot with precision while his thumb firmly circles on my clit, creating a torrent of pleasure.

My brain is so disoriented with all the sensations he is drawing out of me. I don't even care how eager I seem as I grind against his finger. I need this, and I will take it while it is being given. The intensity builds, and I sense the impending eruption of my climax.

"Jonah," I moan out digging my nails into his bare chest.

He leans down, bites my neck, and starts sucking.

As the sensation intensifies, I can no longer contain it. Waves of pleasure ripple through my body, and my core surrenders to the ecstasy, gripping him tightly while pulsating, every inch of my body quivers in his hold.

"Jonah," I cry out again, panting and moaning into his chest, my hips rocking as I ride out the waves of pleasure. My body convulses and tightens so hard on his fingers I feel I could snap them. Even as I come down from my orgasm, I want to restart all over and have him fuck me again the same way.

"How many women has he fucked with these fingers?" my intrusive thoughts decide to make themselves known. *"How many women's cum has he had dripping down his hand?"* Deciding I'm not going to hurt my own feelings right now, I look up at him, bringing myself back to the present, as my orgasm comes to a stop and my breathing begins to slow. "Sorry," my whisper comes out breathless. "It's been a while," I say, embarrassed that I came so quickly.

"I'll wager I cum faster," he grins as he continues kissing my neck. "You were right," he exhales.

"About what?" I pant.

His fingers slowly slide out of me, causing a final gasp to escape my lips. "The other amazing things you were mentioning."

"Is that so?" I quip back, enjoying the feel of his mouth on my neck.

"Mmhmm," his deep groan vibrates my skin.

Reaching up I wrap my arms around his neck, loving the feel of us pressed together like this. Closing my eyes, I allow myself to fully enjoy our sexual encounter.

"How long do we have?" I question playfully.

"Maybe five minutes," his mouth moves to a new spot.

"Think you can cum in that amount of time?" I salivate just thinking about putting his cock in my mouth. I want to suck on him. I *need* to suck on him.

"Without a doubt," he removes his mouth, locking eyes with me for only a moment before his lips clash against mine.

He tastes so good.

While his tongue moves against mine, I feel his fingers brush against my leg, gently wrapping around it as he shifts his body away from the mirror.

"Think you can walk?" he grins.

"I'm not sure," I admit, still reeling from my orgasm.

"Then I'll carry you," he responds earnestly.

"No," I insist, gripping his hand wrapped around my thigh.

As I slowly bring my trembling leg down from the mirror, I place it on the floor and straighten up, making sure my unsteady legs can hold me upright.

My legs, panties, and his entire hand are soaking wet. "Here," I say, grabbing my apron and wiping his hand with it. "That should get you by until you can wash your hands."

"Who says I'm going to wash my hands?"

"Me," I tease. "Your family is going to be here soon, so unless you don't plan on touching anyone, you need to wash your hands."

All sexual tension evaporates at the mention of his family, and I almost feel awkward. I seem to have a knack for making things weird without even meaning to.

"Well, isn't that something," I jest, looking at the mirror where there's an impression of my leg and finger marks from my attempt to steady myself.

"This is undoubtedly my favorite piece of art in this hallway," he stares admiringly at it.

"Until I clean it off," I joke.

"You will do no such thing," he says playfully, though there's a hint of seriousness in his tone.

My legs have stopped trembling, and we need to get our disheveled clothes back where they belong. I push on his chest with both my pointer fingers, signaling for him to scoot back. As he complies, I see fresh claw marks on his chest, lightly bleeding.

"Oh my gosh, Jonah," a shock resonates through me. "I made you bleed," I stare wide-eyed as I pull his shirt open more to inspect the marks.

He glances at the mirror while buttoning his shirt. "That's nothing compared to what I did to your neck."

I turn to the mirror and discover three prominent hickeys on my neck. Panic crosses my face, while his lips curl upward. "Give it a couple of days, and we'll both be healed, baby," he says, kissing me on the cheek as I continue pulling down my collar to examine my neck more closely.

"Your parents are coming, Jonah!" I exclaim, not finding a couple of days fast enough for them to heal.

As I gaze at them, I can't deny their undeniable allure. My attention lingers on the marks left on my neck by his mouth. These imprints will stay for days, offering me constant reminders of this unforgettable moment, until they eventually fade away as I'm sure this moment will to him.

"I don't think they'll be checking for hickeys their son may or may not have given someone, and I can guarantee they won't be unbuttoning my shirt to inspect for scratches. Besides, I think they're sexy," he taps three fingers on my three hickeys.

I adjust my dress, ensuring that my newfound hickeys are not noticeable, and we step out of the small alcove in the wall. My cheeks are flushed from our recent activities. My brain repeatedly reminds me not to appear nervous or guilty, but if someone were to ask what we were just doing, I'd probably respond that he was fingering me before I could stop the words.

Walking side by side, he reaches down and intertwines his fingers with mine. When we reach the end of the hall, Giles is promptly standing there, as if he has been waiting for Jonah to finish up.

"Giles, hi!" I exclaim, feeling a bit embarrassed, realizing he would have heard everything we just did. If I thought my face was flushed before, I can only imagine the darker shade of pink my cheeks are now. I can feel them radiating heat.

Was I loud?

I don't think I was.

I've never heard myself before.

"Miss Kalyn," he smiles, "It's always good to see you."

"You too, Giles," I attempt to release my hand from Jonah's. However, he tightens his grip and looks down at me mischievously.

"Well, I should be going," I say awkwardly. Then glance at Jonah and give him a look, signaling for him to release my hand.

He holds it for a moment longer before relenting and loosening his hold, allowing me to withdraw mine.

"Gentlemen," I say as I take my leave.

"Bye, baby," Jonah calls after me.

I turn and grin at him as I continue walking away.

He smirks, and Giles stands smiling next to him.

CHAPTER

Seventeen

KALYN

Shay, Amber, Lilly, and I are all peeking out a sitting room window that is tucked away near the front door so we won't be seen, to observe Jonah's family's arrival.

Lilly comments on the curvaceous woman, wearing a form-fitting dress, high heels, and bright red lipstick. Her light brown hair, the same color as Jonah's I notice, is meticulously pulled up into an elegant bun, each strand seemingly in its perfect place. "That is Mr. Everett's mother, Antoinette," she says pointing.

Even from a distance, her intimidating aura is palpable.

The towering man who emerges from the car is unmistakably Jonah's father. He exudes an air of entitlement about him. He is impeccably dressed in a tailored suit and carries himself with a sense of superiority.

"That gentleman right there is Mr. Everett's father, Sr. Beaumont Everett," she says, pointing toward Jonah's father.

"Who is that?" I ask, observing a stunning brunette stepping out of the vehicle, wearing a short skirt and a top struggling to contain her fake boobs. Even from a distance, her beauty is obvious.

"That is Mr. Everett's sister, Eliza," she says.

"Ugh," Shay grimaces. "Imagine being a part of such a flawless-looking family," she continues staring out the window.

Giles and another man are removing luggage from the rear of one of the vehicles, and Giles is engaged in a smiling conversation with an unseen individual.

My eyes shift to Jonah descending the front steps of the mansion, making his way toward his family. The joyful sound of a child calling his name reaches us, accompanied by the patter of small feet approaching. It's a scene that catches me off guard.

"Jonah!" A little girl, maybe five, with light brown hair matching the rest of the family's, races toward him. Her hair meticulously curled into perfect ringlets, exclaiming with glee, rushes from where Giles stands right into Jonah's embrace.

"Bug!" he calls back to her, scooping her up in a warm hug, twirling her around in a full circle, their laughter harmonizing in the air. Witnessing this heartwarming moment, my own heart softens.

"That is Mr. Everett's little sister, Adeline. She was the surprise of the century," Lilly playfully remarks.

I watch as he puts her down, and her little hand instinctively reaches for his. His mother strides towards him, enveloping him in a hug that initially appears reciprocal, but he attempts to pull away while she persists in holding on.

Eliza embraces him next, and he teasingly ruffles her hair. "Dick," she exclaims, landing a gentle punch to his arm.

"Son," a stern, low-pitched voice says, reaching out for Jonah's hand and then pulling him into a firm hug.

"Hello, father," Jonah responds in a tone I can't quite decipher. There's a hint of strain, perhaps tension, underlying his words.

"What a lovely surprise," an unwelcome voice chimes in, almost singing. "I had no idea you all would be coming," Jenevieve says cheerfully as she descends the grand steps, her arms outstretched as she happily greets Jonah's family.

"Jenevievc, darling," Mrs. Everett calls out, extending her arms for a hug. "It's so wonderful to see you," they peck each other's cheeks, hardly touching for their embrace.

Taken aback by the unfolding scene, I inquire with a hint of confusion. "Jenevieve is acquainted with the Everetts?" I get out, hoping my voice doesn't sound shaky.

"Yep," Lilly replies. "They're hoping Jenevieve and Mr. Everett will tie the knot," she adds casually.

This revelation hits me like a freight train.

"Why on earth?" Amber questions, mirroring my confusion. "They would actually be perfect together," she adds after only a moment of thinking it over.

Her words strike a pang in my stomach, even though I am aware she's oblivious to my feelings for Jonah. But the mere thought of him with another woman elicits an unexpected pain.

Shay is the one who snaps me out of my self-pity thoughts. "Ew, they would be awful together. Jenevieve is an insufferable woman," she scoffs.

Lilly chimes in. "Jenevieve comes from wealth too—she and Eliza have been friends since they were in school together. Jonah and she only reconnected after she and Eliza graduated high school and Jenevieve happened to run into him by chance at a business conference," Lilly explains, rolling her eyes and air-quoting "chance."

I recall the day I met Jonah in the hallway on our way to lunch, there was a certain sadness in Jenevieve's eyes—a heartbreak that seemed incongruent with her seemingly heartless demeanor. If both families are eager for them to be together, why aren't they an official couple? It feels like I've inadvertently stepped into the middle of their situation, and I fear I may unwittingly become the catalyst for their families' discord.

We observe her moving around, embracing and kissing everyone, and I feel an unwelcome twinge of jealousy. I wish I didn't harbor such emotions, but they still manage to creep in.

As they all turn toward the mansion, Adeline extends her arms toward Jonah, prompting him to effortlessly lift her. Jenevieve runs her nails down Jonah's back, a gesture not lost to his parents, who exchange approving glances with one another. The subtle gesture makes my stomach churn, instantly causing cramps as if I might vomit right here and now.

The four of us stand up and race back to the maid's quarters, hearts pounding all the way back.

"Why did that feel like we were going to get in big trouble?" Amber remarks with a giggle as we catch our breath, gathering in Shay's room.

We were permitted to leave work as soon as Jonah's parents were close to arriving that Friday morning. Jenevieve instructed us all to disappear, and we gladly complied. The image of Jenevieve being welcomed by Jonah's family, and her hand on his back, replays in my mind. I can already predict that I'll spend the weekend fixated on the entire situation and his family being here. Even being in a completely separate part of the house where I won't see or hear them, I still feel suffocated merely being under the same roof.

"Want to go spend the weekend in town? We can escape the chaos for a couple of days, let everyone settle in," Shay suggests.

"YES, please!" I exclaim before she can even finish asking.

"Let's pack and blow this popsicle stand," she says, clearly sensing my need to get away.

We invite Lilly and Amber to join, but they decline, opting to stay in case "anything good happens." Shay and I quickly gather overnight bags and hurry to her jeep.

"This feels like we are being naughty," I say to her, adrenaline coursing through my body.

"It's exciting!" she exclaims.

WE SPEND THE WEEKEND AT A CHARMING BED AND BREAKFAST, EXploring local shops and indulging in meals at quaint restaurants. We went for a swim in the bed and breakfast pool and enjoy each other's company. Shay talks about Jonathan the entire time, and I love hearing about their incredibly romantic love. Their connection gives me hope that true love does indeed exist.

Although Shay would have had to notice the hickeys scattered across my neck, she never brings them up or indicates she has seen them. That brings me relief because I don't want to delve into the explanation of how they came to be on my neck. They make me feel somewhat dirty and angry stemming from Jenevieve's actions—her nails trailing down Jonah's back, leaving me questioning if there's something more between them. What if I'm foolishly caught in the middle, unaware that he's involved with both of us? Brad 2.0?

The weekend goes by faster than I had anticipated, and the thought of returning to the mansion already makes my stomach turn. We opt for a later check-out, allowing us to remain until seven. After grabbing dinner, we stroll through a flower garden, watching the sunset.

"I'm thinking of staying a couple more days," I tell Shay.

It seems she grasps that persuading me otherwise is useless, as she looks at me sympathetically and simply responds with an "okay."

"Do you want to come back with me so you can at least get your car?" she offers.

"Oh no, I'll be fine. Thanks for offering though."

"Fine, but you're taking my jeep," she insists.

"Absolutely not," I assert.

"What do you plan on doing without a vehicle?" she asks, confused.

"I plan on using my Lambor-feeties," I say, holding my feet out in front of me.

"Have I told you how much I love you?" she chuckles.

"No, actually you haven't. So, I will wait."

"I love you," she casts a glance my way, her expression betraying her remorse for leaving me here.

"I love you, too," I respond as she reaches over and grabs my hand. We sit here for a bit longer, both of us silent, and it feels peaceful.

"Where are you going to stay?" she asks.

"I was thinking of sleeping on this bench actually," I say with a straight face, wanting to see her reaction. When her head whips in my direction, I smile wide.

"I was going to see if that sweet little cottage was available," I reply. It's a tiny cottage hidden away from the main road, surrounded by trees. It looks as if you step from reality directly into a Thomas Kinkade painting. As soon as I saw it, I told Shay I needed to live in it. She laughed and said it would be perfect for a sweet old lady that baked fresh chocolate chip cookies and passed them out to anybody going by.

"Okay," she nods. "I should be heading back. Let's get you over there and checked in."

I appreciate her staying as long as she did since I could see Jonathan was texting and calling her nonstop today. I assume he is eager to have her back. These two are disgustingly precious.

After leaving the front desk, I give Shay a thumbs up as I walk back to her jeep. "All set," I try to convey a sense of contentment through my words to comfort her.

I am excited to stay longer, but I'd be even more excited if she was staying with me. I genuinely enjoy her company, though I understand her eagerness to return to her man.

"Are you sure you don't want to come back with me?" she asks with a hint of sadness.

"I'm positive," I respond, pulling my bag out of the back seat.

"Fine," she gives in, sounding defeated. "Don't worry about work. I will have Jonathan take care of it. We don't want you sick at the mansion in your puking state while Mr. Everett's family is there," she winks at me.

"You really are the best. Drive safe," I gently close the jeep door and she starts to back out. I wave goodbye to her, and she continuously blows kisses as she drives away.

I kept it from Shay that I had reserved the cottage for a full week, anticipating that she might object to me staying that long.

I walk down the little paved trail to the cottage tucked in the woods. It is surrounded by nature's beauty with a soothing creek running beside it. Hiking trails weave through the trees, and I fully plan on going for hikes while I am here.

I walk to the front door, unlock it, and step inside, locking it behind me. Setting my bag down, I glance around.

The cottage is just as cute on the inside as it is on the outside. It's cozy, with an open layout combining the bedroom, kitchen, and living room into one harmonious space. The bathroom is in its own private area.

The furniture and bed have precious floral prints reminiscent of my mother's taste. This nostalgic touch adds an extra layer of endearment. Even the drapes carry the same floral theme. The wooden floors are softened by rugs strategically placed in the center of the living room and at the foot of the bed.

I SPEND THE NEXT WEEK VENTURING THE TRAILS GETTING ACQUAINT-ed with the town, discovering that this getaway was precisely what I needed. However, as Saturday approaches, the thought of returning to work dampens my spirits. My time here has been truly enjoyable—I read two books, indulged in some Netflix, which is something I never do, and think about getting my life back on track once this year is over.

A sense of sadness sets in as I think about my time here ending, leaving to move on to my next chapter in life, knowing Shay will stay because of Jonathan, and Jonathan will stay for Jonah. Shay is someone I envision sharing a lifelong friendship with. However, I dread the thought of hearing anything about Jonah once I am gone. I picture Shay accidentally mentioning him and inadvertently hurting my feelings. Or worse, inviting me to her wedding, with Jonah undoubtedly in the wedding party.

As nighttime descends, the soothing sound of raindrops draws me to the back patio, where I rock in the porch chair, captivated by the calming rainfall.

Later, while lying in bed, thoughts of Jonah invade my mind—the memory of his smile, mouth, and specifically… his hands, fueling a surge of arousal within me. My hands venture downward, slipping inside my panties, as I imagine his hands taking control. Recalling the sensation of his fingers sliding in and out of me, eliciting moans. The memory of his bites on my neck and passionate kisses, accompanied by the sounds of our shared moans, plays vividly in my mind.

Twenty minutes crawl by, and I only find myself annoyed that I'm unable to get off. Not even close. And sexually frustrated. *'Perfect,'* I think to myself. *'Thanks for not working,'* I say to my body, removing my hands from under the blankets and dropping them onto the fluffy bedspread.

The following morning, awakened by the cheerful chirping of birds, I decide to extend my stay for an additional week. With enthusiasm, I make my way to the bed and breakfast overseeing the cottage, only to discover it is already booked for the upcoming week. Undeterred, I try to secure a room at the bed and breakfast, to find that it too, is fully reserved, thanks to a town-wide art exhibit.

As I walk back to the cottage, I pass two older ladies sitting outside a coffee shop talking.

"Excuse me. I'm so sorry to bother you. What day does the art exhibit start?" I ask, hoping it starts this weekend so I can attend.

"What art exhibit, honey?" one of them replies.

"The one that's in town," I respond, confused.

"There is no art exhibit," they both seem confused.

"Do you know why all the rooms at all the hotels are booked up?"

Again, they look confused and glance at each other. "The rooms never book up, honey."

"Right," I smile at them. "Thank you, have a wonderful day." I wave and walk off.

'*Okay, so she just didn't want to reserve the cottage for me,*' I admit to myself. I've been a good guest—quiet and respectful. What did I do to make her not want me to stay here? An uneasy feeling begins to settle in. I would have assumed that any money coming in is better than no money, and my money is just as good as the next person's. Yet, she has an issue with me, and I can't quite understand why.

When I return to the cottage, I walk past it and head up my favorite trail. The trail has a lot of inclines, which is nice as it gives my ass a good workout.

I leisurely hike for an hour until I realize I don't have any water to drink, and my mouth is incredibly dry, so I make my way back down. My ass is on fire from the hike, but the exercise feels good.

As I clear the trees to the cottage, I grab hold of a tree trunk, pulling my leg up toward my butt to give it a good stretch, doing the same thing to the other side. Then, I lean forward to stretch my legs and back. The burn from this stretch feels amazing. I continue doing various stretches, spreading my legs wide, leaning to one side and then the other.

My body aches with pleasure.

Standing upright, a smile crosses my face as I think about how beautiful it is here. Stepping toward the little cottage, I halt in my tracks. Jonah is sitting on the back patio, rocking in the same chair I sat in the night before. I curse my legs to continue moving as they momentarily forget what they were supposed to be doing.

"What are you doing here?" I ask, confused, trying to steady my tone even as my body shakes violently from the unexpected presence of him. My nerves suddenly awaken all at once.

"That's funny, I came to ask you the same thing," he rises from the chair and gazes down at me.

I retrieve the cottage key from my pocket, intending to insert it into the lock.

"It's already unlocked," he informs me.

"I made sure to lock it before I—You have a key to MY cottage?"

"I do," he grins proudly. "Well, actually, I have the main key to the cottage," he adds, holding up the master key.

"Why?" I ask, placing my key back in my pocket, and true to his words, the door is already unlocked. I push it open, entering with him trailing closely behind.

"Because I own it," he replies, amused.

If he's the owner, why would she not want me to stay another night? The realization hits me. "YOU!" I exclaim, turning towards him. "That sweet little lady at the bed and breakfast lied to me!"

"She did what her boss told her to do."

"Why would you do that?"

"Because I want you home," he declares honestly.

"You realize how rude that was, right?" I articulate, still feeling upset. She had me thinking I did something wrong, and I've been racking my brain trying to figure out what it could be.

"Possibly," he replies, leaning against the wall near the back door. "You know what's not rude? I packed your bag for you so we can get going."

"Excuse me? You didn't," was I away long enough for him to pack my bag? Was there anything embarrassing he could have found?

He folds his arms across his chest and points toward the front door where my bag is neatly packed and waiting.

"You're super lame, you know that?" I walk over to where it sits, picking it up, and head out the door, leaving it wide open behind me.

Jonathan is sitting in front of the cottage in Jonah's black SUV. Upon spotting me, he waves his hand in my direction without fully detaching it from the steering wheel, a broad smile plastered across his face. I smoothly settle into the passenger seat, conscious that this choice might provoke Jonah for one of two reasons: either he anticipated sitting here, and I've claimed it instead, or he usually sits in the back seat being chauffeured around and was expecting me to join him back there. Regardless, I secretly hope he finds this move bothersome.

"Okay, we can go now." I close the door behind me.

He greets me with a friendly, "Hi, Kalyn," as we both watch Jonah locking up the cottage and approaching the vehicle.

As he reaches my door, I feign ignorance, pretending not to notice him. He taps on my window, prompting me to reach over and lock the door keeping my eyes straight ahead. Without missing a beat, Jonathan unlocks it, and Jonah pulls the door open.

"Let me get the door for you, baby," he offers, reaching over pulling open the backseat door.

"Oh, no, thank you," I force a smile and attempt to close my door, but he grabs it, keeping it in place.

"I insist," he flashes a charismatic smile back at me.

Turning to Jonathan, I look for assistance. "He will make us sit here all day if you don't get in the back with him," Jonathan states honestly.

With a sigh, I step out of the car, passing by him. "You smell nice," I mutter irritably and climb into the backseat. I notice a smirk forming on his lips as he shuts the front passenger door, moves on to close my door, and starts circling the car.

"You know, if we're fast enough, we could probably back up before he can get in," I remark, only half joking.

He settles into the car, closing the door behind him, and Jonathan starts to reverse.

I don't understand why he decided to come get me when his family is visiting. I'm surprised he even thought about me at all since I assumed he would be so preoccupied he would have forgotten my existence. Even if only momentarily.

Unaware that I've been fidgeting with my fingers, I suddenly feel his hand intertwining with mine. Bringing our clasped hands to his lips, he plants a tender kiss on my knuckle. It's a simple gesture, yet it fills my stomach with fluttering sensations.

Leaning over the seat with the utmost delicacy, he whispers, "Can I have a kiss?" My gaze shifts from his eyes to his inviting lips and back to his eyes. Despite my initial attempt to stay upset, he's too damn sexy.

Noting my hesitation, he adds, "I'll settle for a kiss on the cheek," he turns his head forward presenting his cheek to me. Leaning over, I cradle his chin, turning his face back toward me, and softly press my lips to his.

Attempting to pull away, he rests his hand on the back of my neck, subtly shaking his head with a smile, and coaxes me back into the embrace. Our mouths meet once more, and a slow, intense kiss unfolds, leaving the world momentarily suspended.

Our kiss is interrupted by Jonathan, breaking through the silence.

"You guys coming?" He exits the car, closing the door behind him.

Glancing around, I realize we're in a garage, and I am starting to think Jonah is magical because time disappears every time we kiss.

"Let me get your door," he offers, stepping out, circling the back to the front passenger door to retrieve my bag, and then opening my door. "Thank you," I murmur shyly as I step out. He takes my hand as he closes the door behind me, leading us up the garage stairs toward the door to the mansion.

Reaching for the doorknob, I attempt to withdraw my hand, but he tightens his grip, turning back to face me.

"We shouldn't be seen together, your family is here," I express my concern, fearing it would only cause more issues.

"My father and sister left a week ago for business. My mother and baby sister won't be on the main floor," he reassures, pushing the door open, and pulling me inside.

Jonah leads the way through an unfamiliar section of the house, with the hallways illuminating as we approach. Upon reaching the main area, distant voices become audible, causing me to tug on his hand repeatedly, urging him to let go. Although he eventually releases my hand, he stays by my side as we proceed. Unsure of his intentions or how to ask for my bag, I just keep walking, allowing him to lead the way.

In the distance, the distinct sound of Jenevieve's heels echoes, and my heart sinks as she comes into view. I've never understood why her heels sound notably louder than anyone else walking in heels. I can't decide if she naturally just stomps around or if she purposely walks loudly so everyone knows she's coming, and they can run and hide.

Her eyes light up upon spotting Jonah, then shift to me, and a subtle look of disgust crosses her face before returning her gaze to him.

"Mr. Everett," she beams, then glancing at me with thinly veiled disdain. "Kaylin, sorry to hear you weren't feeling well. You look… well-rested. I'm glad the other staff stepped in to handle your work." Her words drip with insincerity.

Choosing not to engage, I turn to Jonah, "I can take my bag now. I'm feeling much better," I say, urging him to play along and just hand my bag over.

"Jenevieve," he nods at her and presses his hand on my lower back, guiding me forward, leaving her standing there. Without even having to look, I can feel her piercing gaze shooting daggers at me.

Arriving at the maid's quarters, he casually walks in without hesitation. In the living room, some of the staff are engrossed in a reality TV show, paying no attention to our entrance. We manage to reach my room undetected.

Feeling the need for a soothing shower, I head to the bathroom, silently hoping that he might join me.

I complete my entire bathroom routine, from washing to dressing and braiding my hair, without him ever coming in. Not even to catch a glimpse.

Returning to my room, I'm pleasantly surprised to find him still here. The bedspread is pulled back, revealing him lying on my usual side of the bed. Though he's partially covered, his bare chest is visible, eliciting a visceral response. His shoes, pants, and shirt are neatly arranged on a chair in the corner, indicating perhaps he's in my bed in just boxers. *Lord help me,* ' I think to myself, biting my lip as I picture him lying there naked.

I move closer, seeing him peacefully sleep, and it is the most incredible sight. Slipping into bed on the opposite side, I lie on my side, quietly observing this breathtaking man. He is undeniably stunning. I take in the details of his face until my eyes grow heavy and sleep wins.

CHAPTER
Eighteen

KALYN

My eyes reluctantly flutter open as I scan the darkened room. Sensing the firm embrace around me, I become aware that Jonah is still in bed with me. Sometime during the night, he migrated to my side, wrapping me in his arms with my back nestled against his chest.

"Good morning," his voice carries a smile, whispered into my back.

This feels like a dream.

The most incredible dream.

"I figured you would have snuck away by now," I respond with a smile of my own.

"Hmm-mm," he disagrees, holding me even tighter.

I secure my grip on his arm. "Do you want everyone to know you're in here?" The options seem clear—he either leaves before the staff wakes up or patiently waits until we are all off to our jobs for the day.

"Mmhmm," he murmurs in agreement.

A soft laugh escapes my throat. "What time is it?" I inquire, unable to turn and glimpse my nightstand clock.

"5:30," he responds.

"Don't you usually start your day at 5:00?" I question, and then realize I only possess this knowledge courtesy of Shay.

"I start when I want to start,"

His voice is so sexy in the morning, I note.

"Your alarm is set for 7:00. You've got another hour and a half before it goes off, why don't you try to get a little more sleep?" he suggests, kissing my shoulder.

"That might be hard when I have a stranger in my bed," I playfully remark.

"Do you want me to go?" he inquires, planting another kiss on my shoulder.

I shake my head no before I say the words. I don't want him to go. I want to stay like this forever. If I could be encapsulated in time forever just like this, I would gladly do so. I fit perfectly in his strong embrace, and I want to enjoy every second of it before it comes to an end, and I have to get up for work.

His arm that is around me moves upward, and his fingers intertwine with mine. My other arm rests on top of his, while my fingers softly trail up and down his arm. I feel so tiny in his embrace. I feel protected.

"If you could be any animal, what would you be?" I break the silence that envelops us.

I sense his smile, and it only takes a brief pause before he answers, "I'd opt for the aquatic life. Specifically, an anglerfish."

His response catches me off guard. "Wait, what? An anglerfish?" I'm genuinely puzzled as I envision a huge, deformed fish that instills fear in other sea creatures.

His smile broadens. "An anglerfish lives in the deep sea, where it's dark and hard to find a mate. When a male finds a female anglerfish, he bites onto the female and releases an enzyme that fuses his tissue with hers. It's called sexual parasitism. Over time he physically integrates into the female. Even their circulatory systems connect. And he eventually becomes dependent on her."

"So, you want to fuse onto a female and live off of her?" I laugh. "Why would you want to do that?"

"It serves a purpose. This attachment ensures a consistent supply of sperm for the female when she releases eggs. If I were to attach to you, it would be to spend every moment with you… And fill you with my sperm." He seals his words with a kiss on my back, followed by a gentle bite that sends shivers through my entire body.

"Ah, so you're envisioning a scenario where it's just you and me, a pair of anglerfish fused together, while I pop out your babies?" I turn my head to look back at him.

"Exactly," he grins. "I haven't even revealed the most intriguing part. It has a pole-like appendage protruding from its head, complete with a bioluminescent light at the end, enabling it to illuminate the surrounding darkness."

"A flashlight on its head?" I question, not sure if he's just messing with me.

"Yes, a headlight," he clarifies, "the soft glow serves to lure unsuspecting prey towards it."

"When I posed that question, I expected a response like a cat, perhaps for their agility and ability to sleep all day, or a dog for their undeniable cuteness," amusement lingering in my voice.

"What about you, baby? If you could be any animal, what would you be?"

I respond with a laugh, "A cat, for their ability to sleep all day, or a dog, because they're undeniably cute."

"Mm, you are undeniably cute, and we can lay here and nap all day if that's what you want."

I lie here thinking about his answer and how random it was, but the best answer I could have ever heard. How is he handsome, smart, and funny?

Curiosity sparks another random question: "What's something that would immediately ruin your day?"

Without hesitation, he responds, "If I woke up and I was an anglerfish," eliciting laughter from both of us.

"What is your favorite word to say?" This time he asks the question.

"Hi," I reply shyly.

"Just a good ol' fashioned 'hi,' huh?"

"Yep. What's yours?" I wait for him to answer, expecting another funny response.

"I have two... Kalyn," he murmurs, then leans in to whisper the second word, "Baby," his voice seductive, while he gently bites my ear.

An electric charge courses through me, and I confess, "I like it when you say the second word."

A low, aroused rumble escapes him as he turns me onto my back, declaring, "Me too, baby," he says as he slides his hand under my back wrapping his arms around me. My arms encircle his neck, and he lowers his mouth to mine. His tongue softly enters my mouth, a fleeting moment interrupted by the abrupt blare of my alarm.

"Good lord!" I exclaim, startled giggles rippling through me as I jolt on the bed in response to the sudden noise.

He lets out a hearty chuckle, rolling over to silence the alarm.

As I rise from bed, I stretch my arms above me and let out a quiet yawn. I notice his gaze lingering on my chest, a smile playing on his lips. Realizing my nipples are peaked and pressing against the silk top, I apologize, crossing my arms to cover myself.

"Don't cover up," he urges, holding his arms out to me. "I like it."

"Oh?" Uncrossing my arms, I climb onto the bed. His eyes intensify with heat as I move toward him, my breasts gently swaying against the fabric. "I have to go get ready for work," I whisper, leaning down to plant a soft kiss on his lips.

He shakes his head no and pulls me on top of him, my legs straddling him as he holds me tightly against his chest.

"I'm going to tell my boss on you," I tease.

"What do you think he will say?" he smiles up at me.

"What do YOU think he will say?" I redirect the question back to him.

"He will praise my efforts."

"You'll have to let me know when you talk to him," I lean down to gently bite his bottom lip, letting my teeth graze across it as I pull away, then climb off him.

Preparing for work, I discard my pajamas, opting for a lace black bra and panty set. Returning to the bathroom, I brush my teeth, and undo my braid, letting my hair cascade down before putting it into a messy bun atop my head. I notice Jonah in the mirror approaching, his clothes are back on with his shirt still unbuttoned. Pausing in the doorway, he fixates on me, desire etched in every feature on his face, mirroring the fervor in my gaze.

He is so sexy.

Breaking away from the doorframe, he strides over to where I stand. Placing his hands on either side of me on the counter, leaning down, planting a kiss on the crook of my neck. I yearn for his hands on my body, resenting the cold counter that gets to feel his touch instead.

"If you don't leave now, you might be seen, Mr. Everett," I intentionally emphasize his last name.

A low growl emanates from his throat. "What did I say would happen if you call me by my last name?" His jaw clenches with intensity.

"I can't remember," I respond coyly, bending forward over the counter, purposely pushing my backside toward him, turning my head to glance back.

I observe his breath catching as I arch forward, and he bites his lower lip, a palpable wave of arousal enveloping both of us. "Well, Mr. Everett?" I coax, my voice steeped in desire.

When I turn my face back around, our eyes lock in the mirror, and he removes a hand from the counter, delivering a sharp spank to my ass, the sound resonating through the bathroom. A hushed moan escapes my lips as the sensation washes over me, his large hand tenderly reaches up and cradles my neck and jaw. Gently pulling me back to an upright position, he lifts my face toward him, planting a kiss on my lips before administering a second slap to my ass. Another moan escapes, and an aroused grin graces my lips.

"I don't think I heard you right the first two times," his voice, low and gravelly.

Turning toward him, I wrap my arms around his neck. "You heard me right the first two times, Mr. Everett," I affirm, craving the feel of his hand on my ass again. As I speak his name, another slap reverberates, and this time, he firmly holds his hand in place as he lifts me onto the counter. Bringing his face to mine, he initiates a passionate kiss, our tongues intertwining and soft moans escaping both of us. I squeeze my arms tightly around his neck as our mouths scour each other's.

Pulling away, I smile. "I have to get dressed, and you need to go before everyone is out of their room," I say as I climb down from the counter.

The sting of his hand lingers as his eyes focus on the mirror. Glancing behind, I meet the spot that holds his gaze, bold, red handprints color my backside.

"I love it," I relish the lingering touch and the marks he's left on my skin.

"Me too," he agrees gazing admiringly at the marks he left. "Have a good day, baby," he utters, leaning down for a final kiss before buttoning up his shirt and making his exit.

I linger for a moment, looking at my backside before deciding to dress in my uniform, wishing I could admire his handprints until they gradually fade away.

CHAPTER

Nineteen

KALYN

Jenevieve resumes her usual unpleasant behavior, barking orders at all of us.

"You will remain invisible. If any of the Everetts walk into a room you are in, you will exit immediately. Nobody wants to see the hired help walking around," she barks.

It has always bothered me how she views the staff as something less than human, like we are filthy animals unfit to be in the presence of wealth. Yet, ironically, she must forget that she's also just "hired help."

Without a word, we all head out in our regular lines, only this time, she stops me.

"Some of us didn't get a week-long vacation," she remarks pointedly, "Since you must be so well-rested, Kaland," she purposely mispronounces my name, "you can work in the stables today," she declares smugly, accompanying my punishment for being absent.

"Wonderful. Thank you," I reply, knowing she only wants people to feel miserable, and it will bother her to know sending me to the stables doesn't bother me. Typically, she would irritate me with this punishment. However, she did get one thing right. I was off for a week, and it was refreshing, and I spent the most amazing night sleeping next to the sexiest man, so I am in good spirits today.

She stares blankly at me, blinking for a moment before she brings her face closer to mine. "Shoo," she dismisses me, her words accompanied with the flick of her wrist.

As I head out to the stables, with each step I take, I can feel his lingering handprint, and I smile to myself. I don't quite make it to the door when Gladys passes by with a tray of tea and stops me. "Kalyn, dear, where are you going?"

"The stables," I reply casually.

"Why?"

"That's where I have been assigned today," I don't want to make it seem like a big deal, so I play it off like I am fine with the job.

"Oh no you're not," she insists.

"It's fine, Gladys. I don't mind," I reassure her. "Have a good day," I add warmly, leaving through the door and closing it behind me before she gets Jenevieve involved, or worse, Jonah.

As I arrive, the pesky stable fly immediately joins me.

"One of these days, you will learn to be a good girl," Brad teases.

"I am always a good girl," I quip back.

"When you decide you don't want to be a good girl, let me know," he winks.

As we enter the storage room, surrounded by other girls preparing for work, I lean in and whisper to Brad, "Now that we're here, I don't think I want to be a good girl." My voice is seductive. I briefly look up at him, batting my lashes, then let my gaze travel down the front of him, pausing on his crotch, before returning to meet his gaze. "Just kidding," I walk toward the supply room, leaving him standing there with his mouth hanging open.

"Hold on," he calls after me.

"You're too easy, Brad," I joke, both metaphorically and figuratively.

After lunch, I return to the stables. As Brad emerges, he spots me, "Wanna see something neat?" he grins.

"There's nothing neat about your little wiener," I retort, continuing back to my stall.

"You have no idea what you're missing out on. But that's not what I was referring to," he clarifies, still walking and not looking back.

I consider the possibilities of what he might mean, but I'm not interested enough to follow him to find out.

As I return with my wheelbarrow, I round a corner and nearly collide with Jenevieve and Mrs. Everett.

"I am so sorry," I exclaim, feeling embarrassed.

"Watch where you are going," Jenevieve hisses. "Sorry, Antoinette. This is why some girls are chosen to work away from the mansion—they don't pay attention," she silently signals to Antoinette that I am a problem. It's as though diligently working where she assigned me is somehow me not doing a good job.

They keep walking, and I overhear Mrs. Everett, "Maybe my son needs to change some staff," giving me a dirty look.

An immediate wave of nausea washes over me. I can't fathom how anyone can tolerate Jenevieve, yet she manages to turn Mrs. Everett against me while maintaining a chummy rapport with her.

The remainder of the day I grapple with irritation and an annoyingly heightened emotional state, yet I manage to keep it together.

Following a refreshing shower, I slip into shorts and a tank top before making my way to the courtyard, my preferred spot for enjoying the fresh air. Taking a seat on a stone bench nestled within the garden, I'm greeted by the sound of the sweetest little voice.

"Do you know how to blow bubbles?" Jonah's little sister asks, holding a container of bubbles. She is so precious—my heart instantly fills with so much joy at the sight of her standing here.

A smile spreads across my face. "Actually, I am known for being the best bubble blower ever," I say, holding my hands out for the bubbles.

"Really?!" She exclaims excitedly and hands them to me.

I twist the top open, grabbing the slender handle of the bubble wand, its tip glistening with a thin film of liquid. I breathe in, and exhale, blowing small bubbles toward her, then dip the wand back in the container, this time swirling the wand around whimsically so a stream of iridescent spheres glide through the air all around us. She giggles and claps the tiny looking orbs between her hands. "You are the best bubble blower! I'm Adeline. What's your name?" She asks, putting both her little hands on my knees.

"That is a beautiful name, Adeline. My name is Kalyn," I reply, putting the bubble container next to me on the bench and gently place my hands on top of hers.

"What do your friends call you?" she asks inquisitively. I can see Jonah in her features, and it makes me wonder if his children will look just like him.

"Just Kalyn," I smile at her. "What do your friends call you?"

"The same as you," she shrugs.

"What?! Your friends call you Kalyn too?" I exclaim, pretending to be shocked.

She giggles. "No silly, they call me Adeline. My brother calls me Bug," she says proudly.

"Wow! I love that nickname."

"Hmmmm," she taps her little finger on her chin. "I'm going to call you Lyn-E. Now you call me something," she giggles excitedly.

I mimic her gesture, tapping my finger on my chin as if thinking hard, then holding my finger up like I have an idea. "I have the perfect nickname."

"What is it?" she asks, jumping up and down.

"I am going to call you Lee-Lee," I hold my mouth open like I just came up with the best nickname ever.

"Yay! That almost sounds like we're sisters, huh?" she exclaims eagerly.

"Um, only the best sisters ever," I match her enthusiasm.

She changes the subject. "Do you like to color?"

I whisper, "Don't tell anybody this, but I'm pretty good at coloring also," bringing my finger to my lips in a shhh motion.

"Me too," she says zealously. "My brother colors with me— he's too big to sit in my chair so he sits on the floor. But it's okay, he can still reach the table. Do you know my brother?"

Her question catches me off guard, but I show no sign it does. "I do know your brother."

"Do you think he's handsome?" she smiles wide.

"Adeline," the nanny calls from the back patio.

"Oops, I have to go, or I'm going to get in trouble," she says, looking sad.

"Well, LeeLee, here are your bubbles back. Your lid is nice and secure," my eyes sparkle, handing her the container of bubbles.

She unexpectedly wraps her little arms around my neck and kisses my cheek. "Good night, Lin-E," she gives me a final wave.

'Okay, well, that was the sweetest thing ever,' I think to myself.

Watching her skip away, my eyes remain on her. I glance up at Jonah's office, curious about what he might be doing. Unexpectedly, I find he's standing in his customary spot, watching me. The sweetest smile on his face.

His watchful gaze makes me self-conscious, yet I love it. He is wonderful and truly has the best little sister ever.

We keep our gazes locked a moment longer, and he pulls his hand from his pocket. Using his pointer finger, he motions for me to come to him.

I respond with a shake of my head in refusal. Instead, I interlock my hands, forming them into a makeshift pillow, and rest my head on it, signaling that I am heading to bed. At this, I see him release a soft laugh and nod his head in understanding.

Over the next few days, Jenevieve keeps me away from the mansion, sending me to work in the stables.

I find myself a tiny bit envious of Shay, as I know she has been working with Jonathan on important documents for Jonah. He starts his workday at five AM and continues most days until the late evening. The staff usually isn't allowed anywhere near his office when he is working because he spends most of his days on the phone conducting business meetings.

I had to work until after seven today because one of the girls said she had a cramp and couldn't keep working.

Gladys had mentioned after my shower from work, I could go to the kitchen and she would have dinner waiting for me. As I make my way, a moaned cry catches my attention: "Oh my back." I see Gladys walking with a tray of tea toward the sitting room where Antoinette usually sits.

"Gladys!" I rush over, removing the tray from her hands, and set it on the table. "Are you okay?" I caress her back in the spot she was just holding.

"Yes, dear, my back is so sore today," she replies, appearing to be in terrible pain, bent over unable to stand straight.

"What can I do?" I ask with concern.

"Do you mind taking this to Mrs. Everett, honey? I just don't think I can carry it," she says, in pain.

"Of course, Gladys," I respond without hesitation.

"Thank you, honey," and then mysteriously stands up straight and walks off, her back pain seemingly gone. *'That sneaky little devil,'* I think to myself, realizing she purposely wanted me to have to bring this to Mrs. Everett. Maybe she thinks this will be a way Mrs. Everett and I can familiarize ourselves with one another.

I pick up the tray and make my way to the sitting room. Upon entering, I find Jenevieve and Mrs. Everett seated across from each other, deep in conversation. It appears that Jenevieve is doing most of the talking.

Adeline is drawing at a table nearby and looks up when I enter.

"Lin-E!" she exclaims, running over wrapping her little arms around my leg and squeezing.

"Hello again, LeeLee," my eyes brighten seeing her again.

"Did you come to color with me?" she asks excitedly. "I am coloring a picture of me and you playing with bubbles."

Jenevieve stands and interrupts, exclaiming furiously, "What are you doing in here?" Not even attempting to hide she's bothered by my presence. I assume when Gladys sent me to bring Mrs. Everett's tea, she didn't realize Jenevieve was also in here. But her anger also appears she is somehow annoyed with Adeline. Which just can't be possible because she is the absolute sweetest.

"I was bringing Mrs. Everett's tea," I hold the tray higher to show the tea.

Mrs. Everett instructs Adeline to go get ready for bed. Adeline hesitates briefly, then tightens her grip on my leg, waves goodbye to me, and exits the room with her nanny.

"Just bring it here," Jenevieve demands.

As I approach them, her eyes track my every step. As I pass by, she carelessly extends her foot, causing me to stumble. Before I can regain my balance, the entire glass china shatters on the floor, hot liquid splashing everywhere, and my palms smashing into the broken glass.

"How dare you!" Jenevieve yells.

"Get out now!" Mrs. Everett stands, also yelling, holding her hands up like she got drenched with liquid even though none of it touched her.

Shock courses through my body as I see a small amount of blood seeping onto the tray where the glass has cut into my palms. The scalding hot water sears my hands, yet the pain is overshadowed by the instant numbness my body experiences.

"I will clean it," I utter, my eyes welling with tears and my hands trembling.

"Get out now, you clumsy fool!" Mrs. Everett screams.

Jenevieve grabs me by my hair, pulling me off the ground and shoving me toward the door.

"She is FIRED!" Mrs. Everett's anger reverberates throughout the room.

"You heard her. You are done here, Karla!" Jenevieve yells. "Pack your bags and get out," before rushing to Mrs. Everett in a comedic way to make sure she is okay.

Reaching the door, tears stream down my face. I hold my palms upright, refusing to look down. The initial glimpse of the shards of glass protruding from my hands made me instantly queasy. My first instinct is needing to find Gladys for help. I rush toward the kitchen to search for her, my legs carrying me forward while everything around me blurs. Along the way, I spot Gladys and Jonathan talking in a corridor. I rush over to Gladys, wrapping my arms around her neck, holding my bleeding hands out, and begin to sob.

"Oh my god, Kalyn, what happened?" Jonathan's shocked words ring out.

"I need help," I cry, still holding onto Gladys. "I have glass in my hands," I whimper.

"Come on," Jonathan takes me by the arm, placing his free hand under mine in a thoughtful attempt to catch any blood that might fall from my hands. Gladys grabs my other arm, and we head into the kitchen where we spend the next hour.

I sit at the metal table, my hands stretched out across it, my head resting on my arm, while Jonathan picks glass out of my hand, and Gladys strokes my hair.

I let them know I didn't want to talk, and the silence eventually allows me time to stop crying, with only the heavy breathing stutters coming through.

"Kalyn," Jonathan says softly, "What happened?"

"I got fired," I respond, my head still laying on my arm. I can sense this isn't what he's after. He wants to know how my hands ended up in this state. But that's all the information I want to provide.

"Fired?" Gladys and Jonathan both utter simultaneously, their voices filled with shock and confusion.

"Yes," I confirm.

"By whom?" Gladys asks, sounding incredulous.

A disbelieving chuckle escapes me. "Mrs. Everett."

I don't even have to look to feel Jonathan and Gladys looking at each other.

"You aren't fired, honey," Gladys reassures me, patting and rubbing my back gently.

"I just want to go."

"Do you want to stay in my room tonight?" Jonathan suggests. "That way, you don't have to explain anything to anyone."

"Yes," I reply, feeling relieved, sitting up and staring hopeful at him.

He bandages my palms and escorts me to his room.

Gladys helps me change into the fresh clothes Jonathan provides for me. Just like Jonah, Jonathan is a big guy. The overly baggy gray sweatpants and baggy tank top fit him perfectly, but I am swimming in them. I make a mental note that one wrong move and my boobs will pop out the side.

I crawl into his bed, resting at the head of the bed against the pillows with my legs pulled toward my chest and my arms wrapped around them in a hug. I was so careful when I was walking. I made sure there was nothing in my way so I could safely set the tea down. Jenevieve knew I was coming and purposely put her foot in front of me. God, she makes me look so fucking stupid all the time.

I barely get settled on the bed when Shay rushes in, climbing on the bed and wrapping me in a hug, causing me to start crying all over again.

I tell her I accidentally tripped and dropped the tray of tea, and my hands fell in it, and how Mrs. Everett was furious with me.

Shay does her best to comfort me, eventually allowing the room to fall silent while she gently rubs one hand on my back. I'm torn between questioning how Jenevieve manages to escape consequences for her actions and realizing I'm a prime example of how she does it. I could report her and ensure everyone knows what she's done, but who would believe me? She has a personal connection with the Everetts, whereas I'm just a hired stranger. Even if they were aware of her behavior, I'm easily replaceable. I find myself caught between a rock and a hard place.

"Where is she?" Jonah shouts, his voice reverberating through the walls.

"In here, sir," Giles responds, extending his hand to indicate Jonathan's room.

Jonah charges through the open doors.

Glancing at him, panic evident on his face, I notice his disheveled hair, like he's stressed. The top buttons of his shirt are undone, as if his shirt was suffocating him and he was attempting to get more air. I wonder who told him? Or what they told him. I don't recall seeing anyone on the phone, but someone alerted him to the incident. I quickly avert my eyes, fearing that making eye contact will trigger more tears.

"Baby," he storms in, and hurriedly kneels on the bed, crawling over to me, his gaze fixed on my bandaged hands. Shay moves out of the way as he parts my bent knees bringing himself between them. There's a flicker of determination in his eyes, a desire to mend what's broken.

"Baby," he whispers, delicately tilting my chin up and pressing his lips to mine. He holds our kiss for a moment and then slowly pulls away, searching my eyes, and then his mouth is on mine again, this time with need. Our lips part, and our tongues begin a magical dance, softly intertwining with one another.

I hoped he wouldn't discover what occurred. Now that I realize he's already aware, I'm relieved he doesn't seem to be placing blame to me or angry about the expensive broken china. Quite the opposite—he seems to only care whether I am okay or not.

His hand glides up the baggy sweatpants I am wearing, grabbing a fistful of the material at my hip.

A moan escapes my lips, and a spark of eagerness glints in his eyes.

He sits back onto his heels, reaching for the hem of the tank top, expertly pulling it over my head. My full breasts gently sway as he removes it and tosses it to the floor.

My first reaction is wanting to cover myself, but as soon as I attempt to move my hands, he seizes my wrists, holding them in place. He gazes in awe at my chest, taking in every detail.

He lets out an unsteady breath.

For the first time ever, I witness sheer arousal consume a man. He gazes at me as though I'm a priceless masterpiece his eyes have just discovered. His gaze alone seems capable of restoring all my confidence. I've never felt more beautiful.

"Baby," he murmurs, this time with a tone filled with enthusiasm, and lust gradually crosses his face.

He leans down, his warm tongue delicately sucking my peaked nipple into his mouth, swirling in a circular motion, nibbling and sucking, before pulling away and placing a kiss on the tip. Then, he moves to the other side, giving the same amount of attention.

I release a quivering exhale, watching his face work wonders on each breast. I intertwine both hands in the back of his hair, clutching tightly, wanting to keep him from removing the contact. I feel the corners of his mouth lifting while his lips remain on my skin.

Once more he sits back.

"No," I protest, not wanting the connection to end.

He grins at me, grabbing both sides of my pants, yanking them off in a single motion.

I sit fully naked in front of him.

His hands are propped on each of my knees holding them open, not even giving me a chance to try covering myself.

Pure amazement floods every feature on his face as he stares down at me. His gaze roams from my breasts, down my stomach, finally resting between my legs.

"Fuuuck," he breathes out.

Lost in the moment, I temporarily forget that Jonathan and Shay are still in the room, only becoming aware when Shay remarks, "Damn Kal, you're hot," as she climbs off the bed.

Jonah responds with a low "mmhmm" of agreement, bringing his hands up to the collar of his shirt and pulling it over his head, discarding it to the floor with the tank top and sweatpants I was wearing. Then he moves back, lowering himself onto the bed. His arms wrap around my legs, and his mouth, warm and tender, delicately parts my lips with his tongue.

My head falls back into the array of large, plush pillows crowding the upper part of the bed. My eyes roll at the incredible sensation coursing through every inch of my body. His tongue is velvety soft, and he skillfully navigates all the right spots precisely when I need him to.

I loop my fingers back in his hair, drawing his face further into my spread legs, not even caring about the pain from the cuts on my bandaged hands. My feet lift off the bed as I raise them closer to my chest, increasing the pleasure and granting him full access to my center.

His arms grip tighter around my thighs, and he buries his face deeper into me. He continues his expert tongue maneuvers on my swollen clit, tracing circles and delicately employing a blend of flicking up and down, and sucking, leaving no area of my slit and entrance untouched.

Moans resonate from my throat as he persists in his tongue work. I lower my feet to the bed, gliding them along the plush fabric of the bedding beneath us. My breathing quickens as an orgasm begins to build. I feel my body growing tense from the overwhelming sensation.

And he stops.

It takes me a moment to come back from the peak of my impending orgasm, confusion attempting to weave through my hazy thoughts. When I open my eyes, ready to ask him why he stopped, I see he has removed his pants and boxers and is kneeling before me, entirely naked, mirroring my state of being nude. I audibly gasp at the sheer magnitude of him. He is sculpted and chiseled in places I didn't know men could be, but moving lower… Damn, that's gonna hurt. I've sensed his size through his clothes, but I've never truly seen it until now.

"Holy shit! You weren't exaggerating," Shay remarks, presumably to Jonathan.

"Shhh," Jonathan hushes her.

"I don't think that's going to fit," I gulp, eyeing his long, thick member standing straight up.

"It will," a seductive smile playing on his lips. "I'll be gentle," he reassures.

Women give birth every day. This is not comparable, but what happens if he literally rips me open. What if an ambulance has to come here! Everyone will know what we did and how I was "injured." Can I even call it being injured? I am mortified just imagining it. I used to think I might be sore after having sex again just because it's been so long, but now, that's going to be a toss-up on whether it's from his size or the time it's been since I was intimate with someone.

He wraps both arms under my bent knees and pulls me further down onto the bed, so I am lying flat. He secures both of my hands above my head with just one of his own. Lowering himself on top of me, the direct contact of our skin and the weight of his body, although he's careful not to exert too much pressure, already feels exhilarating and my worries evaporate. Following the line of my neck with his tongue, he gently nibbles at the hollow. With his free hand, he glides his fingers down my side to my leg, easing between my thighs and wrapping his large hand around his thick shaft.

He delicately places his cock against my wet entrance, my moisture coating him. He glides his tip between my slit, sliding it up to my swollen clit and pressing small circles on it.

Another moan escapes my lips as my hips arch off the bed, up towards him. His breathing becomes labored and shaky with arousal, a warm rush that brushes against my ear as he nibbles on its sensitive curve. Each gentle bite sends tingles down my spine. His voice, a husky whisper, caresses my senses. "It's going to be a little uncomfortable at first, but I will go slow, baby," awaiting my approval as he slowly slides his penis back down my slit to my entrance.

"Okay," I breathe out, a soft sigh escaping my lips as I release one hand from his grasp and wrap it tightly around the arm that holds my other hand in place. He leans down, placing his soft lips against mine, and with measured care, a gasp escapes my parted lips as I feel the first gentle intrusion, a mere inch of his length penetrating me.

My body instinctively reacts, muscles tightening in response to the overwhelming pressure. I cling tightly to his hand intertwined with mine, and clutch his arm, digging my fingers into the firm flesh as I surrender to the exquisite agony, squeezing my eyes shut. I'm completely engulfed by the intense stretching, and it feels as though my body can't accommodate his size.

"You okay, baby?" he moans, expressing concern through his pleasure.

"Mmhmm," I murmur, giving my body time to acclimate to the stretching sensation.

"Hey," he quietly says, and my eyes flutter open, meeting his intense gaze.

Passion ignites in his eyes as he inches deeper. A whimper of pain mixed with pleasure surges out of me, then met with the feeling of something inside me tearing. Although it's not the exact area I anticipated would rip from his size, I'm still not surprised that it did happen as he works himself inside me.

My body involuntarily responds, my inner muscles tightening down around him in a desperate attempt to alleviate the intense stretching. My hand shoots to his hip, pushing against it, so he doesn't push in any further. It's painful, yet my brain and pussy have different ideas of what they want. My brain begs to stop immediately, while my core yearns for more.

"Fuck baby, don't squeeze so tight," his voice trembles, attempting to control himself. "You're making it hard to impress you, if I cum before I can get it all the way in."

I let out an aroused laugh, trying to stifle it. Sensing a hint of relaxation, he seizes the moment, withdrawing slightly before gradually pushing in even more. My hand remains on his hip, giving myself a sense of control, if the pain is too intense, I possess the power to stop him. Then, with perfect precision, he repeats the same motion, withdrawing again before pressing back in to the same depth.

My breath catches in my throat, trapped in the vortex of pleasure and pain. My mouth forming into a silent "O", mirroring the ecstasy coursing through my veins, and reflecting it on my face.

He lowers his mouth to mine, initiating a passionate kiss. His hips moving slowly in and out of me, without going in further.

With every thrust, my body responds eagerly, becoming increasingly slick with arousal, while my core tightens around him. My hand relaxes, tracing a familiar path back up his torso, reclaiming its place wrapped around his strong arm. Sensing my plea, he inches in, taking his time as he moves to new depths, my body stretching for the first time to a man this size, his hips moving rhythmically in and out. His entire large, muscular body undulates on top of me, as his body comes up, his thrust propels my body in tandem.

"Yesss," I cry out.

"Can I go all the way in?" he breathes out, asking for permission.

"Mmhmmm," I moan.

Our mouths rejoin as he withdraws his shaft momentarily, then skillfully guides it back in, filling me so full and leaving himself buried. My face frozen with a breath caught in my throat as I process all the sensations. He stills, buried to the hilt, his body seeming to have an entirely different struggle than mine. It's been years since having his cock buried in a woman, yet he remains in control over his urge to rush this and finally take his release. When my breath finally escapes, it is a stuttered exhale of desire.

Easing out, he presses right back in, withdrawing, and pushing back. The harmony of extreme pain and euphoria prompts a passionate moan much louder than I had intended. My fingers grip his skin, digging in, seeking to release the pleasure and pain in various ways.

Despite the discomfort, it's undeniably gratifying. I wrap my legs around his waist, urging him closer, while arching my hips toward him to grant him better access. An invitation for him to drive his shaft into me deeper.

He glides back and forth with measured rhythms, gradually increasing the intensity as we get acquainted with each other's body. His steady pressure has my legs trembling. Our moans harmonize, each one fueling the other's desire. I reach my arm down, grasping his lower back, pulling him into me with increasing urgency.

The contradicting sensations have me craving him to penetrate me more forcefully, as if I can't comprehend the amount of pleasure my body is experiencing. I need him to show me he's really in me, and hard. My legs clamp even tighter around his waist as I beg him for more.

"You want harder?" he moans.

"Please," I cry out.

He slides his arm under my ass, lifting it off the bed. The profound fullness and depth of his penetration in the transition of positions evokes a sensation so intense, I fear I'm going to wet the bed. My hand immediately releases his back, flattening between us as I pin my sensitive folds together keeping whatever this is suppressed.

His hand intercepts mine, reaching down, drawing it back up, securing his arm beneath my armpit to prevent any escape.

"I need to use the bathroom," I plead, feeling some sort of urgency building.

"You don't," he pants out, continuing to drive into me with force.

"I think I do."

He smiles, his pelvis drawing in and out, "It's called squirting, baby."

"I don't want to," I say embarrassed as the spot he keeps hitting makes my core grow tighter.

I attempt to withdraw my hips from him, making an effort to retreat into the mattress, using as much force as I can, but he is too strong. He holds me in place, his movements picking up speed.

"Wait," I plead as a newfound sensation begins to ripple through my body, igniting every nerve ending. With each thrust, a deep urge surges, building with an inexorable force. My entire body tightens, unable to move as a surge of warmth radiates from my core, spreading like wildfire. I gasp in astonishment as a torrent of pleasure envelops my senses. My back arches towards him and my pussy convulses, my features contort in ecstasy, as breathless moans fill the air.

He withdraws his cock, watching my body writhe and shake as clear liquid squirts out of me. He pushes all the way back in and withdraws fully, liquid flowing again, only this time my pleasured moans cry out, and a hunger stirs in the depths of his eyes, awakening an intense longing that demands to be sated.

"Fuck," I bite my forearm. What the fuck just happened? That's never happened to me before. I'm sure I'm going to be mortified once my clarity returns. But right now, I want to feel it again.

He moves down the bed, burying his face in my pussy, lapping up all the liquid and eating me passionately. Slipping two fingers inside, he begins rocking them back and forth on my G-spot as another rush of liquid builds and squirts out. He's licking and sucking me the same way he does my tongue when we kiss, causing my hips to come off the bed and gyrate against his hand.

He pulls his head back, biting my inner thigh, slowly withdrawing his fingers before tracing his tongue up the curves of my body, licking his way back up to my mouth, sliding his tongue in, giving me a tantalizing taste of my own intoxicating essence.

"My goddess," he breathes, positioning his cock at my entrance, and easing back in, though this time my body has already endured the initial discomfort of being stretched open, making it an easier endeavor.

My core zealously attempts to draw him in more than he physically can, engaging in a fervent dance of rubbing, clenching, and slurping on his shaft. Beads of sweat form on his hairline, and breathless moans escape our parted lips.

Once my body readjusts to his considerable size and I start to relax, he effortlessly lifts me onto his lap, his throbbing penis still inside me. With a swift motion, the pillows scatter to the floor as he positions me on his thighs, pushing my back against the headboard. My legs coil tighter around his waist, while my arms envelop his neck. His incredible smile meets my gaze, emitting a low grunt before initiating slow and forceful thrusts, this angle allowing him access to go even deeper than before.

He grabs handfuls of my backside, squeezing firmly. "Incredible," he lets out guttural moans.

I release my legs from his waist and press the balls of my feet into the back of his calves as he relentlessly thrusts into me, evoking cries of ecstasy. My orgasm building, accompanied by a tingling sensation across my skin.

He continues this rhythm a moment longer before repositioning me, turning us towards the end of the bed, laying me down flat on my back. His body nestles with mine as he settles on top of me, intertwining our fingers and securing our hands above my head. Our mouths reconnecting. I sense his impending orgasm approaching, mirroring my own.

He drives in and out of me over and over, each thrust sending shockwaves through my body. His pace escalating until he's vigorously driving into me. With each powerful thrust, I feel him delving deeper—so much deeper than I ever thought possible. He is pounding into tender depths of me, that will surely have aches in the aftermath. Even with this knowledge that I will pay the price later, in this moment, the pleasure outweighs any future discomfort.

My screams ring throughout the room. Though I will be embarrassed later to find out how many others in the house can hear me, I find myself unable to stifle them, lost in the throes of ecstasy.

Bringing his mouth into the crook of my neck, he begins sucking and biting. Chills envelop my body as our orgasms burst out together, the room filling with our intertwined moans. My hands grip his, relaxing only to tighten again, his member pumping inside me, the extending release unleashing a four-year buildup. My pussy constricts around him, releasing the same pent-up tension within me.

I know it's not solely due to the length of time since I last had sex, but this is the most extraordinary orgasm I've ever experienced. The intensity surpasses any idea or experienced orgasm I've ever known, and I realize I've barely scratched the surface of its potential. Even as I'm still descending from the pleasurable peak, my body still pulsating around him, the desire to feel it all over again is already surging, a craving for the unparalleled bliss he has awakened.

As our climaxes subside, his thrusts slow, creating a moment of an incredible and magical connection. My legs shake uncontrollably while he leaves himself buried inside me as he relaxes on top of me, never exerting his full weight.

We linger in this blissful state, our breathing falling into sync.

Replaying the intensity of this encounter again and again, slowly drifting off to sleep.

I OPEN MY EYES AS I FEEL MY HANDS, POSITIONED ABOVE MY HEAD being unwrapped, and I glance up to see Jonathan mouthing "sorry" while holding up bandages. "You bled through. I'm just going to change them really quick," he whispers as he unwraps fresh bandages.

I nod in agreement and keep my head tilted upright, observing as he efficiently unwraps and inspects the cuts on my hands using his phone's flashlight to see. Then begins re-bandaging each hand back up.

"All done," he smiles at me and stands, gathering the soiled bandages. "Night, Kal," before departing.

Jonah shifts on top of me, emitting a low "mmm" as he nuzzles his face into my neck, his arousal returning. I realize at some point while we were sleeping, he must have withdrawn himself from inside me because I can feel his hard cock nestle against my still-wet slit. I don't know how much semen he left in me, but I feel like my ass is laying in a puddle, presumably everything that has seeped out.

"Can't sleep?" he whispers.

"Jonathan changed my bandages," I respond back in a whisper.

"Mmm," an understanding resonates from his throat.

He reaches down between us, gripping his arousal, his face still in my neck. "How are you feeling?"

"Maybe you should find out."

He sits up on his elbow, gazing down at me, and with that, he examines my entrance with his fingers, presumably checking for moisture.

Pretty sure that's all you," I tease, as I can feel just how wet I still am.

"Let's add to it," he guides his tip to my center. Despite the swelling from our prior sexcapade and the ensuing friction, it still feels amazing as he works himself back inside me. Getting past the initial discomfort of him entering once more, it quickly becomes incredibly pleasurable.

This time, however, he takes it slow, both of us relishing the sensations. My hands roam his solid body, heightening my arousal.

He leans down, drawing my nipple into his mouth, and a moan escapes my lips.

Filled with confidence, I gently push on his chest. He resists at first, but when I continue trying to push him off, he looks at me with a hint of confusion, but I bite my lip seductively, assuring him that we're not finished yet.

He withdraws his cock, rolling over, resting on his back, a smile playing on his lips as I gradually position myself on top of him. His face beams with sheer pleasure and excitement. Straddling him, I observe the growing anticipation in his eyes. Reaching between my thighs, I grasp his shaft and align it with my entrance.

Now, it's my turn to take charge, and I savor the moment. Holding onto his shaft, I use it to draw circles around my entrance before slowly sinking myself on him.

As I gradually slide up and down on him, gripping his chest for stability, moans escape both our lips. Once I'm fully positioned all the way down on him, stretching to accommodate his size, I allow my body a moment to adjust.

Slowly, I initiate a rhythmic rocking of my hips, ensuring he remains fully immersed in me. Holding onto his chest for a moment longer, before I quicken the pace, with him gripping my waist and ass. The motion continues, transitioning from rocking back and forth to circling my hips on him, as I move my hands from his chest to my full breasts, squeezing them with each pass.

"Yes, baby, don't stop," he moans breathlessly.

I maintain the motion until I sense my orgasm building once more. Lowering my hands from my breasts, I reposition them on his chest, firmly planting them as I lean forward and start sliding up and down on him—slowly at first. With the assistance of his hands on each cheek, he joins in, pulling me up when I ascend and helping guide me down as I slide back onto him.

Our pace quickens, and I tilt my head back. "Jonah," I moan loudly.

Smiling, he thrust his hips upwards into me until we both climax again. My vagina tightening around him as he spills inside me for a second time. My hips resume the rocking motion back and forth on his shaft as wave after wave of my orgasm course through me, my body shaking and convulsing on top of him.

I gradually ease my hips to a standstill, savoring the sensation of him still submerged, as I regain control of my breathing. Looking down at him, I see his complete immersion in our shared moment, even as his arousal subsides.

As our breaths return to normal, I leisurely withdraw from him, relishing the soft sound of his pleasure-filled moan as I do so, before rolling onto my back beside him, feeling the lingering echoes of our intimacy.

"I'm not sure who's typically in charge of cleaning duties in here, but I might need to volunteer for laundry duty tomorrow," I tease, glancing at Jonah, then at myself, and finally at the bedding. His head remains on the bed, and he turns to look at me with a smile.

"It definitely looks like a crime scene in here," he jokes, seemingly unfazed by the blood scattered across both of us and the bed.

I burst into laughter.

"I didn't want to alarm you, so I didn't mention it," he says as he rolls over to face me. "Are you okay?" he asks, tracing his fingers along my belly.

"I've never felt better," I grin at him. "I think something ripped inside of me though," I recall the feeling of something tearing as he was first penetrating me.

"Typically, you would feel that when you lose your virginity. Unfortunately, you had to feel it a second time. You shouldn't feel that again," he reassures me.

"I think that is where the blood came from. I'm not on my period," I say to him, hoping he doesn't think I just got period blood all over him.

"I wouldn't care if you were. But that is one room checked off," he muses.

"One room checked off for what?"

"You moaning my name," he smirks, referring to the first day we met, and he said his name would echo off every wall in this house from my moans.

Not even ten minutes pass of silence and I feel his erection pressing into my leg again.

I glance at him, holding back a laugh, as his face innocently nestles in my hair.

"Do you see what you do to me?" his penis flexes toward me.

Rolling onto my side, I push my bottom back against it. "Well?" I turn my head to face him.

"My naughty girl," he says eagerly through gritted teeth, propping himself up on his elbow. He grasps his shaft and positions it at my entrance. Once it's in place, he releases his hand and spanks my ass. The sound reverberates around the room, and my body is flooded with ecstasy.

Bringing his hand to my throat, he grabs hold, pulling my face towards his as his tongue finds my mouth and he shoves himself into me once again.

CHAPTER

Twenty

KALYN

I awaken groggily, feeling a dull ache between my legs. True to his word, he had mentioned on the first day of meeting that he was going to fuck me raw. I stretch my arms across the bed, expecting to feel his soft skin, only to discover it's empty. After the fourth time of going at it, he gives me a bath, sort of. We more so sat in his huge bathtub with the water running, while he cleaned me off with a hand towel as I held my hands up to avoid the water.

Opening my eyes and glancing around the room, my gaze stops as I watch Jonah approaching the bed, clad in dress pants and an unbuttoned white shirt, revealing his smooth bare chest.

"Good morning," he utters, bending down, planting a kiss on my lips, holding a cup in his hand.

"Coffee?" I ask, eyeing the cup.

He sits on the edge of the bed, responding, "Nope," with a smile, extending his hand out for me to take the contents in the opposite hand. He places two pills in my palm. "Someone mentioned they don't like the smell of coffee, so I quit drinking it… except on business trips," offering me the cup. "Water," he adds, holding it out to me.

Attempting to sit up, I notice the dull ache while lying down is nothing compared to the stinging pain between my legs when I sit up. "Ow," I unintentionally vocalize.

"I'm sorry, baby," his tone conveys a hint of guilt, knowing he is the one who caused the rawness. This sensation is entirely new to me. Despite the pain, there's a certain satisfaction in acknowledging it was us together, creating an incredibly passionate moment that left me sore.

"This is what I get for going so long between having sex," I didn't realize that over four years of no sex would make me so incredibly sore. Was it the extended friction of our intimacy or perhaps his size contributing to the discomfort?

He watches me swallow down the medicine and removes the cup from my hand, placing it on the nightstand. "That was Tylenol in case you were wondering," he smiles. "You just take random pills from strangers without knowing what it is? I'm gonna have to watch you more closely," he teases, lightening the mood as he sets the cup on his nightstand.

"Umm, I don't let strangers inside me," I delicately bring my legs toward the direction of the bed where he stands.

"Good girl," he draws his face close and presses his lips against mine. "Because if you did, I would have to commit murder," he adds, breaking the kiss. Before leaning back in with sheer amusement on his lips as our mouths connect once more.

"Yeah? You'll kill the men who've put their dicks in me?" Fortunately for him, my list is rather short, comprising only three individuals. Well, make that four now, as of last night.

"They will regret ever putting their dick anywhere near my girl," he playfully bites my lip, drawing it into his mouth.

Realizing it must be early, considering he's already dressed for work, I decide to change the subject. "I'm scared to ask, but what time is it?" The room's blackout curtains make it impossible to tell.

"Well," evading a direct answer, "That depends. If you will do what I want, the time doesn't matter. I'll wait for the medicine to kick in, and Giles to come back with some medicine to relieve the rawness. Then, I'll bury myself in you again," he declares, kissing me once more. "But I know you better than you think," he walks to a nearby chair, grabs my work uniform by the hanger, and brings it over to the bed. Placing panties, a bra, and socks on top of it, he lays the ensemble on the side of the bed. He gazes at my still nude body for a moment before leaning over on the bed, grabbing my ankles, being mindful to keep my legs slightly spread, and gently pulls me until my butt is right on the edge.

"I'm sure Jonathan will enjoy you doing that," I tease. We removed all the bedding last night because they were covered in fluid. They now sit in a heaping pile by the door.

"I don't care if he does or not," he nonchalantly remarks, completely unbothered that he just pulled my bare vagina across Jonathan's mattress.

"I had your uniform brought up," he remarks. "One that fits properly," his eyes wander over my body, and he bites down on his bottom lip.

"I can't wait. It was a full-time job all on its own trying to drag that colossal tarp around, I expect back pay for the troubles," alluding to Jenevieve's habit of providing me with oversized uniforms. At first, I thought of this as a simple oversight on her part. But as she continued providing only me with uniforms that were way too big, I realized she was intentionally doing it.

Jonah grabs my panties and slowly begins helping me into them. When they reach my thighs, I hold onto his arm while I reposition myself on my knees. He trails his fingertips down my legs until he reaches my black lace panties. His head between my breasts, he places a kiss on each nipple and slowly pulls my panties into place. Deftly grabbing for my bra, again helping me into it. Handling it effortlessly, he snaps it at the back. He has clearly handled many bras.

"Is this some kind of fetish?" curious about the maid uniforms.

Jonah lets out a mock sigh, denying it and revealing, "That would be my mother."

"A way to distinguish the help?" I half-heartedly tease.

"Something like that. So, if you feel like ditching that uniform and wearing your regular clothes, I have it on good authority your boss gives his permission," he playfully spanks my bottom.

Wrapping my arms delicately around his neck, "Does my boss also want to pay all my bills?" I bring my lips to his.

With a serious tone, he responds, "Yes."

"Well, Mr. Everett, lucky for you, you get a good, reliable worker out of me," I take hold of both sides of his shirt and begin fastening the buttons.

He leans down, planting a kiss on my forehead. "I'd prefer to have a good..." Shifting his focus, he kisses my nose. "Wet," he whispers against my cheek. "Horny," he quietly remarks, placing a kiss on my other cheek. "Did I say horny?" He looks into my eyes before his lips find the sensitive skin of my neck. "Beautiful," he gently nips at my neck. "Woman," he says with a grin, "to be around all the time, even on my business trips," he concludes.

"You want me sprawled out naked, ready to take your cock anytime you need," I question teasingly, lifting a brow.

"I want you," he states simply.

"I want you, too," I respond, kissing him.

I reach for my uniform and push on Jonah's solid chest to make room, allowing me to maneuver off the oversized bed. As I slip on the uniform, I notice that this time it fits flawlessly—perhaps a bit too flawlessly, as the top reveals a hint of my breasts and the dress is shorter than the usual uniforms.

Jonah confesses innocently, "I made some small alterations to it." He looks me up and down as if he is going to devour me right here.

Amused, I respond, "I can see that. For everyone's enjoyment, I presume?" Knowing that everyone is going to be staring at my uniform. I went from being the only one with a uniform that was way too big and now I am the only one with a uniform that is quite… revealing.

"I need her other uniform back, Gladys," he says in a slightly higher pitch, to call for Gladys, accompanied by pure amusement.

"Shh," I cover his mouth with my hand. "That was just a joke," I assure him, joining in the laughter as I glance at the door wondering if anyone heard him.

"Although, now that I look at you in this, a maid outfit might be a new kink," his eyes flicker with arousal.

"Oh? Do you need me to dust the baseboards, Mr. Everett?" I seductively bite my lip.

"I need a lot more than that from you," he envelops me in a comforting embrace, resting his head atop mine. The sensation of having my arms around him is undeniably comforting. Glancing toward the nightstand, I check the clock, and it reads 9:10 AM.

"It's not!" I exclaim.

Jonah appears confused about what I am referring to.

"It's not actually nine in the morning," I anxiously reveal.

"Babe, it's fine," he reassures, attempting to soothe my concerns.

"No, it's not," I insist. "I hate being late," I hurry to the chair where my work shoes are sitting on the floor, quickly slipping them on before heading out the door.

Descending the stairs, I catch the sound of Mrs. Everett delivering stern reprimands. The team I typically work alongside is lined up in front of her, arranged against an oversized sofa. Jess sees me approaching from the side, shooting me a nervous and apprehensive look, motioning for me to join them in line, shifting to make room for me.

While Mrs. Everett diverts her attention to the nanny, speaking in a hushed conversation, I seize the opportunity to blend into the line between Katy and Jess. The persistent discomfort between my legs grows more noticeable with each passing moment. I attempt to find a more comfortable position, shifting my stance several times, before finally lowering myself onto the couch. Leaning to one side brings a fleeting relief to the discomfort, and I patiently await to discover the cause of Mrs. Everett's agitation.

Upon concluding her conversation with the nanny, Mrs. Everett redirects her attention to the lineup of maids, landing on me as if she's suddenly become aware of my presence, then looks down at my bandaged hands. It almost looks like sympathy crosses her face, but she quickly sets it aside as she plunges back into her heated tirade.

"Someone better confess immediately," Mrs. Everett demands. "Someone infiltrated my room in the middle of the night and stole a million-dollar red diamond necklace. You'd better come clean now!" she exclaims.

Silence hangs heavy in the room, enveloping us in a collective sense of bewilderment at her accusations. Everyone remains standing, their faces a mix of confusion and concern. Well, everyone except me. The discomfort between my legs makes it excruciating to stand or sit for too long. Yet, I'm hesitant to draw further attention to myself by shifting positions. In the brief time I've been here, it's become apparent that we're being accused of theft from her room.

Personally, I find the accusation incredulous. Jonah's generosity is well-known among the staff—as he overpays us. Stealing jewelry would be a foolish risk, especially considering the legal repercussions. Well, unless one ventures into the black market, but that's a realm I'm unfamiliar with.

"I'll have all of you fired if someone doesn't confess right now," she threatens, growing angrier.

"I found it," Jenevieve declares, storming into the room with her signature heels clicking.

"Oh, thank god," Mrs. Everett sighs in relief as Jenevieve returns her necklace. "Where was it?" she asks, sounding relieved.

Jenevieve scans the room, her eyes landing on me, then moving down to my chest, noticing the alterations to my uniform. Her eyes flare with fury as she darts her eyes back up to mine. "Callous," she hisses, stomping in my direction. Her anger seems to intensify because of my new uniform. "Can you explain why I found Mrs. Everett's diamond necklace in your bags, packed with all your belongings?" she questions, looking menacing.

"Well," Mrs. Everett snaps. "You get fired and think you can leave with things that don't belong to you, girl? I'm filing charges against you, thief—you'll be arrested for this!" she accuses me.

I struggle to even comprehend that they are trying to blame me for stealing her necklace. I have never stolen anything in my entire life. Yet the accusation instantly makes me feel like I am somehow guilty.

"I didn't take anything," I say frantically.

"Stand up when you're being spoken to," Jenevieve commands, abruptly lifting me to my feet by my arm. Her eyes scan over my body as she pulls me to my feet, her grip tightening on my arm as she returns her focus to my face. I gather she is not a fan of Jonah's alterations.

"I'm sorry," instant discomfort between my legs fills my body when I am jerked into a standing position.

"I saw her go into Mrs. Everett's room," Vanessa chimes in. "Last night, I was coming back from getting a snack and saw her sneaking away from the maid's quarters, so I followed her. I saw her come out with the diamonds. I'm sorry for not saying anything. I was scared," Vanessa says, sounding concerned and glancing at Jenevieve and Mrs. Everett.

I stare at Vanessa stunned, my mouth hanging open in disbelief. I can't believe what I am hearing. She keeps her eyes forward, yet I see the faintest twitch of her lip as if she finds this funny.

"Thank you for speaking up now," Jenevieve acknowledges.

"How dare you," Mrs. Everett says looking furious at me.

"Enough!" A loud, thunderous voice echoes throughout the room, causing everyone to stand even straighter.

Jonah and Jonathan stand in the doorway.

"Mr. Everett, your mother's diamond necklace was stolen by Kal—" Jenevieve begins before Jonah cuts her off.

"I said enough!" he yells again. Everyone in the room jumps once more by the inflection of his voice. I've never heard him sound so angry. What if he believes I took his mother's diamonds? The mere thought makes my stomach churn. I envision him yelling at me, declaring that he never wants to see me again, and instructing me to leave his house immediately. The prospect of walking out in shame, with the lingering ache between my legs from last night's events, adds to the distress. He'd regret our intimate encounter for the rest of his life.

"My diamonds were stolen, son," Mrs. Everett says, her voice tinged with hurt, as she holds it up to show him.

"When did this happen?" he questions angrily.

A look of delight crosses Jenevieve's eyes. "We don't know a precise time, but we found them in Kaylin's bag," she informs him.

"What. Time?" Jonah asks again.

Vanessa speaks up, "It was around midnight, sir," she says confidently as if she is being exceptionally helpful, even though she knows she didn't witness me taking anything.

He walks confidently to the center of the room, positioning himself between his mother and me, ensuring that we both are still able to see one another. "Tell them," he says, staring between his mother and Jenevieve but addressing me. Everyone in the room stands still, not sure who he was speaking to.

I remain silent.

"Tell them," he repeats, only this time he turns his head to look at me.

Staring back, I seal my lips together and subtly shake my head no.

"Speak when Mr. Everett demands it," Jenevieve hisses at me. Her eyes conveying she believes he is about to send me flying out the front door.

"Tell them what you were doing at midnight," he says, staring at me. "Or rather, who." This appears to be something only he and I understand as everyone else in the rooms seems to completely miss that last part.

Jonathan lets out a muffled snort before clearing his throat and mouthing sorry to those of us who were brave enough to look over at him. I shoot daggers in his direction thinking somehow he is going to get me in even more trouble.

"Speak girl," his mother demands.

"Jonah, stop, please," I plead, not wanting everyone in the room to find out I was having sex with the boss last night.

"How dare you refer to him so informally, girl," Mrs. Everett barks.

"Get out!" He shouts louder than the first two times he already has.

Wearing a haughty look, Mrs. Everett declares, "You heard him! Leave!" fixing her gaze squarely on me.

"I am telling YOU to leave, Mother," he turns his head toward her, blindsiding her completely.

"Jonah?!" she says, looking horrified. "You can't possibly be serious. This girl stole from me." She points her finger accusingly at me.

"I assure you it wasn't her," he says, trying to steady his tone.

Vanessa speaks up, "Sir, I saw her doing it."

He turns toward her, "What is your name?"

"Vanessa, sir," she says innocently.

"Do you make a habit out of lying, Vanessa?" he questions, only he doesn't want an answer. "You didn't see her take anything, admit that you lied," his voice remaining calm.

"I promise I did, sir. I know it was her," Vanessa insists, trying to convince him.

"We are telling you the truth, Mr. Everett," Jenevieve pleads for him to believe her.

"It wasn't her," he barks again.

"Why are you defending the help, son?" his mother asks, stunned.

He meets my eyes, his gaze unwavering, then strides over to me. Grabbing the collar of my uniform between his first two fingers, he pulls it to the side, revealing the hickeys he left on my neck during our encounter last night for the entire room to see. I can see out of my peripheral that Jenevieve looks horrified. He softly rubs his thumb over them. "How are you feeling?" he asks softly.

"Fine... Sir," I respond, feeling my cheeks flush. It feels like any interaction between us carries an unspoken understanding like everyone in the room is somehow aware that we were frantically grinding on each other all night.

Our eyes remain locked, then he looks to Jenevieve and then to his mother. A wicked smirk slowly forming on his face. "You want to know why, mother? Because I was fucking her last night," he declares, causing an audible gasp around the room.

"Excuse me," she spits, appalled, while Jenevieve looks like someone punched her in the stomach, adding to the look when she grabs at her stomach as if somehow her dress became too tight, restricting airflow to her.

"You heard that right," he says, maintaining eye contact with her. "I was fucking her. And during the time you claim to have seen her," he says pointedly to Vanessa, "She was riding my dick," he grins proudly. "And she was late today because I kept her up all night having sex with her. My cock was buried so deep in her pussy, she wouldn't have been able to sneak off to do this unthinkable act you are accusing her of doing. And while you pack your bags, she will be back in my bed. Don't expect to see her the rest of the week for work." He looks at Jenevieve. "I plan on fucking her until she can't walk," he says amused. Then turns to me. "Sorry baby," his eyes remain intense as he brings his hand to my cheek, softly brushing his knuckles along the skin. Cradling my chin, he tilts it upward, pressing his lips to mine.

"You have got to be kidding me! You are still sleeping with your staff Jonah?" his mother says disappointed, cutting through the tension in the room.

"Why do you concern yourself with who I am sleeping with?" he asks, lacing his fingers in mine. "You no longer need to concern yourself with that, Mother. Kalyn is who I'm sleeping with. In a year, Kalyn is who I will be sleeping with. In ten years, Kalyn will still be who I am sleeping with. Do you get it yet?" he states dryly to her.

Everyone appears totally shocked. When he starts walking, he guides me out of line and I fall in stride beside him, wanting to flip Jenevieve off behind my back, but know just this is doing more than a simple finger gesture could do.

"Find out who stole my mother's jewelry," Jonah says to Jonathan and proceeds to pull me out of the room, leaving everyone behind us staring stunned.

CHAPTER
Twenty-One

KALYN

Today started amazingly.

Then turned to shit.

Back to amazing.

Then ending in shit.

I have never been fucked so many times in one day. Yet every time Jonah and I finish, one of us got a second wind and went right back at it.

When I can finally peel myself off him, I sneak back to my room to shower and take a much-needed nap. I am overly tired and sore.

Upon waking, I dress in comfy shorts and a loose-fitting tank top. I decide to go see what Shay is doing and maybe see if she wants to watch a movie.

As I close my door and walk past Amber's partially open door, I hear the sound of crying and muffled conversation. Without waiting for a response to my tap, I enter to find Shay comforting a visibly upset and tearful Amber.

"Amber, what's wrong?" I notice her sitting cross-legged on her bed, with a stack of used tissues in her lap and fists clenched, her face resting on them.

"GET OUT OF MY ROOM!" She looks up abruptly, sharply instructing me to leave, her tone suggesting that I'm somehow responsible for her distress.

Shay gives me an apologetic glance.

Confused, I search for some sort of explanation. She responds with a subtle eye roll, hinting that Amber might be overreacting, and resumes comforting her. Despite feeling a twinge of guilt for somehow unknowingly upsetting her, I do as she says, closing the door behind me. I'm confused, unable to pinpoint anything I might have done, yet my stomach churns with unease. I've always disliked it when people were mad at me, especially people I care about.

Guided by emotions, I head to Jonah's office with the certainty that he'll be inside. Without knocking, I open the door and find him and Jonathan engaged in casual conversation, tossing a small football back and forth in the sitting area by the window.

As I enter, Jonah catches the football and tosses it back to Jonathan, his eyes shifting to concern. "You okay, baby?"

I just walk over, climb into his lap, straddling him, wrapping my arms around his neck—his arms instinctively encircling my waist.

"What's wrong?"

I keep my face nestled in his neck. "Amber is mad at me and I don't know what I did," I let out a sigh.

"You smell nice," he remarks, planting a kiss on my shoulder.

"So do you," I murmur with my mouth mashed into his shoulder.

His fingers trace up and down my back while he and Jonathan pick up their conversation. I sense a subtle movement as I hear him catch the small football once more before tossing it back to Jonathan, their easygoing conversation continuing.

I awaken when I hear Shay's voice, not even realizing I had dozed off. Lifting my head, I notice her settling into the chair next to Jonathan's, propping her feet on his lap and reclining back. I stand up, adjusting my position on Jonah's lap to face Shay.

With sympathetic eyes, she gazes at me.

"Can you talk about it?" I inquire, careful not to pry if Amber prefers nobody knows what's going on.

"I will, but I need everyone in here to promise not to lose their minds," she casts glances at me, Jonah, and then Jonathan.

Jonathan raises his hands distancing himself from the situation. Shay shifts her gaze back to Jonah and me, raising a questioning brow.

"I'm cool," I respond, mirroring Jonathan's gesture by raising my hands. I study her expression, anticipating that the situation might be even worse than I initially imagined, given the prolonged pre-conversation she's having with us before she reveals what's going on.

"Mr. Everett?" She looks at Jonah as if anticipating he will be the one getting upset by what she is about to say.

"I'm here for support," he tightens his arms around me.

"Okay," she claps her hands on her thighs. "Amber has had a crush on Brad since she started. He started showing her attention here recently, which she assumed meant he liked her, and she slept with him," she scans the room, searching for reactions.

"So, she's upset with me because I warned her about Brad being a player?" My mouth hangs open, unable to comprehend how she could twist this into me being the villain instead of addressing the fact that he's a known dirtbag.

"No, she's upset because Brad wants nothing to do with her now," Shay corrects.

"And she's angry with me because?"

"You all promised to keep your cool," she points at me and Jonah, as if signaling that the upcoming information might make the situation worse.

"Yes," I agree, growing somewhat impatient at her dragging this out.

"She's upset because, well... while they were having sex, he, uh, was moaning your name," her usual relaxed features contort with concern. Her brows draw together as she shifts her gaze between Jonah and me.

Jonah draws in a breath, releasing it with a firm grip on my leg before relaxing it.

"You both promised to stay cool," Shay reminds us, pointing both index fingers at each of us.

"We're cool," I affirm, running my hand up and down his forearm.

"I know I don't even need to ask, but she believes you and Brad have been having sex, and that's why he was moaning your name," as the conversation continues, her discomfort seems to escalate, etching itself across her features.

"What!" My exclamation reverberates through the room. "WOW!"

"I've assured her you haven't. She's simply fixated on that notion because she's feeling heartbroken," Shay attempts to clarify, offering a justification for the current situation.

"Unbelievable. That dipshit sleeps with anyone willing to fuck him, and she gets upset with me for him doing exactly what I warned about?" My annoyance grows as I realize her anger is directed towards a situation outside of my control. Relaxing against Jonah, I rest the back of my head on his chest.

His breathing is steady, and instinctively, I start synchronizing my breathing with his.

"I should confront him," locking eyes with Shay for any type of reaction on whether she thinks that would be a good idea or not. "I don't care what kind of dirty talk he wants to do, but he crossed a line sleeping with Amber." Reflecting on our past discussions, I recall the countless times he emphasized that I wasn't his type—not that it holds any significance or that I seek validation from him. Still, why would my name surface during an intimate encounter with someone else? When Jonah and I are intimate, my attention is entirely dedicated to him.

"Maybe he's expecting you to confront him?" Shay proposes, offering a potential insight into Brad's mindset.

"What a loser," I remark, absentmindedly extending my foot toward the coffee table, only to fall short by a foot. Giving up on the attempt, I let my foot drop back down.

Guilt begins to wash over me. I've known how Amber felt about Brad for months now. The thought of finally being intimate with Jonah, only for him to moan someone else's name, makes me feel sick to my stomach. And then to have the person's name he moans be one of my friends would only make matters worse. It pains me that she's hurting, and I wish there was something I could do to ease her hurt.

"Fucking douche," I inadvertently say out loud.

CHAPTER
Twenty-Two

JENEVIEVE

I sit at the mansions bar, gutted by the earlier events. The intensity of my hatred for her consumes me. She is a low-life piece of trash that isn't even worthy of his time. Every fiber of my being despises her. Thoughts of him slipping away from me overwhelm my mind, and tears escape from my eyes. I've loved him since middle school, and now I'm losing him to a girl he hardly knows. I am better than her in every way. How can he be so blind? I am far more superior, and he is making a terrible mistake. The tears start to flow uncontrollably.

In an attempt to numb the pain, I lift my glass, signaling the bartender to refill it.

I tried to push her away. Assigning her chores nobody wants to do. Yet, no matter how I treat her, she never caves. She is stronger than I originally gave her credit for, I'll give her that. I must confess, the act of striking her brought the most satisfying pleasure that I haven't felt in a long time. The urge to strike her again is compelling—the thought of delivering a resounding slap across her face fills me with a perverse longing.

I'm engrossed in my melancholic thoughts when I sense her passing by.

"You know I remember you from that night," I say taking another sip of my golden liquid. Tear streaks of mascara cascade down my face I notice in the mirror behind the bar.

She stops walking and looks over at me. I continue, "The night of the Gala, he looked dashing." A couple more tears free themselves from my eyes. "We had sex previously, but that night, it felt different. Jonah… Jonah, Jonah, Jonah," I say his first name the same way she does, then repeat it, loving the way it feels on my tongue. The way he allows her to say it yet corrected me when I did the same after being hired to work for him, fills me with even more anger. "Jonah fucks the orgasm right out of you, as you clearly found out," I hold my glass up, giving her a cheer, seeing her staring at me with a look of pity. This little bitch had his penis inside her, and then walks around flaunting her trashy hickeys.

"I was aware that during his business trips, he would have sex with flight attendants or someone from the office, sometimes even other staff here until I threatened each and every one of them, and they stopped doing it. He eventually learned not to mix personal business with pleasure here. While he was home from business, he had needs, and I was available for him anytime he needed. The night of the Gala was flawless. Everything unfolded seamlessly," I reminisce, my thoughts returning to that evening.

THE GALA

Today, I find myself unusually irritable. The gala is tomorrow evening, yet Mr. Everett hasn't extended an invitation for me to accompany him. He has never brought anyone with him previously, but lately, he has been having sex with me more often. I presumed this was due to his developing feelings for me, and I expected an invitation. My family is convinced that Mr. Everett and I will eventually be wed. They approve of him, considering him the ideal man for me—wealthy, influential, and often away on business, granting me the freedom to spend as I wish with all the money I could dream of spending. It doesn't hurt that he's also attractive. My sister, on the other hand, married an older wealthy man, and she despises having to share a bed with him, stating he stinks and sweats all over her and his penis is so tiny she isn't even sure when he puts it in.

I've grown accustomed to Mr. Everett's desires and preferences in bed. Once we are married, we will be having sex completely different. He will have to diversify our intimate experiences. I yearn to wrap my arms around him and watch him while he has me, yet he prefers the position where he takes me from behind. He has always been a tad on the rough side when having sex. If his penis size weren't so substantial, his forceful thrusts might not be perceived as too rough. Initially, the intensity was painful, but now, my body craves it.

My mother calls me every day asking if he has invited me to the Gala yet, reminding me that all the most important business people will be there and it will be good for Father's business for people to see Mr. Everett and me as a couple. I had hoped he would ask me to join him by now so I could hear in my mother's voice how proud she is of me, but it hasn't happened yet.

"Get to work," I tell the maid's as I stride down the hall, still seething over the omission.

Rounding the corner, I encounter Giles, who promptly shifts his gaze to the floor when he passes me. It's laughable, as I know he often whispers lies in Mr. Everett's ear about me. Maybe that is why Mr. Everett hasn't asked me to accompany him yet. Puny little weasel.

After he disappears from my view, his footsteps come to a halt, as if he's hesitant to say something.

"What is it, Giles?" I demand, turning to face him. I hate it when he talks to me. He has nothing of value to ever say and he only ever wastes everyone's time.

He looks at me for a moment, pondering. "Nothing, ma'am," he says and resumes walking.

"Mr. Everett," I chirp in a tone that conveys my delight at seeing him when I turn back around.

"Giles!" Jonathan calls after him, prompting him to pause and head back toward where Jonathan and Mr. Everett are walking. Mr. Everett rolls up the sleeves of his button-up work shirt mid-forearm—he is so sexy, I smile to myself staring at his muscular arms.

"Jenevieve," Jonathan greets me.

"Jonathan," I make an effort to appear anything other than disgusted, even though I can't tolerate him. His persistent wide snicker only exacerbates my irritation.

"Well," Jonathan inquires, "Are you coming tomorrow?"

I'm puzzled as I'm not sure what he's referring to. "Coming?" waiting for him to elaborate.

"Stop," Mr. Everett interjects, addressing Jonathan.

"To the Gala. Giles was coming to offer you the opportunity to attend," he continues, his gremlin little smirk still plastered on his face. "Did you not ask, Giles?" Jonathan's stupid devilish grin grows wider as he turns to Giles.

"It must have slipped my mind," Giles responds, knowing damn well it didn't slip his mind. This is exactly the kind of thing that makes Giles such an unlikable person. He was sent to do one task and he couldn't even complete it. He will find himself out of employment as soon as Mr. Everett and I are married.

Sure, it did, I think to myself, annoyed. "I'd love to go, Mr. Everett, thank you."

"If you can get a dress made in time," Jonathan adds, his tone tinged with amusement. I don't know why Mr. Everett surrounds himself with fools on purpose. Jonathan is probably the biggest one yet, with Giles being close behind if not even for first place. Jonathan thinks he is so clever, always wearing his sneaky little grin any time I come around. Maybe he feels the need to drive a wedge between Mr. Everett and me because he wants him all to himself. Jonathan is the one who encourages Mr. Everett to sleep with other women. They share in all the women while they are away on business trips. Jonathan always taking Mr. Everett's leftovers.

Little does he know, I already had a dress made because I knew Mr. Everett would come to his senses. "I will have a dress."

Mr. Everett appears stressed as he lets out a loud sigh. "Let's go," he says to Jonathan, and they continue walking down the hall. Jonathan stares me up and down as he walks by with a devious smirk on his face, appearing to be up to no good.

"Just fix it," I exclaim, my hair not sitting exactly how I want it.

"Yes, Jenevieve," the small hairstylist with oversized glasses says, casting glances at the mousy girl doing my makeup. "I am going to be on the cover of every magazine," I assert, gazing at myself in the mirror. I've never encountered someone as beautiful as myself, a fact that may be unfortunate for them but proves to be incredibly fortunate for Mr. Everett.

After an hour, they eventually perfect my hair and makeup.

With the assistance of one of the maids, I slip into my snug, gold, glittering dress for the gala. Gazing at myself in the mirror, I'm aware that tonight, I will be the most stunning woman at the event.

Exiting the Gala after a delightful evening, we make our way to Mr. Everett's blacked-out SUV. I open the door and sit down, parting my legs to him as he approaches, finding that I have liquid courage to spice things up tonight, I give him a seductive smile.

"Want it?" I ask, lifting my dress even higher.

He hesitates for a moment, contemplating, then jerks me out of the SUV, turning me around and tugging my panties down. He unzips his pants, his impressive shaft springing free, and he deftly sheaths it with a condom, discarding the wrapper on the ground. He spits on the tip, using his hand to move the saliva down. Gripping his member firmly, he plunges it forcefully inside me in one expert motion. I let out a moan from the incredible sensation, sinking into the leather seats of the SUV. He pounds into me relentlessly, his grip on my hips bruisingly tight as he pumps into me hard, shoving the entirety of his length in and out. I feel his penis pulsate as he finds his release, then pulls out abruptly, peeling the condom off his shaft and tossing it on the ground before making his way around the vehicle zipping up his pants and climbing in.

"Pick those up," Jonathan instructs me as I pull my panties back into place, referring to the condom and wrapper.

"If you don't need anything else tonight, I will see you at the office tomorrow," Jonathan slyly says to Mr. Everett, with a blonde I've never seen before standing behind him.

"Have fun," Mr. Everett responds.

I look down at the discarded trash and roll my eyes. The help can clean it up. That's what they are paid for after all, and climb onto the leather seat.

During the drive, Mr. Everett and Giles engage in discussions about business matters and the Gala. The conversation becomes monotonous, prompting me to divert my attention to scrolling social media, specifically browsing wedding dresses. However, even that loses its allure after a while.

Setting my phone aside, I get on the floor at Mr. Everett's feet, a subtle move that halts the conversation, providing a welcome relief from Giles' incessant chatter which I find increasingly unbearable.

"What are you doing?" he asks, his voice tinged with annoyance as he looks down at me. Yet, I can read through his irritation, the weariness born from a long night of obligatory mingling with people he couldn't care less about.

"Cleaning you up," I respond seductively, as I unzip his pants. I love this part—feeling his soft member in my mouth and savoring it growing hard as I suckle. The taste of the condom isn't exactly to my liking, but I'll bear it to bring him pleasure. Especially with the amount of money tonight brings his business, which in turn will benefit me.

As his penis stiffens, I find my mouth can only accommodate about a quarter of his size. Nonetheless, I lace my fingers together behind my back, maintaining a rhythmic suction and pulling motion on his girth.

His arousal intensifies as he reclines in his chair, placing his hand on my head and pushing it down beyond my comfortable limit, triggering a reflex that makes me gag. But I persist.

Even as I feel him sit back up, I continue my rhythm, only stopping when he becomes entirely flaccid.

Perplexed, I gaze up at him, assuming he has dozed off, only to discover him staring out the window fixated on something with an unfamiliar look on his face. Returning to my seat, I glance at Giles, who is observing him through the rearview mirror.

Baffled by his focus, I follow his line of sight and spot a blonde woman descending the steps of a brownstone, tears streaming down her cheeks. At first, I entertain the notion that he might feel sympathy for her.

However, as I shift my attention back and forth between him and the woman, a different sentiment lingers in his gaze. She begins walking, casting a glance at our vehicle, tears still flowing. A honk from the car behind us startles her, prompting her to quicken her pace. While he keeps his eyes fixed on her.

I notice his renewed arousal and return to my position on the floor, enclosing my mouth around him once more. However, this time, his body responds differently, going limp again.

"Get off me," he demands irritably, prompting me to quickly return to my seat. His whole demeanor changes in a matter of seconds and I can't comprehend why.

"Drive," he instructs Giles, who promptly complies, while he deftly zips up his pants as we lurch forward.

'That was peculiar,' I think to myself, feeling a twinge of hurt from the sudden rejection.

In the following weeks, I witness various female staff summoned to Mr. Everett's office, emerging in tears while he yells and breaks things in the aftermath. There is even a period when he left for a business trip, extending for six weeks, only to come back even more angry.

The business trips become more frequent, with him only ever returning one day a week.

I need to know where he is going. Knowing he will be leaving soon, I get a rental car and position myself down the road. I trail him for seventeen hours, only to discover him pulling up to a small diner where he lingers for the next nine hours. It doesn't take long to discern the reason behind his visits—she is here… working.

Tears stream down my face as I watch. Eventually becoming overwhelmed with sadness, I walk over to his car, open the door, and climb in. He looks completely shocked to see me.

"What the fuck are you doing here?" he shouts, his tone filled with anger. I lean over and kiss him.

Pushing me away, he wipes his mouth and orders me to get out.

"No," I insist, demanding to stay.

"Get out of my vehicle, Jenevieve!" he yells, rage filling the entirety of his face.

Jonathan exits the front seat, opens the back door, and instructs me to get out. I remain motionless.

"If you want to keep your job, you'll leave now," he spits out.

Tearfully, I comply with his wishes.

Kalyn

"I don't understand why he let four years go by?" I mutter, my confusion palpable. Yet, my words are not directed solely at her—they're an attempt to unravel the enigma within me.

Jenevieve emits a sinister cackle. "You don't get it, of course you don't. You're a silly little child," she says, casting a sharp glare in my direction. "Mr. Everett isn't one for committed relationships, Mr. Everett fucks," she remarks. "What Mr. Everett excels at is generating wealth and striving to please his parents. Do you know what would mend his relationship with his father? Marrying me. Our fathers are close friends who've jointly planned our wedding and even envisioned their future grandchildren."

I recoil at the mere suggestion of Jonah and her having children.

She goes on, "Mr. Everett wasn't inclined to settle down just yet, which is why I overlooked his involvement with other women. I love him and would do anything for him. However, he's undergone significant growth in recent years and is now prepared to embrace a more stable life," she adds, her demeanor shifting.

"You were merely a means to an end, Kalyn," she declares, correctly using my name for the first time. "He was a man who was with a new woman every other day. When he began experiencing erectile dysfunction the night of the Gala, he believed that you, the heartbroken pathetic girl, could somehow remedy him," she snorts. "As time passed, I believe he started to feel like nobody, not even you, could resolve his issues," she adds, shooting me a disdainful glance. "He eventually chose to abandon the idea of being with you. He stopped driving to your work," she says villainous.

"The day you showed up, I felt like I was going to have a heart attack at the sight of you. It's evident you don't fit in here," her eyes beginning to fill with tears. "I believed he forgot all about you. But the day he saw you here... God, imagine holding so much power over someone you've never even met," tears start streaming down from her eyes. And she shakes away whatever thought she was going to say before she says it out loud.

"Jenevieve, I had nothing to do with—" she cuts me off.

"I'll release you from your contract if you agree to depart immediately. I'll personally cover your entire year's salary, and you can start anew... somewhere else," she implores, her gaze fixed on me.

"I'm not going anywhere, Jenevieve," I assert decisively.

"The thing is Kalyn, he was, is, and always will be mine. You have borrowed time with him, but it will always be Jenevieve and Jonah Everett," Alluding to her last name being Everett. "Not you, Kalyn, and Mr. Everett," she says, emptying the contents of the glass into her mouth and standing up.

"Enjoy him while you can, I'll be coming for what's mine," she says and begins clicking out of the room.

CHAPTER
Twenty-Three

JONAH

My recent business trip was lackluster overall. While the professional side went smoothly—I managed to close all my deals—the real highlight is seeing her again upon my return. Four weeks away from her felt far too long, and I've resolved never to stay apart from her for such an extended period again. Jonathan is chauffeuring me to the diner where she works tirelessly six days a week. Her only reprieve comes on Tuesdays, which she reserves for laundry and errands. Knowing today is Thursday, I'm certain she'll be on shift from two PM until closing at ten.

Every visit to the diner ignites a whirlwind of nervous anticipation within me. We make it a habit to park in the familiar spot right in front of the diner's windows, perfectly positioning ourselves to catch her in action at the tables inside. Arriving thirty minutes before her shift begins is our routine, knowing she has a habit of arriving early, typically twenty to twenty-five minutes before her official start time. There's a thrill in catching glimpses of her up close as she passes us on her way into the diner. Her arrival always holds an element of surprise, considering she has to round the corner of the diner, making her timing uncertain. It's during this suspenseful period, I eagerly await her arrival.

As the minutes tick by, I catch myself glancing at my watch constantly and scanning the surroundings. "Did we miss her?" I ask, my gaze darting around. By now, she should have arrived, yet I've kept my eyes glued to her usual route, but there's no sign of her. I periodically scan inside the diner for her and still nothing.

"Definitely not," Jonathan reassures, glancing around as well.

"I don't see her in there," I note, feeling a surge of nerves as another twenty minutes slip by and there's still no sign of her.

This is unusual for her.

Where could she be?

"Maybe she's sick?" Jonathan offers.

"She never gets sick," I respond, getting out of the car.

"Where are you going, Everett?" Jonathan calls after me.

Ignoring his question, I open the diner's door, the bell chimes, signaling a customer's entry. "Welcome, sir. Sit wherever you'd like," the owner greets me from behind the counter.

"I'm not staying," I tell him. "The girl who usually works today, is she sick?"

"Kalyn? I had to let her go," he says, looking pained. "Business slowed, but since I let her go, it's almost non-existent."

I could have told him that. She was the only reason people continued coming in here daily.

"Is she at home?" I hold my breath waiting for his answer.

"I don't know," he replies sincerely. "I've tried getting a hold of her for weeks, and she isn't responding. If you reach her, let her know I want to offer her the job back."

"Yeah, I'll let her know. Thanks."

"Hey, what's your name?" Milo calls out to me. "If I hear from her first, I can let her know you stopped by."

"It's alright. I'll go track her down," I respond, turning to exit the diner. Returning to the SUV, Jonathan stares expectantly at me, awaiting an update. "Drive to her apartment."

"Is she sick?" he asks, confused.

"They had to let her go… I was gone, and she was let go. She's probubly been a mess," I feel my chest grow heavy, knowing I wasn't here to make her feel better.

Arriving at her apartment, we pull up in front of it. I notice that the curtains have changed, and there's the sound of a child playing and yelling inside. A man descends the stairs, and as he walks past my window, I roll it down and ask, "Excuse me, the girl who used to live there," gesturing towards her apartment, "did she move?"

He looks back to where I'm pointing. "Kalyn? The pig ass manager evicted her," he says, his voice tinged with irritation. "He made advances on her, she turned him down, and he had it out for her since then. Gotta go, man, laundry," he gestures to the overflowing laundry basket.

We drive to the main office, my chest thundering. I stride in, the manager quickly rising from his desk. "How can I help you, sir?" he asks, his voice trembling.

I march over, seize him by the throat, lift him up, and slam him against the wall. "You like hitting on women that don't want you?" I spit the words at him.

"I don't know what you're talking about," he mumbles.

"You evicted someone recently," my face inches from his.

"Kalyn?" he stutters. "She was behind on rent."

I turn and shove him in his chair, slamming his face into the pile of papers on his desk. "Look again," I hold his head down. "I think you will find she was never behind," I am seconds away from kicking the shit out of this scumbag. I don't even need to hear the details of what he tried to do to her. My mind is already filling in the gaps, and I'm having to use all of my self-restraint to not permanently harm him.

Without moving, he concedes, "Yes, you're right. She wasn't behind," both of us knowing she was in fact behind on her rent.

"*Exactly,*" *I lean down close. "If you pursue her in any way, whether hitting on her or thinking she still owes this dump any money, I will come back, and we can have a more… intimate conversation." I sneer at him. "Would you like that?"*

"*No sir,*" *his voice still trembling*

"*Bitch,*" *I say, smashing his head down into his desk again before walking out.*

Back in the SUV, I pound my palm against the dash in frustration. "Fuck!"

Jonathan remains silent.

"*Giles, she's disappeared. I need her located,*" *I frantically blurt out as Giles answers my call on the first ring.*

"*Yes, sir,*" *Giles responds via the SUV's speaker system.*

As we drive, I spot her friend Sam strolling down the sidewalk with earphones in. "Pull over," I direct Jonathan, turning to see Sam behind us. He complies instantly, and I leap out of the car before it is at a complete stop.

"*Hey,*" *I call to Sam as I approach him. "I'm looking for Kalyn."*

He removes his earbuds, "Sorry, what did you say?" holding them in each hand, appearing confused that a stranger is randomly approaching him on the street.

"*Kalyn, where can I find her?*" *I repeat, a sense of urgency in my voice.*

"*I don't know, man. Maybe tell her to reach out to me if you end up finding her,*" *he responds, sounding annoyed. "I've been calling and texting her constantly, and she's ghosted me," a hint of hurt in his voice.*

"*You have no clue where she might have gone?*" *My irritation growing. This fucking idiot calls himself her best friend, yet he has no idea where she went?*

"*No. If I did, do you really think I'd be aimlessly walking around, hoping by chance I run into her? I still call her every day, and she's been gone for a month,*" *he says pathetically.*

"*Have you called the police?*"

"*No, I didn't think of it,*" *he admits, but the realization that he probably should have called the police is settling in on him.*

"She's been missing for a month, and you didn't think of it?" I retort, anger bubbling up. "Your solution is to walk around like a fucking moron, hoping you run into her. What the fuck kind of logic is that?"

"Look, I don't know who you are, but I've tried getting a hold of her. If she wanted to be found, she would be found. Kalyn does whatever Kalyn wants," he says, putting his earbuds back in and walking off.

I return to the SUV, angrily instructing Jonathan once again to drive.

It doesn't make sense where she would have gone. If she got evicted and let go from her job, why did she not move in with Sam? For an hour, I struggle to focus on anything other than finding her.

When Giles's name appears on the SUV dashboard during an incoming call, I promptly answer it.

"Giles. Have you located her?"

Giles hesitates, and I urge, "Giles, did you find her?"

"I did, sir," he finally admits, still hesitant.

"Where is she?" my frustration growing.

"Sir, she's here," he says hesitantly.

"Here?" I question, uncertain about his meaning.

"At the mansion. She's a new hire, sir. A maid," he clarifies. Jonathan and I exchange shocked expressions.

"Get me home," I instruct him, and he understands my urgency and flattens the gas pedal.

CHAPTER
Twenty-Four

I try not to let Jenevieve's words affect me, but I'm extremely bothered. Although Jonah has never hurt me, her comments make me feel hurt by him. The fact that she claims I am living on borrowed time only fuels my disdain towards her. It makes me wonder, what if she is right? Losing Wyatt was an excruciating experience, my first true heartbreak. It took me years to heal from that pain. However, with Jonah, I fear that I wouldn't be able to survive such heartbreak. The mere thought of it makes my heart ache and fills me with utter dread. My heart would wither and fall from my chest.

Adding to the complexity is Jenevieve's affluent background and the friendship between Jonah's father and her father. Will they ever be able to accept me? Coming from a humble family, my life has been defined by struggle and sorrow. I simply don't believe I have the strength to endure another heartbreak.

These are the moments when adulthood loses its appeal.

I knock on Shay's door, finding her engrossed in typing on her laptop. She looks adorable with her pink glasses perched on her petite nose and her hair neatly braided into two pigtails. She relaxes in a chaise lounge chair reminiscent of the one I usually occupy in Maeva's office, only Shay's exudes more elegance. As I enter, she looks up and smiles.

"Hey," I walk towards her.

"Hi," she responds, sitting up and lowering her feet to the floor. She removes her glasses and puts them on the keyboard. "I was just finishing up some documents for Jonathan. Come in, hun," she invites, waving me over.

"I need someone to talk to," I admit, my tone filled with defeat.

"Of course!" she exclaims, setting her laptop aside and joining me on her bed.

"I'm here to vomit all my problems on you," I let out an exasperated sigh.

"There's no one else I'd rather have vomiting their problems all over me," she responds happily.

"It's about Mr. Everett," I begin. "Jonah," I correct myself. Her smile widens.

"You don't even know what I'm going to say," I reply playfully.

"Continue," she maintains her grin.

"I honestly don't even know where to start."

"Okay," Shay responds. "May I?" She asks permission to offer advice. "Mr. Everett is head over heels for you, and the way I see you looking at him, it is mutual." She pauses and adds, "Not to make this about myself, but you guys kind of gave me a complex after the other night. I've already told Jonathan he better step up his sex game. Mr. Everett was tossing you around that bed like a ragdoll. Damn, that was hot, Kal," theatrically rolling her eyes back. "And I've heard about his massive dick, but I wasn't expecting that," she widens her hands for emphasis.

Laughter spills out of me.

I ask the question knowing I am only going to hurt my feelings when she tells me the answer. Yet, I ask anyway. "Besides Jenevieve," I pause, "has anyone else here slept with him?"

Shay appears uncertain about how to respond.

"Who?" I ask, already sensing the answer in her hesitation that someone here has been intimate with him.

"Claire," she straightforwardly admits. "He got rid of everyone else, except Jenevieve and Claire. Or rather, Jenevieve ran everyone else off."

"Wow," I'm stunned. Claire is always busy tending to the horses, exercising them, and braiding their manes. She has always been pleasant towards those of us working in the stables, maintaining a quiet demeanor and keeping to herself. I can't even picture her and Jonah having that sort of relationship. "Why did he keep her around?" I question, feeling a sharp pang in my chest.

"She's excellent with the horses," Shay answers honestly. "And besides, she doesn't live here. Even if she did, you've got nothing to worry about, Kal, I think they had sex a few times and that was it. She never seemed upset afterward, and he never mentioned it," she reassures me.

I draw my knees into my chest, running my hands up and down my shins.

"What's this about? What's going on in that pretty little brain of yours?" she inquires, tucking my hair behind my ear, her hand lingers for a moment before she lowers it.

"Well," I begin, "Jenevieve decided to enlighten me on how she and Jonah used to fuck all the time. She even went as far as discussing their future marriage and the names of their future children, which their parents have apparently already chosen," I reveal irritated.

The idea of miniature versions of Jenevieve walking around sends shivers down my spine. But imagining those tiny people being miniature Jenevieve and Jonah's… I can barely stand the thought.

"Jenevieve is delusional," Shay remarks.

"She was sucking on Jonah's cock when he first saw me," I add, tinged with a disbelieving laugh.

"And she hasn't done it since," Shay remarks. "If she felt the need to tell you something intimate like that, it's because she's feeling threatened by your presence. The truth is dawning on her that her fantasy world is crumbling, and you make it harder for her to continue trying to entertain the thought."

"I'm so bothered by this," I admit. "Like, really bothered. What was the purpose of her telling me all that?" I question aloud.

"To make you feel precisely how you're feeling now, and it worked. Let me paint a picture for you: Jenevieve was a girl who had a crush on her best friend's older brother. He went off to college, and she graduated high school. Two years later, she purposely found a way to cross paths with him at a business conference just to reconnect. As a favor to his family, he hired her. She remains in his employment due to their family connection. Her parents are eager for a marriage between them because he's rich as fuck. I mean, who wouldn't want their daughter married to a sexy billionaire? If Mr. Everett truly wanted her, it would have already happened."

"What if I'm not good enough for him, or his family decides to never accept me?" I feel utterly deflated.

Her expression turns resolute. "First of all, absolutely not. Your worth is not something we are even going to question. You two are equals. And secondly, I am going to tell you what my mom once told me: 'If a thought begins with 'what if,' it's an intrusive thought. Meaning, it's not coming from you.'" She gives my hand a reassuring squeeze, hoping her words offer some comfort.

"I'm going to have to start charging my intrusive thoughts rent. They're taking up a lot of brain space," I rest my head on

Shay's shoulder letting out a sigh. "Does the thought of Jonathan being with other women not bother you? Like past women?"

"I will straight-up pussy punch any bitch I see that has ever been with him," she responds, causing me to sit up and look at her before we both burst into laughter.

"Okay, so this rage I am feeling is normal?" I ask, still smiling.

"Hun, if you weren't bothered by the thought of Mr. Everett being with other women, I'd question if you even have feelings for him."

JONAH IS IN HIS OFFICE WITH GILES, JONATHAN, AND DAME, THE MAN I saw from security during the incident with the intruders. They are all seated in front of the large windows. As I enter, the lively banter dies down.

"Hey, Kal," Jonathan greets me with a smile.

I approach Jonah and stand in front of him. "You've had sex with other women," I state, placing my hand on my hip and popping it out for emphasis.

He shifts in his seat, smiling at me. "Hi, baby."

Shay walks in and takes a seat on Jonathan's lap, wrapping her arm around his neck.

"You've had sex with other women," I repeat, staring at him, waiting for his response.

"It feels like I'm missing the entire conversation that led to this," he comments, looking at me and then at Shay.

She raises her hands in an innocent gesture, humor dancing in her eyes. "I'm not the one who had sex with other women using your dick."

Jonah leans forward, reaching for me. He wraps his arms around each of my thighs, lifting me onto his lap so I am straddling him.

"I..." Jonah pauses, searching for words.

Dame playfully whispers, "Don't say another word until your attorney arrives."

The room erupts into laughter.

"Do I need to get rid of all of them to make you happy, baby?" he asks sincerely.

"Maybe," I reply, crossing my arms in front of me. This action pushes my breasts together, and I watch his eyes immediately wander down.

Jonathan joins in, "I didn't even know he was interested in women."

"I wasn't," Jonah's eyes fill with desire as he stares a moment longer. "I've never been attracted to a woman until you," a smile playing on his lips as he gently brushes his fingertips against my cheek.

"Actually, now that I think about it, YOU have had sex with other women too," Shay remarks, looking at Jonathan.

"Whoa, whoa, whoa," he raises his hands defensively. "I'm not the one on trial here. Everett is," he points a finger in our direction.

"No, we're discussing you now," she taunts.

"I don't think I like this," Jonathan protests, laughing.

"I prefer this much more," Jonah snickers, his eyes fixed on Jonathan.

"Oh no no no, Mr. You're not off the hook," I poke his chest.

"But, Jonathan," Jonah interjects, redirecting attention to Jonathan.

"Both of you," I say, looking back and forth between them. "How dare you not think about us when you were having sexual relations with other women before you knew us," I tease.

"Gross," Jonah says, feigning a shudder at the mention of other women.

"I was thinking the same thing. The thought made me so sick to my stomach I couldn't even find the words to vocalize it, I almost hurled," Jonathan adds.

"Listen, Linda," I jokingly say to Jonah, "I'm here to be mad at you. But you're making it really difficult."

I feel him flexing in his pants, indicating he's aroused. He looks at me with a seductive expression and my heart races.

Biting my lower lip, I draw it into my mouth, and a wave of intense emotions passes between us as we lock eyes.

"I believe it's time for us to call it a night," Giles suddenly suggests, sensing the shift in the atmosphere between Jonah and me.

Everyone else catches on, and they begin to stand as well.

"Your room or mine?" Jonathan asks, patting Shay's butt as she climbs off his lap.

"Actually, you guys stay. We're going to bed," Shay declares, gripping my hand and pulling me to my feet, leading us towards the door. "Have a good night, guys. Reflect on past choices and perhaps regret them," she smiles at me as we leave. I steal a final glance at Jonah and notice his mouth hanging open in disbelief, his hand pressed against his hard member.

"That was absolutely thrilling," I exclaim as we walk back to our rooms, linked arm in arm.

"I bet Giles is still back there, trying to scoop their jaws off the floor as we speak," looking back towards where they are.

I head to my room, with her following closely behind. "What are you doing?" I ask, my cheeks still hurting from the laughter.

"Sleeping with you. You know damn well both of them will try to sneak into our rooms tonight, attempting to have their way with us. And they don't get to tonight," she states, coming in, locking the door behind us, and settling onto the bed.

"Have I told you lately you're the best?"

"So are you," she responds sincerely, turning around and fluffing the pillow behind her.

We fall asleep in each other's arms, only to wake in the morning on opposite sides of the bed. As soon as my alarm goes off, I groan and quickly silence it. I lightly give Shay's butt a spank, urging her to get up.

"If I had known you woke up looking like such an angel, I would have insisted we share a bed every night just so I can see your angelic self right when I open my eyes," I smile at her, noticing her bed head.

"I know, it's hot, right?" She waggishly puckers her lips in a kiss and rubs her messy hair. Heading to my bathroom, she bursts into laughter when she sees it for herself.

After getting dressed and ready for work, we head out right on time to join our usual line. Jenevieve barks her orders and casually mentions that Mr. Everett left this morning on business. Although it wasn't necessary for her to share this information, it bothers me that she knew before I did, and that I'm finding out from her. It also makes me wonder if I could be the reason he left and if he was upset with me because of last night.

"Do you think they left because they're upset with us?" I whisper to Shay, my stomach feeling uneasy.

Shay responds nonchalantly. "Who knows? Maybe they can have a good cry together and come back feeling better." Her quirky remarks always manage to lift my spirits.

Everyone begins to scatter to their assigned duties, but I can't focus on a single word Jenevieve had said. My mind is consumed with thoughts of upsetting Jonah. However, as soon as she stomps in front of me, my mind goes completely silent.

"Care to take a guess where you'll be today?" Her face twists into a wicked sneer.

"Aren't you too old to be playing games with 'Little girls'?" I reply bluntly.

Her eyes widen before narrowing into thin slits. "You'll be where you belong... with the animals," her nostrils flare. "Now, shoo."

She is such a pussy. She waits until Jonah is gone before sending me back to the stables. Little does she know, I've been itching to confront Brad and give him a piece of my mind.

As morning passes, I still haven't seen him. When I return from lunch, my first mission is to go find him.

Finally, I spot him fiddling with horse saddles. I walk over to him, leaning my back against the wall next to him. Closing my eyes, I tilt my head back and lightly touch my throat in an intimate gesture. I let out heavy, panting moans, "Ahh... ahhh... Kalyn," before abruptly stopping and locking eyes with him. "Who do you think did it better?" I ask, challenging him.

His eyes brighten. "I require an immediate replay so I can provide a truthful response."

"How could you sleep with Amber? You're a repulsive pig. Did you know she hates my guts because of you? What kind of big-ass loser moans someone else's name during sex? Are you dumb, heartless, or all of the above?" I vent my anger.

"Are there any other options?"

"You tell me. What do you call that disgusting behavior?" I question.

"An accident."

"An accident? I'll show you an accident when I accidentally stab you with a manure fork," I snap.

"Kalyn, I'm sorry—"

"Oh no. No. You don't get to say my name. You've already said it too many times with other women. How does that even happen?" My anger escalates.

"Brain fog," he replies plainly.

"Brain fog? You are going to blame that on brain fog? Please elaborate," I gesture openly as if signaling he has the floor.

"Sex feels good."

"I know it does. But that doesn't explain how stupid shit falls out of your mouth while having it." Having a conversation with him is like talking to a toddler.

"I don't know, Kalyn. I was having sex and you popped in my head, and I guess your name slipped out," he says as if it weren't a big deal.

"How does another woman pop in your head?"

"Sorry, slip of the tongue. You're on my mind a lot, and your name is the name I think about when I'm cumming."

His lips curve up in a wicked smirk as the words come out of his mouth.

"I literally want to rip your lips off your face and stomp them all over in the dirt."

His head falls back, and he lets out a belly laugh.

As I narrow my eyes to thin slits, I fold my arms across my chest, anticipating a response. But his amusement only persists, and my frustration only grows.

"Who hurt you so bad, you became such a lousy human?"

"It's just sex, Kalyn. People have it every day. Everyone knows I don't want anything but sex. So, they can't really cry about it when all I take is sex."

"Why Amber?"

"I didn't intentionally say your name with just Amber. Ask the last five people I've slept with, they probably all have similar stories." He is acting like this is some sort of joke.

"You're a loser. You know that? I hope you end up alone and miserable." I go to walk off and then turn back to him. "On second thought, I think you and Jenevieve would be the perfect match. Never speak to me again," I storm out of the stables.

I spent the entirety of the remaining day feeling bad for evidently upsetting Jonah. I contemplate various ways to mend the situation. By the end of the day, I've sifted through my emotions and have come to the realization that if he's genuinely upset, then he can be upset. And if he's simply busy with work, then that's okay too.

Once the workday concludes, I return to my room to shower. I scrub my body diligently, wanting to rid myself of the lingering horse manure smell. Afterward, I apply lotion to my entire body and make my way to my closet in search of something comfortable to wear before I head to Shay's room to see what she's doing. I slip on a rose gold silk nightgown with a daring slit up the right side, extending provocatively up to my hip, paired with matching silk panties. I love how it feels on my skin. It hugs my body perfectly. While it's not transparent, it doesn't leave much to the imagination. The fabric is soft yet incredibly thin, and I can't deny feeling sexy in it. It's peculiar, considering I'm surrounded by other women, and it's meant to wear to bed.

I make my way to Shay's room to show off my nighty and find both Shay and Lilly are excitedly wearing new pajamas as well. Shay's pajamas consist of a matching silk top and shorts set, while Lilly's are baggy cotton pajama pants with a button shirt.

"Well, well, well," I exclaim with excitement. "Looks like we're having a pajama party." I jump into Shay's bed to join them.

Shay smirks at me, "Hello, boobies," wagging her eyebrows mischievously.

I lie back on her bed, running my fingers along the fabric on my stomach, "Have you ever felt pajamas this soft in your entire life?"

"I'm not sure," Shay reaches over to trail her hand across my stomach. "Nope, that's incredibly soft."

Shay turns her attention to Lilly. "Anything new with Theo? Anything new *between* you and Theo?" She emphasizes the last part, knowing that Lilly is well-informed about everything regarding Theo.

Theo is the go-to guy in the mansion for fixing or replacing things. He has been working for Jonah for as long as anyone can remember, and Lilly has had a crush on him since she started three years ago. He's usually quite serious, but I've noticed that he does have a sense of humor every now and then.

He often wears a ball cap, which initially led me to believe he might be hiding thinning hair. However, I've observed that he always removes it whenever a lady addresses him, which I interpret as a gesture of respect. His thick black hair is long enough for him to run his fingers through it straight back before placing his hat back on. He also keeps his face shaved—a theme in this house that people have whispered about—if Jonah has a new haircut, all male staff inevitably follow suit and get a similar haircut. When Jonah grows stubble, the rest of the staff grows stubble. I wonder if the hair is a work requirement or if people just want to emulate him?

"We waved at each other this morning when he was changing out light bulbs. He dropped his towel, and I picked it up and handed it to him when he came down from his ladder to get it," she beams as she reminisces on the moment they shared.

"Girrrrl," I happily draw out, "Did you literally just say Theo proposed to you today?"

"It appears he did, huh," she playfully retorts. "What about you, Kal? Who has caught the attention of those pretty green eyes?" She leans on her elbow, flashing a smile and batting her lashes at me.

We are mid-giggles when Shay's bedroom door suddenly bursts open, and Jonah walks in.

"Jonah!" I exclaim sitting up, audibly confused why he is here instead of away on business like Jenevieve mentioned earlier. He locks eyes with me and strides over to the bed with a low growl in his throat, swiftly scooping me up and putting me over his shoulder.

"Ladies," he states curtly as he walks out of the room with me dangling over his shoulder.

As we make our way out, Amber emerges from her room and stops dead in her tracks, mouth hanging open in astonishment. Other girls in the hallway stop their conversations as we pass by. I'm sure this sight looks odd, with our boss carrying me down the hall, my long hair cascading past his waist. I can feel the curious eyes following us until we completely disappear from sight.

He carries me slung over his shoulder through the mansion, up the grand staircase, and into a part of the mansion I've never been to before.

He briefly pauses in front of two massive double doors, gripping one doorknob, heaving the door open. It leads into an enormous bedroom. The intoxicating aroma of his captivating scent fills the room.

It's *his* room.

It exudes elegance, cleanliness, and a distinctly masculine ambiance, covered in black and silver. The bed, the largest I've ever seen, undoubtedly tailored to accommodate his huge size, is neatly made. He comes to a stop just next to it and lowers me to my feet. I feel a mixture of excitement and nervousness.

I stand there, uncertain of what I should be doing. However, my unsettling thoughts are quickly interrupted as he unbuckles his belt, creating a sharp whipping sound as he removes it. He smiles and effortlessly lifts me off the ground once again, this time cradling my ass with both of his large hands, while my legs instinctively wrap around his waist and my arms encircle his neck. He crawls onto the bed, making his way towards the pillows, laying me down and positioning himself so he is straddling my body, raising my hands above my head. I am so entranced by the breathtaking man above me I don't realize he is tying my hands above my head until he starts moving back down the bed.

"Can you move your hands?" his sultry voice fills the silence.

I tug at the fabric that binds my wrists, and while my arms have enough slack to move comfortably, they are tied just tight enough I can't get my hands free if I try, but it doesn't hurt. As I tug at the fabric again, I notice the incredible smile forming on his face again. Each time causing a nervous flutter in my stomach.

Maintaining eye contact, he undoes the top buttons of his shirt, each one revealing a tantalizing glimpse of his sculpted body underneath. As he brings his hands to the collar of his shirt, he effortlessly removes it, revealing his enticing body. The sight of him causes my mouth to water, and I have to swallow to prevent myself from choking on my saliva.

He positions his hands on either side of the mattress, inches away from my chest, his intense gaze fixed on me. A flush creeps into my cheeks as his eyes roam over my body, igniting a desire within me. I feel his arousal growing while being restrained in his slacks.

He releases a low, aroused exhale, his palm pressing firmly against the bulge in his pants. "You," he breathes out huskily. "Drive me absolutely wild."

With deliberate slowness, he begins to move downward, his gaze fixated on where my nightgown falls at my ankles. Placing a hand on each of my feet, he glides them up my legs, ensuring the silk material rises with his slow movements. Pausing as his hands reach my panties, making them visible, he savors the sight before him, his breath hitching. Leaning in, he nips at the fabric just above my slit, eliciting a sharp inhale of breath from me.

With measured intent, he continues sliding my nightgown up my stomach, gradually revealing more of my skin with each languid movement. His lips leave a trail of kisses along my exposed flesh, igniting anticipation. Halting just below my breasts, he pauses, his gaze smoldering with desire.

My heart races so intensely it feels as if the pulsating rhythm echoes throughout the entire house. Instead of freeing my breasts from the confines of my nightgown, he teases me by nibbling at the hardened peaks through the fabric, sending shivers down my spine and prompting me to tug at my restraints, unable to contain a whimpered moan of pleasure.

I sense the curve of his lips forming as he switches to the other breast, lavishing it with the same tantalizing attention. My head instinctively tilts backward, surrendering to the overwhelming sensations as my eyes flutter closed. All coherent thoughts dissolve into a haze.

At last, he lifts my nightgown to expose my breasts fully, and in an instant, his mouth hungrily descends upon them, his lips and tongue eagerly lashing and sucking.

I let out a soft moan, needing more of him. Ever so slowly, he raises my nightgown, stopping when it covers my eyes. "I can't see," I whisper, my breath catching in my throat.

"That's the point." His hands glide down my body, starting from my neck, caressing my breasts, and then trailing off, leaving shivers in their wake. Having my hands tied is a new experience, and it's almost suffocating not being able to free myself. With him on top of me, my chances of getting out of this position are zero percent. And now, with him covering my eyes, I feel disoriented. Even though I know I'm safe with him, feeling trapped is making my palms sweat.

Even though my vision is almost completely obscured, I catch a glimpse of him through the bottom of the fabric. He keeps his gaze fixed on my body, his chest rising and falling heavily, as he unbuttons and unzips his pants. Once he removes them, I can see the outline of his length and girth through his boxer briefs.

"It looks bigger than before… It won't fit," I gasp, my voice barely audible.

He grins and confidently declares, "It will." With that, he removes his boxers, revealing himself in all his glory.

He slowly leans down over me and presses one of his knees between my closed legs, and they instantly part for him. He pushes his knee into the back of my knee, causing it to bend as he continues pushing it out until he has enough space to do the same thing with the other leg. As my legs widen, creating enough space for him to position himself between them, he trails his thumb along the outside of my silk panties, tracing my throbbing slit until he reaches my soaked entrance. Pausing momentarily, he glides his thumb back up, each motion making my panties wetter. My hips move, yearning to shove my body harder against his finger.

"Do you like that?" he whispers.

"Yes," I moan.

Shifting his body on the bed, he smoothly slides his knees beneath my legs, guiding them up to straddle him. Positioning himself slightly over me, one fist rests on the bed while the other confidently grasps his shaft, pushing the tip against my entrance, the only barrier being the fabric of my panties. I imagine he can feel just how soaked they are. He begins rubbing deliberate circles around my entrance, exerting just enough pressure to push the fabric inward half an inch, sending waves of pleasure rippling through me. It feels so incredible I roll my head leisurely side to side with each circle he draws. I even have a moment of clarity where I tell myself if I don't stop moving my head side to side, I am going to rub all my hair off in the back.

He completes another full circle before trailing his tip up the fabric covering my slit. My panties are so wet that he effortlessly slips between my lips, pushing the fabric in with him. Reaching my clit, he applies added pressure on that sweet spot, tracing it several times before descending back down. Once again, he circles my entrance before slowly gliding back up to my swollen bud.

I can't discern his breathing amidst my own heavy panting, but the urge to release a loud moan overtakes me. He guides his tip back down to my entrance, exerting pressure against the fabric before sliding back up. This time, he slowly slips the tip beneath my panties, gradually inserting the entirety of his length between my folds. With the palm of his hand, he pushes into his shaft, filling every inch of my slit and then some with his thick member, causing me to fully arch my back off the bed.

"Oh, God," I gasp.

"Just call me Jonah," he whispers playfully, as he sensually glides his length up and down me slowly. Finding a steady rhythm, he carefully lowers on top of me, ensuring he doesn't put his full weight on me. His left arm wraps around mine, intertwining our fingers. His other hand explores my curves, stopping at my hip and sliding his hand under my backside, cupping and squeezing. Nibbling at my earlobe, he trails down my neck, alternating between bites and licks, all while continuing his tantalizing movements along my slit.

"Jonah," I moan, craving him to fill me. He withdraws himself, and I feel the softest brush of his finger down my slit, causing my hips to arch towards him. I usually love his touch in any way he gives it, but right now, the gentleness of it is driving me crazy. I had a craving last night that went unfulfilled, and now I ache to satisfy it.

"Please," I pull on the restraints, trying to bring my hand to his and force him to touch me.

My plea lands on deaf ears because he continues trailing his finger lightly up my slit, barely giving me anything and then trailing it toward my center, almost making it to my entrance before he trails back up to my clit, circling it softly and doing the same thing, working his way back down.

"Jonah," I bite out, frustrated.

He pushes the tip of his finger into my entrance and my mouth clamps shut, waiting for the pleasure of him inside me. But he doesn't give me any more, he continues drawing slow circles and pulling out.

"Quit fucking with me," my eyes begin to prickle with tears.

He ignores me and repeats the same movements two more times, slowly circling my clit with no pressure and lazily drawing down, barely penetrating me.

"What the fuck are you doing?" I snap.

"You don't like it?" his voice is almost mocking.

"No!" I tug on the restraints, hoping maybe my anger will free me from them and I can finger my own damn self. But they hold steady.

"Hmm," his voice rumbles.

"Untie me."

His finger pushes in to the second knuckle, still not deep enough. "You're so wet, baby," he continues circling. "I'm so horny," his teeth sink into my hip bone.

"Then stop fucking around and fuck me."

"I should since I've had blue balls since that stunt you pulled last night."

... So, that's what this is about. Shay and me leaving them last night. He's messing with me now.

"I'm sorry," the first tear springs free, not because I feel bad for what we did, but because I am so sexually frustrated.

"Are you though?"

"Not as sorry as you will be," I retort.

"Are you threatening me, baby?" he rips my panties off, eliciting a gasp from me at the suddenness of the fabric being torn away from my body, and his shaft pressing into my center with no barrier holding him back.

My body yearns for more, and a sensuous moan falls from my lips.

"Did you threaten me?" he murmurs as he thrusts his pelvis into me.

"Yes," I moan in response.

He can interpret that however he wants because right now, the only thing I'm panting about is how good he feels.

With a urgency, he thrusts his hips in and out of me until he is fully submerged. Each thrust causes my breasts to sway, eliciting a deep growl from his throat. Then, the bite of his teeth on my nipple sends a surge of excitement rushing through me, causing my back to arch off the bed.

He hungrily forces his mouth to mine, and I kiss him with increased fervor. He reciprocates with equal passion, causing my hips to arch toward him despite the constraint of his size. The sensation is overpowering, his fullness stretching me until it feels like my hips are being pulled apart. The pleasure is so intense, my moans audibly ring out.

"You liked that huh?" He breathlessly grins, his lips seeking mine eagerly. Our mouths move urgently against each other, eliciting a moan from him. I tug at the restraints, yearning to wrap my arms around his neck, but they hold me securely in place.

"Fuck," he moans, barely withdrawing and pushing back in impossibly deeper. My body eagerly welcomes him, tightening and pulling at his cock to penetrate me more. "Fuck, baby," his voice trembles as he continues to push in and slowly pull out, gradually increasing the depth each time.

"Deeper, Jonah," I moan, as I thrust my hips against him. "Deeper," I plead. Granting my request, he withdraws slightly before plunging himself completely inside me. It's mind-blowing. "Holy shit," I cry out, feeling an orgasm building.

Reaching down, sliding his arm under my leg, lifting it to his side, and holding it against him, he thrusts in and out of me. He moves with such precision—every thrust he hits places inside me I never knew existed. Without missing a beat, he releases my pinned leg and unties my hands, swiftly removing my nightgown the rest of the way, tossing it to the floor.

I was tugging on the restraints so tightly I didn't even realize until he freed my hands. I can feel the tingling sensation as the blood rushes back, circulating through my veins. Suddenly, I feel nervous now that I can see him after being blindfolded the whole time.

A flicker of excitement crosses his face as he pulls me onto his lap, pressing me against the headboard, my body propped on his thighs as he drives into me from this angle.

I firmly grasp the headboard above me, using one hand for support, while my other arm encircles his neck. As he thrusts in and out, I rhythmically bounce on his lap, synchronizing our movements together. The sensation is so contradicting; he is going painfully deep, yet I slam down on him hard repeatedly because it feels so good.

His arm securely embraces my waist, while his other hand rests atop mine above us. Each motion he makes feels methodical and intimate. Our hands remain in close proximity, and he attentively avoids applying any weight that might cause discomfort.

My hips gyrate on him, allowing his shaft to fully rearrange my insides, and it feels incredible. His eyes close, and his mouth parts as he pants, while I continue my tantalizing rhythm of my hips.

Beads of sweat form on his hairline, trickling down his face, and his chest glistens with perspiration. I watch as a droplet of sweat glides down his cheek, and I instinctively lick it away. I'm uncertain if it catches him off guard or arouses him, but his eyes flicker open, and we lock gazes. Urgently he lashes his lips against mine, while he resumes thrusting in and out of me. I tightly wrap my legs around his waist, desperately trying to keep him completely inside. Every aspect of him feels incredibly pleasurable.

As he increases the intensity of his thrusts, I release my hold on the headboard, and encircle his neck with both arms. My head tilts back, and I moan in pure ecstasy.

Slowing his pace, he asserts himself with commanding thrusts, filling me completely and maintaining the intimate connection of our bodies. Gripping my hips, he rocks them back and forth along his buried length. In the dim light of the room, our moans ring out and our breathing becomes heavy.

Normally I would find it awkward and uncomfortable to sweat during sex. But I would gladly lap up every drop of sweat off this man. Gliding against each other, with the sheen of perspiration coating both of our bodies, I find it incredibly sexy.

Hours seem to pass, yet time stands still when I'm with him. I'm certain I won't be able to walk tomorrow. I am almost positive our intense friction would have already dried my arousal but him orgasming twice already has kept renewing the slickness.

"Jonah!" I exclaim, frantically scratching at his back as the impending orgasm intensifies. "Jonah," I moan again unsure of what I'm begging him for.

"Cum for me, baby," he grunts, rocking my hips on his shaft.

My body tenses as I feel it reaching the edge, and in a surge of intensity, my climax erupts, constricting and releasing around his solid member. My body vibrates and I pinch my eyes shut as he continues forcing my hips to rock on him. The pleasure becoming almost too much to handle.

He slows his movements as the ripples of bliss subside. He flashes a wicked grin, pulling me off his shaft, my legs trembling uncontrollably as he flips me on the bed, repositioning me on all fours, grabbing my hips and pulling them back toward him as he enters me once more. I moan out as he fills me, my head falling back as I take his full length. He laces his fingers through the back of my hair, squeezing and pulling me onto my knees towards him, drawing me into his chest.

"Jonah," I cry out in pleasure. His hand finds its way to my throat, and he squeezes. It's a sensation I've never experienced before, and initially, it startles me. But as he tightens his grip on my hair and thrusts into me, a rush of pleasure washes over me, overpowering any fear. I feel my face flush with heat, yet I can still breathe, even with his hand limiting some of my oxygen. When he eases the pressure on my throat, he turns my head toward him, our mouths meeting in a passionate kiss, and our tongues move together in a frenzy.

His hand ventures down between my legs, skillfully circling my clit with the fingers that were just at my throat. I don't know what has gotten into me, but I want his hand back on my throat. Taking control, I guide his hand from my hair to my neck, tilting my head back so he can position his grip back under my chin, as I intertwine my fingers with his, resting my head against his shoulder. I can feel his lips curve up at my boldness as he turns his face towards me.

"You want me to choke you again, baby?" he asks as he begins to squeeze. "You look so pretty when your face is red," he pants into my ear before releasing his grip.

I gasp for air as he releases my throat and guides me forward on the bed, his body following mine. My legs are spread wide, my lower back arched as his body folds over mine, and he thrusts into me from behind. I want to feel my stomach to confirm he is actually penetrating as deep as it feels, because this angle feels like he is puncturing my chest cavity. My brain must be in a euphoric state because no pain receptors are alerting me to the trauma he must be causing on my insides. Instead, my body draws him in deeper.

Propping himself on his forearm, he secures his grip on my throat again, turning my face towards his. He presses his lips to mine, squeezing my neck again, moans still managing to escape my lips as I feel another orgasm growing.

"Cum for me, baby," he pants in my ear, his voice low and husky.

I feel his release as he drives into me hard, his hand on my throat squeezing even tighter as he continues thrusting. "Fuck, baby," he groans, his pace quickening as he goes deeper. My back arches, every nerve electrified as the intensity peaks, my body pulsating as my orgasm erupts out of me again. Muffled moans ring out as he releases my throat, pushing me flat onto the bed as he thrusts quicker in and out of me, his cock filling me with his seed, sending waves of pleasure coursing through me until I'm left lying there convulsing with the aftershocks of my release.

He remains buried inside of me, his weight pressing down on my back as we both lie there, breathless and panting. I can feel a subtle shift in the bed, and he produces a towel from somewhere. It appears he was prepared for this little rendezvous.

As he withdraws from me, he delicately places the towel beneath me, anticipating the inevitable release of fluid that will seep out.

"We wouldn't have to go through this extra effort if you used a condom, Mr. Everett," I continue laying there with my eyes closed.

His teeth gently bite my butt. "What have I said about you addressing me like that?" he questions, his words followed by a slap where his teeth just were.

I relish the feel of his hand against my skin, reveling in the lingering sting it leaves behind. Yet, I can't ignore the warm trickle of his essence leaking out of me.

"I'm just saying, all of that could be contained in a condom," I remark teasingly.

"I don't want to wear a condom," he lays on his side next to me, his fingers tracing exquisite patterns along my back, sending goosebumps rippling across my skin.

"You'll wish you put one on when we end up with a surprise," I grin, my body growing heavier as relaxation seeps in, my eyes too heavy to open.

"I'm trying really hard to put a surprise in your belly," he says playfully, kissing my shoulder.

"You'll be a good daddy." My words coming out slow through a yawn.

"And you'll be the most amazing mommy… in nine months," I sense his grin as he shifts closer to me.

I want to respond by saying I would love nothing more, but sleep creeps in and takes me with it.

CHAPTER
Twenty-Five

JONATHAN

Everett warned his mother would be back to scold him some more after he announced to everyone he and Kal are fucking. I just hoped I didn't have to be involved when she showed up.

Mrs. Everett charges through the house, heading straight for Everett's room, where I know he and Kal are most likely fucking. The confirmation comes as we approach the door, and the unmistakable sounds of their moans, intertwined with explicit screams ringing out.

"Harder, Jonah," as the thrusting sound of skin-on-skin contact radiates through the door. "Harder," she screams again, only this time even louder.

Trying to divert Mrs. Everett's attention, I propose, "Mrs. Everett, why don't we go wait in his office?" I suggest hoping she will accept the invitation to get the fuck away from this door.

Unyielding, she refuses, determined to confront Everett directly. "I am not moving until I speak with my son," she seethes, each word spat out with intense conviction.

"Fuck, baby, you're so tight," Everett moans. "Ride me, just like that... oh, fuck," he continues, accompanied by Kal's subdued moans.

The explicit sounds persist, reverberating through the closed door. Struggling to find a solution, I grapple with diverting Mrs. Everett's attention downstairs. The sex sounds coming from behind these doors is undoubtedly the last thing any mother wants to hear in the current situation.

"You like it when I fill you with my cum, baby?" Everett remarks, the pace of his thrusts quickening and Kal's screams intensifying.

With those words, Mrs. Everett's eyes widen in shock, and an unmistakable fury emanates from her. The idea of Everett potentially impregnating Kalyn has her seething. In a burst of anger, she lunges for the door handle, but I swiftly step in front of the door, determined to prevent her from entering. Standing tall, I loom over her, steadfast in my commitment to keep her out.

"Move aside, Jonathan!" she scolds me sternly, waving her hand in a dismissive gesture.

"Yes, Jonah, just like that!" Kal screams again.

"You take my cock so good," Everett groans, audibly gritting his teeth. Mrs. Everett looks at me angrily, "You don't want to test my patience, Jonathan."

"That's it, baby, take my cum in your tight pussy," as she moans out her orgasm loudly, with him following moments later.

I stand in front of the door, vigilantly blocking her from entering. She patiently waits outside, while the sounds of laughter and hushed conversation dominate the bedroom. Mrs. Everett's impatience becomes apparent, and I fear she might erupt into screams. Swiftly, I send a text to Everett, alerting him that I am currently blocking the entrance to his room to prevent his mother from entering. His phone emits a single beep, and I discern the sound of him picking it up from his nightstand. Subsequently, hushed conversations ensue from inside the room, accompanied by the hurried pitter-patter of Kal's tiny feet rushing to the bathroom.

"I believe it's a good idea for us to head to Everett's office," I suggest, uneasy at the thought of her entering the room where Everett was just balls deep in Kal. She responds with silence as if my words are not directed at her.

Shortly after, Everett forcefully swings open his bedroom door, and I quickly step aside without a chance to exchange words with him. Mrs. Everett immediately begins scolding him.

"Bring her out here," Mrs. Everett seethes upon seeing Everett.

He lingers in the doorway, jeans hanging low on his hips, pulling a T-shirt over his head. Her eyes widen with fury as she notices the bite marks on his chest and neck. "There's no convincing me now that she's worth anything more than that disgusting mouth she was just using," she hisses at him.

Unfazed, he walks past her down the hall, prompting her to follow him. She continues scolding all the way down the hall as they vanish down a flight of stairs.

Entering the bedroom, I head toward the slightly cracked bathroom door. Peering inside, I don't spot Kal. Pushing the door open, I step into the spacious bathroom and make my way to the extensive walk-in closet. There, I find her dressed, seated on a chair beside the center island dresser. Leaning against the door frame, I gaze down at her as she sits cross-legged, playing with her fingers. It's evident she's engaged in a silent internal struggle. I don't want her upset, knowing that the only thing she's guilty of is making my best friend happier than I have ever seen him in all our lives.

"I couldn't hear a thing through the door," I reassure her with a lie, hoping to lift her spirits.

She gazes at me, seemingly searching for the truth. "Mrs. Everett couldn't hear Jonah and me having sex?" she asks, her shoulders tense until I assure her once more. While I don't condone lying, I choose not to disclose this minute detail to spare her additional pain.

"Not a peep," I grin.

A sigh of relief escapes her. "I probably would have died."

Returning her smile, I'm aware that she would be embarrassed to discover just how much we could hear. I can only imagine the discomfort of not being liked by your partner's mom. Adding the knowledge of being heard during sex would undoubtedly compound the awkwardness.

We lapse into silence, and then she confesses, "We get carried away sometimes with our dirty talk," smiling innocently.

"Don't we all," I sheepishly respond.

Her smile lingers for a moment before fading away. "What am I not seeing with Jenevieve? There must be something. I mean, Jonah's family is smitten with her, his mother is here yelling at him because he wants a sexual relationship with me. So, what am I missing?" She seeks answers I can't provide.

The truth is, Jenevieve has always been difficult. Even during her time with Jonah, she treated everyone like shit, and her behavior escalated after Jonah ended their relationship. It was as if she believed she could justify being a bitch to everyone as a means to alleviate the self-inflicted misery caused by her actions, holding onto the hope that Jonah would eventually come back to her.

"You're not missing anything. What you witness is precisely what Everett has always seen," I assure her, recognizing that my words may not bring much comfort. Jenevieve possesses a demeanor that has constantly made her feel superior to others. Moreover, she harbors a belief that she and Everett are destined to be together, though I don't know how much Kal knows about Jenevieve and Everett's past, and I'm not about to get tangled in that mess.

"Jonah's family will never accept me, will they?" she asks, and I empathize with the reasons behind her concerns. She cares deeply for Everett and the prospect of his family not accepting her bothers her.

I push myself away from the wall, prepared to make my exit. "To be perfectly honest, I don't believe they have much affection for me either. Their bond is strong, and it seems to extend exclusively to their tight-knit family," I admit, acknowledging the undeniable truth of the matter. She falls silent and pulls her legs to her chest, wrapping her arms around them as if to hug herself.

"Alright, I think I'll go find Shay," I stare a moment longer at her. "And Kal, you have one thing very wrong. Everett doesn't just want a sexual relationship with you. He wants a relationship with everything that comes with it." Determining she probably could use some alone time; I step out of the doorway and head out.

CHAPTER
Twenty-Six

KALYN

I sit on Jonah's desk with my legs crossed, as he leans back in his chair, holding a pen, and pressing it to his lip.

"What about a wombat!" I enthusiastically suggest. We're brainstorming the most unique animals.

"No way!" he disagrees. "Why a wombat?" His gorgeous face mixed with confusion.

"I feel like it's pretty obvious. They poop cubes! Literally cubes. Then use the cubes to mark their territory, I don't know if they actually do, but they could probably even build their house out of their own poopsies," I say, amazed, my hands gesturing as if unveiling some astonishing revelation.

"That's tight," Jonah responds, leaning forward in his chair and typing on his computer, pulling up wombats. "His house would definitely smell like shit," he jokes.

Laughter erupts between us until a throat is cleared, causing our amusement to subside. He looks up from his computer and I turn to look toward the door where his mother stands.

"I need a word, son," she says curtly.

"No, we are good—" he begins.

"Actually, I need to go to the restroom. I'll come back," I interject, climbing off his desk. As I attempt to leave, he grabs my hand, pulls it to his mouth, and kisses my knuckle, giving me a reassuring smile when he releases it.

Mrs. Everett keeps her head straight ahead, yet her eyes follow me as I walk away, disdain etched across her face. Jonathan said they didn't hear anything yesterday but I have a nagging feeling that they certainly would have heard something. Especially with how quickly Jonah left the room and was gone for over an hour afterward.

She spent the night and I knew she would be leaving today. So, I shouldn't be surprised she is here now. I am just embarrassed that she knows what we were doing.

"Mrs. Everett," I offer a polite nod as I pass by, but she offers no signs of acknowledging my words.

Exiting Jonah's office, I leave the door partially open, mirroring the way he had it when I initially entered. I prefer leaving things as they were set by someone else.

Shay stands on the other side of the door, her finger to her lips, signaling for me to be quiet and listen.

"What are you doing?" I mouth to her, not expecting to see her standing there.

"WE are eavesdropping," she states.

"You can't be serious, Jonah," we hear her scolding. "She is only after your money."

Shay and I exchange wide-eyed glances. Given our circumstances, anyone might easily jump to the conclusion that the girl with a modest background, having lost everything, is now involved with the rich boss solely for his money. What outsiders fail to grasp about our relationship is that he had set his sights on me long before I ever knew who he was.

"Right there, Mother, you just said it right there... MY money," his tone almost frightening with anger. "I don't care about money; I'll live with her anywhere she wants."

"I didn't raise you this way. You are out of control," she declares, her voice growing more stern.

A brief silence ensues before his mother adds, "You have nothing to say, son?" Her tone carries irritation.

"Not to you, no. Go be disappointed in me from the comforts of your own home," he replies, urging her to leave.

"Your father will be so upset," her words seem to carry an underlying significance.

"Shocker," he responds flatly.

"Jonah," she pleads. "Jenevieve is perfect for you," she insists.

I must have some sort of reaction to hearing this because Shay grabs my hand and squeezes it in a comforting gesture.

I hear a condescending snort emanating from him. "Perfect for me? How did you come to that conclusion?"

"Oh Jonah, don't be so dense," she retorts. "You both come from similar affluent upbringings. Your fathers are close friends."

"How does my father's friendship with her father have anything to do with me?"

"Jonah, at thirty-three, it's time to settle down and think about starting a family. I see the appeal in that girl," she remarks, pausing before using the word "appeal." "She's a fun time for now, but long term, it won't happen," she states honestly. "Jenevieve is for the long term, darling."

"Fun time for now? Kalyn isn't just a fun time for now. She's the only one," he asserts, trying to convey his conviction.

"Jonah, being part of this family means understanding your responsibilities. Marrying Jenevieve is your responsibility. Carrying on the legacy of both our families is your legacy," she emphasizes.

"We're finished, Mother. I won't marry Jenevieve, drop it," he declares resolutely.

"Yes, you will," she responds sternly.

"Tell Ethan to marry her if you're so eager to have her as a daughter!" he shouts.

She retorts sharply, "Your brother is already fulfilling his duties for the family."

Jonah roars. "Was that part of fulfilling his family duties when I yielded to your wishes and started dating her, only to walk in on my brother and girlfriend having sex?!" he exclaims. "It's already bad enough you forced me into keeping her under my roof."

"And you haven't contributed a penny of her salary," she hisses back.

"Nor would I, I never wanted to see her again."

"Are you really going to punish the rest of your family because your brother and Jenevieve made a mistake?" she questions.

"Perhaps one time could be considered a mistake, Mother, but sneaking around, getting pregnant by him, only to have an abortion—that's not a mistake. It's disgusting. Frankly, it's not just about them. It reflects poorly on you for still demanding this of me."

"She ended the pregnancy for you, Jonah!" she hisses.

"No, she terminated the pregnancy for herself. And Ethan. He only slept with her because he needed to take what was mine. He never wanted her. He wanted to take from me."

I've heard enough. Learning that he and Jenevieve actually dated is an emotional blow that has me gasping for breath. I'm not prepared to hear any more details. I stand up and walk away, tears streaming down my face.

"Kalyn... Kalyn, wait," Shay calls after me, hurrying to catch up, grabbing my arm.

"I'm okay, Shay. I just need some rest," I wipe away my tears with the back of my hand.

Shay appears remorseful. "I'm so sorry. I shouldn't have made you listen. I honestly didn't know any of that, Kal."

I retreat to my room, shutting the door behind me. Once alone, my tears begin cascading down my face. I thought everything Jenevieve told me was bad enough. Now, learning that Jonah was involved romantically with her makes me feel like someone is sitting on my chest, restricting my oxygen.

The love and affection he gives me was once shown to her. I feel betrayed, yet these feelings aren't valid since he didn't betray me at all. We didn't know each other even existed at the time.

I sometimes dream of my parents, and for the first couple of moments upon waking up, I can feel the power of their love. Nobody else on this planet could hold a candle to their love for one another. There is no lingering worry about anyone else breaking the bond they shared.

I thought I had that with Wyatt, but it always seemed to lack those true feelings, which I chalked up to being actually broken from all the heartache in my life. I feel all those feelings and so much more with Jonah, yet it feels like I am having to fight for him with another woman, and it feels awful. I can't decide which would be worse: if the other woman was nice or the fact that she is an actual monster.

When I ponder things of purity, like a newborn bunny, my heart fills with warmth. It's a similar feeling to the purity I sense from Jonah. While opposite to that is the way my skin prickled the moment I laid eyes on Jenevieve. Without even exchanging a word, I felt a sinking sensation in the pit of my stomach. Some individuals exude positive energy, while others emanate malevolence. I believe it's more probable for purity to be tainted by evil than the other way around. I dread that Jenevieve would dismantle the remarkable man Jonah is beneath the protective walls he has erected.

Adding to the already shitty situation, the revelation that she cheated on Jonah with his brother and even got pregnant by him is truly devastating. I didn't even know he had a brother. Lilly never mentioned anything about a brother when she was telling us about each of them the day they arrived. I wonder if Ethan sleeping with Jenevieve is the reason why he didn't come. To make matters even worse, Jonah's parents are funding Jenevieve's salary to ensure she stays employed within Jonah's household, ensuring she is always near him.

The extent of their cruelty is beyond comprehension. Jenevieve is an even bigger scoundrel than I originally believed, and I didn't think she could be any worse than I already thought. But apparently, I was wrong. Who would do something so terrible to someone. Let alone someone as wonderful as Jonah. The mere idea of being under the same roof as Jonah's mother or Jenevieve right now feels unbearable.

On impulse, I decide to go see my parents. It's been a while since I visited, and I have a lot to talk about. I grab my floral luggage bag out of my closet, tossing in essentials. Wiping away tears, I stash a couple of tissues in my purse for the drive. Car key in hand, I lift my bag and head out. Just as I reach the elevator, Jenevieve intercepts.

"Where do you think you're going?" she hisses.

Ignoring her, I push the elevator button, waiting for the doors to open. Her clicking heels approach, and as the doors part, I step inside, only for her to grab my arm with a vice-like grip.

"I asked you a question!" she snaps, her gaze piercing into me, and the strong hold on my arm signals her irritation at my lack of response.

Pulling my arm from her grip, I snap, "Get your hands off me," while pressing the elevator button to take me to the garage.

She must notice the tear streaks on my face. Despite knowing I am upset, she still dares to lay her hands on me… again, even with Jonah in the house. She is clearly confident I won't go tell him.

"You have work in the morning. You're not allowed to leave the premises," she declares, narrowing her eyes.

Meeting her gaze, I retort, "Then tell Jonah on me." With that, the doors close, leaving her stunned in my wake.

CHAPTER
Twenty-Seven

KALYN

"Hi, Mom. Hi, Dad. Hi, Grandma," I greet, settling onto the grass and fixing my gaze on the shared headstone of my parents, situated beside my grandma's headstone next to my father's side. My parents' memorial stands tall and grand, a beautiful structure meticulously crafted and gifted by my mother's dearest friend. Beside it, my grandma's marker is simple, a modest, flat one—a lovely tribute that, though not as extravagant, was all I could afford.

I absentmindedly pluck at the grass, grasping one blade at a time, rolling each between my fingers before letting it drop and move on to a new one. I've never been adept at this—conversing with the headstone. They never seem to respond.

However, this is an improvement from the hour I spent in my car, mentally encouraging myself to get out and walk over to them while I absentmindedly pluck strands of my hair out, wrapping them mindlessly around my finger, and unraveling it again.

"I, uh... I'm really failing at this whole life stuff," I wipe a free-falling tear from my face with the sleeve of my sweatshirt. "I really miss you guys," my voice trembles. "I just don't understand why you guys had to die that night and I survived." Tears begin streaming down my face faster.

"Grandma, I appreciate everything you did to raise me as best as you could," I trace my fingers along the lettering on her grave-stone. Memories flood my mind. "You used to talk about Mom and Dad all the time. Mom, I can still remember your hugs. The absolute best hugs," I wrap my arms around myself, reminiscing about the warmth of my mother's embrace. She would always squeeze me, kiss my head, and call me 'her most beautiful girl'—a feeling of pure happiness back then. The love bestowed upon me by my mother is a yearning I've carried since her passing. The affection and care she showered on me during those early years made every year without it nearly intolerable.

"And now I'm all alone," I murmur, hugging my knees tighter as tears flow even faster.

Strong arms envelop me, and I catch the comforting scent before he speaks. "You'll never be alone ever again, baby," Jonah whispers in my ear.

My sobbing intensifies at his words and him being here. Just feeling the warmth of his embrace has me hugging my knees tighter because I instantly feel comforted in his presence. He keeps his arms firmly wrapped around me, briefly shifting one to grab something. Then, he moves my long hair out of the way, bringing his hand tenderly to my eyes and wiping away tears with a tissue.

He repositions, settling his legs on either side of me, and resumes his position, wrapping his arms around me.

As my sobs begin to quiet, we sit in silence, gazing at their headstone.

"Hello, Mr. and Mrs. Bell, I'm Jonah," he introduces himself, and I lean back into his chest, feeling his arms tighten around me. "You have an incredible daughter. You would be really proud." Nestling his face a little closer to mine, my fingers lace between his, and I slowly draw them lazily up and down his in a soothing motion.

"Don't stop," I whisper, urging him to continue talking.

"I've always been a bit on the serious side, but your daughter has brought out laughs in me I didn't even know were possible," he continues. "When she's nervous, she plays with her fingers. She eats like a bird, nibbling and picking at pieces of food," he shares things about me I never knew he noticed. "She sings to herself while she works," I can hear the smile in his words as he speaks. "Even when people aren't kind to her, she offers kindness to them. I had the privilege of witnessing a heartwarming moment between my baby sister and Kalyn. Kalyn was blowing bubbles, and my sister, jumped around, clapping her hands to pop them. I hope these are the moments you get to see with her, the pure, kind, and wonderful person she is," he shares this sentiment while tenderly planting a kiss on the side of my head, then settling his cheek in the very spot where he placed the kiss.

His sweet words bring fresh tears to my cheeks. "Thank you," I murmur in response.

"They passed away when I was six in a car wreck," I explain, the memory of the incident absent but the heartbreak still vivid. "I survived without a scratch. My grandma later told me that responding officers mentioned all they could hear when they arrived was me calling for my mom to wake up. I suppose my mind blocked it out," I say sadly. "My therapist says I have survivors' guilt."

"I'm so sorry, babe," he embraces me tighter. "I've never truly felt like I belonged. Avoiding all forms of friendships with anyone, I feared that if I let people in, they would leave too. Sam seemed to be the one person who consistently said and did the right things—the only person I allowed to get a foot in the door," I express metaphorically. "However, in my true Kalyn fashion, I made sure to disappear, ditch my phone on the side of the back roads, and not even talk to him for the last four months. I am on a roll," I take a crack at dry humor.

"You could go see him, offer an apology, and invite him to our home," he suggests.

Our home. My heart flutters at the mention of '*our* home.'

"I'd really like that," I smile.

"It's only a thirty-minute drive. Come on," he encourages, prompting me to sit up.

My trips to the cemetery are tinged with discomfort. Although it's meant to provide solace to those visiting their loved ones' graves, I often feel awkward here. However, on this occasion, I find myself genuinely at ease, and I credit that newfound comfort to the presence of this wonderful man.

Rising to his feet, he extends his hands out toward mine. Meeting his gaze, I place both of my hands in his, and with a gentle tug, he assists me in standing upright. His arms encircle me, drawing me into a secure and comforting embrace.

"Goodbye, Mom, Dad, Grandma," I address each of their headstones. "I love you."

"It was so nice talking to you," Jonah also acknowledges their headstones.

His tender words bring a tear to my eye as I gaze up at him. With his hand cradling my face, he delicately brushes away the free-falling tear and presses his lips to mine before enveloping me in an even tighter hug.

As we walk back toward my car, I realize Jonathan, whom I assumed brought Jonah here, isn't waiting for him.

"How did you get here?" I ask, confused.

"I took a cab," amusement filling his words.

"You did!"

"I did. First and last one ever," he adds.

"That bad, huh?"

"All I'll say is he had rotten eggs for breakfast with a side of sewage to wash it down," his tone serious.

Laughter ripples through me, and he joins in. "I wish I was joking," he remarks as we approach my pride and joy: my magnetic gray Rav4.

"Her name is Estelle," joy rings through my voice as I refer to my vehicle.

He whistles, "Impressive, she's almost as beautiful as you."

I retrieve my key from my pocket, but he swipes it from my hand, unlocking the passenger door and holding it open for me. "M'lady," he gestures for me to climb in.

"Do you know how to drive?" I ask earnestly, devoid of poking fun. I seriously am unsure if he knows how to, and I certainly don't want him learning on my little beauty.

His mouth drops open in animated shock, and I smirk as I climb in. He leans into the open door, grabbing my seatbelt and stretching it across me. "Yes, I know how to drive," he plants a kiss on my lips. "Or do I?" he taunts, grinning as he rises to shut my door. He strolls around the front of the car, still wearing a satisfied smile. He smoothly settles into the driver's seat, fastening his seatbelt, and turns to grin at me.

"The key goes in the ignition right here," I lean over, playfully pointing out the spot for him.

"You're the most precious smart alec I've ever seen," he teases.

I'm somewhat surprised to discover that he's an exceptionally good driver and confident behind the wheel. With his left hand casually propped on the wheel, his right hand delicately holds mine, his thumb tracing up and down the side of my thumb.

I observe our intertwined hands. His hands are undeniably good-looking.

"A penny for your thoughts," he says to me, eyes focused on the road.

"I was just thinking, you have really nice hands. You could be a hand model," still admiring it in mine.

"You think so?" he keeps his wrist on the wheel but lifts his hand up to examine it.

"I do," I express. "Put your hand up to mine," I suggest as we pull up to a stop sign.

He lifts his hand off the wheel, holding it up. I release our grip, grabbing his hand with both of mine. Locking eyes with him, I place his middle finger in my mouth, my lips and tongue closing around it. His lips part slightly, a subtle gasp escaping as he watches me immerse his finger, suctioning to it and slowly pulling my mouth off.

Biting my teeth into my bottom lip, I flutter my lashes innocently at him. "Penny for your thoughts, Mr. Everett?" I say seductively.

He gazes at me, momentarily appearing speechless.

"Um," he clears his throat, "...that was sexy," he admits after a pause. "I have something a bit bigger if you're in the mood for something to savor," he adds, a touch of humor in his voice.

"Oh? Are you going to show me?"

He nods, glancing at the rearview mirror, prompting me to look behind us.

"We're in the middle of nowhere. No one will see us," I reassure, unbuckling my seatbelt and pushing the gear into park. Positioned on my knees in my seat, I lean over, taking charge as I unbutton his pants and enjoy my time slowly lowering his zipper.

He releases the brake and shifts back in his seat. He rests his left hand behind his head for added comfort as he watches me slide my hand into his pants and pull out his already erect cock.

Anticipation and desire reflect in my gaze as I shift my attention from him to his arousal. My mouth waters at the enticing sight. As I hover above him, I part my lips, allowing a trickle of saliva to glide from the edge of my tongue to the tip of his arousal. The intensity in his eyes flares with heat as I carry out the act, using my hand to stroke his member while spreading my saliva around it. A low moan escapes his lips, urging me on. With a firm grip, I lower myself, delicately taking the tip into my mouth and swirling my tongue around it. Another soft moan escapes his throat. "Fuck, baby," he groans, entwining his fingers into my hair and tightening his grip.

I gradually slide my mouth down his shaft, settling into a rhythm with a coordinated motion of my hands rotating up and down. He's so thick my small hands can't even fully wrap around the entirety of his shaft.

His breathing quickens. My hand, initially on the center console, moves over the top of his hand in my hair, signaling my need for him to grip tighter. He complies, tightening his hold, prompting me to shift my arm back to the console. The sensation of him in my mouth and the intensified grip on my hair elicit slow, pleasure-filled moans as I continue to pleasure him. His moans heighten my arousal to the point a mere touch of his hand between my legs could lead to an orgasm.

He maintains a tight grip on my hair, attempting to pull me away, but I resist, continuing to suck.

"I'm going to cum, baby, move," he utters, a mix of urgency and arousal in his voice.

I respond with a throaty moan, maintaining my suction.

"Babe," he murmurs in a final plea for me to move.

Moans and strained breaths break free from him as he releases his warm liquid into my throat. Feeling his pulsations, I adjust my rhythm, making sure to swallow every last drop. As the pulsating subsides, I slowly withdraw my mouth, licking up every remaining trace.

"Was that also sexy?" I flash a smile at him wiping the side of my mouth.

His face lights up, and he grabs my face between both hands, initiating a fervent and passionate kiss.

"I'll take that as a yes," I grin as he withdraws, interpreting his response as an affirmative.

He reclines his head on the headrest, letting out a heavy breath. After a brief silence, he composes himself. "Damn, baby, that was incredible," while zipping up his pants. Putting a hand on the gearshift, he shifts into drive and lightly slaps my thigh. "My tongue is coming for you next."

As we approach the imposing, modern structure, my stomach tightens with anxiety. I nervously wipe my palms along the sides of the seat, fixating on the building through the window. Sam holds the position of a senior accountant, and unfortunately, is still employed in the same building where I once worked… where Wyatt still works, as far as I am aware. Thankfully, he is on a different floor, but it still has my nerves firing.

I'm nervous to see Sam, I know he's going to be upset with me. Yet, my unease is heightened even more by the presence of Wyatt somewhere in the building because I want to punch his nose through his skull.

"You okay, babe?" Jonah asks, resting his hand on my thigh.

I keep my gaze fixed on the building, briefly hearing Jonah's words but unable to tear my eyes away from the structure. "Huh? Yeah, I'm fine," I respond, stealing a glance at him before returning my attention to the window.

His eyes reflect concern, and though I would have elaborated, fate intervenes conveniently. Sam strolls across the expansive outdoor entrance space.

Swiftly unbuckling my seatbelt, I exit the car and stride toward him.

"Sam," I call after him, quickening my pace. "Sam," I repeat, attempting to catch his attention. Engaged in conversation with a woman, they momentarily pause to identify the source of the voice. "Sam... hi," I greet as I finally reach him.

"I'll meet you inside," he tells the woman, who responds with an "okay," glancing at me before returning her gaze to him. She hesitantly walks toward the building.

"How are you?" I ask nervously.

"How am I? Kalyn, you left without so much as a goodbye. I didn't even know what happened to you. And all you have to say is how are you? Unbelievable," he responds, angrily. And rightfully so.

"I'm sorry, Sam," I say, hoping he can sense the sincerity of my apology. "Will you give me a chance to explain, I'll tell you everything," I plead.

"No need, apology accepted," he says, turning to walk away.

"Sam, please," I beg, grabbing his arm, urging him to stop. "Just talk to me."

"What's the point? So you can just walk out again?" he retorts.

"I got fired and evicted. What was I supposed to do? Cry about it in a cardboard box under a bridge?" In my heart, I knew he wouldn't understand the situation, and it's one of the reasons I hesitated to reach out in the first place. Now, feeling overwhelmed with emotions, I gathered the courage to come and apologize, but he is shutting me out completely. I get why, it's just frustrating, and my heart feels like its crumbling into pieces.

"You know damn well I would have helped you," he asserts, turning to meet my gaze, hurt evident in his eyes, and it weighs heavily on me. I feel so guilty, yet I'm at a loss on how to mend the situation.

"I didn't want you to feel sorry for me. I didn't want your pity. I needed to get by on my own," I hope he can see this from my perspective.

"Pity? You believe I would have pitied you? Unbelievable! You hold quite a low opinion of me, don't you?" his voice still etched with hurt.

"No, but I know you, and I know you would have tried to fix the situation," I respond candidly.

"Yes, I would have, Kal. That's what friends do. What friends don't do is leave without a word," he states, still glaring at me. "But congratulations, you succeeded in getting by on your own," he says, looking at me. Then, noticing Jonah leaning against the passenger door of my car, he lets out an incredulous laugh. "I'm glad he was able to find you. He nearly ripped my head off for not calling the cops when you took off. Looks like you made everyone worry for nothing," he remarks, turning towards the building and continuing on his way.

His words halt me on the sidewalk. What did he mean by *"glad he was able to find me?"*

I remain in a state of bewilderment, watching as Sam walks away. Trying to understand his words.

"Kalyn," Jonah says delicately, taking hold of my hand. "Come on, babe," he encourages, guiding me back towards the car. I want to run after Sam, gravel on my knees until he forgives me, but I keep walking away. I can feel Sam watching me, yet I don't turn around.

Jonah opens the car door, and I step inside, putting my seatbelt on. After closing the door, he walks around to the driver's side.

As he shuts the door, I ask, "Sam said he was glad you were able to find me. What does that mean?" I turn to Jonah, but he doesn't say a word, keeping his gaze fixed ahead. "Well?" I press, trying to understand Sam's words.

Jonah starts the car and pulls away, a noticeable silence settling between us.

"Jonah?" I persist, unwilling to drop the subject. While it seems unlikely that Jonah and Sam would have crossed paths before, they somehow did, and there's no apparent reason for them to have done so.

"I've already told you, you're mine," he asserts.

"Yeah, you mentioned that a time or two, but what did Sam mean?" When would he have had time to talk to Sam?

Jonah maneuvers the vehicle with a familiarity that suggests he knows the area well. We're leaving town in the opposite direction we arrived, surrounded by trees on both sides of the road. Eventually, he turns onto a dirt road. I recognize the path—it leads to a large, dilapidated mansion. As we continue down the dirt road, I notice that the once-overgrown driveway appears altered, the overgrown weeds cleared as though a car had been here often.

The driveway unfolds, revealing a still eerily run-down mansion, triggering memories of the spooky tales shared every Halloween about the haunted estate. The stories were scary enough to deter anyone from venturing here, as fear loomed over the place. Even as we pull up, I can't shake off the eerie energy, witnessing the ominous structure up close for the first time.

The circular driveway, now overrun by weeds except for the single set of tire tracks that have flattened down the weeds, paints a stark picture of neglect. A round fountain sits at the center, once beautiful, now holds stagnant, swampy water at its base. Vines crawl up the sides of the mansion and the six imposing pillars at the front.

The once-white mansion now stands weathered and peeling, with paint flakes drifting off.

"What's going on?" I ask, puzzled. He remains seated, gazing blankly out the window, lost in thought.

He unbuckles his seatbelt and opens his door. "Showing you."

CHAPTER
Twenty-Eight

KALYN

I watch as he walks around the front of the car. Reaching my door, he opens it and extends his hand for me to take.

"I'm not getting out. This place is haunted," I stare at him.

"Come on," he continues holding his hand outstretched.

I hesitate, weighing my options. I could die from a ghost or squatters brave enough to break in. But both scenarios seem like nothing with Jonah here to protect me. Reluctantly, I accept his hand as he leads me to the broad staircase. On either side of the steps, sit two stone gargoyle statues, each stoically peering out from their perch.

As we pass by the one on the left, Jonah puts his hand into the gargoyle's mouth, retrieving something and clutching it in his fist. Leading me up the stairs to the expansive wrap-around porch, he inserts the item—which I now know is the key he obtained from the gargoyle's mouth—into the door and unlocks it.

"Jonah," I whisper in disbelief. "This is trespassing," I glance around to make sure nobody sees us.

"You're not a fan of breaking rules, are you?" he remarks, with a slight sense of humor.

"No, I'm not, and I don't like breaking into abandoned houses," I confess nervously as he opens the door.

Upon entering, I stand in the doorway, shocked to see the seemingly abandoned house isn't quite abandoned. The entrance leads into a spacious foyer with a large round table sitting on top of a dark burgundy rug. To the right, a staircase ascends with intricate railings, leading to the upper landing. Off to the left, a living room with contemporary furnishings is neatly placed.

"I'm so confused," I scan the room. Jonah presses his hand on my lower back, encouraging me further into the house, closing the door behind us.

"I own it," he declares plainly.

"What do you mean, you own it? You just happen to own an abandoned house in the same town I lived in?" I direct my eyes toward him.

"No," he replies candidly. "I don't just happen to own an abandoned house in the same town you lived in. I bought it to be near you," he confesses, his eyes meeting mine, not an ounce of shame or embarrassment in them.

"Excuse me," I blurt out, taken aback by his words. "You're creepy," I state, staring at him before glancing around the house.

Why did he purchase a house just to be close to me? We were complete strangers. Judging by the significant investment in this house, he must have spent quite a substantial amount of time here. How could he claim it was to be near me when he never attempted to even talk to me? He never made any effort to interact with me.

"I wouldn't describe myself as creepy, I just knew what I wanted."

"That makes it even creepier because you knew you wanted me and just stared at me from afar… like a creep," I respond. "Continue," I urge, my attention shifting to wandering the living room.

He watches me, leaning against the pillar that leads from the entryway to the living room, his hands in his pants pockets.

"*I* hadn't encountered you until that day in the hall, and the table incident, which I'm sure you recall," I emphasize the word "I," playfully glancing back at him. "Jenevieve told me… about the night of the Gala. What I'm curious about is how things transition from you seeing me get my heart broken by my cheating boyfriend, to owning a house where I lived and what Sam was talking about."

I settle onto the couch, all the while he doesn't move from his position. "So?"

He stays silent.

"You drop a massive shit on me, and now you're the one with nothing to say?" I laugh, flabbergasted.

"I have a lot I want to say, things I want to do," he responds, still leaning in the same position.

"Well," I extend my arms encouraging him to elaborate.

"How much did Jenevieve tell you?" he lifts an eyebrow.

"That she was sucking your cock when you saw me. That you watched me at work," I divulge. "You know, the worst part of all this, Jonah, is that in our entire conversation, what bothers me the most is that Jenevieve had her mouth on your dick." The more I dwell on the idea of her being intimate with him, the stronger my irritation grows. It makes me want to lash out at her for simply being her and to punch him in the dick for allowing it.

The thought of someone so awful bringing him pleasure infuriates me. The sexy moans that I have loved and enjoyed, reveling in the satisfaction of eliciting them, are probably the same moans he was making as she was pleasuring him. He probably even held her hair the way he holds mine and kissed her with the same passion he gives me.

He pushes away from the door frame, striding purposefully toward the couch. "Jenevieve has never felt my tongue between her legs," he utters, placing a knee on the couch beside me. Leaning over, he positions his arms on either side of my head on the back of the couch, his face merely inches from mine.

"Then I feel sorry for her," my voice catching in my throat. His proximity, hovering over me like this, erases my previous frustrations.

"Oh yeah?" A hint of arousal in his tone.

"Mmhmm," keeping my lips pressed together.

A seductive expression on his face sparks my arousal, needing him to be buried inside me.

Obviously, four years was too long to go without sex. He is turning me into a nympho.

"Why me?" I ask as the escalating sexual tension permeates the room.

His expression suggests that my question has seemingly deflated his sexual energy. Releasing a heavy exhale, he slumps onto the couch beside me, stretching out his arms on the backrest and leaning back. "I might come off as a snob, questioning why this sexy, rich guy wants me," playfully placing the back of my hand on my forehead and tilting my head back in a melodramatic manner. "But I need to know."

"It was something my mother said," turning his head while keeping it reclined on the couch to meet my gaze. "She said, 'One day I would open my eyes, and the love of my life would be there. I would instantly know that she was the one, she would outshine every other woman.' I didn't fully grasp what she meant. Nor did I give it a second thought. I enjoyed being with women—I had been with many, but I wasn't the settling down kind of man, and I've always known that... And then I saw you." He turns his head, closing his eyes. "Time came to a standstill—I couldn't take my eyes off you—my heart was racing so fast. I tried everything to fix my dick—I had numerous women attempt to arouse me. I tried fucking, but my thoughts were consumed by you, and I couldn't get aroused. So, I went back to see you... to see if maybe that night I was just having an off night. I didn't expect anything out of it. But my erection came back the moment I saw you again. You have been the only woman I have thought about since that day, the only woman that I can get hard for."

"Why do I sense that when your mother said that—she intended for you to open your eyes and realize Jenevieve was the one for you?" I fully understand his mother's underlying message.

"Yes," he concurs.

"Jonah, I overheard your conversation with your mother," I admit.

He turns his head back toward me, grinning. "I figured, hence the hours of chasing you to this place," he teases.

I smile but press on, "I heard what she said about you and Jenevieve and what she did with your brother," unsure of my intentions with even bringing it up.

"It was a long time ago," he assures, sounding completely unbothered by it anymore.

"Still, I'm sorry that happened to you," reaching my hand out and placing it on his lap.

He lowers his hand, intertwining his fingers with mine, then guides me into his embrace, wrapping me in his arms.

"Well, this took an unexpected turn," I jest.

"You mispronounced 'romantic'," he says in response.

"Oh, are we just going to breeze past all of this?" I gesture whimsically around the room.

"Does it change how you feel about me?"

"Yes," I respond honestly. "It turns me on," I admit.

He spanks my butt, "My naughty girl."

"Exactly how much do you know about me?"

He releases a breath, indicating he might be well-acquainted with my story. "I want to learn everything about you directly from you," he eventually replies.

"Why didn't you come into the diner and have a conversation with me? Wouldn't that have been a simpler approach?"

"We ordered food one of the days we were outside," he responds.

"Who is we?"

"Me and Jonathan."

"You did?!"

CHAPTER
Twenty-Nine

JONAH

I sit in the backseat, jitters coursing through me as we approach her work. Seeing her again is what gets me through these extended business trips. Today marks the sixty-third time I've laid eyes on her. Although our interactions are non-existent, the excitement and nervousness persist each time.

"You good, Everett?" Jonathan asks, cutting through the silence. "You're shaking the entire fucking SUV," he stares through the rearview mirror.

Even though she and I have never exchanged words, I feel anxious. I take extra care to ensure my appearance is just right, meticulously adjusting my hair, even though I know it will end up disheveled from running my fingers through it by the end of her shift. My attire always leans toward business, though I skip the tie and suit jacket, opting for a more relaxed look. Today, we ran late due to oversleeping after a late-night flight and arriving at the rundown mansion in the early hours, causing us to fall into a deep sleep.

Rushing to get ready this morning, Jonathan informs me of the expected on-and-off rain throughout the day. I choose black business slacks and a white button-up shirt, neatly tucked in. I grab my black peacoat just in case and hastily pull it on. We hurry to the car, aiming to reach her workplace as quickly as possible. It's been two weeks since I last saw her, and the longing to see my girl is unbearable.

As we arrive at the diner and find our customary spot on the busy street, Jonathan shifts the car into park. With seamless fluidity, he leans his seat back, retrieves his phone, and promptly sends a text to his girlfriend before immersing himself in the latest news updates.

My usual routine involves arriving at the diner half an hour before her shift starts to catch a glimpse of her walking by. Today, however, we're only fifteen minutes early, and luck is on my side. We wait just a short two minutes before I spot her rounding the corner. My heart momentarily pauses—she is the epitome of beauty. Clad in jean shorts and a black t-shirt, her hair is braided, hanging over one shoulder. As she walks, she swings her folded-up umbrella in her hand, subtly mouthing along to the music playing in her ears.

Each time I see her, I remind myself she doesn't know who I am, resisting the urge to jump out of the car, press her against the building, and shove my tongue down her throat.

"She really is…"

"Don't even finish that sentence," I snap at Jonathan, who has a knack for articulating things fucking stupid. I don't want to hear him say she's sexy, or I'll have to deal with his feisty girlfriend after breaking his nose.

"Pretty, I was going to say pretty," he clarifies, holding his hands up in a gesture of innocence.

I continue to watch her as she enters the diner, disappearing into the back before reemerging, working on the computer behind the counter. Then, she comes around the counter, tying her apron around her waist and helping customers.

She's incredibly beautiful, to the point it's almost unbearable. Despite understanding that she's just doing her job, witnessing her smile at any man in there sparks a pang of jealousy—it's not me she's smiling at.

I crave her.

I need her.

One day, I'll have her spread out beneath me, screaming my name. But for now, I'll sit here, as I always do, watching my baby work.

I often wonder if the owner is aware that his diner is a ghost town until her shift begins, at which point it becomes overly busy. The influx of customers persists throughout the day, and people always request to be seated in her section. I observe men fixate on her, lingering long after finishing their meals, and it sparks instant anger in me.

I can tell she remains oblivious to the impact she has on people—men and women alike are drawn to her.

The day unfolds, marked by intermittent rain and an earlier onset of darkness than usual.

"I don't even know what her voice sounds like," I absentmindedly remark while watching her attend to a group of men, all smiling at her. She returns to the register to process their payment, and they remain focused on her, whispering amongst themselves. Watching her pick up the phone, I see her multitasking as she prepares a receipt and pen for the table she just walked away from.

"Odd question, is there any way you can come out to my car and take an order? My leg is broken, and I can't walk. We're in the black SUV," Jonathan says, and I see my girl turn her head to peer out the window… directly at us. My neck can't turn fast enough to catch Jonathan subtly waving to her.

Mouthing to him, attempting to get his attention to hang up, but he pretends not to see me. "Thanks, appreciate it," he says, before ending the call.

"What the fuck did you just do?" I exclaim.

"We woke up late, been sitting here for six hours, she still has three hours to go, and I'm starving. We didn't have time to grab food on the way, and you're about to hear her voice," he responds, donning a fake mustache that's not even properly adhered to his face—obviously fake.

"What the fuck is on your face?"

"I picked it up from that quarter machine at the gas station. Got five of em. Do you want to put one on?" Reaching into his pocket and producing four more round plastic balls, each containing a rolled-up mustache.

"That looks ridiculous," I remark.

A soft tap on the passenger window makes every nerve in my body tingle. I lower in my seat and pull the collar of my coat up around my face. It feels too soon. What if she doesn't like me? What if she isn't what I imagined? What if she has a raspy voice from years of smoking?

"Hi," the most enchanting voice I've ever heard in my entire life fills my ears, captivating my senses entirely.

"Hey, thanks for coming out here," Jonathan says to her.

"Of course, not a problem," she replies, friendly. "What can I get you?" She takes her pen and notepad out of her apron. It feels surreal that she is right here. She is close enough that I can reach out and touch her.

Jonathan places his order, but I am utterly entranced by her. Her scent envelops me, intoxicating my senses with its allure. Her beauty, up close, exceeds all expectations, leaving me breathless. Her complexion is flawless, her full pink lips appearing slightly wet after she subtly licks them while she smiles, writing down Jonathan's words. How is she more stunning up close? She is sheer perfection. I can't bear the longing that grips me as I realize she isn't mine yet.

"And that should be everything?" Jonathan says, breaking me from my trance.

"Perfect. I'll put a rush on it. Do you guys want a cup of coffee or anything?" She looks at Jonathan and then, as if time slows, turns toward the back seat, meeting my gaze for a split second before I shift my eyes to Jonathan, prompting her to do the same.

"That would be awesome," Jonathan responds.

"I'll be back soon," she smiles and walks back toward the diner. I can't even be mad at him. The woman I am going to marry is… flawless… perfect in every way. She could tell me she lives with cockroaches as pets, and I would learn to love them. She is everything I dreamed she would be, and now her scent lingers with us. I rest my head back on the seat and inhale until my senses adapt, and I can no longer smell her.

True to her word, she returns within minutes, holding two coffees and tapping on the window. Jonathan rolls it down, and she hands him one, cautioning, "Careful, it's hot." Reaching between the seats, she hands the other one to me, still smiling as Jonathan takes a sip. I find myself staring at her beauti-

fully small fingers wrapped around the cup, and my mind instantly replaces the cup with a different image—her small hand around my dick.

As I reach out to take the cup, our fingers touch, and an electric jolt seems to surge between us, snapping us both out of the moment.

"Sorry," she says innocently, "If the coffee doesn't wake you up, that shock should do the trick," she teases. "Let me know if you guys need anything else. I'll come back soon." And she walks back inside.

Fuck, I need her. The desire to pull her into the car and make love to her overwhelms me. The thought of her walking back into the diner with her pussy sore from me fucking it fuels my arousal.

But, at this moment, that would scare her. The realization causes my once-hard cock to instantly go flaccid.

I notice a cook ringing the bell for two takeout orders, and she swiftly collects them, placing each in a bag along with napkins and silverware. She heads toward the door, again walking in our direction.

"Hey," I call to Jonathan, who's engrossed in his phone. He sits up as she waits at the window, and he starts rolling it down. She hands Jonathan his food and unexpectedly reaches in the window pressing the unlock button on the car door and comes to my door pulling it open to hand me my food—food that I hadn't ordered. Jonathan must have ordered something for me.

Completely caught off guard, I sense my hands may be noticeably shaking as I take the bag from her and place it on my lap. "I put napkins in the bag. Silverware too if you need them," she addresses me directly. "I don't bite," she softly pokes my chest, "hard anyways." Her smile grows wider before stepping back and closing the door.

I watch in complete shock as she returns inside. Stunned, I remain motionless until a single beep from my phone prompts me to pull it out of my coat pocket. Jonathan has sent me a video capturing the entire interaction, and I watch it over and over, grateful for his foresight in recording it.

"You can thank me by paying for dinner," he says, continuing to eat. "This is pretty damn good food," he adds, looking down at his meal and munching on a fry.

He's right. The food is decent.

An hour passes, and Jonathan calls her to signal we're ready to pay. Despite her attempt to cover the cost, he insists. She returns with the total, and after handing her a fifty, he tells her to keep the change. She nearly makes it inside before tapping on the window again. Handing him a hundred-dollar bill, she mentions it was unintentionally placed in the middle.

"Nah, that was intentional," Jonathan says. "He wanted to compensate for your troubles," he motions to the back at me.

She smiles and looks to the back between the seats, "Thank you. Perhaps I can give you ten back, and you can buy him some new glue for that mustache—it looks like it's having a hard time staying on his face." A laugh unintentionally escapes my throat.

Her mouth hangs open with a smile still playing on her lips. "I just heard noise come out of you," she remarks, acting as if she can't believe it.

"He actually bought me the mustache, says it makes me look like a pornstar. I was gonna FaceTime my girlfriend and see what she thinks," Jonathan shares.

"I think she's going to love it," she replies. "Thank you again. Have a good night," she waves intentionally acknowledging me.

As the diner closes, I observe the lights flickering off, and she emerges, heading toward a car that pulls up on the road. She waves and climbs in the passenger side. The first time I saw her with this guy, an immediate impulse to confront him for being near my girl crossed my mind. After some investigating, I discover he's her long-time friend, a guy named Sam, and their relationship is purely platonic. Giving me instant relief, but jealousy that he gets to be near her like that still settles in.

We head home afterward. The drive feels both long and too short, engrossed in the video clip of her and me—playing it repeatedly. I even have to grab my cell phone charger to replenish my phone's battery, which I drained watching the same footage over and over. Zooming in on her full, pink lips as she talks, her petite nose, and her captivating green eyes, I marvel at her beauty.

"Until next time, baby," I murmur at my phone, tucking it back into my pocket as we pull into the garage at my mansion.

CHAPTER
Thirty

KALYN

"**Y**ou came out and took our order. You were so gorgeous up close. I didn't think you could get any more beautiful, and when you stood in the window of the SUV, my heart was racing. And you smelled… God, you smelled so good." He closes his eyes as if remembering smelling me for the first time. "It was raining out. You were wearing shorts and a black T-shirt, with your hair braided. When you brought out the food, you tapped on the window and talked to Jonathan—he was wearing a hat and a fake mustache.

My mouth drops open animatedly. "Shut. The. Fuck. Up," emphasizing each word. "I remember that!" The recollection flashes in my mind—walking out to the car, perplexed by his fake mustache that stubbornly clung to one corner, constantly trying to roll inward on the other. While taking their order, he persisted in attempting to affix it to his face, only for it to inevitably peel back up. I couldn't fathom why he was donning a disguise, but I didn't pass judgment. That entire night, as I lay in bed, the memory lingered, contemplating the inexplicable surge of electricity between me and the guy in the backseat. It almost felt like a sign of a deeper connection, but he showed no interest and made it abundantly clear by refusing to utter more than a couple of words to me.

"I was trying to gauge things. Over time, I felt like I knew you, truly knew you. I thought you'd see right through me pretending to be a stranger to you. It just became a routine in my days watching you work. I was returning home from a four-week business trip out of the country, the longest I had gone without seeing you. When I returned, you weren't there. It was the worst feeling. I went by your work, apartment, and saw Sam walking, so I asked him if he knew your whereabouts," he exhales, as if recollecting that day stirs up memories.

"Did you not put the flyer on my door?" I guess I was thinking this whole time that perhaps he put it on my door himself.

"No," he replies honestly. "I'm still trying to figure that one out."

"Well, you might want to give them a raise when you figure it out," I tease, giving his side a soft pinch.

He remains silent.

"Why did you seem so upset when you saw me there? I mean, you spent so much time sitting at the diner watching me, why wouldn't you have been happy that I was in your home, a lot closer to you?" Recalling how angry he seemed, my stomach dropped when he stood next to me and then questioned why I was in his house. I felt singled out and embarrassed.

"I had envisioned every scenario of sweeping you off your feet and bringing you *home*, only to discover you were hired as staff. Jonathan drove a hundred and twenty all the way back. I tore through the house looking for you. Gladys said you were at lunch. My nerves were on edge as I braced myself to see you—inside my own house. Not through the barriers of glass, but face to face. When you finally came into view, a mix of excitement and nervousness washed over me. I wondered if you would recognize me, if our touch would reignite that electric spark between us. Approaching you, the intoxicating scent that clung to you consumed my senses. I stood frozen beside you, my senses going wild as I took in your fragrance. Then, I caught sight of your face," he pauses, his voice heavy with emotion. "I couldn't comprehend what I was seeing. Your beautiful face had… bruises…. Fuck!" he exclaims, sounding disappointed.

Minutes go by and he feels tense.

"Baby, tell me what really happened?" his tone deflated.

"Okay," I agree. "I will, but only if you promise not to overreact," I look up at him.

He meets my gaze, shifting his eyes between mine. "Okay," he nods.

"Jenevieve adamantly didn't want me there. She made it known from the moment she met me. The first day of work, she slapped me... twice, actually," I let out an astonished chuckle, recalling her mistaking me for whispering when it was Vanessa. "I had never been assaulted before, and I tried quitting, but she kept threatening me with the contract I signed. I just thought she was a drill sergeant type, so I kept my head down and did my work. But no matter what others did, she blamed it on me. She made me work through lunch if someone else didn't finish their work. It was always mucking stalls, which was a good workout, and it had to get done, so I didn't mind. Amber struggled with horse feed at the end of our shift on one of the extremely hot days, accidentally tripping over a hose, and spilling a bucket. Jenevieve saw the mess, took the other bucket from her hand, and knocked me out when she swung it across my face. Shay and Brad offered to take me to the hospital, but I refused. So, Shay spent the entire night changing out ice packs on my face to help reduce swelling." I explain and wait for him to say something.

Recalling the major things Jenevieve did to me feels almost absurd when spoken aloud. She truly embodies the definition of pathetic. When he remains quiet, it prompts me to look up and ask if he has any questions. His head is leaning back on the couch, tears streaming down his face.

"Oh, babe, no," I murmur, pulling myself from his embrace and climbing into his lap. I wrap my arms around his neck, my heart breaking at the sight of his sadness. "Please don't," I plead, my voice a whisper against his neck, holding onto him tighter. His handsome face appearing defeated is a sight my heart can't bear. "Baby," I wipe away his tears with my thumbs and press my lips to his.

He responds to the kiss, igniting an uncontrollable desire within me, urging me to be closer to him. My hands move down to his pants, rubbing up and down on his already thick member.

Urgently, we begin unbuttoning each other's pants, our hands working quickly with the need to get them off immediately before the moment passes us by. He lifts me, laying me on my back on the couch as he situates himself on his knee between my legs, one foot still grounded on the floor. Swiftly, he removes my shoes and pants, discarding them on the floor, followed by my sweatshirt. With equal haste, he sheds his shirt, unveiling his sculpted torso, then lowers his pants, not bothering to fully remove them.

He hovers over me, reconnecting his mouth with mine. He reaches down between my legs, gripping his shaft and guiding it to my entrance. With a gentle push-and-pull motion, he eases in until fully immersed. Moans and labored breathing escape us as he wraps his arms tightly around me, initiating a rhythmic pumping, moving in and out with deliberate motions.

My fingers coil in his hair, while my other hand clutches the edge of the pillow behind me, my body arching to meet his every thrust. My breasts sway up and down with every rock of his hips, and he lets out a low groan as he pulls my nipple into his mouth, sucking hard before pulling his head back, allowing his teeth to graze over the peaked point, then doing the same thing on the other side.

He continues in his rhythmic thrusts, syncing perfectly with my desires. With each motion, he increases the force, penetrating deeper. The sound of our bodies slapping together fills the room, blending with our shared moans and ragged breaths.

Our movements are guided by emotions—mine, by the profound intensity of him coming to find me, talking to my parents' and grandmother's headstones, and recounting our initial interaction that I was unaware of. His emotions are guided by the pain of recalling my face with bruises and finally hearing the truth of what transpired.

"Don't stop," I plead, as he precisely hits the exact spot I need him to. His thrusts persist, and I tighten my grip on the pillow before releasing it, digging my nails into his back, eliciting pleasure-filled moans from him. His skin is slightly damp from sweat, and my fingers can't seem to find traction, allowing them to glide easily down his skin, digging my nails in without feeling like I am ripping his skin apart. Our bodies entwined feel as though they were cut from the same fabric, destined to be together. My arms encircle his broad torso, my petite limbs wrapping around him, creating a truly exquisite sensation.

As the anticipation of my orgasm intensifies, my body tenses with each forceful thrust, drawing me closer to reaching that peak. With my legs wrapped firmly around his waist, I pull him in closer, fully arching my hips off the couch to meet his every movement, holding him in place so he drives in even deeper. My moans escalate into screams as my orgasm erupts out of me.

Every muscle in my body tenses as my climax cascades out of me. Jolts of pleasure cause my pussy to contract on his shaft as my body releases waves of bliss. My nipples harden to the point they feel as though they could cut through his skin. I writhe beneath him, my body contorting as though I'm being pushed beyond my limits, as he continues to thrust into me until he reaches his own climax. Even after he stops rocking, his cock continues to pulse inside me.

He lies limply on me once he finishes, our breathing gradually syncing as it slows. We revel in the aftermath of the intimacy, layered in shared sweat. I softly run my fingers up and down his back, his skin prickling with goosebumps, but he remains still. I stare at his shoulder, admiring the delicate scattering of freckles across his muscles, prompting me to place the gentlest of kisses upon them.

He lets out a muffled laugh, his body quivering, goosebumps layering his skin even more.

"Did that give you the eebie-jeebies," I giggle, noting his reaction to my soft touches.

"It tickles so good," he muses, his face still nestled in my neck.

"I think that means a ghost walked through your body," I giggle, continuing to trail my fingers on his back. "How much did this couch cost?"

"Just a few pennies, baby. Why do you ask?"

I realize it's not true. This must be an expensive couch—correction, expensive for my budget. "I think when you remove your penis, there's going to be a flood of semen," my belly tightens as laughter escapes me. The movement causes my core to clench around his shaft again, drawing a moan from him.

He sits up on his forearms and leans down to kiss my nipple. I watch him, and my lips grow jealous of my own nipple for receiving his affection. Resting his chin on my chest, he stares up at me, total contentment in every feature.

"Do you have any furniture cleaner somewhere around here?" Hinting at my intention to clean up the couch from the impending mess we're about to make.

"No need," he snakes his arms under my waist, lifting me from the couch while keeping himself inside me, carrying us toward the foyer and up the stairs.

At the top of the stairs, to the right, are double doors that he walks to and opens them wide, revealing a spacious master bedroom. It too is designed with a minimalist touch, with a large black wood-framed bed with a fluffy white comforter. Two sitting chairs and a center table are situated at the far end— directly in front of the balcony. On the right wall, an entrance leads to the master bathroom, which he walks us straight to, not allowing me much time to look around. There, he turns on the shower and steps inside. Once under the water, he gently lifts me by my waist as he withdraws himself placing me on my feet. Just as I expected, his fluid seeps down my leg, joining the water on the floor, circling the drain, and eventually disappearing.

I shouldn't be surprised, but all my shower necessities are already neatly arranged in here. Something that would have been done back before I knew him. I chuckle as I watch him pump my favorite shampoo into his hands and begins to lather it up.

"Turn around," he instructs, indicating that he wants to wash my hair. Following his request, I turn, and he proceeds to scrub my scalp, delivering the most wonderful scalp massage in the process. Afterward, he rinses the shampoo out of my hair, paying extra close attention not to get any water in my eyes.

"Thank you," I turn my head to the side to look back at him, offering a smile.

"Always, baby," he leans his head down pressing a kiss on my shoulder.

Opting to spend the night here tonight and head home tomorrow, we decide to order pizza. After a short drive into town to pick it up, we return to the not-so-abandoned house. It still feels peculiar being here. It's odd that an entire remodel happened and not a single story circulated around town about it. Then again, it's far enough back from the road that nobody would have noticed work trucks coming and going. Especially if they did it during the hours nobody would have noticed. I do find it amusing he left the exterior unchanged. Maybe it's his way of keeping people from wanting to come near it or to avoid attracting attention to himself.

The evening unfolds with us enjoying romantic movies, indulging in pizza, and cuddling on the couch.

"Is this what you envisioned for us?" I ask, my back against the couch, lying on my side with my body wrapped around his as we both watch the movie. Our situation might seem unconventional for a romantic film, but it's uniquely ours, and I cherish every second of it. However, I wonder if this aligns with his desires. He's expressed his vision of bringing me home, but what scenarios did he imagine unfolding to lead us to this point?

He turns his head toward me, gazing affectionately for a moment before responding. "Not exactly. I thought I would be the one to sweep you off your feet and somehow convince you to move in with me. Yet, here you are, living in my home, and I'm still actively trying to sweep you off your feet."

"And if you do succeed in sweeping me off my feet?"

He reaches down, grasping my ring finger and pressing a kiss on it. "I will put a ring on it. Then spend the rest of my life doting upon you."

"What if I put a ring on your finger first?" I smile at him.

He stares back at me, a playful gleam in his eyes. "Fuck it... nothing else has gone according to plan. Put a ring on my finger, baby. I'll marry you."

This incredible man wants me—wants to be exclusive with me, and judging by his words, might even want to marry me. I wonder if my parents had a hand in this. Maybe in the spiritual realm, influencing Jonah to me. We have an undeniable connection, even the slightest touch between our bodies triggers powerful electric shocks. I am more than willing to spend the entirety of my life with him. And every life after this.

The morning dawns, and I dress in some clothes Jonah conveniently already had here. After ensuring the house is secure, we descend the large staircase at the front, with him briefly pausing at the gargoyle to return the key to its mouth. He walks me to the passenger door of Estelle, unlocking and opening it for me. Once I am comfortably inside, he closes the door and walks around the front of the car, opening the driver's door and getting in.

"Do you mind if we grab breakfast before we leave?" I ask as I buckle my seatbelt.

"Of course not," he replies, starting the engine and shifting into drive. "Where are you thinking?" he asks as he makes his way down the long dirt road.

"Milo's Diner."

He rests his hand on my lap, flashing a smile. "Milo's Diner it is."

Even though I got laid off from here, I feel a sense of contentment when we pull up. Milo was so good to me. Business slowed down so much, and I knew he was struggling to pay the bills. I understood why he had to lay me off, even though, at the time it really sucked. But I wouldn't be here with Jonah if he hadn't.

As we enter the diner, the familiar chime of the bell above the door greets me. It's a sound I've grown accustomed to, a nostalgic reminder of my time working here. Yet now, it merely serves as a signal to Milo that a customer has arrived.

"Sit wherever you'd like," he calls out, his body turned toward the cash register as he puts the money from another customer inside. Closing the til and turning to greet his customers who just walked in. "Kalyn?" His face transitions through various emotions as he hurries around the counter to wrap me in a heartfelt hug. "How are you, kid?" His eyes glisten with tears as he speaks.

"I'm really good, Milo. How are you?" I ask, pleased to see him.

"I've sure missed you," he says, holding me at arm's length so he can look me over.

"Milo, this is Jonah Everett. Jonah this is my previous boss, Milo," I properly introduce them, recalling Jonah saying he came in here looking for me.

They shake hands, and Milo remarks, "Nice wording, kid. Thanks for not calling me your *old* boss—I might have had a heart attack hearing the word 'old'," he jokes. "Well, sit wherever you'd like, and order whatever you'd like—it's on the house," he adds as he walks back around the counter.

Choosing one of my familiar tables, Jonah pulls out the chair for me next to the window, taking a seat across from me. When Milo returns to our table, he brings two glasses of iced water. "Anything besides water to drink, Mr. Everett?" Milo asks Jonah, knowing I usually always just settle for water.

"Water is fine, Milo. Thank you," Jonah responds.

Jonah stares absentmindedly out the window. I can see he's completely lost in a memory, and I wonder if it feels surreal for him to be on this side of the window, staring out. I can practically envision a scene with us sitting here, while simultaneously having Jonathan and him sitting in his SUV staring in. It's unbelievable how much things have changed since he first saw me, since he sat outside the diner watching me. Now we sit here together.

We place our orders and engage in a pleasant conversation with Milo as he moves around the back of the counter, creating a warm and familiar atmosphere. It feels as if no time has passed since I was last here, like I just finished a shift a couple of days ago.

A couple more groups enter while we're here. Milo attends to them, leaving Jonah and I immersed in our conversation. Unbeknownst to me, the door chimes again, and I'm startled as the chair next to me is pulled out. I look up to see Sam sitting down.

He extends his phone toward me, and I stare at it, confused, as I glance between him and the device. "What?"

"You've obviously got a new number—put it in my phone," he insists, still holding it out.

"I actually don't have a phone anymore," I admit.

He laughs, dismissing it, "Right," as if I'm not being serious.

"I'm not kidding. I threw it out the window when I left town and never got a new one," I clarify.

He seems to sense my honesty. "Can I give you my number so she can text me sometime?" Sam turns to Jonah.

"No problem," Jonah replies, taking his phone out of his coat pocket. "We'll get her a new phone immediately," he assures Sam.

"Does this mean you really, really forgive me?" I ask hopeful, turning my entire body toward Sam. I'm sure my face is covered in desperation.

"I could never stay mad at you, Kal," he responds sincerely. I wrap my arms around him in a hug before he can even finish his sentence.

"Thank you," I whisper, holding him tightly. "And again, I'm so sorry, Sam."

When I release him, he speaks to Jonah. "I'm Sam," he introduces himself, extending his hand across the table to Jonah.

"Jonah Everett," he replies, shaking Sam's hand.

"So, uh, how do you two know each other?" Sam asks Jonah and me. I take a sip of water, glancing at Jonah to come up with an answer to that.

"I was fortunate enough to have her as my waitress," he states casually, taking a sip of his water and fixing his gaze on me, silently inquiring if that response suffices.

"I'm currently a maid in his home," I add cheerfully. "You should come visit! You'd love his home."

"*Our* home," Jonah corrects.

Sam appears perturbed by Jonah's words, and I can't help but think it stems from the numerous times he pleaded with me to move in with him, and I consistently declined.

"Well, Sam, I appreciate you coming. I've missed you so much," I convey my happiness to him. "We've got a long drive ahead, so we need to hit the road. But I'll text you from Jonah's phone to check in and plan a time for you to come visit." I stand, pulling him into a tight embrace.

We bid farewell to Milo, and he urges us to visit again soon. Jonah insists on paying for our meal despite Milo's attempts to refuse. I'm not certain of the amount Jonah gave him, but it was enough to render Milo speechless before he pulled Jonah into a heartfelt hug.

DRIVING DOWN THE LONG DRIVEWAY, WE APPROACH THE MANSION. Gradually, it towers into view, its sheer size continues to amaze me. As I take in the details, I notice we're not turning toward the staff parking garage.

"Ummm," I point as he passes it. "Babe, you missed the turn," I say, glancing back.

"I missed the turn to the staff parking," he explains, his voice seemingly pleased with himself.

"Ohhh," I realize he is going to have me drop him off at the front door, and then I can go back and park. Assuming he must not want to walk through the staff parking garage. But then I am confused even more when he veers off to the left driveway. "Wait, where are you going?" I ask, looking at the rectangular driveway we just passed.

"I'm going to park," he replies, continuing to drive towards the far left side of the mansion where a large garage door is open.

"No, Jonah. I still work for you," I say concerned.

"Fine," he concedes. "Your boss demands your car be parked by his," he smiles.

As he pulls into the enormous garage, its sheer size is impressive. Capable of comfortably fitting thirty or so cars, but I'm taken aback to find only a modest five vehicles currently dispersed throughout the spacious area, leaving a surplus of unclaimed space. Parking Estelle in a generously open spot near a large black truck, I convey my surprise. "I thought you'd have more cars than this," I scan the surroundings.

With a flicker of amusement, he clarifies, "Two of them belong to Jonathan," before stepping out of my car and walking around to open my door.

"Thank you," I say, as I step out, heading to the back of the car to retrieve my bag. Lifting the trunk door open I go to reach inside but Jonah beats me to it, grabbing my bag and placing the strap on his shoulder.

"Cute," I remark sarcastically, pulling down the door to close.

"Glad you think so, I think you're pretty cute too," he quips, leaning in for a kiss, his free arm wrapping around my waist.

"Hey, I just want to make sure there won't be any issues... you're not planning to slap anyone or... fire anyone," I mention, referring to Jenevieve.

"I won't fire anyone, and I'll keep my hands to myself... with one exception—you," he says playfully.

"I'm fine with that," I say seductively, wrapping my arms around his neck and leaning in for another, more passionate kiss.

"Alright, alright, you two. You've had a couple of days to swallow each other's tongues," Jonathan comments, leaning in the doorway with his arms crossed.

We pull apart, laughing, our arms still wrapped around each other.

"Incoming in three, two, one," Jonathan announces.

"Kalyn," Shay says, entering the door just as Jonathan counts down. She hurries to me, tightly wrapping her arms around my neck, breathing into my hair. "Don't do that to me," she says, sounding worried.

"I'm sorry, Shay," I apologize, feeling remorseful. "Well, you've had your time with her," Shay remarks to Jonah, pulling me towards the door she just came through. "You can have your boyfriend back," she adds, referring to Jonathan.

"Hi, bye," I say to Jonathan as I walk past him.

He laughs, "Hi, Kal."

We make our way down the hall from the garage. "Where the fuck did you go?" Shay asks sounding worried.

"I needed to take a break and get some air," I explain, not wanting to delve into my family or details about Jonah. "Is Antoinette still here?" I ask, concerned about her potential reaction.

"No, Jonah made her leave... I'm the one who told him you left," she apologizes.

"It's okay," I reassure her. "It was... enlightening," I add, unsure of how else to express all the information Jonah gave me back at his rundown, not-so-rundown house.

"Feel like going for a walk, or are you tired?" she suggests, pointing to the courtyard.

"I'd love to go for a walk," I respond eagerly. I enjoy walks, and the courtyard behind Jonah's home is the most incredible one I've ever seen.

We meander through the beautiful winding pathways, admiring the flowers and meticulously sculpted shrubs, just catching up. Shay informs me about everything at work, detailing how Jenevieve made subtle jabs at me even in my absence. Which shouldn't surprise me, yet it does. I try to give her the benefit of the doubt repeatedly, but she makes it really hard.

A vast pond sprawls across the landscape, its tranquil surface reflecting the surrounding greenery. Perfectly sculpted waterfalls cascade gracefully. The sound of flowing water is so soothing, I feel it would be the perfect spot to sit and talk.

"Do you mind if we sit here for a while?" I ask pointing at the flat rocks intentionally placed around the edge of the pond.

"Not at all," she responds with a sunny disposition.

We discuss the beauty on the walking trails, acknowledging that living here feels like a dream, and then break off into silent calmness.

"Something is weighing heavily on me, and I want to talk to you about it," Shay breaks the quiet as she gazes at the water before turning to look at me.

"Of course, Shay. Is everything okay?" I ask, a little concerned.

"It's about you," she responds.

CHAPTER
Thirty-One

SHAYLA

I pick up the phone to the familiar voice of my boo, "Hi love," I excitedly greet as soon as I answer the phone, hopeful for his return as it has been a month since we last had sex. "Are you almost home?"

"Hey hun, we've made a pit stop for gas, but should be back in about five hours. By the way, there's a new girl that was recently hired. Can you keep an eye on her and let me know anything you find out about her," he requests, surprising me with his unusual ask.

"Who?" I cautiously ask.

"Her name is Kalyn," he reveals.

Chills envelop my body. Why does he want information on Kalyn? It's not jealousy that I feel by his request, but rather a sense of unease. "Kalyn is the new hire I DID befriend, but I won't spy on her, Jonathan," I assert, feeling irritated that he would even ask me to do this to my friend.

"You don't have to spy, honey, just keep an eye on her. Let me know if there are red flags… or even green ones," he reassures.

"You're essentially asking me to spy on her, and I won't do it," I bite out in frustration. Just the thought of doing that to her makes me feel I should be arrested for being the worlds biggest douche canoe.

"It's not for me, it's for Everett," he states, catching me off guard.

I find this entire phone call bizarre. Johnathan minds his own business, and he definitely doesn't concern himself with other women. But I wasn't expecting all of this to have anything to do with Mr. Everett. "What? Why?" I ask, bewildered.

"That's her," he discloses, his tone indicating a sense of urgency.

Her? It takes me a moment to even realize what he's talking about. When it registers that he's talking about the unsuspecting woman Mr. Everett has been infatuated with for years, my mouth goes dry. "Like HER?!" I blurt out, my jaw dropping. How am I just now finding out about this? Mr. Everett practically worships the ground this woman walks on. Why would he have anyone spy on her? I thought he wanted to marry her? Why did he bring her to work for him if he still wants someone to spy on her?

"Yes," he confirms. "Everett is out of his mind," his voice tinged with concern.

The sound of him retrieving the pump nozzle from the car echoes through the phone as he gives it a shake to get rid of any falling gas drops before hanging it back on the hook.

"Did he not know she was being hired?" I'm trying my best to make sense of everything he's telling me, but this is a lot of shit to unpack.

He sighs, "No, he found out a couple hours ago. I have to go—he's walking back to the car. Love you, honey."

"Love you too," I reply solemnly, my mood deflated from this call. "Oh, hun, I need to warn you… there was an incident, and her face is really beat up," I hold my breath, waiting for his response.

"What do you mean her face is beat up?" he whispers angrily on the other end of the receiver, not allowing me time to explain what happened. "Everett is going to murder us all. I have to go. See you soon," and then ends the call.

Mr. Everett is going to be furious when he sees her face. I stand here, clutching my phone, contemplating how I will even face her, knowing full well *the countless stories I've heard about Mr. Everett and Jonathan's encounters outside her work. Many times before they would return home, Jonathan forewarns me of Mr. Everett's heightened anger due to his failed attempts to jerk himself off, leaving him with massive blue balls. During these times, I wait for Jonathan in his room instead of the garage. When Mr. Everett is in these moods, me excitedly waiting for Jonathan to arrive home only seems to agitate him more.*

Countless times, I've felt the urge to track this woman down and shake some sense into her for failing to acknowledge Mr. Everett's obsession with her. I wanted to shove them in front of each other and yell, "There, just fuck already!" And now, in just five hours, they will be face to face.

I think of her working in the other room, having no idea this is taking place. I understand Mr. Everett's infatuation with her. The moment I saw Gladys with her, I knew I had to befriend her. I even consider her one of my best friend. Not only is she beautiful, but she is so funny, and compassionate. Mr. Everett doesn't even realize how much trouble he is about to find himself in when it comes to her.

As Jonathan and I lay intertwined in bed after finally making love that night, I confess, "My hands were drenched in sweat when I heard him approaching. He stopped right beside her. I can only imagine how fast his heart must have been racing."

I was on high alert, attuned to every sound, fully conscious of my surroundings, knowing he would arrive soon. I didn't know how this would all play out. Would he wait for her to finish lunch, or would he storm into the dining hall, causing a scene? Considering he is reserved—I instantly strike that option off the list of possibilities. But then remember, emotions might prompt uncharacteristic behaviors to emerge. Like him just finding out the woman he is in love with is now working in his house.

Or for instance, my own spontaneous decision to fly practically across the country just to see the man who captivated me at the airport while waiting for our flight, talked with me throughout the entirety of our flight, before parting ways. This behavior is unprecedented for me. Yet, he made me want to do it. Jonathan made me need to do it.

"He was already out of the car before I parked. Gladys told him she was at lunch, and he was long gone by the time I got in the house right after him."

"Jenevieve looked shocked when she saw him. I guess you guys returned earlier than expected?" It dawns on me they were back a couple of days earlier than planned.

I don't pay Jenevieve any mind. I can't stand her, and she isn't worth a single ounce of energy to think about. She confidently strode down the hall beside us, making sure to stomp her heels as she walked. Her entire demeanor immediately changed when his footsteps resounded down the hall. Her face lit up when she saw him, only to falter faintly when he stopped next to Kalyn. A knowing look in her eyes. She knew who Kalyn was. She knew what Kalyn meant to him. And Kalyn, she had no idea what was taking place.

"We went to the diner, and she wasn't there. He punched the dashboard so many times I thought he was going to make the airbag deploy," his expression remains serious. "I'm just gonna feel bad when she's being plowed by that bull-dozer," he jokes. "God, he's gonna destroy her insides. She's gonna be shredded and stitched back up daily." He pretends to shudder at the thought.

"Shut the fuck up," I playfully hit his shoulder.

He turns his shoulder away from me holding his arm up in a protective gesture as he continues teasing. "He's gonna have to fuck her for the first time in the hospital because she's gonna have to go right into surgery immediately after."

Laughter fills the room, and I welcome the respite from the seriousness of today's events. After a moment, the room falls silent.

"What's wrong?" I turn on my side to look at Jonathan.

"She's his kryptonite. He thinks she is going to solve all of his problems. I just worry what will happen if even she isn't able to get him working again," each word heavy with defeat.

"Have you seen her?" I ask rhetorically, my shock evident. "I have the sexiest man alive, and I still want to bang her. If she can't fix him, he's doomed for life."

"What if she doesn't reciprocate his feelings?" he meets my gaze.

"Well luckily for everyone, she does. You should have seen them today. The chemistry between them was so intense if someone had lit a match, the entire town would have exploded. The sparks between them made us all feel hot—well, all of us except Jenevieve," I add, my face contorting in disgust.

"I'm surprised she's still amongst the living," he remarks. "I thought he was going to kill her for Kalyn's face."

"He almost hit her," I interject, recalling the moment he nearly backhanded her. I secretly wished he had. I would have loved to see her brought down a few notches.

"Doesn't surprise me," he adds.

"The only reason he didn't was because Kal stepped in and blamed herself for getting hurt," the words come out sounding shocked as I remember the situation. "Speaking of which, she must know who Kalyn is, right? I mean, Jenevieve is a bitch to everyone, but I've never seen her be so cruel to someone in my entire life."

I remember Kalyn telling me three days after the fact, that Jenevieve had backhanded her. I was seeing red. I was off her bed storming toward the door, nearly there before Kalyn raced after me, blocking the door. I was seething with rage, ready to go kick the shit out of Jenevieve.

But Kalyn stopped me, saying she didn't want anyone fighting her battles. She warned that if I didn't keep my mouth shut, she would never confide in me again. That night, as we lay in her bed, she opened up to me about her struggles to trust others. She didn't know how to open up, yet, sometimes, all she wanted was for someone to just listen to her—a way to vent her frustrations. She explained how it would make her feel like a coward and she would be more embarrassed to have someone else confront Jenevieve. She assured me she could handle Jenevieve on her own.

At the time, I was unaware of Mr. Everett's feelings for her. Now, I am glad I kept my mouth shut. This is going to be better than walking into a candy store as a child, getting to fill a bag with an assortment of your favorite candies. The joy I will feel watching Jenevieve crumble under the heartbreak she will face. Kalyn will emerge victorious. All the suffering she endured at the hands of Jenevieve will be worth it because she will triumph in the end. This time… the villain doesn't win.

"Yeah, she definitely knows who she is. Kalyn's face is burned in her memory from the night everything went down," he states matter-of-factly.

"Wasn't she with Mr. Everett that night?" I ask, trying to clarify the details.

Jonathan snickers, "She was sucking his dick when he saw her for the first time, and his dick went limp in Jenevieve's mouth. It hasn't worked since then. Except for the times he would watch Kalyn at work," he adds. "God, I think about how he must have felt to see her walking down the hall only to be up close to her and find bruises all over her face."

"Poor Mr. Everett. Poor Kalyn, to be treated so poorly, and she doesn't even understand why," feeling compassion for both of them.

CHAPTER

Thirty-Two

KALYN

Shay fixes her gaze on me, her expression filled with worry. "Are you upset with me for not telling you I've known of Mr. Everett's feelings for you?"

I take a moment to gather my thoughts. "No, I'm not angry, and I can't say I wish you had told me because I believe it unfolded as it needed to. I just can't shake the feeling that I was somewhat of a joke," I respond honestly, pausing as I contemplate my words. "Who else knew who I was?"

She hesitates briefly before admitting, "I found out the day Mr. Everett returned. Gladys, Giles, and Jenevieve knew. I believe that's everyone." She shares the information sincerely. "But you are the furthest thing from a joke. Quite the opposite. We were all so enamored by you. It was like we got to see the real you without you feeling like you had to be something you're not."

Some things are starting to make sense, while others remain shrouded. I understand Jenevieve's animosity towards me, her resorting to physical harm or starving me in an attempt to vent her anger for the woman that has Jonah's affection being in his house. But Brad's behavior puzzles me. He's a flirt with everyone, and initially, I interpreted his annoying conversations as lame attempts to flirt with me. However, he bluntly stated that I wasn't his type, yet seemed bothered by seeing Jonah and me holding hands. Despite never making a move on me, he always appears... jealous? It feels like we're trapped in a circus, and I'm the clown on constant display, walking on the tightrope.

"Gladys knew?" I exclaim, taken aback. "Is that why she hired me?" It did almost seem like she was waiting for me the day I first arrived in the staff kitchen. And then she led me straight to my bedroom, as if she already knew it was meant for me. Even though she claimed all the suites had the same amenities, I later discovered that mine was almost twice the size of the others. It had been deliberately overlooked when assigning rooms to employees to avoid any potential conflicts. Yet, Gladys deemed me worthy enough to have the largest bedroom.

Shay maintains a concerned look, "If you ask me, I think she might have been the one who had someone place the flyer on your door."

I burst into laughter. "Sweet Gladys?! Do you really think she would?"

Shay leans into my shoulder, "I'm ninety-nine point one hundred percent sure it was her."

What is the actual likelihood of Gladys orchestrating something like that? It requires a lot of time and planning, not to mention finding someone willing to make such a long drive for a two-second task. Or did she find someone local to do it? Somehow, a flyer *did* mysteriously appear on my door, and as far as I am aware, my door only. It all seems like an awful lot of effort to go through just on the chance that someone would apply for the job.

Conversations with Shay flow effortlessly. She's open-minded and gives the best advice. I feel bad that she worried about whether to tell me she's known about Jonah's feelings for me since the day I met him. After all, I am the one who told her I didn't want her saying anything to anyone about me. I guess that could also extend to even myself. She always has good intentions and is incredibly kind-hearted. She loves passionately and fiercely protects those she cares about. I believe she thought she was doing the right thing by not telling me everything about Jonah.

Honestly, I think she made the right decision. Besides, if she had gotten involved, things could have gotten worse for everyone. I can't imagine how I would have reacted if I hadn't been given the time to slowly process what was happening between Jonah and me. I still don't fully understand what we're even doing...

After a full week back home, Jenevieve is acutely aware that Jonah and I were away together, but nobody knows where we went, not even Shay. I can only imagine Jenevieve has attempted to gather information from anyone she could, but since nobody knows anything, she wouldn't have obtained any answers, leaving her incredibly bothered by this lack of knowledge.

She has likely already concocted her own version of what she thinks we were doing, which would only exacerbate her frustration. Although, I'm willing to bet her mind wouldn't even entertain the possibility that he and I were intimate. So, the story she created wouldn't have hurt her feelings as much as the reality actually would.

Today, her anger is palpable, although it hardly deviates from her perpetual state of a scorned woman. So, at least shes consistent. While she gives orders, she expects us all to look at her while simultaneously demanding we avoid direct eye contact with her. It feels like an immature power play, feeding into her sense of control.

The slight puffiness under her eyes hints at her losing sleep most likely from not being able to figure out where Jonah and I were.

I always bring out the best in her.

My spidey senses remain on high alert when she is near, making it easier for me to know when I am about to be punished for something. She gives orders arrogantly and then stiffly shifts her head to look at me before she abruptly changes where I will be for the day. She remains in place as everyone disperses. As I approach, her eyes stare me down, and I know she is going to do something—my reflexes kick in when she reaches her long pointed claws out toward me and tries grabbing me by my arm.

"You might want to think twice before you put your hands on me."

She lowers her arm, her face contorting with even more disdain. "You are useless… go work with your own species," she sneers. "Stables," she orders bluntly, pointing for me to go.

Without another word, I turn to leave, with her following behind, probably because she gets some sort of satisfaction from watching me have to do the shitty chores she appoints to me. I imagine she stands at the window, watching me until I am fully out of sight whenever she sends me to the stables.

Today, I grow a stronger backbone. Ignoring her instructions, I don't head for the stables—I walk in the direction of Jonah's office. Although I have no plans on actually interrupting him with this matter, I still find it amusing when she realizes what I am doing and nearly runs after me, yanking on the back of my uniform and telling me she decided she wants me dusting today after all.

Cleaning the stables wouldn't have been so bad if Brad wasn't going to be there. I make every effort to avoid him, as I am still mad over everything that went down with him and Amber. She still won't talk to me even though I always say hi to her when I see her and try my best to have conversations with her, only to be met with silence.

Throughout the week, news spread like wildfire that Jenevieve would be leaving on Friday for a whole week, and I couldn't be happier. She turns her departure into a grand affair, making sure everyone is aware she's leaving as if she believes people are genuinely interested. The atmosphere in the house noticeably relaxes the moment she exits.

"I have a surprise for you," Jonah whispers in my ear as I stand at my bathroom counter after my shower, wrapped in only a towel.

"Oh?" I squeeze a small dab of moisturizer onto my fingertip, twisting the cap shut before smoothing the cream over my face. Wiping my fingers on my towel, I turn to wrap my arms around his shoulders. I can't recall him ever giving me a surprise before, and it piques my curiosity, even more so by his timing. With Jenevieve's absence, he already appears more relaxed, which makes me instantly wish she would just never come back.

"Mmhmm," he wraps his arms around my waist and effortlessly lifts me onto the counter.

"When do I get this surprise?" I raise a brow.

Truth be told, I've never been a fan of surprises. However, the thought of him taking time from his busy day to do something for me makes me feel special.

He glances at his watch. "In an hour," sounding rather pleased with himself.

"Does my surprise entail anything specific?" I trace my finger down the front of his pants, secretly hoping it involves him taking me to my bed right now.

"Absolutely not," he grins. "Get dressed and meet me by the front door." With his arms wrapped around my waist, he gently pulls me off the counter, setting me back down on the floor before pressing his lips to mine. "See you in a bit," he nudges my face with his nose and strides out of my bathroom.

He kept the details of my surprise a secret, leaving me unsure what I'm supposed to wear. I loosely curl my hair, apply a light layer of makeup, and find a pink floral dress in my closet, pairing it with sandals.

As I approach, I see him peering through the glass by the front door. Sensing me approaching, he turns his head, a smile forming on his face as he scans my appearance. Withdrawing his hands from his pants pockets, he walks over to me.

"You are stunning, baby… I believe your surprise has arrived," he towers over me, and, in his playful manner, he zombie-walks behind me, his arms straight down in front of me, chin resting on the top of my head as we walk toward the front door.

"You're deliberately slowing me down," I tease, as he sticks to the back of me like a backpack.

"Anglerfish," he whispers, followed by a belly laugh. As he removes his arms from in front of me, he reaches out to pull open the front door.

Outside, I spot Sam at the back of a car, a man in a black tuxedo handling his luggage.

"Sam?!" I exclaim, my voice brimming with excitement. He lifts his gaze, and a happy expression appears.

"Hey, Kal," he grins, and I eagerly rush down the steps, throwing my arms around his neck.

"Oh my gosh!" I hold onto him tightly. "You're really here!" I sigh, savoring the moment. This is a better surprise than I could have ever imagined. Jonah must have coordinated with Sam to arrange this visit for me. My heart swells at Jonah's thoughtful gesture and the presence of my best friend.

Releasing him from the hug, we turn towards the house. Jonah is leaning against the doorway, while Sam takes in the surroundings.

"Damn, dude, this is an incredible place," he comments to Jonah, his eyes scanning the massive house.

I recall being in his shoes, finding it hard to grasp the size of Jonah's home. Now it feels familiar, although there's nothing ordinary about it. Walking up the stairs to the entryway, Jonah stands up from the doorframe, exuding contentment.

"Where's your king's cloak, your royal highness?" Sam jokes, bowing to Jonah.

"I wear that... and only that in the bedroom," Jonah retorts with a smirk.

"TMI," Sam snickers, holding his hand up as if to try to stop the words from entering his ears.

"How long are you staying?" I ask, snaking my arm around his as we walk inside.

"Just a couple of days. I only took today and Monday off work, I go home Sunday night," his tone upbeat yet tinged with a hint of disappointment.

Giles approaches as the man who helped Sam with his bags enters. Giles swiftly takes the bags and heads off with them in the opposite direction of my room, which confuses me as I assumed Sam would just be staying with me. Then I realize Jonah must have also thought of this and decided against it, arranging a separate sleeping space for Sam.

We walk through the house, showing Sam around. Jonah guides us to a suite near his room where Sam will be staying. Along the way, we pass by Shay and Amber, who are engrossed in conversation, walking somewhere together. For a moment, I hesitate, wondering if Amber will ignore me if I try to introduce her to Sam. I don't want to give Sam any reason to think things are bad here.

Shay's face lights up when she sees us. "You must be Sam. Kal talks about you all the time, and I've been trying not to slip up the last couple of days about your visit," she says, hugging Sam.

"Hey," Sam responds, returning the hug. "I guess I can't stay mad at you for taking my place as Kal's best friend when you're this nice."

I glance at Amber, hoping she's open to an introduction, and she returns my gaze warmly. I take this as a sign she won't make a scene if I try to talk to her.

"Sam, this is my friend, Amber," I introduce, as he extends his hand, giving hers a gentle shake in greeting.

"It's a pleasure to meet you, Amber. I've heard so much about you as well," he says with a smile. "I believe there's one more person from the group you always talk about, right? Lilly?" He looks at me for confirmation.

"Yep, she's around here somewhere," I reply, scanning around us.

"Well, I'm sure we will see so much more of you during your visit. It was nice to meet you, Sam. We're on our way to go watch a movie," Shay announces, linking arms with Amber and tugging her along, as Amber stares bashfully at Sam.

"Nice to meet you too. See you guys around," he calls after them.

As we enter the suite where Sam will be staying, his eyes widen as he lets out an impressed whistle. "Damn, maybe I'm not going to leave after all."

The room looks like a fancy suite in a high-end luxury hotel. "Me too! I have never been in here, but I can't wait to stay in here with you," I say, smiling as I flop onto the bed on my stomach.

Jonah comes up behind me and gives my butt a light smack. "Nice try, baby. You'll be staying with me."

"I'll be right back," Sam excuses himself, as he walks towards the bathroom, closing the door behind him.

"I am going to fuck you so good tonight, babe," I roll onto my back and pull on Jonah's shirt, bringing him between my spread legs, kissing him passionately.

"So you like your surprise?" his voice low as our lips remain touching.

"I love it, thank you," our kiss intensifies.

"Okay, you two. No need to break in my bed before I sleep in it," Sam jokes, emerging from the bathroom.

The following evening, I find myself walking back towards Jonah's office when I unexpectedly come across Amber.

"Hey, Kalyn," she says nervously.

"Amber, hi," I respond happily.

"I was hoping we could talk."

"Of course. Want to go for a walk outside?" I gesture towards the courtyard, to which she eagerly agrees.

It's been a while since Amber and I had the chance to talk privately. Whether she wants to yell at me or try to patch things up with me, I figure the courtyard is the perfect setting to talk privately. I still feel bad for everything that happened with her and Brad. Since she distanced herself, I've been in the dark about how she's been holding up. Shay and Lilly never bring it up. Then again, Shay spends all her free time with me or Jonathan. I hope Amber hasn't taken that as Shay taking sides. But seeing them yesterday heading to go watch a movie together in the home theater suggests she must not have thought too much about it.

"I want to apologize for the way I have been behaving," she says as we slowly stroll along the beautiful paths out here. "I was foolish to think you would have been having relations with Brad. I was so infatuated with him that I didn't listen to anything anybody else said about him. I was so blindsided when he said your name… you know. It made me angry at you. And I can see now that my anger was misguided. I'm really sorry," her eyes welling with tears.

"I would never hurt you like that, Amber," I say sincerely. "But also… I've been kind of seeing Mr. Everett for a while now."

Her expression becomes animated. "Okay, so when I saw him carrying you out of Shay's room, I was literally stunned frozen.

Everyone started whispering, and Jess was like, 'They've been sleeping together for a while now, they aren't even that secretive about it,' and continued on like it was no big deal, while the rest of us couldn't even move. Then Shay acted oblivious about it and Lilly just kept her mouth shut. So, how is it? He's so…intimidating. Is he always like that?" She speaks rapidly.

"One question at a time," I playfully remark. "Shay and I were teasing him and Jonathan the night before, hence him carrying me out of her room like a sack of potatoes. Jess caught on because we always get partnered to clean, and Jonah isn't trying to be secretive to anyone," I explain as she interrupts me.

Her mouth opens wide, "Jonah! You call him by his first name?!" She grabs at her chest and clenches her shirt. "Okay, is Jonahh, as well-endowed as everyone whispers about?" she says his name as if she is not supposed to be saying it.

"And then some," I smile.

"I knew it! I bet he's incredible in bed," she rolls her eyes dramatically.

She's absolutely right. He is amazing in bed. "The best I've ever had," I answer honestly.

"Does Jenevieve know? She's meaner to you than anyone else!" she says, finally piecing everything together.

"Oh, she knows," I say, thinking about how much she knows. She is all too familiar with me. I'm sure she thinks about my ultimate demise every second of every day.

"How'd she find out?"

"Jonah told her… and half the staff… and his mother, the day Mrs. Everett's diamonds went missing. Vanessa decided to lie and blame me for the stolen jewelry, and Jenevieve claimed to have found the necklace in my room. I guess Jonah felt that was the perfect time to let everyone know that I couldn't have been the one who took them because he was fucking me all night. Oh, and letting everyone know that during the time they were supposedly stolen, I was riding his cock," I say as I watch her mouth hang open.

"Holy shit."

"That's funny, that's exactly what I thought when he said it," I chuckle.

"Is he as intimidating in a private setting as he is all the time?" she asks. "Like I feel nervous just thinking about him."

"I don't think so. Then again, I have gone to work with his semen still inside me. So our perceptions of him are quite different," I reply.

"That is so sexy. Is his… semen in you right now?" she raises a brow and looks over at me.

"Maybe," we both laugh. "Come on, you can come hang out with us." I take her hand and lead her back inside toward Jonah's office.

"Is he gonna mind if I come into his office?" she asks nervously.

"Of course not," I open the door and walk inside. Sam and Jonah are sitting in lounge chairs, engaged in conversation. Amber looks anxious, so I subtly pull her arm and guide her forward. Walking over to them, I point at an empty chair next to Sam for her to sit in, and playfully tug Sam's ear as I walk by as a way of saying hi. Then make myself comfortable on Jonah's lap.

"Hey, babe," I turn my head towards him and give him a kiss.

"Hi, baby," he responds, his gaze softening as he looks at me.

"Hey, Amber," Sam greets her with a wave as she takes a seat.

"Hi, Sam," she nervously responds, waving back.

"So, what were you guys talking about?" I ask, leaning back and lacing my fingers in Jonah's, wrapping his arms around my waist.

"Our favorite topic… you," Jonah grins, pressing his nose into my cheek.

"Oh goody, can't wait to participate in this conversation," I muse.

"Too late Kal, we've already shared all the secrets before you got here," Sam adds.

"Well, I probably could have been helpful to this conversation, but I suppose you guys know best," I tease.

"How did you two meet?" Amber asks Sam, glancing between the two of us.

"We met in middle school. We have been best friends ever since," Sam recalls happily.

"Was she always so pretty?" Amber asks, smiling at me.

"She used to wear her sweatshirt with the hood up and gave everyone dirty looks, no one dared to approach her," we both laugh.

"And yet, here you are," I tease him.

Sam was the only one who made any attempt to get to know me. After weeks of him persistently trying to be my friend, I decided, why not? Then realized he and I got along perfectly.

As the night goes on, Amber noticeably relaxes, and Shay and Jonathan eventually join us. We spend the evening engaging in random topics and laughing. It feels really good to spend time with friends, enjoying each other's company. When it's time to call it a night, Amber invites Sam to accompany her on a walk, and he agrees enthusiastically.

We all part ways, and Jonah and I make our way back to his room for the night.

THE WEEKEND WENT BY FAR TOO QUICKLY. I HUG SAM GOODBYE, holding onto him tightly, not wanting him to leave. "I'm just going to hold you hostage here and never let you go," I say, tears welling up in my eyes.

"Your boyfriend is already giving me a death stare," he teases, and I reluctantly let go of him. "Kal, I don't want to step on your toes, but I was wondering… would you mind if I asked Amber for her number?"

"Of course not. Amber is great," I reply, feeling excited that he's interested in her. Unlike Brad, Sam is a genuinely good man. If things get serious between them, I have no doubt he will treat her like a queen.

I walk back to Jonah and wrap my arms around him, while Amber talks to Sam. We go back inside, and I glance back to see he is putting her number in his phone, both smiling.

Feeling tired, I yawn. "Give me a kiss, I want to go to bed."

"What does a kiss have to do with it?" he asks, smiling.

"Are you going to walk me to my room?" I assumed we were going to go our separate ways from here since we just spent three nights together.

"Yes. Let's get you to bed," he replies and takes my hand.

I start walking toward the maid's quarters when he tugs my arm, pulling me back toward him. "Hmm-mm," he says, leaning down to kiss me. "Wrong way," he whispers and begins walking in the direction of his room, and I eagerly follow.

CHAPTER
Thirty-Three

KALYN

I find myself casually propped against the L-shaped counter in the second kitchen, a distinct departure from the expansive staff area. Unlike the latter, it almost feels "normal" in here except for its oversized dimensions, but it is beautiful, with sleek black cupboards and pristine white marble countertops. It appears more akin to a standard, well-appointed kitchen. Even though I highly doubt Jonah has ever ventured in here before. Nevertheless, it remains stocked with fresh produce, impeccably maintained, and cleaned spotless.

From this viewpoint, I have a clear vantage point across the kitchen, extending into a fully furnished living room with cozy couches and meticulously arranged decor. A generously sized TV, hanging on the wall, is currently playing a Hallmark movie that has me completely captivated.

Jonah approaches from behind, brushing my hair aside and leaving tender kisses on the exposed skin beneath the delicate straps of my loosely draped dress.

"Hi, babe," I greet him with a smile as he works his way up my neck.

"You smell amazing," he remarks, his member pressing against my backside. He continues to graze kisses on my neck, then softly nips at my ear. "I got you something."

"Oh?" I turn my head to the side to look at him.

He brings his mouth to mine, our tongues intertwining.

"Yes," he responds, kissing me again. I can hear him place something on the counter in front of me. I break away from the kiss and glance down to find he got me a new phone.

I stare at it. "Well, ain't that somethin'," I grin at him. He taps the screen, and it illuminates with a photo—a selfie he captured of me peacefully asleep in his arms on the couch at the abandoned mansion. In the picture, he's holding me, a smile on his face, with his head resting against mine.

"You better stop right now, Mr. Everett," I declare, "or I am going to get down on one knee right here, right now," I joke as I open my phone.

"Is that a promise, Mrs. Everett?" he counters, his voice a seductive whisper brushing near my ear.

"It might be," I tease back, browsing my phone. Noticing two new messages, I click on the messages icon, revealing two conversations—one labeled 'Sam,' while Jonah's contact name reads 'Your Jonah,' which makes my heart instantly swell with emotion. Choosing Jonah's first, it begins with a cheerful "FIRST! Hi baby," instantly bringing a smile to my face. The second is from Sam, with a conversation between Jonah and Sam unfolding inside.

JONAH

Hello Sam, this is Kalyn's new phone. Bringing it to her now.

SAM

> Hi Jonah, thank you. Saving her number.

SAM

> Kal, text me when you get this.

SAM

> Miss ya.

"Thank you," I murmur softly, leaning into him, his chin resting on my shoulder, his arms wrapping around my waist, as we both peer at the phone screen.

"You're welcome."

I pull up the camera on my phone. "We need a picture where we can both smile." Raising the phone, I snap a photo. My heart floods with joy as I see the pure happiness reflected in both of our faces. I navigate to his contact and replace it with this picture, ensuring I'll see it every time he calls.

Jonah releases his embrace and settles on the floor beside my legs, leaning his back against the cupboards. "What are you doing?" I smile down at him.

He grabs my thigh closest to him, parting it as he situates himself directly beneath me.

"What are you doing?" I ask again, staring down at him, my breath slightly heavier and tinged with desire as he locks eyes with me. His hands roam up my legs beneath my dress, and in true Jonah fashion, he rips my panties away.

"Jonah!" I exclaim, attempting to suppress the excitement coursing through me. I am unable to protest further as his warm tongue slides between my slit.

"Jonah," my words coming out as an aroused exhale.

I grip my fingers in his hair to steady myself as I stand over his gorgeous face. I stare down at him as his eyes remain closed, while he continues devouring me.

My breathing quickens as the delightful feeling of his tongue circling and gliding over my swollen bud heightens. Tilting my head back, my hips begin to sway rhythmically on his tongue. I shift my leg onto his shoulder, granting him better access, and he eagerly seizes the opportunity to bury his face even deeper, squeezing tightly around my thighs.

He maneuvers his tongue in ways I have never felt before. With delicate caresses transitioning seamlessly into assertive pressure, he tantalizes every inch of my sensitive area. As he glides down to my entrance, he teases the outer edges, and then his tongue penetrates me. He delves in and out, exploring my core, as my panting grows louder. I need him deeper. I need him in and on every part of me. Pulling him into me by his hair and urging him closer, I press my hips into his face. In response, a primal groan rumbles from him, sending vibrations coursing through me.

I hear the dreadful click of Jenevieve's heels from a distance.

"Jonah, stop," I say through a breathy moan, scared Jenevieve will stab me if she sees us. But he doesn't stop. He moves his grip from my thighs to my ass and squeezes tighter. "Jonah, stop, someone is com—" I try to get out but find my body leans forward on the counter as he slides his thick middle finger inside me, and begins rocking it on my G-spot while licking and sucking my swollen bud. "Fuck," I sigh, my eyes rolling back. I bring my hand back down and grab a handful of his hair, tightening my fingers and pulling him into me once more, crushing my thighs around him as I feel my orgasm growing.

Jenevieve enters the room opposite the counter Jonah and I are behind. His fingers maintain their steady rhythm, rocking back and forth, then in and out while licking my pussy. I make my best attempt to look like I am not currently using his face as a chair. If he doesn't ease up on his movements, I fear I will cum all over his face.

Gripping his hair tighter, I try to push myself off him, only to be met with his unyielding strength, pinning me in place, tethering me to the overwhelming bliss.

I've noticed she's not only incredibly controlling but also very nosy. I assume she comes in here to see why the TV and lights are on, probably hoping to catch someone in here so she can yell at them. As she rounds the corner and sees me, she abruptly stops. It's as if she almost believes her mind is playing tricks on her because there is no way, on God's green earth, that me of all people would be in this part of the mansion, and that she would have to see me outside of business hours. After she gathers her thoughts, she looks furious.

"What are you doing in here?" she hisses, her disgust palpable.

"Hi, Jenevieve," I manage to say, my voice trembling trying my best to hold back my orgasm as my core clenches.

Jonah has an unwavering rhythm, and I know I'm going to succumb to the orgasm that's building. His finger relentlessly stimulates my G-spot, and when I think it can't get any more intense, he withdraws his finger, only to immediately replace it with two, stretching me wider.

Involuntarily, I lower myself, opening up even more for him. Every part of my body aches to rock against his fingers and tongue. At this point, I don't even think I can speak a coherent word. My body and brain are giving in to him.

"What are you doing? Answer my question!" she demands.

My free hand, not entwined in his hair, reaches for the side of the counter. I grip tightly, anchoring myself in position as I make my best attempt to withhold my imminent release in front of Jenevieve, knowing I will regret it as soon as the high is over. In my current state of brain haze, I'm finding it less hard to care that she is here.

"I… uhh…" the words come out in a breathy gasp as I grip the counter tighter, shifting forward as he continues fingering me and working wonders on all my sensitive spots.

"Miss Jenevieve," Giles intervenes from behind us, no doubt seeing what is occurring on this side of the counter but drawing no attention to it. In fact, he is so nonchalant over it, I wonder if he somehow missed me sitting on Jonah's face.

As my knees begin to tremble, I bite my lip, and my eyes flutter closed in anticipation.

"May I have a word with you?" Giles strides across the kitchen, extending his hand toward the doorway Jenevieve just came through, clearly intent on escorting her out of the room.

She glares at me but reluctantly acquiesces, exiting the room and he trails after her. I don't think they could have made it fully out of earshot before my orgasm explodes out of me, and I begin grinding on Jonah's face riding the waves, my vagina muscles squeezing around his fingers.

"Fuuuuck," I moan, feeling my body jolt as I begin to finish. Jonah's fingers slow, and his tongue now gently rubs my clit.

He turns his head and softly bites my thigh as he removes his fingers, eliciting another moan from my lips. Finally, my body gives in, collapsing onto the counter, my cheek resting against the cool hardness of the surface as I allow my breathing to steady.

Jonah stands behind me and lays his body over mine, wrapping his arms widely around me as if in a protective position. He kisses my shoulder and then rests his head on mine.

I hear Giles's footsteps returning, lingering momentarily before he quietly exits again.

I'm not sure I can even walk right now. My legs feel like they are jelly.

Without asking, Jonah picks up my phone placing it in his pocket. Then, effortlessly scoops me up, carrying me to his bedroom where we spend the rest of the night together.

I awaken to the faint sound of the shower turning on. Slipping out of bed, I pad quietly to the bathroom, where I discover Jonah standing, his skin glistening with sweat, every muscle of his naked form on display. "Did you just finish your workout?" I ask, my expression softening as I appreciate the captivating sight before me.

He turns his head, returning the smile. "Indeed," he confirms. "Care to join me in the shower?" He gestures subtly towards the running water, a playful glint dancing in his eyes.

"My hair is still damp from our shower a few hours ago," I mention, smiling and crossing my arms. "I suppose I didn't give you a good enough workout last night," I tease.

"Oh, but you did," he responds, walking over to kiss me before heading to the shower. I watch through the glass, mesmerized, as he steps under the water, looking up, allowing it to cascade over his face. Each droplet that lands on him follows the contours of his body, flowing down. He begins washing away the sweat, and the simple movement is so utterly sexy, I feel myself starting to become aroused. The rising steam gradually veils my view, leaving only his silhouette visible until the mist shrouds my view.

At this point, I have two options: get in the shower with him and have amazing morning shower sex, which will undoubtedly make me late for work, or be responsible and force my legs to carry me out of here, allowing me to be on time for work and giving me sexy thoughts to carry me through my workday.

The clock on his nightstand reads seven in the morning, and I make my way back to the maid's quarters. With a sense of ease, I begin to prepare for work, methodically dressing in my uniform and loosely braiding my hair. Before leaving, I go to my nightstand and send Sam a good morning text, wishing him a great day at work, then set my phone back down.

"Good morning," Shay greets as we both step out of our doors simultaneously. "You look remarkably refreshed," she grins. "And you are walking so well. It seems you're getting accustomed to being plowed by an Arizona Iced Tea can," referring to Jonah's size as she looks down at me walking.

"Well, that's quite the mental picture to start the day with. Thanks for that," I quip.

"Jonathan wanted to play with toys last night. I'm a little sore today, but it was so worth it," her face is mixed with satisfaction and mischief.

"Are you two finished?" Jenevieve stands in front of us, glowering down between us.

"He has a couple more we are going to try tonight. I can't wait," Shay continues, ignoring Jenevieve to finish what she was saying. Then turns to face her. "We are now. You could have waited before interrupting our conversation," she says, annoyed.

Jenevieve carries on as if Shay didn't say anything to her, striding along the rows and doling out commands to the rest of us, seizing every chance to shoot me a glare. In response, I offer her a wide smile, just for good measure. This momentarily disrupts her composure in frustration, but she regains her focus and proceeds to instruct all of us on our cleaning assignments for the day.

Shay and I are dusting a hallway on the third floor, yet my attention keeps drifting to the window.

"I want to go camping."

Shay comes up beside me and looks out the window where I am looking. "It won't be that exciting, but I'm sure Jonathan has a tent somewhere around here. Do you want to set it up in the trees over there?" She points to the wooded area off to the far side of the courtyard.

"Not here, dork. I want to pack my car with camping gear and actually drive to the mountains."

"I never pictured you for the camping type," she glances in my direction and then back out the window.

"In the summers, Sam's family used to take me camping with them. I've missed it. Just the thought of it brings back such vivid memories. I haven't been since high school, and I want to feel the freeing sensation of being in the woods again. I miss being surrounded by the sounds of running water, the birds chirping, and the smell of the crisp morning air when you first step out of the tent. I miss the smell of nature and the crackling of the fire as little embers dance their way toward the night sky," I say with a wistful sigh, lost in nostalgia.

"I love camping. Jonathan mentioned wanting to go somewhere for the three-day weekend Mr. Everett is giving the staff for the holiday."

My face lights up. "Wanna go on an adventure?!"

"Duh!" she excitedly claps her hands.

Throughout the week, we discuss our upcoming camping trip, and Jonathan eagerly joins. To prepare, he and Shay venture out after work one of the days to procure camping gear, considering we have none. They purchase a fantastic double camping tent that we can share. It has two sleeping rooms and an additional space at the entrance. All three areas of the tent can be unzipped to allow a wide-open space or zipped up for privacy walls.

They also get us comfortable air mattresses, cozy blankets and pillows, a kitchen tent, fold-out tables, coolers, and chairs. They will go grocery shopping the day before we leave to stock up on food and drink items, and Shay and I compile a list of all the essentials we will need: from first aid kits and bug spray to bear spray and various other necessities we anticipate might come in handy.

We extend an invitation to Amber and Lilly. Amber excitedly tells us that she invited Sam to join, and he said yes, while Lilly said absolutely not. Things with Amber and Sam have apparently been going really well, and I couldn't be happier for the two of them.

Sam also calls and texts me, letting me know he and Amber are happy and is interested in pursuing a relationship with her.

To liven up our trip, Shay invites some of her and Jonathan's friends who will meet us at the location Shay has picked out for us.

I haven't asked Jonah if he will come with me yet. Shay and Jonathan are at odds on whether they think he will come. Shay believes Jonah will willingly go along with any request of mine, no matter how ridiculous it might be. On the other hand, Jonathan suggests that Jonah wouldn't want to get dirt on his suit, even if there's a chance he will "get pussy" out of it.

ON THURSDAY AFTER WORK, SHAY AND JONATHAN HEAD OUT FOR their shopping expedition as planned. While they are gone, I have been tasked with talking Jonah into coming with us. Since I know he is still working, I make my way to his office. Over time, I've become accustomed to our interactions. I usually knock softly on his office door while entering, never waiting for permission. He never seems to mind. In fact, his beautiful face lights up every time I come in unexpectedly, so I continue doing it.

"Hello, baby," he greets, looking up from typing on his computer.

"Hi."

Approaching his desk, I take a seat on it right in front of him. He leans back in his chair, his elbows on the arm rest, clasping his hands together on his stomach. I slide my slippers off onto the floor and loop each of my feet into the arms of his chair, pulling him closer to me. This maneuver wouldn't be possible if he didn't willingly move forward towards me, and I appreciate his willing-ness to fill the space between us.

"Let me tell you about my boss," I begin, leaning forward and seizing the collar of his shirt, drawing him closer. "He's this in-credibly sexy man," I pull him in for a kiss when his face is near.

"And guess what? He's giving his employees a three-day weekend. So, Shay and I came up with a plan for the time off. I'm extending an invitation to you to join us. I figure I need something good to look at while we're away," I shrug my shoulders casually, as if it's no big deal.

Curiosity spreads across his face.

"We're going camping," I announce, beaming at him, hoping to ignite some excitement in him.

He freezes and appears to be questioning if he heard me correctly. He blinks, processing my words while his gaze remains fixed on me.

While camping is clearly something he's not thrilled about, I'm hopeful he'll join. I want to share every experience with him. However, if he decides not to come, I'll understand and will still be excited for our adventure nonetheless.

"If you don't want to come you don't have to. But we leave tomorrow," I give him a kiss, then swing my legs over him before stepping down from the desk and slipping my feet back into my slippers.

He rises from his chair and joins me as I reach back to him, our hands intertwining naturally. Leading him, I guide us to the garage where Jonathan and Shay have just returned.

"What's up," Jonathan calls cheerfully as he steps out of his truck.

"Show us what you got," I eagerly exclaim, fists balled at my sides, joyfully bouncing in place.

Jonah's gaze fixes on my chest as he licks his bottom lip, then leans over, effortlessly wrapping an arm around my waist and lifting me off the ground. My legs instinctively wrap around his waist, and my arms encircle his neck.

"Are you wanting to get bent over the tailgate and fucked right now, Ms. Bell?" He spanks my butt before moving closer to the tailgate so we can see what they got.

I grin back at him. "Is that all I have to do to turn you on, Mr. Everett?" I tug my tank top down slightly to reveal more of my bare breasts, stopping just short of exposing my nipples.

His breath hitches, and he tenses his jaw, delivering another spank.

He sets me on the tailgate, and I turn to face Shay, who's seated on the opposite side. One leg is bent while the other swings lazily back and forth. Jonah stands beside me, his hand resting on the side of the truck where the tailgate is open.

They go through each item one by one, organizing and removing tags from the camping gear as they do. Seeing everything they have heightens my excitement to begin our adventures tomorrow.

Jonah's lack of enthusiasm is palpable. I wrap my arms around him, and he embraces me back. "You don't have to come. But if you do, you'll for sure be cumming," I grin at him.

WE LAY IN BED AFTER HAVING OUR WAY WITH EACH OTHER, BOTH OF us on our backs. His arms spread out wide, while mine rest comfortably above my head.

Sitting up, I swing my legs off the side of the bed. "Thank you for the release, Mr. Everett. We leave tomorrow if you'd like to join. If not, I will see you when I see you," I move to get off the bed but am pulled back by strong arms, pinning me down beneath him.

"Nice try, baby. I could just tie you to my bed right now and have my way with you all weekend instead," he leans down biting my neck.

This man, this beautiful man. The things I would do for him. "You wouldn't have to tie me up…" I let my words trail off.

When he gets up, I lift my head to watch after him as he walks toward the bathroom. "Come help me, baby. I have packing to do."

"Eeee!" I squeal, climbing off the bed and chasing after him.

We spend the next hour laughing non-stop as he keeps grabbing business attire, and I have to replace them with shorts and t-shirts that have never been worn. It seems like the tags were removed, the clothes washed, and then put away here to never be thought about until now.

"Is this what you guys do? Just hang out in the closet naked?" Shay's voice startles me from the doorway.

We both look over and see Jonathan and Shay with amused faces. We're still sharing playful banter as he continues suggesting bringing his work desk and extension cords to plug his computer in. He even tries to talk me into going camper shopping right now instead of sleeping in a tent.

"Yes, you guys are way overdressed," I tease back.

"I will undress if this is leading to an orgy," Jonathan cracks, and Shay instantly hits his chest with the back of her hand.

"As you can see, Shay won," I motion my arms toward Jonah's bags, as if I were Vanna White on Wheel of fortune.

"Was there a bet going whether I'd go?" Jonah asks, intrigued.

Simultaneously, Jonathan, Shay, and I all deny it in various ways, attempting to convince him otherwise, before bursting into laughter at our own absurdity.

Jonathan strides in and grabs Jonah's bags. "I'm taking these before you decide you don't want to come." He strolls out of the room with Shay following behind, waving goodbye to us.

Just one half-day of work tomorrow and we take off immediately after. I can hardly wait.

It's 1:30, and I'm already showered and prepared to go. Shay came in my room a little bit ago, mentioning she was going to head to the garage and finish packing the remaining items we are taking, instructing me to meet her out there when I'm ready.

I head to Jonah's office, hoping to find him there. As I approach, I notice Jenevieve entering ahead of me. Stepping closer, I position myself just outside the slightly ajar door, listening in.

"Mr. Everett, you look… what exactly is it you are doing dressed like that?" Her tone carries a hint of flirtation and curiosity. "Are you going somewhere?"

"I'm leaving for the weekend," he replies, the sound of his typing still audible from his computer.

"Where on earth are you going dressed like that?" she asks again, her tone laced with amusement.

I haven't seen what he looks like yet, but he could be wearing a Speedo and I'd still want to ride him.

"Is there anything you need help with?" I see her standing at the side of his desk with one leg propped out in an awkward, sexy sort of pose.

"It's a three-day weekend, Jenevieve. Why not fly home and visit your parents, or… I don't know, go do something," he suggests, shutting down his desk computer then closing his laptop, unplugging it, and tucking it into his desk drawer, locking it afterward.

When he stands, I see he's in black shorts that show off his sexy, tanned, muscular legs, and a white t-shirt with black Nike shoes. She has lost her mind to not be panting at the sight of him.

I am not particularly keen on having a confrontation with Jenevieve, so I hurry off to get ahead of them. I barely make it to the corner before Gladys calls after me.

"Oh hi, Gladys," I say, masking any sense of urgency to get myself as far away from his office as possible.

"Hello, Mr. Everett," Gladys turns her attention behind me, and I turn to see Jonah and Jenevieve approaching.

She scrutinizes me from head to toe. I'm wearing distressed jean shorts with a white tank top, sporting the same Nike shoes as Jonah, that he got for both of us. I watch Jenevieve scan me again, landing on my shoes and then shifting her focus to Jonah's shoes, back to mine, and finally up to my face. She appears to have pieced things together. Suddenly, her lips tighten as if she's trying to suppress her anger.

"I packed everything you asked me to pack. Jonathan came by to pick it up a little bit ago. I also slipped in a surprise for you," she winks at me.

"Thanks, Gladys. I should get going," I awkwardly turn and attempt to slink away.

"Gladys, Jenevieve," Jonah nods to each of them and follows after me.

When he catches up, he slaps my butt.

"Jonah," I scold him, grabbing his arm and pushing it away. I glance back, hoping Jenevieve and Gladys have left, but they're still there, watching us intently. Gladys with a beaming smile while Jenevieve looks like her head might explode. My eyes shift away when Jonah wraps his arm lazily around my shoulder and pulls me to him. It's too late to pretend we aren't leaving together, so I wrap my arm around his waist in response.

CHAPTER
Thirty-Four

KALYN

"Why are we doing this again?" Jonah's voice carries a hint of frustration as he and Jonathan wrestle with the tent poles.

Grinning at him, I offer a playful response. "Because, nature, babe." I watch with enjoyment as they persist grappling with the double tent.

Jonah sounded like a child in the front seat of the truck repetitively asking if we were almost there every half hour on the drive here, never failing to amuse Shay and me. Each time he asked, we exchanged knowing glances and stifled giggles. In the rear-view mirror, Jonathan's eyes betrayed a subtle amusement, evident in the crinkle lines next to his eyes.

Jonah lets out a long sigh, sarcastically mocking. "Nature? Sure, why not just sleep on dirt, rocks, and bugs when we have a perfectly comfortable bed at home. Bears, nah, they won't eat us," he continues his irritated rant.

"Is it bad that him being a crybaby makes me want to force him to shut up by sitting on his face?" I grin at her.

"Is it bad that I will pay you to sit on his face to get him to shut up?" Shay retorts, and we both laugh.

We head to the truck and start unloading other supplies. Beginning with the kitchen tent, we make lively conversation as we work diligently putting it together. Then, we proceed to arrange the fold-out tables by placing our supplies and food on top, ensuring everything is neatly organized, and the coolers are positioned conveniently under the spacious tabletops for easy access. Though it's just a brief three-day camping trip, Shay and I prefer a well-organized setup.

"Think they are purposely acting like they don't know what they're doing so we have to set everything else up?" I muse while observing Jonathan and Jonah still struggling with the tent. They're currently holding open the directions while they point at different spots on the paper, then to piles of equipment on the ground.

"Either they are purposely taking their time so they don't have to help, or we should reconsider bringing them camping again because this is almost pathetic at this point," she teases. "I can't believe you actually convinced Mr. Everett to come."

"He didn't resist much," I reply, still watching him. "I told him I was coming whether he did or not, so he packed his bag."

"I doubt he's ever had a speck of dirt on him. This is going to be quite the experience for him," she jokes.

"He'll handle it fine. A bit of fresh air will benefit all of us," I add confidently. "Jonah got us matching shoes. I went to his office to show him mine, and Jenevieve happened to be there. When they came out, she saw our shoes and her eyes looked like they didn't know which shoes to focus on. She looked like a bird as her head shot back and forth between them. It was so weird," I recall, remembering how odd she looked.

"She has probably never seen a pair of exercise shoes in her life," Shay quips. As we arrange a couple of chairs in the corner of the kitchen tent, she casually asks, "What are your thoughts on Amber inviting Sam?"

"I'm completely fine with it. Amber is fantastic, and I know what a great guy Sam is. According to each of them, things are going really well," I reflect on my conversations I've had with them.

"Is Mr. Everett okay with Sam coming?"

"He's never vocalized any concerns. I don't see why he would mind. After all, Sam is coming for Amber," I assure her, nodding with satisfaction as we complete the setup.

"Uh-huh," Shay responds, with a hint of skepticism in her tone.

Exiting the kitchen tent, we head towards the firepit, where rocks are neatly stacked around the edges of a pit dug into the ground. A large log is positioned at one end of the firepit for seating. Beyond the log, there's a clearing leading to dense trees. Following the path through the trees leads to a creek fondly referred to as "the bathtub" for the weekend.

Armed with a variety of fold-out and camping chairs, we start arranging them around the fire pit. Shay had mentioned she wasn't sure if the other campers would bring their own chairs, so she brought enough for everyone just in case.

We stare at the chairs, now neatly arranged, and I scan the surroundings, searching for firewood. Shay and Jonathan brought a little bit of firewood, along with an axe for chopping more if necessary. Actually, now that I think of it, I would love to watch Jonah shirtless chopping wood.

"Let's go find some sticks for the fire," I suggest, and head toward the trees. After gathering armfuls of sticks, pieces of wood, and even picking up litter left by previous campers, we return to the fire pit and unload our findings. Though it is currently incred-ibly hot out, we anticipate it's going to get cold at night.

Seeing that the guys still haven't managed to figure out how to put the tent up, Shay and I plop down in chairs around the firepit. "Do you need our help?" I ask, only half-teasing. They proceed to whisper to each other out of earshot.

Letting out an exaggerated sigh, "If only the tent was up, we could be having sex right now," I grin at Shay.

Jonah responds irritably, "I'll show you nature. I'll fuck you right here in the dirt."

"Mmm, I might like that," I call back.

I hear the crunching of gravel under tires as another car pulls up, and Sam and Amber step out. "Hey Kal," Sam waves in my direction and heads straight to Jonah and Jonathan.

"Hey Sam," I wave back, then turn my attention to Amber as she walks over to us and takes a seat next to Shay while Sam lends a hand to the guys. Sam was a Boy Scout and grew up camping, so I have every bit of confidence he will have the tent put up in no time.

Shay extends her crossed foot toward Amber, giving a gentle push on her leg. "This will be your guys' first-time having sex, won't it?" she raises her eyebrows suggestively.

Blushing, Amber admits, "Yes, if all goes well. I really like him," she confesses, the joy reflecting all over her face.

Curious, Shay continues her probing, "Oh, it will go good. You can ride him all weekend. Did he seem excited when you invited him?"

Amber's smile remains plastered on her face as she recounts, "He was hesitant at first, work and stuff. But I told him Kal talk-ed Mr. Everett into going, so I won't give up until he agrees too. Which he did," she adds proudly.

In just ten minutes, the tent is up, just as I knew Sam would have it. He then moves on to getting our mattresses inflated. Jonah and Jonathan help by making the beds. Though I can't see them, I imagine Jonah occasionally glancing over at Jonathan, trying to follow his lead. It's clear Jonah isn't accustomed to making beds himself, having relied on others to do it for him for so long.

Sam then goes to his car and pulls out his and Amber's tent from the trunk, then searches for a spot to set up.

"Put it next to ours, there's plenty of space," I call out.

But Sam shakes his head with a chuckle. "No thanks, I've heard the stories of you four," he quips, setting his tent down on the opposite side of the campsite from ours.

I playfully argue, "Oh come on now, we aren't that bad," trying to persuade him as Jonah walks up.

"I need water and my dick sucked," he says, wiping sweat off his face with the hem of his shirt, leaning down to kiss me.

"I can help with both of those," I raise my water bottle to him.

"I know you can. Come on," he takes a sip of my water and extends his hand to help me up. Once I'm on my feet, he lifts me over his shoulder, carrying me back toward the tent. I drumroll on his butt, spanking each cheek while laughing.

Inside the tent, he sets me down on my feet, and without hesitation, I instantly kneel before him. "Do you wanna fuck my mouth?" I seductively whisper, my fingers deftly undoing the button and zipper on his shorts, taking my time as I do so. I slip my hand into his boxer briefs, grasping his throbbing hardness and pull it out.

He gazes down at me, his hand moving to my hair, fingers entwining and gripping firmly as I approach his shaft, maintaining eye contact. With a tender lick at the tip, he exhales heavily. Another lick follows, this time my wet tongue swirling in a full circle around his tip, before I envelop it in my mouth all at once. I subtly move my head back and forth, the wetness of my tongue gliding up and down his length, coating him in moisture.

As I pull off, I hollow out my cheeks, earning low rumbles of approval from his throat. Then proceed in a rhythmic combination of sucking and slurping, my hands rotate on his shaft as I work him into my mouth.

He grips my hair rough, exactly the way I crave, and begins thrusting his hips, forcing his member deeper into my mouth. The intensity is so alluring, it draws out harmonious moans from both of us with each forceful thrust. His size is overwhelming, stretching my jaw as he pushes in deep. I open my throat as wide as possible, eager to accommodate him fully for his release.

I close my eyes, enjoying the taste of him, but he tightens his grip on my hair. "Look at me while I fuck your mouth," he groans.

My eyes hesitate to open, and he increases the hold on my hair. When I finally meet his gaze, a surge of arousal floods over me at the intensity in his eyes.

"That's it, baby, keep sucking." I grip his member tighter as I stroke him, my other hand delving into his defined hip. He tastes so good, and him watching me only heightens the pleasure.

"Fuck baby," he groans as his body tenses with his growing orgasm. Knowing I'm the cause of his pleasure makes me want it to never end.

I continue sucking as his thrusts pick up speed. My hand moves from his shaft to his other hip, creating a buffer between the depth of his thrusts and the depth my mouth can handle. Saliva trickles out of the corners of my mouth, and tears leak from my eyes as he holds my head against his thrusting hips, the sensation sending shivers down my spine.

I feel his shaft grow impossibly firmer, and I hold his hips tighter.

"Want it in your throat?" he asks as his member starts to throb.

"Mmhmmm," I hum, eliciting his eyes to roll. I want to taste him—I want to swallow every drop of him.

"You're so sexy," he says, gripping my hair tighter before he explodes.

I continue to suck as he shoves his length deep, spilling out. I feel the warm liquid flowing down my throat as he finishes with strained moans, the rhythmic motion against my mouth ceasing.

With a final suction, I slowly withdraw my mouth, offering a coy smile up at him as I delicately drag my hand across my lips, cleaning up the remnants of our intimacy.

"My naughty girl," he grins, his eyes still sparkling with desire. "Come here," he beckons, sitting on the air mattress, extending his arms toward me. Following his instruction, I crawl toward him. Upon reaching his knees, I stand up, then gracefully climb into his lap, straddling him. I can feel his erection pressed between us.

"Hi," he whispers, kissing my chest.

"Hi," I whisper back, lightly combing my fingers through the sides of his hair.

He places kisses along my chest, collarbone, and neck. Tilting my head back, I willingly offer better access for him to continue.

"You're gonna make me have to commit murder," he says as he reaches his hand up, grabbing the edge of my tank top, pulling it below my breasts, releasing them from their confines.

"Why is that?" I smile.

"I don't like how good you are at sucking cock."

"Why would that make you have to commit murder?" I muse

"There's only one way someone learns to suck cock like that."

"Are you jealous, babe?" I find it utterly sexy that he is jealous of me giving head to other men in the past. Two other men to be exact.

"Painfully," he admits, taking my breast into his mouth.

"Shall we discuss the way you fuck? I am almost afraid to talk about those numbers," I tease, though the amount of women he has been with probably exceeds what I think. The idea of it makes me feel like we might end up in orange jumpsuits together because it makes me also want to commit murder. Only I'd probably have hundreds of women to off.

"Let me show you how I fuck," his mouth moves to my other breast.

Wrapping one arm around behind me, he loops his hand between my legs, pressing two fingers on my sweet spot. His other hand grips my breast his mouth isn't sucking on, encompassing it entirely. He sucks on my nipple, softly biting down, while rubbing slowly back and forth against my shorts.

He rubs my swollen bud, pausing only long enough to remove his mouth to ask, "Do you like these shorts?"

"Yes," I breathe, "don't rip them," my hips begin to rock on his finger.

"Take them off," he urges, his breathing heavy.

Leaning back, I rest one hand on his knee while the other grabs hold of his shoulder. With a seductive shake of my head, I silently refuse, continuing to rock my hips on his fingers that are working their magic through my shorts.

"I need to be inside you," his voice strained with arousal.

"No," I respond panting.

"Let my fingers be inside you," he pleads.

I persist in grinding on his fingers, which continue their skilled work on the outside of my now-soaked shorts. As my orgasm builds, my hips rock faster on his fingers, and my moans become more audible. My belly tightens, and my head rolls back, my hips swaying rhythmically back and forth.

Suddenly, he flips me over, laying me on the bed, popping open the button on my shorts and sliding them off, along with my panties, tossing them behind his shoulder. He positions my legs over either side of his shoulders and eagerly begins sucking and flicking my clit with his tongue. *Why was I fighting this incredible feeling?*

His tongue moves with finesse, its so soft and wet, so experienced. My hips rock greedily against his face and my orgasm approaches.

My fingers loop in his hair, pulling him into me closer. He guides his fingers that were holding my slit open to my mouth, and I willingly take them in, suctioning onto them while holding him in place with my thighs.

When he pulls his fingers back, my tongue and lips trace their length until he withdraws them fully.

I feel the slickness from my saliva trickling down my already drenched slit, as he slides down to my core, plunging his fingers deep inside.

"Yes," I gasp as my back arches off the bed.

His fingers and tongue move in perfect harmony as he continues to stimulate me.

I remember the first time I felt this feeling that is building, I was positive I needed to pee. Now that I know that's not what it is, I welcome the feeling. The pleasure is so intense I feel like I lose all control I have over my own body.

My body trembles as he withdraws his mouth to watch as my orgasm cascades out of me, and like before, when he removes his fingers, clear liquid squirts out. He plunges his fingers back in, repeating the motion, causing more liquid to spill out.

"Fuck," I moan as he immediately focuses on my swollen bud, licking and sucking on it while my body pulsates and shakes with pleasure.

He brings his fingers back to my mouth, and I eagerly suck on them, tasting my own essence. My orgasm washing over me in waves of bliss, accompanied by muffled moans as I suck harder on his fingers.

As my orgasm subsides, and he allows my body a moment for the convulsions to fade, he removes his fingers from my mouth. Securing his arms around my thighs, he begins tracing kisses hip to hip. I raise my arms above my head, savoring the amazing sensation.

"Well, okay then," I let out a sigh as I lie there, waiting for my breathing to regulate.

Raising my head, I glance toward him, appreciating the incredible man between my legs. "Give me your phone," I extend my hand toward him.

Without hesitation, he hands it to me. I angle the phone to capture the moment, ensuring everything from my chest down is in the picture. The result is as sexy as I envisioned—my rounded breasts pushed into perfect peaks by my tank top, my nude lower half and legs wrapped around him, with only my loose blonde braid as the identifying feature.

Returning his phone, he looks at the picture with a smile and comments, "That's sexy." After a moment of admiring it, he casually tosses it onto the bed.

He grabs my legs, placing them so my feet are on the ground. I discern the sound of him unzipping one of our bags. Then, he repositions himself between my legs, still on his knees, leaning down to plant a kiss on my lips. Holding up a pair of exercise shorts with a single finger, he appears pleased with himself. "Your other ones are soaked," he notes, then moves back, sliding my feet into them and pulling them into place.

As I stand, I tug my shirt back up and make my way out of the tent. He reaches out, grabbing my shirt, pulling me back, wrapping his arms around my chest. "Where do you think you're going?" Arousal still evident in his tone.

I smirk, "I'm going to hang out with friends and enjoy the fresh air."

"I want to make out… and do other stuff," he replies seductively.

"You can and will... tonight. Put that weapon away and come back out," I say, sliding my feet into my Birkenstocks, unzipping the tent, and walking out.

As I emerge, I notice some new faces gathered around the fire pit, suggesting the other campers have arrived.

"Seems someone had a little premature ejaculation," Jonathan jokingly whispers out the side of his mouth to Shay, loud enough for all of us to hear.

With quick steps, Jonah falls into stride beside me. "She sucked my soul right outta my dick," he jokes back.

"Do you guys realize they've been gone for thirty minutes?" Amber asks, missing their sarcasm.

"I thought he couldn't get it up, that's why we didn't hear Kal screaming," Jonathan barely gets out before Shay hits his chest.

"We'll see who's laughing tonight when we outperform you," I retort.

"This is true, I want to be thrown around and manhandled like you. I'm joining you guys," Shay says playfully.

"The more, the merrier," my lips curl up.

"I'd manhandle both of you, but the only one that will really be getting manhandled is me by Everett if I touch Kal," Jonathan jokes, prompting laughter from everyone.

Jonah takes a seat beside me in our fold-out chairs, holding my hand and lightly nibbling on my shoulder. "I don't share," he asserts.

"WOW! I thought we were friends, Mr. Everett!" Shay pretends to be upset, but her expression gives away her amusement.

"Will this be your first time?" Jonathan asks Amber and Sam while mindlessly striking a stick against the rocks surrounding the fire.

Amber looks instantly embarrassed, preferring the strangers to her who joined us not to know anything personal. She is really reserved and quiet around other people she's not comfortable with, while Sam appears unbothered.

"Jonathan!" Shay exclaims, hitting his arm again.

"You can't go camping with a bunch of horn dogs and be a prude. It's sex, that's the most PG way I could have asked," he laughs, shielding himself from her.

CHAPTER
Thirty-Five

JONAH

I take in the lively banter. It's dark out, but the fire is ablaze, and it feels good. All the women went to bed, but we could still hear their giggles an hour ago, leaving me unsure if they'd actually fallen asleep. Around the fire, only five of us guys remain, with one occasionally playing the guitar. Everyone, except me, is drinking.

Joining our group are six additional campers, invited by Jonathan and Shay—two couples and two solo guys. They all seem easygoing, making our conversations flow effortlessly.

"Hi, babe," I hear the sweetest voice as Kalyn approaches, an oversized blanket draped around her. Her disheveled hair suggests she might have dozed off. I notice a peculiar look in Sam's eyes as he watches her that bothers me. I'm aware of her magnetic presence and know many people are drawn to her, I see it everywhere she goes. However, his gaze is longing for her, almost possessive.

"Hi," I greet her with a smile, putting my foot down so she can sit on my lap. To my delight, she goes a step further, straddling me while holding onto the blanket, opening it up, and securing it around my neck so we are both wrapped in it. "Can't sleep?" I ask, leaning in to kiss her soft lips.

"No," she responds, shaking her head. "I'm cold," she murmurs, adjusting on my lap, inadvertently positioning her plump pussy against my cock.

"Sorry," I whisper, uncertain if sitting on my erection is uncomfortable for her.

"I like it," she responds quietly, reaching between us to position herself more comfortably. The voluptuous curves of her pussy and ass feel incredible with just her sitting on me. I unconsciously flex against her, and her body responds by her hips rocking back against me. Both of our bodies reacting to the other.

I trace my fingers up and down her smooth back while the guy with the guitar begins singing again. His voice is quite good, and he knows how to play the guitar. The conversations fade into background noise as I rest my head against hers, enjoying the feel of her warmth wrapped around me. Though I'm not ready to admit it to her yet, I'm glad she pushed me out of my comfort zone and had me come along. This moment right here is my idea of perfection. My body feels completely at ease.

My thoughts are interrupted by a random question from Jonathan, who, having been drinking, is engrossed in a random story and repeatedly seeks clarification on details. As he launches into the tale, his animated gestures draw laughter from everyone. Even I can't help but laugh.

I briefly think Kalyn might have dozed off because she is so still, until she is re-situating the blanket, bunching it in one hand, and then slides her free hand between us, freeing my cock from my shorts and stroking it up and down a couple of times. I'm unsure if she's about to provide a discreet hand job, but I'm captivated, glancing between her and her hand.

Locking eyes with me, she whispers, "I'm not wearing panties," as she continues stroking me softly. When she bites her teeth into her bottom lip, a surge of desire courses through my veins, and my cock flexes in her hand. She locks eyes with me again as she lifts up and shifts her silk night shorts to the side, positioning me at her wet entrance.

I can't take my eyes off her as she starts lowering herself down on me, and I can feel my penis contending with the tightness of her pussy. I know it's always slightly uncomfortable for her at first, but I revel in the knowledge that my cock is stretching her tight pussy to accommodate my size. Any time she is sinking herself onto my shaft, her eyes pinch closed and she draws her lips into her mouth as she bites down from the discomfort. It never lasts long, and I should probably be concerned that she is in pain while doing it, but I'm consumed by how fucking sexy she looks, and I eat that shit up.

I'm only a few inches inside, and it's evident she's grappling with the tightness as I penetrate her. She stops lowering, steadying herself by placing a free hand on my hip to prevent going down any further. Her legs tremble as she hesitates, and when she goes to withdraw, I grab her hip with one hand, holding her in place. With my other hand entwined in her hair, I draw her head back, capturing her lips in a passionate kiss. Pushing my tongue into her mouth, she pushes her tongue back. I anticipate that our kiss would ease her tension—my girl loves kissing. Maintaining our passionate kiss, I feel her inching up before lowering again, releasing a trembling breath as I fill her deeper.

Her pussy is a revelation, unlike any I've experienced before. I believed my cock would never be the same again after years of not being able to fuck, or get aroused for that matter, but ever since being with her, it seems to have a perpetual vitality. My cock has found new life with her. When I'm in her pussy, restraining my orgasm becomes a challenge. Every moment I'm torn between a desire to flip her over and pound her pussy to make her squirt, and a contrasting need to take it slow, savoring every moment, every breath, and every piece of her.

Her breath catches as I guide her down to take my entire length inside her. The snugness of her pussy preventing my release. Her eyes flutter closed, and her head tilts back. Her chest rising and falling with each breath as she experiences every sensation coursing through her all at once.

Gradually, she begins to sway her hips in a gentle, rhythmic motion, accompanied by soft, breathy moans near my ear. My fingers trace the contours of her shorts, slipping underneath the fabric, grasping her round ass.

My jaw clenches with each subtle movement of her hips, the increasing pleasure heightening the intensity of the moment. Her hips sway, her body caressing mine, and every rock backward, her ass glides up on my shaft, the movement causing my eyes to roll.

Her arms tighten around my neck, maintaining her rhythmic rocking motion as she glides up and down on me. I nibble on her ear, and then my attention is caught by Sam, who appears to be fixated on her, observing her. He looks as if he is contemplating whether he can discern if we are having sex, a yearning for her, and a readiness to bolt at any moment. Unaware of my gaze, he remains entirely focused on her.

Jonathan interjects with a playful comment, "Blink twice if you guys are soaking right now," addressing both Kalyn and me. She turns towards him, flashing a smile before her eyes roll and her face returns to one of elation. "I keep catching movement in my peripheral, and I can't tell if you're fully fucking right now, or dry humping" he adds proudly. The consumption of alcohol removes any filter from his unguarded speech, allowing his unfiltered thoughts to flow freely.

Another guy, sounding impressed, chimes in, "Did you say they are fucking right now?" This prompts the guy to launch into a story about his own escapade with a girl he met while camping. He stumbled upon a woman from a neighboring campsite while galavanting the trails. He seized the opportunity, bending her over a tree and fucked her right there. Only later did he discover that her husband was also camping nearby, and he spent the rest of the camping trip trying to avoid them. "I blew my load in her. Hopefully she didn't go home with more than just that secret. I don't want some kid knocking on my door in twelve years saying I got mommy pregnant while camping," he jokes, and everyone laughs except for Kalyn and me. I don't even know if she heard him.

I drown out the rest of his story as I feel her squeezing around me, signaling the imminent release of her orgasm. Bringing my thumb down to her engorged bud, I delicately trace circles on it. Her movements and breaths become strained, and I revel in the intense sensation of her pussy constricting around me repeatedly. With each contraction of her pussy, she's gripping my cock so tight it's almost painful but so goddamn sexy.

As her breath gradually steadies, her grip on my cock remains firm. "Can we go to bed?" she asks, her words spilling out as moans, barely restrained, yearning to be unleashed.

I respond with a smile, planting a kiss on her. "Yes."

"Do you want to cover him," she nods to my cock still buried inside her.

"Nah, he's just gonna come right back out," I'm indifferent to who sees my dick. In fact, I want Sam to see what I am working with. I want him to see that my dick is dripping with her cum.

With deliberate slowness, she eases herself off me, her nails digging into my shoulder as another moan leaves her beautiful mouth, fully wrapping the blanket around herself. I stand, my erection still long, thick, and gleaming with her moisture, has the conversation quickly shifting to the size of my cock and how it could fit inside her. Everyone participates in the discussion except for Sam, who appears genuinely shocked, fixated on my cock, while his body language gives away he's pissed. Just as I had hoped.

"Did you guys cum?" Jonathan asks, a mischievous grin directed at me.

"She did," I say proudly. "Night fellas," I call out to them, seizing my dick and quickening my pace to fill the space between her and me. I wrap my arm around her shoulder and kiss her hair when I catch up.

I unzip the tent, holding the fabric open, motioning for her to enter first. In the pitch-black interior, the netted window allows moonlight to filter through. I zip the main area of the tent and turn on the heater in the shared space so we can all get warm. It's freezing in here and I wonder how Shay has managed to remain sleeping alone with it being so cold.

I join her in our space to find her undressed. My grin widens, appreciating the curves of her voluptuous body. Her captivating breasts are truly exquisite, the most beautiful pair I have ever seen. They are a masterpiece, allowing me to cradle them easily in my large hands, with them subtly spilling over. It feels as though they were crafted specifically for me—full and firm, with perfectly shaped nipples adding to their allure.

As I approach, I lean down to draw one of her nipples into my mouth. She moans, wrapping her arms around my neck. As I release her nipple, she loosens her embrace, prompting me to shed my shirt, letting it fall to the ground, followed by my shorts, leaving us both exposed.

She turns and gracefully moves onto the mattress, assuming a position on all fours. Lowering onto her forearms, she widens her legs, bouncing her ass a few times. "What are you waiting for, Mr. Everett?" she extends her arms upward, placing her head on the mattress. I marvel at the stunning sight before me.

I finally have her.

She is entirely mine.

Without hesitation, I position myself on my knees between her open legs, directly behind her. Running my fingers along her wet slit, confirming it's still ready for me, I align my cock at her entrance, and she immediately pushes her hips back toward me. She's greedy, and I love it. Wasting no time, I thrust my entire length inside her, eliciting a loud moan from her.

My shaft is slick with her arousal, facilitating a rhythmic movement as I thrust in and out. With each forceful penetration, she screams in ecstasy.

"Jonah," she moans, pleading my name, and I respond by pushing all the way in, my palm flat on her back, pausing briefly before withdrawing partially and slamming back into her. Her pussy clenches tightly around my cock and I smack her ass with my hand and grip it firmly. I can see the red mark already beginning to show and I slap the same spot even harder. She cries out and her head tilts back as she lets out another moan.

"Do you like that, baby?" I spank the same spot again.

"Yes," she pants.

"Show me how much you like it," the slap of my hand hitting her flesh fills the air.

In response, she widens her legs further, arching her back to lift her backside even higher, initiating a rhythmic bouncing motion on my cock.

Grasping her hips with determination, I persist in drawing her back onto me, aiming to penetrate deeper. Succumbing to the intensity of the moment, I thrust forcefully, feeling myself stretching her core, eliciting a soft whimper from her, her hands clenching the blankets as she buries her face in them to muffle the pain.

Halting immediately, I yield control to her, allowing her to set the rhythm with her bouncing and rocking motions. Her movements are slow, feeling for anything that may be too painful. I reach my hand between her thighs and begin rubbing circles on her clit, igniting her moans again. Her hips regain speed and she begins rocking back and forth, swaying against me and I sense her impending climax. Shes clutching the blankets as she cries out, her pussy tightening, and her motions quicken.

"Fuck, baby," I grab her ass, squeezing.

She moans, her back arching up as she lets out passionate cries into the blankets, as her climax erupts. Her convulsions create a rhythmic massage on my cock, coaxing my release as I shoot my load into her. There's an incredibly erotic sensation in the act of filling her with my semen as if leaving an indelible mark of possession.

CHAPTER
Thirty-Six

KALYN

It's lunchtime, Jonah and I spent most of the night having sex, performing oral on each other, making out or cuddling. We slept in, missing breakfast but Shay and I prepared lunch for everyone. After serving the food, we gather around the unlit firepit, sharing random tidbits about ourselves.

"I've never had a boyfriend… Officially," I admit honestly.

"What are you even talking about?" Shay questions playfully.

"You know in elementary school when a boy would give a note to a girl they liked, and it would be like 'do you want to be my girlfriend?' and you got to check yes or no. I never got a note," I smile. "I'm still bothered by this," as if the note is what signifies an actual relationship.

"Oh, yeah? Well, I went to a private Catholic school, and Tom Wilkins passed me a note in class that said, 'Meet me in the bathroom and I'm gonna put my finger in your hole, and then you'll be my girlfriend.' Mrs. Eusoff took the note as it was passed to me and read it aloud to the entire class without pre-reading it. Then, our parents got called, and Tom had to read the note to our parents. So, yeah, I can't relate," she flips her hair.

"Ughh. Tom Wilkins," I playfully shudder, as if I even know who he is.

"That guy sounds like a p.i.m.p.," Jonathan comments.

Shay chuckles and chimes in, "I'll bet I wasn't the only girl who received a love note like that from him. I didn't make it to the bathroom, so he probably put his finger in someone else's hole. I know my hole never got filled."

"The confidence has me turned on and I haven't even had the privilege of meeting this class act," I remark.

Jonathan joins in, teasingly asking Shay, "Well? Did you fuck Tom Wilkins?"

"Umm… no. I was classy—I lost my V card at prom with my boyfriend, whom I'd been dating for two years, thank you very much," she jokingly tilts her nose upward in a snooty gesture.

Turning his attention to me, Jonathan probes, "What about you, Kal? Who took your V card?" Sam and I share a quick glance before averting our eyes. I can sense Jonah noticed, as his hand, which was gently rubbing my shoulder, briefly stiffens and hasn't fully relaxed since. I try my best to collect myself from the unexpected question. "I'm actually still a virgin," I attempt to divert the conversation away from me.

"Anal doesn't count, am I right?" Jonathan interjects, attempting to lighten the mood.

Shay's jaw hangs open. "Can you imagine?" She gazes at me in astonishment. "You'd definitely need to be stitched up after," accompanied by an exaggerated look of pain.

"He's never even offered," I tease.

"Have you ever?" she questions.

Once again, Sam and I share a knowing look before I simply respond, "That's not my thing."

"Girl, you don't even know what you're missing out on," Shay smiles at Jonathan.

"It's true, it's amazing," Amber chimes in.

"I'll take your word for it," I laugh.

Sam and I had almost all of our firsts with each other. Our first kiss, our first time, we even tried anal. I guess we can't even consider it trying, since we did it more than a handful of times, and it did feel good. But it didn't feel right to continue, especially when I could see Sam's growing feelings after each time, the way he would try to hold me when we finished. I just wanted my release and then to move on with my day.

There is a knowing tension lingering in the air as the other campers resume asking random questions to each other. Feeling a bit uneasy about the direction of the conversation, I opt to invite Shay for a hike so I can talk to her. "Hey, Shay, lets go for a hike?" I widen my eyes at her, hoping she catches on to my need for a one-on-one conversation.

"Yes!" she responds enthusiastically, instantly picking up on the subtle hint I was giving her.

Amber chimes in, "Sam and I will come too," as she glances at us and then at Sam.

Jonathan stands. "Get up, Sasquatch. We are going hiking. Maybe wear a reflective vest so nobody accidentally tries to shoot you," he taunts Jonah.

I instantly feel bummed that they all invited themselves when I wanted to talk to Shay privately.

As we head back to our tent, Shay mouths "sorry" to me.

I dress in lilac workout shorts paired with a matching sports bra and casually tie my hair into a messy bun atop my head, throwing on my backpack loaded with water, energy bars, and other essentials. When selecting my outfit, I had chosen it with the intention of Jonah appreciating how it accentuates my figure, particularly the way it hugs the curves of my ass and highlights my chest. However, I soon realize that the earlier conversation about virginity didn't sit well with him, and he didn't appear as excited as I thought he would with the outfit I chose.

Enthusiastically, Amber urges us to pick up the pace as Shay and I are dragging our feet toward one of the trails. "Come on, guys, this is going to be fun!" she exclaims excitedly.

Shay and I stroll side by side, with Jonah and Jonathan trailing behind us. The walk unfolds in a picturesque setting—thick trees allowing glimpses of sunlight, random flowers dot the landscape, and a creek flows on our right. The trail diverges in different directions, but we follow Amber's lead.

After an hour of walking, we stumble upon a hidden waterfall. While not massive, its beauty is undeniable. "Let's take a break here," Amber calls out, and everyone disperses to explore the surroundings.

"He is pissed," I whisper to Shay as we walk off toward the waterfall.

"I'd say. I can't believe you never told me you lost your virginity to Sam," she responds in a hushed tone.

"It was so long ago. It doesn't even feel like it ever happened now," I admit. "Do you think everyone noticed? Or am I being paranoid?"

"Everyone noticed," she says unfiltered. "And just because it feels like it never happened to you, doesn't mean it feels that way to Sam. He stares at you with little puppy dog eyes."

"Oh stop, he does not." I look over at him, as if to prove a point to both of us, meeting his gaze, he smiles and waves.

"Mmhmmm," she gives me the 'I told you so' look.

"Oh whatever," I quip back.

"Puppy dog eyes," she repeats.

Jonah remains on the trail, bending over to stretch. "I'm gonna go try to suck his dick," I tell her, wanting to get out of this awkward situation I put myself right into.

"God, please let him accept, for all of our sakes," she responds, only half kidding.

As I approach him, I feel out his mood. "Is this your first time hiking?" I ask. "Or rather, traipsing," I correct, as this isn't much of a hike.

He stands upright, shifting his weight to the opposite side, stretching his side as I speak. "Nah, I've been hiking before," he states flatly.

Raising an eyebrow, I pose another question, "Have you ever gone swimming in a random pool of water in the middle of nowhere with a mysterious waterfall?"

"I'm not getting in that water," his tone unchanged.

"While everyone else is soaking their feet, do you want to sneak away and soak something else?" I suggest, running my finger down the front of his T-shirt.

He continues stretching, "Sure."

Well, that settles it—he's definitely bothered.

I stand there, briefly considering whether to walk away, but I opt to join him in the stretches instead. Spreading my legs, I bend to one side, mirroring his movements. I switch sides as he does, following his lead. I notice that he repeats the stretch on one side, taking into consideration that I am following his movements. Despite having already stretched one side, he performs it again, ensuring that I can stretch both sides.

"I love the outdoors," I admit, taking in the peaceful surroundings. "But it's a bit unnerving, thinking anyone could be watching from a distance without you knowing," I remark, looking around at all the thick trees.

I picture someone dressed in camouflage, laying on their stomach with a scoped rifle, surveying us through the lens. That's what they always portray in movies anyways, as they make their plan on when to attack.

"They would regret it if they tried anything," he asserts, standing confidently.

"Well, I'm certainly not worried with you being here. Anyone catches sight of you, they'll skedaddle real quick," I say, eliciting a laugh from him. "There it is." I poke at his abs, and his smile widens. He reaches his arm out, wrapping it around my neck, pulling me into a hug.

"Where did you learn your tactical skills?" I inquire, recalling the night at the mansion when two intruders managed to get in.

"When you have money, people feel entitled to it. They'll go to extreme lengths to get their hands on something that isn't theirs. I chose to learn to protect myself and what's mine," he responds, holding me tighter.

"How did you learn to do that thing with your tongue?" referring to his remarkable tongue skills while eating pussy or kissing.

"Well," he pauses, "Growing up, our chef used to let me lick the batter off the blender blades," he responds.

I burst out laughing.

"I licked it clean as a whistle," he includes.

"I think I've stumbled upon chupacabra footprints over here," Jonathan announces to all of us.

Jonah and I turn in the direction of his voice, seeing what he is talking about. When we see the rest of the group heading over to him, we follow.

There are large, dried animal prints in the mud and Jonathan pokes at them with a stick. "Yep, that's exactly what these are, I can tell by the manicured nail marks."

"Indeed," Sam confirms.

"Good thing we're not goats," I remark.

"They've evolved. Now they snatch people, eat them, and any body part they consume becomes a part of their body," Jonathan continues.

"Are you serious?" Amber asks, debating whether his words hold any truth.

"Sniffing your fear" Jonah plays along with the story.

"That's right, they do. I forgot about that," Jonathan says.

"Yeah, yeah, yeah," I roll my eyes. "And every twenty-three years for twenty-three days, they get to feed, and they also go by Jeepers Creepers."

"Yes! You've heard the tales too!" Jonathan exclaims, a look of astonishment on his face.

"Are we safe out here?" Amber asks.

"He's an idiot, Amber. Just ignore him," Shay says, as Jonah and I stand, preparing to walk away.

"I'm gonna keep walking," I inform them, noticing they're still fixated on the prints. Jonah takes my hand and guides me back toward the trail. Eventually, everyone follows suit, and we hear Shay scolding Jonathan for being a moron. Her scolding him always amuses me. I just love her so much.

"Mr. Everett, do you think there's anything out here that could hurt us?" Amber questions.

"No," Jonah says flatly.

"Come on, Amber, you were the leader of our hike. Go lead," I encourage her.

"I'll lead," Sam says, walking past us, taking the front of the line. This puts a pep in Amber's step, and she hurries to catch up with him, engaging in conversation as they walk.

"I need a wizard staff to help me hike," I vocalize a random thought, scanning the forest for a suitable stick. Jonah immediately grabs my hand and pulls me off the trail. "Where are we going?" I'm bursting with excitement.

"My baby wants a wizard staff. My baby gets a wizard staff," he declares, tromping through overgrown grass. After ten minutes, he finds a tree that appears dead or dying and effortlessly snaps off a branch. He places the leafy end on the ground and stomps off the tip. Handing it to me, it's the perfect height for a walking stick.

"Thank you," I smile, examining it. "I don't think you're any match for me now, Mr. Everett," I point the stick at him. "This is a lethal weapon, and you don't want to m—" he grabs my stick before I can finish letting him know he doesn't want to mess with me and my big ass stick, jerking it towards him, causing me to collide into his arms. "Well, okay then," I say, stunned. "You have an unfair advantage," I try to justify his quickness.

"Yeah? What advantage?" He leans down to kiss me.

"You're big. Really big," I offer, knowing it's the best I've got.

"That is shaky logic at best. My size should be a reason for me not being fast. Try again," he suggests.

"Well, I blinked for a second, and you waited until my eyes closed," I say, then chuckle at how ridiculous it sounded.

"Are you saying I process speed faster than most, or that you blink incredibly slow?"

"You tell me, do I blink slow?" I gaze up at him.

"Your blinks are perfect," he releases my staff, intertwining his fingers with mine, and guides us back toward the trail. Although everyone is now out of earshot and sight, we continue following the trail in the direction they were headed.

"We need a bag of marbles to drop on the trail so we know where we are going. Look above the trees and tell me if you can see everyone else," I suggest.

He tickles my neck, eliciting a laugh. "Is that a tall joke? You think I'm a giraffe?"

"Shut up," Shay calls out when she sees us, holding up a stick she picked up. "You got a lightsaber too?!"

"Nah, dawg, this is a wizard staff," I respond proudly.

"You come walking out of the forest all majestic as fuck with a wizard staff, and I'm the bridge troll that found a stick over yonder," she quips, and we crack up.

"I don't know, from where I stand, that looks like it could be a wizard staff. Maybe a little short, but definitely a wizard staff," I look at Shay's short stick. Her stick looks like she found it on the ground, while my stick was ripped off a tree by my big, strong grizzly man.

"I just wanted to hit something," she whacks her stick on the trail.

Pretending to tuck my hair behind my ear, I nonchalantly point my finger at Jonathan.

"I saw that," he takes Shay's stick from her hand and whips it in my direction.

"Don't start with me," I poke my stick out to him, and he clashes hers against mine.

"I am not to be blamed for any injuries you are about to sustain," I warn him.

We hear the crunching of twigs snapping in the distance and look to see Sam and Amber returning. "Mom and Dad are coming back—we're in trouble," I note their annoyed expressions.

"Kal, go see why they look like someone pissed in their cheerios," Jonathan says.

"Lucky me," I tease as I start walking toward them.

"Ready to head back?" Amber asks dryly.

I glance between her and Sam, getting nothing in response. Sam stands there with his hands in his pockets, like he doesn't know why she appears so annoyed.

"Sure," I turn back toward Jonah, Shay, and Jonathan. "We are heading back."

"Here, Kal, let me carry your bag," Sam says, grabbing the strap to my backpack.

"Oh, I'm good, Sam, thanks though," I keep my arms in the straps.

"I insist," he smiles, tugging on it once more.

"Okay... sure," I say hesitantly, letting the straps fall off my shoulders. I purposely kept it on, knowing my outfit accentuated my round ass, and I didn't want to make Jonah feel bad after earlier. I don't need to rub salt in the wound.

He takes my backpack, and I continue walking. Passing Jonah, I see his head shoot down to my ass, and his hand immediately squeezes, firmly cupping the cheek with his fingers between my crack and my cheek. He keeps his hand there for a moment before patting my bottom a couple times, then lazily drapes his arm around my shoulder.

"I can bounce a quarter off that thick ass, baby," he grits his teeth, kissing the side of my head.

"Kal, remember that time we were camping, and we got sticks like that and slept next to them in case someone came into our tent? Uncle Tony got drunk and came to our tent by accident, and you beat him on the head with the stick," he reminds me, humor evident in his tone.

Looking at Jonah, I declare, "I already told you, I'm lethal with these," showing him my stick. "That was an example of 'you're gonna learn today,' and Uncle Tony learned that day," I laugh, reminiscing about hitting him with a stick. It was a tent full of girls and Sam. Back then, Sam wore glasses, and he wasn't wearing them, so when the tent opened, and a shadow came in, I grabbed the stick and hit. It was over before Sam found his glasses.

"Uncle Tony still talks about that. He said for a 14-year-old, you hit with the force of a man," the memory making him laugh.

"I forgot about him. How is he?" I ask, curious where he is these days.

"Still drinking daily," Sam responds.

"That's unfortunate," I express sadness for Uncle Tony's struggles.

"Is it supposed to rain?" Amber asks out of the blue, cutting through the conversation.

"I don't think so, why?" Sam inquires.

"I keep getting drops on my face," she explains, as I start to feel a few droplets myself.

"Rain won't kill you," Jonah states.

Looking irritated, Amber retorts, "It might not kill me, but I don't want to be soaking wet."

As the rain intensifies, everyone picks up their pace, and I grab Jonah's hand, shaking my head no to him as I pull his arm to bring him closer. Without a word, I draw him into a kiss—a passionate kiss—right there in the rain. I know it's cliché, but my life has been everything but, and I am going to seize the moment and live in the present.

Jonah bends down, his hands cupping my bottom as he lifts me. My legs wrap around him, our bodies entwined as we stand there kissing in the pouring rain.

I let go of my wizard staff as he strides over to a large rock and moss-covered wall, pressing me against it. Our mouths move more frantically as I reach out for anything to steady myself on, propping myself up on rocks jutting out of the jagged wall.

One at a time, he coils each arm beneath my legs, drawing them towards my chest and deftly pulling my shorts upward until the fabric settles on my raised knees. He maintains a tight hold on me, pushing me into the wall. His hand finds its way between us, releasing his thick, hard member and pressing it firmly against my eager opening.

He begins working it in slowly, his hips making their way inward, then withdrawing, only to press back in. As he feels the slickness coating his shaft, he emits a low grunt, thrusting his cock into my core, withdrawing only to thrust in deeper and harder. My hips shoot upward as he stretches inside me, and I'm not completely ready to be filled so full yet. My pained moan rings out through the rain, and I look down to watch his cock fuck me.

My chest rises and falls with shallow breaths, my nipples peaked through the fabric of my sports bra. Removing a single hand from the wall, I release both breasts from the bra, pulling the material just below them. His eyes light up at the sight, igniting a hunger in him that he unleashes.

I've never experienced penetration from this angle, and it feels incredible. The initial thrusts are a bit uncomfortable, but with a minor adjustment, he seamlessly inserts himself perfectly.

Amidst the fervor, with the rain coming down so hard and my hands struggling to hold on to the slippery rocks, I start to worry we might slip.

"Babe, I can't hold on," I tell him as my hands turn red from gripping so tight to the rocks.

"Let go baby, I got you."

Removing one hand from the wall, I wrap it tight around his neck, trying to make sure I won't slip right out of his hold. As his strong arms envelop me, I relinquish my hold on the wall, confident he won't let me fall. With each thrust, he presses me deeper into the wall, continuing to drive in and out of me.

The thunderous rain pounding all around us drowns out our whimpered moans as he rocks his hips. His movements are quick and determined, each thrust slamming deep and hard into my center before withdrawing just to slam himself back in. We're soaking wet, but his grip stays firm on my waist as he drives into me with relentless passion. He feels incredible.

"Faster," I moan, my voice melding with the rhythm of the rain. I stare down at him pounding into me. "Faster," I repeat, and he squeezes my waist, thrusting fast and hard. "Yes," I cry out as he continues the movements until my body tightens and releases in orgasmic bliss. I moan out in ecstasy as I writhe against him, gyrating my hips against his pelvis until I feel his release, his head bending down to bite my neck… hard. A primal yell of arousal escapes my lips.

He remains inside me, his lips seeking mine as our mouths hungrily move against each other. My arms are fatigued from holding onto the sharp rocks for so long, but they find refuge in his strength, knowing he can effortlessly hold my weight. Even being drenched, it doesn't appear to be a struggle for him.

As our lips part, our faces remain close, our eyes meeting in a fiery gaze. In this moment, every emotion surges between us. They say eyes are the windows to the soul, and in his, I find a connection that spans lifetimes.

He shifts his gaze downward while he withdraws himself, my own eyes follow his line of sight, enjoying the last sensations of our intimate connection concluding as his member fully comes out. I clench my core, to keep his semen from spilling out, not wanting it to accidentally get on the outside of my clothes.

One arm at a time, he disentangles himself from beneath my knees, as my feet find the ground. My entire body is sore, but the moment I look up at him, all I can think is *'worth it.'*

"We'll be better sheltered from the rain here than if we try to walk back," I suggest as we adjust our clothing.

"Whatever you want, baby," he leans against the wall, taking the space I was just in and pulls me close to his chest.

"I sure do enjoy you when you're wet, Mr. Everett," I tilt my head up toward him, my chin resting on his chest.

"Oh, yeah?" he grins mischievously.

"Rifle and scope watching," I remind him of my earlier fear, as his face suggests he's ready to go again.

"Lucky them, they would've gotten to stare at my ass," he jokes.

"That is lucky for them," I reply as he leans down to kiss me.

We stand beneath the trees, enduring a couple hours of rain before trudging back to camp hand in hand. Jonah heads toward the tent, but I pull him in the direction of the creek.

"What are you doing?" He lifts a brow, covered in mud and dripping wet.

"We are going to clean off," I say, smiling.

The hot day makes the creek water refreshing. I step in first, submerging myself and toss my sports bra at him. "Come in," I call as I discard my shorts. He grins, sheds his shirt and shorts, and joins me. The water is just barely to my knees, allowing us to easily sit and be submerged. Lifting my hand from the water, I use it to clean the mud from his face, and we continue the ritual of wiping mud off each other.

"We don't have towels," I realize when we are ready to get out. "Come on," I grab his hand, pulling him out. I bend down and pick up our clothes, trying my best to keep the muddy garments away from my clean body.

"You gonna give that to me?" he questions as we walk through the wooded area between "the bathtub," and our campsite.

"Give what to you?"

Slapping my bare ass, he whispers, "Your ass."

I don't even know how to respond to that. That kind of sex isn't something I'd normally be interested in anyway. Besides, Jonah's size alone is almost too much to handle. I can't even imagine how he'd make that work. I assume with him even mentioning it, he has performed anal on women before, and he's never mentioned anyone getting seriously hurt. Shay and Jonathan do it often, and she's never mentioned any issues either. Quite the opposite, she loves it. How does one prepare for someone as well-endowed as Jonah? It would probably have to be a spur-of-the-moment thing, because right now, in a sober state of mind, the thought of it sounds painful.

Emerging from the tree clearing, a few individuals are by the fire, wrestling with damp chairs. They look up at us as we walk by, and I offer an apologetic smile and a wave, mouthing "sorry" to them and keep walking. Sam exits his tent, spotting us, and stares.

Jonah acknowledges Sam with a casual, "What's up," wrapping his arm around my waist. It drifts over my backside, settling on my hip as we quicken our pace to our tent.

Upon entering, it's evident that Shay and Jonathan are napping, their wet clothes left at the entrance of our tent as they lie uncovered in their bed. Zipping our tent closed, Shay opens her eyes, and I mouth an apology for waking her before retreating to our section. Flipping my head down, I regather my hair into a messy bun and kneel to rummage through my luggage for clothes, while Jonah sprawls on the bed, knees bent, feet on the ground.

I retrieve a pair of panties, socks, jean shorts, and a tank top from my bag. From Jonah's bag, I grab boxer briefs, shorts, a T-shirt, and socks. When I peek into his second bag to see what he packed, I notice three new pairs of shoes, each with matching smaller pairs. He's arranged matching shoes for me for every pair he has. It's such a considerate gesture, one that I've never experienced, and though I shouldn't be surprised by anything he does, I still find myself surprised, just staring at the shoes. I become more grateful for his thoughtfulness now as I realize I wouldn't have had any shoes to wear if it weren't for him. I hadn't anticipated the rain. I suppose I should have checked the weather report beforehand.

I set his clothes neatly on the bed beside him and proceed to get dressed. I can see his breathing has steadied and his eyes remain closed letting me know he has fallen asleep. I head out of the tent, pausing to stare at how much mud is on the ground and how ruined these new pair of shoes are going to get from the mud. But it's either these or my Birkenstocks. And my Birkenstocks equal muddy toes to go along with them.

I exit the tent and walk to the kitchen area, avoiding the mud puddles as I walk. Rifling through the cooler for sandwich ingredients. I proceed to make myself a sandwich, singing quietly to myself, and stop when I hear the kitchen tent opening. I turn and see Sam coming in.

While I typically don't dwell on past sexual encounters with Sam, I find a strange relief in the fact that Jonah now knows about it, albeit indirectly. I've noticed a growing connection between Sam and Amber. Given that Sam is my best friend, I anticipate he will be coming around more often, and I wouldn't want too much time to pass before addressing the topic with Jonah. Not that I think it's a major issue, but perhaps it's something he would prefer to know. We haven't discussed it since, and I assume if it bothered him, he would bring it up. Thankfully, he seems to be back to his usual self.

"Hey, Sam. Want a sandwich?"

"Please," he responds appreciatively. I grab a few more slices of bread, and craft sandwiches for both of us and add some chips to our plates.

"That's all she wrote," I say, handing him his plate. We sit in the corner of the kitchen tent on the two chairs Shay and I had placed the day we arrived.

"Damn, you still got it," he praises, savoring a bite of his sandwich. I take a bite and agree with an mmhmm as I wipe the corners of my mouth with my napkin.

"Jesus! Kal! What the heck happened to your neck?" he exclaims, leaning in to inspect it. I had completely forgotten about Jonah biting me. "Are you okay?" He asks loudly with concern.

"I'm fine," I brush his comment off, not wanting to make a big deal about it.

"That doesn't look like you are fine," he sits on the edge of his chair trying to get a closer look.

"I said I'm fine Sam. We get a little carried away sometimes," I defend uncomfortably, referring to our sex.

"Kal, that looks bad," he continues staring.

"Okay, Sam, don't look if it bothers you that much. Damn," I say, sitting back and taking a bite of my sandwich.

"I worry about you, Kal," he says with concern.

"Well, don't. It happened in the heat of the moment. I was having an orgasm, so I didn't even feel it," I confess. I notice his rapid eye blink, momentarily caught off guard by that statement. Then he sits back and continues eating his sandwich. Typically, I would feel bad for the way I worded that statement. But he is making a bigger deal out of this than he needs to, and it instantly irritates me.

The air in the tent seems to thin out, making it hard to breathe. I have the urge to stand up and walk out, but my body refuses to move, keeping me seated.

"The last time I went camping was with you," he breaks the silence reminiscing.

"I bet you're smiling like that thinking about my lip swelling from that bee sting," I recall vividly the camping trip where bees stung everyone in the tent, but I was the only one with a face attack.

He grins, "It was cute."

"Yeah, it wasn't," I respond. "It hurt so bad."

"I know. I remember changing your ice."

"Thank you, Sam. For everything. Especially after... you know," I say, not wanting to utter Wyatt's name. Sam stood by my side in the aftermath of everything that transpired with Wyatt. I was utterly broken, in pieces, and Sam was a constant presence, offering support every single day even though I must have been miserable to be around.

"You're my everything, Kal. I'd do it all over again a million times," he says, smiling.

Uncertain about what to say, I take another bite of my sandwich.

"Maeva called me a while back, wanting to know if I knew how to reach you. You should probably check in with her," he mentions, catching me off guard. I've distanced myself so much that I never told her about the new job and me moving. Or getting fired and evicted.

"Did you tell her where I am?" I inquire curiously.

"No, it wasn't my place," he reflects.

"Thank you."

"Hi, guys," Amber beams, entering the tent.

"Hey," I respond to her as she walks over to Sam, kissing him on the cheek and sitting on his lap. Taking Sam's empty plate, I rise, discard them in the trash, and then start preparing a couple of sandwiches for Jonah, anticipating he will be hungry when he wakes up.

I listen to Sam and Amber talking, loving the sound of her cheerful conversation with him. Once Jonah's sandwiches are ready, I turn to leave. "See you guys later."

Emerging from the tent, I spot Jonah strolling towards me, wearing the clothes I laid out for him. And the matching pair of shoes to the ones I picked for myself. He is so precious.

Each time our eyes meet, butterflies dance in my belly. "I made you sandwiches. I thought you might be hungry when you woke up," I present the plate to him and press my lips to his as he leans down.

"Thank you, baby," he responds, smiling as he walks over to the chairs around the firepit and takes a seat. "That's a damn good sandwich," he adds, his eyes widening with surprise.

I playfully hold out my left hand, twisting my thumb and pointer finger around my ring finger. "Tell me about it."

He leans over, gripping my chin with his hand, turning my face toward him, and pressing his lips to mine. "I will," his voice velvety as he says it, then pulls my bottom lip between his teeth.

"Did you guys get lost?" Amber asks as her and Sam approach, sitting across from us.

"We were just making memories," I turn to look at Jonah who meets my gaze and grins at me.

The rain dried up over the next couple hours and the guys were able to get our fire going just in time as the night grew colder. Sitting around the crackling fire, Jonah holds me close as I relish the warmth, closing my eyes to soak in the comforting sounds and conversations around us. In moments like these, with him by my side, I wish time would stand still.

Shay, Jonathan, Jonah and I all went to bed at the same time. The guys decided to bet who could last longer and so the night unfolds with Shay and I being the ones to tap out after we both agreed our vaginas were going to be rubbed raw.

"Just a little longer," Jonathan pleads with Shay.

"No, go fuck your boyfriend, my ass and vagina are swollen," Shay retorts.

I let out a laugh, looking over at them, they are in the same position as us, Shay and I are on our stomachs and the guys are on their knees straddling us as they take us from this angle.

"That means you too," I turn my head to look at Jonah.

"Pull out first," he tells Jonathan.

"On the count of three," Jonathan replies.

Shay is the true MVP of this game because she unexpectedly moves forward, causing Jonathan's penis to slip out.

Jonah's laughter bubbles out as he gradually withdraws from me.

"You are both losers," I tease as I pull the blankets back and climb in.

"Technically, we won," Jonah says as he climbs in beside me and wraps his arms around me.

"It was an unfair advantage," Jonathan says, planting a kiss on Shay.

"My pussy has its own pulse right now," she laughs.

"Girl, same," I reply.

CHAPTER
Thirty-Seven

KALYN

Shay and I woke up early and went for a walk. By the time we get back, everyone is waking up. We make breakfast and dish up the plates. When we finish eating, Shay and I go to the kitchen tent and start cleaning up the breakfast mess.

"Let me do that," Sam comes in taking the dishes out of mine and Shays hands.

"Are you sure?" Shay asks, as Amber enters.

"Yes, we got this," Amber replies, stepping in to help Sam.

"Go, both of you," Sam tells us.

"I'm leaving before you change your mind," I hurry out and Shay follows.

The guys are gathered at the back of one of their trucks, engrossed in a discussion about guns and inspecting them closely. I gently trace my fingers along Jonah's back to grab his attention, leaning my head on his bicep.

"Shay and I are going to walk to the waterfall and take some pictures," I inform him.

He wraps his arm around my shoulder and plants a tender kiss on my forehead. "Just you and Shay?"

"Yes."

He reaches into the truck bed, retrieving a small black container attached to a key ring. Sliding a red tab over, he demonstrates, "Slide this over and push down. It's pepper spray," he advises, arming us with a small bit of protection.

"Thank you," I murmur, rising onto my tiptoes to press my lips against his as I take the container from his hands.

"Waterfall only. Don't wander anywhere else. I want to know where to look for you if you don't come back in a couple of hours," he instructs.

"Waterfall only," I affirm.

"Good girl," he pats my ass.

As Shay and I make our way to the waterfall, she holds up her container of pepper spray. "I'm surprised they gave us these. They probably think we are going to spray ourselves in the eyes," she quips.

"Let's find sticks. Double protection to defend ourselves with," I suggest, scanning the area until I find one. Though it won't do much damage, it might deter an attacker, with one hundred percent certainty of pissing them off if we were to hit them with it.

We chat and absentmindedly whack at the trail and trees as we pass.

When we get to the waterfall, we take turns capturing pictures of each other. Telling the other one how to pose when we are the photographer.

"Wanna take some sexy ones for the guys?" Shay raises her eyebrow mischievously.

"Jonah would ring both of our necks if we exposed any private parts out here without them around," I tease, though I know it's the truth.

"I don't see the problem. I recall someone enjoying being choked," Shay retorts playfully as we settle on the rocks, dipping our feet in the clear water, basking in the warm sun.

We are gone for four hours, and it doesn't even feel like we were gone even an hour. On our way back, we pass the spot Jonah and I had sex, and I show Shay. Though now in the sunlight, I'm surprised my back isn't cut up from the jagged wall I was pressed against.

When we get back to camp, I see Amber seated by the firepit, enjoying a sandwich. "Where's Jonah?" I inquire.

"He's been summoned to chop wood," she gestures towards the trees.

Following the distant sound of wood being chopped, I navigate through the trees toward him. Emerging from the foliage, I discover my handsome man, just as I had imagined: shirtless, muscles rippling, glistening with sweat as he swings the axe high above his head, splitting the wood with force. However, what I don't anticipate are the admiring gazes of nearby campers.

"How much are you being paid to put on this show?" I tease, leaning against a tree in the shade, crossing my arms over my chest.

"Not nearly enough."

"You gonna have any energy left when you're finished?" I raise a brow to him.

He adds another log to the chopping stump, wiping his brow with his forearm. "Your ass will be the first to find out," he declares, swinging the axe and sending wood pieces tumbling to the ground.

As he continues chopping, I watch the girls chatting amongst themselves before heading our way. Jonah isn't paying attention and I decide not to tell him, curious to see how this plays out. I will give them kudos, it takes balls to approach someone you find attractive, especially when they are with another woman. They giggle amongst themselves as they approach, bumping into each other along the way.

"Do you want to come to our camp next? We could use some firewood too, especially with the cold night ahead. All we brought were these," one of the girls gestures to their scant attire of short shorts and bikini tops.

All that time staring at him and that's all they came up with to say? Boring.

Jonah glances at them, then back at me, and I flash him a wide grin.

"Or we have a shower, if you want to freshen up. You worked up quite a sweat there," another girl chimes in.

"We do! We have a camper with a shower," the blonde in the middle eagerly adds.

"I'm good," Jonah declines, resting the axe against his shoulder.

"All finished?" Jonathan emerges from behind me. "The clean-up crew is here."

"He's finished. These ladies even offered him their camper's shower," I inform Jonathan, gesturing one hand to the three girls standing a couple feet away from Jonah.

"Baby, go do it, you're so sweaty," Jonathan urges Jonah with a flick of his wrist.

The girls exchange glances, their expressions suggesting they now perceive Jonah and Jonathan as a couple.

"Do you want to come with him?" the blonde asks Jonathan with an encouraging smile. Even with this new knowledge of the relationship between these two random guys, they are still eager to have Jonah at their campsite, inviting Jonah's "boyfriend" along.

I chuckle and roll my eyes as I head back to camp.

"Let's go for a walk before the guys rope us into carrying all that wood back," Shay seizes my arm and leads me towards one of the trails behind our tent.

"Fine by me. Apparently, Jonah is going for a shower at an RV in the camp next to ours," I remark, rolling my eyes.

"Excuse me?" she halts, gaping at me.

"Oh, those girls were practically swooning over him. They offered him a shower because he worked up quite a sweat," I mimic air quotes for emphasis.

"And he accepted?!" she exclaims incredulously.

"Yes, with his 'boyfriend'... Jonathan," I laugh. "Even with them masquerading as a couple, they were chomping at the bit for them to return to their camp."

"Well, we absolutely have to spy," Shay declares, gripping my arm as she steers us back towards the direction of the other camp.

This is one of the many things I admire about Shay. She doesn't put up with bullshit. When she's concerned about something, she doesn't waste time entertaining imaginary scenarios. I would currently be stewing over Jonah being naked around a bunch of gawking girls, and then my intrusive thoughts would slip in, playing out scenarios of them taking their turns sucking on his dick.

My stomach knots at the mere thought of it.

As we stand concealed behind a large tree, we observe their camp. True to their word, there's a large, upscale camper with lights shining from within. An older couple sits outside in folding chairs engaged in conversation.

They've got four vehicles parked in the clearing, and I assume there are other campers around. I've heard the distant sounds of four-wheelers, so perhaps they're off riding elsewhere.

"There they are," Shay grips my arm, and we both hold our breath, watching the camper door swing open.

The girls emerge first, followed by Jonah and Jonathan. Jonah's hair is wet, and he remains shirtless but has changed into a new pair of shorts.

"At least Jonathan wasn't naked in their camper," I comment, noticing his dry hair.

"That doesn't help him any, given that he would have been alone with those girls while Mr. Everett was showering," Shay remarks as we keep our eyes fixed on them.

They're all standing in front of the older couple, engaged in conversation. We can't hear what's being said, but the older gentleman's expression appears surprised. He rises from his seat, shakes Jonah's hand, and pats his back as he continues chatting. I can't tell if the man knows him personally or by reputation, but he seems eager to continue conversing with Jonah, and the girls appear smitten. They can't be much older than twenty-one.

We linger there for half an hour, exchanging occasional comments as we try to piece together what's happening. When they finally start to move and wave goodbye, Shay and I quickly retreat from the tree and take a longer route up the mountainside to avoid crossing paths with them accidentally.

"My bed or yours?" Shay asks as we walk.

"For what?"

"Couples sleep together. They can sleep together," a mix of amusement and irritation in her tone.

Even though I'm feeling a little jealous right now, I get to play the voice of reason. "We can't be mad at them for Mr. Businessman wanting to take a proper shower. We all expected Jonah to struggle with this, but he's been a total champ this whole time."

"We can certainly be mad at them."

"Are you hangry, my love," I smile at her. "Or horny? Because I will go down on you right now if that will make you release some of that pent up tension," I nudge her arm.

She lets out a laugh. "I need your soft touch, Kal," she wraps her arms around my shoulder, and we continue along the path. "Tell me about Sam. Is he big?"

"Compared to Jonah, not even close. But stand alone, yes."

"My first time—his dick was no bigger than a thumb," Shay holds up her thumb, inspecting it for comparison. "It's always the guys bragging about their size that you have to side-eye."

"I was so sad and angry the night Sam and I had sex. It probably would have hurt if I wasn't full of other emotions. Neither of us knew what we were doing, and I just slammed down on him and rode out my anger. And afterward, my stomach cramped so bad that I thought I injured myself. But it was just that first penetration pain."

"Was the anal also driven my emotion?" she asks curiously, simply wanting to understand more.

"My grandma passed away."

She doesn't say anything but nods in understanding.

"Amber is lucky. I don't say it out of jealousy, but from knowing Sam, and his family. They're all amazing."

"I know. I'm honestly surprised you guys didn't end up married. Especially from the city you are from. The first time I met Sam, Amber and I were both like 'Holy shit! He's sexy.' No wonder Mr. Everett feels a bit unnerved by him," she says it as though she's privy to something I'm clueless of.

"Jonah is not unnerved by Sam," I nudge her with my elbow.

"Oh yes he is. You are so oblivious, Kal. It's cute," she nudges me back.

"You're cray cray."

"Sam would move mountains to be with you, and Jonah will bring the world down if he ever lost you. And you, my dear, are like a flower child frolicking through a meadow," she laughs. "Sam is actually exactly my usual type," her admission catches me by surprise.

"I can't picture you with anybody other than Jonathan."

"My family HATES tattoos. Imagine their surprise when I brought him home," she bites her lip with widened eyes as she glances at me.

I knew Jonathan had full arm sleeves and half of his leg covered in tattoos, and I could catch glimpses of them peeking out from his button-up shirts when he left some buttons undone. But last night, when our tent was unzipped between our rooms, I could see his entire chest, which was completely covered in tattoos. His artist must be phenomenal because each piece of art is incredibly well-done. Now that I think about it, I probably looked like a creep, staring at his chest while we all lay in our beds talking.

"How does your family feel now?"

"It's Jonathan," she gives me a knowing look. "They love him more than me. My dad told him no neck or hand tattoos because our wedding pictures need to look normal and not give my grandparents a heart attack, and he agreed."

"Why are you two not married yet?" I always forget they aren't officially married, and it catches me by surprise every time she refers to him as her boyfriend or when I catch sight of her finger without a ring on it.

"We don't talk about marriage very often. I guess neither of us think about it too much. We are comfortable. The only thing that might move things along is Jonathan wanting to share a room. I won't do it until we are married. But I am old-fashioned in the marriage department. He has to get the ring and propose. I'm not going to beg for someone to marry me, and I don't want to guilt trip anyone into feeling like they need to propose. He doesn't bring it up, so neither do I."

Shay's an old soul in a young, beautiful body. She is wise beyond her years, and I would say Jonathan doesn't know how lucky he is to have her. But he truly does. He's so madly in love with her, and she with him. They are adorably perfect together.

"I think it's the uncertainty. Like right now, we could fight and decide we are done and go our separate ways. Or we can fight, and I can go back to my room. But once we are married, we become one. You fight with me, plant your ass down because there's no walking away. But you also better make damn sure this pussy is the only one you want for the rest of your life because cheating is unacceptable." Her views for her marriage are black and white.

"I've never thought much about getting married," I admit.

"Well, that's fine. Mr. Everett has thought of all of that for the both of you," she states. "And I better be a bridesmaid."

"Same to you," I shoot back.

"Maid of honor," she corrects. "And obviously we already know our first-born children are either going to be best friends or betrothed to one another," she laughs.

"God help us all if Jonah and I are the ones with the daughter," I tease.

"Mr. Everett will ring my poor little son's neck," she adds.

"Will you keep working once you guys are married? In the mansion, I mean?"

"I don't have to work now if I don't want to. I get bored with Jonathan gone, so I keep busy by working around the mansion, but truthfully spend most of my days sending Jonathan tit pics. He wants me to go on their business trips to the office with them but it's boring. I sit at his condo all day doing nothing," we watch as a squirrel with two little babies stops on the trail in front of us, looking in our direction before darting off through the trees.

"I think that was a sign you are going to have twins," I tease. "Once you have babies you can be a mom full time. That will keep you plenty busy," I look over at her to see how she reacts to a future with Jonathan babies.

"Yeah, *we* will be real busy taking care of our babies," she says, emphasizing "we."

"Don't include me in that," I joke.

"Oh, I'm including you. We will be big and pregnant together," she grins proudly.

As we reach camp, barely clearing the trees, someone calls out, "there they are," and Jonathan comes rushing out of our tent looking worried.

"What the fuck, babe. You didn't even tell anyone you were going for a walk," he tells her, walking over to her and pressing his mouth to hers.

"I'm mad at you," she says, pushing him away with no force at all.

"I'm going to take a nap," I say to her as she holds my fingers until they eventually drift apart.

"Everett is out searching for you. Get the lube ready because your ass is done for," he calls over his shoulder.

When I get in our tent, I slip my shoes and socks off before sinking into my bed with a sigh, relishing the feeling of relaxing.

Voices drift in, muffled and indistinct, until Jonathan's voice breaks through, announcing, "She's in the tent," from just outside.

I can discern Jonah's footsteps quickly approaching, but the smooth opening of the tent suggests it's not him who unzips it.

I pretend I'm sleeping, but his large presence is palpable even with my eyes closed. He either knows I'm faking or doesn't care if I really am sleeping because large hands grab my ankles, dragging me to the end of the mattress. My eyes shoot open, and I see a very naked Jonah kneeling at the end of the bed, his eyes dark as he grabs the waistband of my shorts, jerking them off, then doing the same to my shirt.

"Jonah!" I exclaim.

He forces my thighs apart, spit falling from his mouth, landing on my slit and sliding down.

"What are you doing?" I sit up on my elbows, my eyes fixed on his movements as he tightens his grip on his cock. Though I told Shay we can't be mad at them, which sounded good at the time, I feel a pang of jealousy as he looms over me, and earlier thoughts of him intimate with those girls flood back. But he is so goddamn sexy, the jealousy begins to dissolve.

Tracing the tip of his shaft along my slit, he spreads the moisture to my already wet entrance. With firm pressure, he pushes his hips into me. "I'm trying to take a nap," my voice trembles with arousal as I attempt to assert myself, making a move to scoot back, even as my desire rushes through me.

He grips my thighs, holding me in place as he pushes in deeper.

"Nap," is the last word I whisper before my legs willingly fall open for him.

He snakes his arm under my back, pulling me onto his lap as he crawls onto the bed, laying me back down so my head lands on the fluffy pillow.

He lays on top of me, hiking my leg up on his hip as he begins rocking in and out of me, nibbling and sucking on the crook of my neck.

"You're upset thinking other women saw me naked," he breathes in my ear.

When I don't answer, he thrusts hard, burying himself inside me. "Yes," the words fall from my lips in a moan that I am unsure he could even decipher.

"Did you think about my cock being in them?"

"Yes," I moan again, my body syncing with him as he grinds his hips in magical ways.

"This cock?" He thrusts harder, showing me exactly what cock he is referring to.

I nod, my brain unable to form words. I did think about it. I thought about it when I saw them staring at him chopping wood. I envisioned him bending them over one by one, their wet pussies willingly accepting his cock. Their arousal coating his shaft, drawing moans from his lips. Him pleasuring them while their bodies bring him pleasure.

He withdraws, and my eyes flicker open in frustration and confusion.

As he gazes down at me, a mixture of anger and longing surges through me. "Yes," I confess, tears welling in my eyes, "I thought about you fucking them."

A sly grin plays across his lips. Rising up on his knees, he grabs my legs, flipping me onto my stomach. Grabbing my hips, he raises my ass, his legs straddling mine as he forces my knees together with his. He grabs his shaft again, positioning it at my waiting center, shoving it in to the hilt.

My head falls into the pillow as I cry out. He withdraws and slams back into me. Another scream rings out. Over and over, he repeats this motion, the blend of pain and pleasure consuming me. With every thrust, I instinctively clamp my thighs tighter around him in an attempt to lessen the impact of his thrust, resulting in me squeezing on him. The blissful sensations vibrate through me as his sexy moans fill the air.

He leans over me, his chest against my back, his weight supported by his forearm while his other hand slides between my thighs, rubbing my swollen clit.

My hips undulate against his finger as I pant into the pillow.

"God, Jonah, don't stop," I gasp, my breath shallow and ragged, my lungs begging for oxygen. My orgasm builds, teetering on the edge, ready to spill over, and he stops rubbing me. He sits up, pushing one knee at a time between my thighs, forcing them open.

I'm spread wide for him, his hand trailing up my spine, his fingers threading through my hair before he grips tightly, pulling me onto his lap. My hips immediately begin to sway against his as we moan in unison.

His other hand grabs my throat, squeezing, my face growing warm as I feel my skin redden.

"Do you think they could handle this?" he murmurs against my cheek, his warm breath tickling my skin, before releasing his grip. I inhale fresh air as I continue to ride back and forth on him.

My arm reaches around the back of his neck, fingers clutching his hair tightly as I begin to rub my clit, feeling my impending orgasm returning.

He grips my throat again, squeezing, repeating the question I never did answer. "Do you think they could handle this?"

I shake my head, my hips picking up speed as I continue to rub circles on my clit, tugging his hair.

"My cock belongs to you, baby," he whispers in my ear as he releases his hand, and I suck in air as he forces me down onto the bed by my hair, driving fast and hard into me. His penis flexes as his orgasm washes over him, and my vagina clenches against him with my own release.

Goosebumps cover my skin as all the incredible sensations surge within. His motion is fast as he pounds into me, even after we both climax, pumping out every last drop.

My body goes limp on the bed, my breathing thick as his hips gradually slow their rhythm. He remains seated on my backside, still buried deep, and I clench my core around his shaft, a subtle way of letting him know I still feel him, knowing he also enjoys this. When I do it again, he lets out a stifled moan and slaps my ass.

"God, you two are fucking sexy," I hear Shay exclaim.

When I look over to the open space between our tents, I realize we never zipped the wall back up, not that the thin fabric would do much for privacy. Jonathan is lounging on his side, his head propped on his hand, while Shay sits in front of him, leaning against him as they both watched Jonah man handle me in the sexiest way.

THE CAMPING TRIP EXTENDED FOR ONE MORE DAY, FILLED WITH HIKES, skinny-dipping, and repeated sex. Shay and I decide we prefer the zip-up portion between our rooms left open, so the guys quit zipping it shut. We are now all more acquainted with each other being naked and surprisingly, it just feels normal. We even openly discuss various topics while lying naked after we were intimate.

We're so lost in our passion that we forget the tent walls aren't soundproof. One of Jonathan's friends joked around the fire last night, warning no one to go in his tent because it's "covered in white fluid…" and that the moans from our tent had him jerking off multiple times at night. Everyone finds this amusing, but I notice Jonah seems unnerved by the comment. So, I rub his leg, reassuring him it's fine. After all, we're camping out in the open wilderness with other people. Of course, they're going to hear us. But later that night, he tells me we're absolutely buying an RV.

The camping trip provided more than just fresh air. Amber shared that she and Sam finally had sex. Her happiness is clear, and I couldn't be happier for her.

As the other campers left, we enjoy a day of relaxation with just the six of us. Reluctantly, we have to leave as our supplies dwindled and real life beckons us. Sam packs up the tents by himself while Jonathan and Jonah pack up everything else, leaving us girls sitting on the large log at the firepit catcalling them.

CHAPTER
Thirty-Eight

KALYN

I've admittedly struggled with confidence in the past, harboring constant worries about how my actions might be perceived. Wyatt broke the little bit of confidence I had, and I never searched to find it again. However, something about the way Jonah looks at me reignites a newfound confidence, as if he sees an unparalleled beauty that surpasses anything he's ever seen. His unwavering admiration has prompted me to act in ways I never imagined possible with anyone else.

We've been back for a week and Jonah has spent hours past when he normally works playing catch up. He started work this morning at 4:30 and it is now past ten.

I leisurely enter his office, finding him absorbed in paperwork while seated in a sleek, armless black lounge chair by the window. Approaching him with a generously sized blanket draped around me, I stand before him.

"Mr. Everett."

Startled, he looks up, and with a subtle reveal, I let the blanket gracefully fall, leaving me standing before him, completely naked. His eyes gleam with surprise, and the papers follow suit, falling to the floor next to his chair. As if he doesn't need to question what I am doing. He instinctively lets every other distraction be tossed aside to give me his unwavering attention.

With a bite of my lip followed by a seductive smile, I approach him, placing each shin on either side of him on his chair, I find myself comfortably straddling him.

His arms snake up my legs, wrapping around me, grasping my backside.

"You've been working so diligently." My hands trace over his partially unbuttoned shirt, completing the task I finish undoing the buttons to unveil his smooth chest. Bending down, I bestow a kiss on his chest, then delicately trace my tongue over his nipple, a move I find quite pleasurable when he does it to me. Wondering if he'll enjoy the sensation, I leisurely guide my wet tongue over his nipple, sensing the subtle reaction of his chest in response. His breath hitches momentarily as he observes my actions. Following his lead, I mimic the gentle bite, careful not to cause any discomfort before withdrawing my mouth. I divert my attention to his belt, skillfully undoing it, pulling it from his pant loops and hold it on one finger, allowing it to slide off and land gracefully on the floor.

Proceeding with a deliberate pace, I start unbuttoning his pants, unveiling his erect member as it springs free when I part the fabric. My stomach instantly swims with excitement as I wrap my small hands around his thick shaft.

"I've been having naughty thoughts today, Mr. Everett," with a seductive gaze, I sensually guide my hand down his shaft and then trace it back up, deliberately releasing my grip. Replacing the touch of my hand, I press my body against his, sandwiching his member between us, his arousal firmly against my swollen bud.

"Oh, yeah?" his voice laced with arousal.

"Yeah," I affirm, kissing him, brushing my tongue against his, savoring the brief connection. Lips lingering, I confess, "I've been wet all day."

His playful response comes with a light spank. "Sounds like you have been naughty. You should have joined me in here sooner," he pants.

"I was busy working," I grin. "It was hard to concentrate on anything else but this," running my finger down his chest then trailing it along the side of his shaft. "I even thought about sneaking off just to touch myself," I confess, locking eyes with him.

With that, he gives my ass another, more firm spank, sending delightful ripples straight to my core.

"I'm offended you didn't intend to invite me to watch."

"Do you want to watch me touch myself, Mr. Everett?" I encircle my arms around his neck and sensually lick his neck right below his ear.

A low hum resonates up his throat with a subtle "Mmhmm."

"Do you want to watch your cock stretch my pussy while I ride you?" I ask, gently biting his ear.

Another affirmative "mmhmm" rumbles up his throat.

Sitting up, I seductively comment, "I can't hear you."

Prompting him to respond, "Yes, baby, I want to watch my cock stretch your tight pussy," he breathes out.

"That's more like it," I smile, bending forward to kiss him.

Rising while still straddling him, I instruct, "Watch me fuck myself with your cock."

His eyes drift to where my hand securely holds him. Bringing the tip to my entrance, my wetness coating him. As I rock my hips back, I press him between my folds, spreading the moisture up my slit to my sensitive bud. Emitting a soft, carnal-filled moan, I use his tip to draw tantalizing circles on my clit, gradually gyrating my hips back and forth, relishing in the amazing sensations.

Releasing his shaft, I glide my wet folds back down his length, feeling him fill my entire slit as I move up and down on him, rocking my hips while my swollen bud revels in extreme pleasure. Despite the intensity, I resist the urge to climax just yet. Descending again, I let out another restrained moan, bringing my hand back to his shaft, gripping it firmly, and repositioning it at my entrance. Pausing, I hover for a moment, creating anticipation in his gaze, making him wait for the pleasure of stretching me open with his girth.

I pause, hovering for a moment, his eyes briefly close, and when they reopen, desire washes over his entire face. I slowly lower myself just an inch.

Gripping his hair and forcing his head back down, I moan, "Watch me."

Gradually lowering myself further onto him and then inching back up, each descent allows him to stretch deeper. Deliberately, I release aroused moans, aware of his watchful gaze, intending to amplify his arousal.

"Fuck baby," he groans, fixing his gaze on my pussy and his cock, wetting his bottom lip, his breaths become labored, and his body tenses.

Working myself down on him until I'm completely seated, I lean back positioning my hands on his knees as I initiate a slow rocking motion; his gaze remaining fixed on my gyrating hips. He keeps his gaze exactly where I want it. I watch his chest rise and fall as his breathing becomes strained.

Leaning forward, my hands firmly grip his chest, I begin a gliding motion, sliding up and down on him, my tightness squeezing his girth, resisting the descent, reluctant to fully engulf him. His hand moves from my hips as he comes up and grabs my breast with his hand sucking my nipple into his mouth, consuming it as moans cascade from my lungs. Observing his eyes shift to the window while still lavishing my nipple, I turn behind me. His gaze is fixed on the reflection in the window of my backside sliding up and down, his substantial size visible with each ascent.

"Do you like watching me, babe?" Smiling at the mirrored view, my ass appears irresistibly enticing, and his throbbing arousal seems almost too big to be penetrating me.

"Yes," he breathes out.

Persistently moving up and down, I shift to a grinding motion. The intensity builds, and I sense his grip tightening as he nears completion. My orgasm lingering on the edge.

Cradling both cheeks, he lifts me off him, his large cock abruptly leaving me feeling empty, still in a state of delirium, I struggle to comprehend why my imminent orgasm has been stopped before it can erupt out of me.

Standing tall, my arms encircle his neck while my legs remain wrapped around his waist, his strong hands gripping my ass. Reaching down between us I attempt to guide his thick member back inside me, but he grins and lifts me higher, denying my efforts.

"Please," I moan, my plea echoing in the air as I beg him to allow me the ecstasy of riding him once more. I don't know how the roles became reversed with him being the one in control, but I want the control back.

Wearing a mischievous grin, he responds with a teasing "no," before lowering us both to the plush white rug next to the large coffee table and two sizable chairs, he gently positions me flat on my back. Kneeling between my parted legs, his eyes flare with desire as he peers down at me.

Removing his shirt the rest of the way, he tosses it on one of the black leather chairs. His chiseled abs have me on the brink of panting. I am undeniably turned on by him and am so wet right now I wouldn't mind pushing him back onto the rug and grinding my pussy up and down his chest and abs until I cum.

A playful smile curves on my lips as I entertain thoughts of all the ways I want to devour this man. The desire to ride him cowgirl style lingers in my mind, envisioning his moans resonating within the confines of his office. Imagining beads of sweat cascading down his face, mouth agape with arousal, as he thrusts in and out of me. I yearn to pleasure him to the point he's blissfully climaxing. His towering presence above me denies me the opportunity, yet my hips still arch toward him, begging for him to fill me once more.

"You're so fucking sexy, baby," he declares, a look of sheer astonishment washing over his features, as if I'm the most beautiful person he's ever beheld. His hands delicately rest on my knees, urging my legs wider apart, and he inhales deeply, savoring the sight before him. Slowly, his hands glide down my thighs, his fingers squeezing on the inside and his jaw clenches in response.

Biting my lip, I gaze up at him, placing my hands above my head in an attempt to patiently await him lowering himself onto me. However, he defies expectations. Instead, he leans down, planting a soft kiss on my inner thigh and then lightly bites his teeth into the same spot.

A sharp exhale escapes me, startled by the unexpected sensation of his teeth on my skin. He switches to a gentle suck on the mark, withdrawing his mouth and delicately licking the area. My hips involuntarily lift off the rug, needing him to put his tongue between my legs.

He smiles as he moves lower on my thigh, repeating the tantalizing sequence of bites, suctions, and licks. Just inches away from my center, I raise my head to observe him. His eyes meet mine as he softly blows on my clit, sending shivers coursing through my body. Witnessing his mouth part, his wet tongue poised inside, he maintains eye contact while lowering himself fully onto his side. His arms wrap tightly around each of my thighs as his mouth finally descends between my wet slit.

The warmth, tender caresses, and moist touch of his tongue elicit an immediate response—my eyes rolling, and my head falling back on the rug, surrendering to him. His tongue brushing between my legs creates an indescribable sensation that engulfs me in a wave of pleasure.

His grip on my legs is firm as he maintains pressure, skillfully tracing circles on my clit and then softly flicking his tongue up and down, each movement sending shivers through my body. Sliding his tongue down to my entrance, he presses it inside, working it over with a thorough, relentless lick. A moan resonates from his throat, vibrating through me, and I can't help but join in with a moan of my own, panting as he continues his expert attention on my sensitive area.

His tongue glides back up to my swollen bud, as he sucks and licks with intensity. My hand descends, entwining in his hair, grabbing a handful and squeezing tightly, evoking an audible moan from him. I pull his face closer, breathlessly urging him on. "Yes," I moan, the pleasure intensifying as he persists in flicking his tongue over me.

His hand moves from my thigh, sliding down my slit, and I need to be filled. Yearning for his fingers to delve inside. The wait is brief, as his mouth continues its expert attentiveness, and I feel the welcomed intrusion of two fingers stretching inside me. "Yes," I moan once more, my hips instinctively bucking off the rug as he skillfully rocks his fingers on my G-spot. My back arches fully off the floor, and he doesn't relent. The rhythmic movements send goosebumps across my body, and I begin to gyrate my hips on his fingers and face, reveling in the exquisite blend of his fingers driving in and out while rocking back and forth on my G-spot.

Each sensation builds, threatening to make me climax at any moment. "Fuck, baby, you're so wet," he remarks, before burying his face between my legs. My fingers desperately clutch at the rug and maintain a secure grip on his hair, grappling for something to hold onto. Lost in the throes of euphoria, I'm oblivious to the approaching click of Jenevieve's heels.

"Mr. Everett, I have the files you requested," Jenevieve announces, screeching to a halt upon seeing us. The files in her hands spill to the floor, papers scattering in every direction. Unable to fully react, I continue panting in the wake of his relentless attention. He shows no immediate intention to cease as he continues licking and sucking on my sweet spot.

"Jon—" I can't even finish saying his name he feels so good.

I want to tell him to stop; we have an audience, but my body has surrendered to him, and I can't find words. His fingers are moving so fast I can feel my entire body starting to shake, my breathing more ragged. As I pull on his hair tightly to get him to stop, he doesn't let up. I am moving against his fingers until my body stiffens and I try to hold the sensations back, but it's too much. I feel the burning spread through my body as the liquid squirts out when his finger withdraws.

"Fuuck," I cry out.

Pulling his head away, he withdraws his fingers, leaving me with an aching emptiness, as he sits up on his knees. I begin to come down from the high, only to realize Jenevieve is still standing there, gaping at us. Instinctively, I wrap my arms around my chest, suddenly self-conscious.

"Get those papers on my desk and get out," he barks at her, redirecting his attention to me. Seizing both of my hands from my chest, he pulls them above my head, intertwining one hand between both of mine, a devilish expression crossing his face. Grasping his thick cock with his other hand, he slides it down the wetness of my slit, teasing my entrance with the tip before pulling it back out. My senses begin to fog over again with pleasure, and I sense Jenevieve still staring, utterly frozen, her eyes wide with horror, shock, and intense anger.

Maintaining a firm grasp on his erection, he eases the tip in a bit deeper, a synchronized moan escaping both of us. Jenevieve scrambles on the ground, hastily gathering the scattered papers. The vibrations resonate loudly, suggesting her hands might be shaking in the process.

Giving my best attempt to focus on me and Jonah, Jenevieve's presence is distracting me. Withdrawing his cock completely my attention snaps back to him as he thrusts his entire length inside me, evoking a loud moan from my lips as the intense stretching takes over once again. The tightness of him inside me wrapping around his thick member has my body arching off the floor, consumed by pleasure.

"Fuuuck, baby," he moans, lowering himself onto me. The weight of his body against mine is utterly exhilarating. I would willingly succumb to death, with his weight stealing every breath, embracing the exquisite sensation as if it were the ultimate bliss. Our mouths meet in a frantic, heated kiss, tongues intertwining as we passionately explore each other. He presses his large arm under my thigh, pulling it higher onto his hip, his arm supporting it as he thrusts in and out of me.

The echoes of Jenevieve's hurried exit, marked by the clatter of her heels, fill the room. Despite the noise and her intrusion, neither of us can muster a reaction, lost in the overpowering sensations coursing through both of us.

Disengaging his mouth from mine, he promptly plants his lips on the crook of my neck, beginning to bite and suck with unrestrained fervor. The deep penetration of his cock, his strong grip on my leg, the weight of his body, and his teeth on my neck ignite every nerve within me. I teeter on the edge, torn between relinquishing to the pleasure and yearning for the primal bite of his teeth sinking into my flesh. Ecstasy courses through my body, signaling the imminent surrender.

Running one hand down his back, my fingers dig into his skin, clawing down and then clamping firmly as his movements intensify, becoming both vigorous and unyielding. "Harder," I pant, a desperate plea for him to unleash a more forceful assault on my insides. Understanding my need, he withdraws an inch before thrusting back into me with a power that causes my entire body to tighten around him. The rhythmic cycle repeats, each thrust delivering an electrifying force that propels us further into the realms of unbridled sensations.

"God, harder!" I scream, the plea echoing in the room. Instantly, he complies, drawing his hips back before forcefully ramming them into me, keeping himself fully pressed inside me. My breath catches in my throat, overwhelmed by the intense pressure on my insides. A tear escapes the corner of my eye at the force of him penetrating me. Noticing, he leans down, licking the tear from my face before pressing his mouth to mine, coaxing me to reciprocate the kiss.

Resuming his powerful thrusts, he slams fully into me, holding the position for a fleeting moment before repeating the motion. Each thrust propels me closer to the edge of release, my senses heightened with every movement. He's truly magnificent, and it's almost surreal that this incredible man is inside me. My pussy tightens around him, and my cries grow louder with each forceful thrust.

I sense his cock growing harder, signaling our imminent climax. Withdrawing halfway, he plunges deep inside me with force and speed. Climbing onto his knees, he keeps himself submerged, leaning over me and pulling my hips off the ground. He slams into me while I reciprocate by gyrating my hips up and down on his shaft, meeting his powerful thrusts. My vagina clenches around him as the waves of my orgasm explode out of me, a culmination of pleasure and ecstasy.

As the pulsations continue coursing through my vagina and legs, a satisfied smile graces my face, the aftermath of that incredible orgasm. He sprawls on top of me, both of us breathing heavily, beads of sweat trickling across our entwined bodies, marking the aftermath of our intense encounter.

His hand gently envelops the top of my head, his arms forming a protective embrace around me. Meanwhile, my hands leisurely trace up and down his back, delicately tickling his skin until they come to a halt on his perfectly round, firm butt. He remains nestled inside me, similar to a cork retaining the liquid that will spill when he eventually withdraws.

His size gradually diminishes, signaling the waning of his arousal. Breaking the silence, or perhaps just the rhythm of our heavy breathing, I tentatively speak, "So, um... are we just going to add to the liquid on your rug or... how do we plan on getting off it without leaking semen everywhere?" I muse, aware of the richness of this mansion and the pricey rug beneath us.

I sense his body shift in response to my words, and I feel the subtle grin spread across his face.

I wait, anticipating a response, but he stays in the same unmoving position. "Perhaps if you stay pressed inside me, we can inch together just enough to shift onto the floor," I suggest, eyeing the wood surface just beyond our reach. Firmly gripping his ass in an attempt to anchor him in place, I subtly try to maneuver us toward the wooden floor. Yet, neither of us budges even a centimeter. He releases a laugh—a glorious, amazing, harmonious sound. The kind of laughter you'd want to record and play on repeat, the most captivating sound I've ever heard.

"Are you ready to get up, baby?" he asks, sitting up on his forearms and peering down at me, an utterly breathtaking sight. I gaze into his piercing blue eyes.

"Yes and no," I confess. "I want you to stay on top of me like this forever, but I'm nervous about getting your semen all over your fancy rug," I admit. I know he can easily replace it, but it feels awkward thinking of someone having to come and remove it, knowing it was stuff from inside me that dripped out ruining it.

Sliding his hands beneath me, he effortlessly lifts me while keeping himself securely inside me. Striding toward the doors of his office, my eyes widen in panic. "What are you doing?" Without checking for any onlookers, he swings the door open and strides out of his office, catching me off guard. "Jonah!" I exclaim, surprised. Clenching my core on him to ensure he doesn't accidentally slip out, even though he remains planted in place.

With ease, he walks across the spacious room, heading for the bathroom on the opposite side. It's the same bathroom I escaped to after Jenevieve and Gladys walked in on me basically dry-humping him.

As we approach the door, Gladys passes by, pausing in surprise at the sight of us. "Hey, Gladys," Jonah greets her casually, unfazed that we are both completely naked and his penis is still deep inside me. Opening the bathroom door, he flips on the light, closing it with one leg to maintain our privacy.

My mouth hangs open in astonishment, attempting to conceal a smile that threatens to take over. "You did not," I utter, shocked by his nonchalant acknowledgment of Gladys.

"You were the one bothered by a rug that is easily replaceable," he replies. Walking over to the toilet, he lifts the lid, positioning himself wide on either side, his arms still wrapped around my waist. Slowly pulling my body upward, he slides himself out of me. As my legs stretch downward, he bends down, placing me softly on my feet. I sit on the toilet to allow his release to spill out.

Moving to the counter, he turns on the water and grabs a soft towel, wetting it to clean any residue off his length, while I finish cleaning myself up. Then I proceed searching for a towel large enough to wrap around myself while Jonah holds his hand out to me as he stands at the door, gripping the doorknob.

"There isn't anything in here you can cover up with, baby. Let's go." His smile suggests a willingness to try and fix my discomfort. "If it makes you feel better, I'll carry you out and use my hands to cover your ass," he grins widely, awaiting my decision. Realizing the lack of viable options to fully conceal myself, much like a playful child, I raise my arms and leap into his embrace. He effortlessly catches me, a joyful laugh emanating from him as I encircle my arms around his neck and plant a kiss on him.

He confidently strides out of the bathroom without a care. Someone lingers in my peripheral, but I purposely avoid identifying them. Acknowledging their presence would only make it more real that someone is witnessing us in the nude.

Back in his office, he shuts the door and heads to the rug we just had sex on, setting me down softly, then pulling on his boxers and pants. Snatching his discarded shirt off the chair, he walks over to me, holding it open to me, exactly like someone assisting me with a coat. He must notice the confused look on my face.

"If I recall, you came in here wearing only a blanket," he remarks, closing the distance between us. Placing the shirt on my arms and pulling it up to my shoulders, turning me, he begins buttoning it up, ensuring my breasts don't accidentally slip out. His smile widens as he observes me in his shirt, though it fit him snugly, it's oversized on me. I catch a whiff of his enticing scent still lingering on the fabric. I feel a renewed sense of arousal.

"You are so beautiful, baby," he whispers, leaning down to softly kiss me.

I can't fathom how he could be any more perfect. Every action, every move—meticulous, and flawlessly calculated.

Taking my hand, he leads us back to the office door. Uncertain of our destination this time, I decide not to question it. Wherever he takes us, I'll gladly follow without a second thought. Exiting, he turns around, picking me up in his arms. My arms naturally encircle his neck as my legs gracefully dangle off one side of his arm.

Carrying me through the house, it quickly becomes apparent that he's leading us back to my bedroom.

Once inside, he gently sets me down on the bed and heads to the bathroom. Returning moments later with panties, a tank top, and shorts.

He bends down to kiss me, and with deft hands, he adeptly unfastens all the buttons he had meticulously buttoned just moments before, pulling the shirt open and gazing down at me. "I will never tire of staring at you," his eyes lighting up as if beholding my naked body for the first time.

Every day, he manages to boost my confidence. I've never felt more assured in my entire life.

"Take a picture, it might last longer," I tease.

His smile broadens as he pulls his phone out of his pants pocket, holding it up, and snapping a picture of me. "I'll use that tomorrow," he places it on the nightstand, leaning back over me, and touching his lips to mine once more.

Picking up my panties from the pile, he guides my feet into them, smoothly sliding them up. He then grabs my shorts, effortlessly slipping them into position, before helping me into my top. As he unbuttons his pants and slides them off, a realization strikes me. "Wait, why am I getting dressed while you're getting undressed?" I find humor in the absurdity of the situation.

He smirks pulling the covers back and then climbs on the bed, laying back onto the pillows with his arms above his head. Removing one hand, he extends it toward me. "Come here, baby," he invites me to cuddle him. Eagerly complying, I crawl up the bed into his arms and lay down, nestling myself into his chest, his arm wrapping around my waist, the other resting on top of mine on his chest.

He traces his fingers across my shoulder as his eyes gradually close. Looking up at him, I observe his breathing becoming steady and heavy as sleep takes over. He appears so peaceful, and unbelievably handsome. I snuggle my face into his chest, placing a kiss to his skin and falling asleep in his arms.

I TRY TO GET OUT OF BED SO I CAN BE TO WORK ON TIME, BUT JONAH is taking me from behind and holding me in place.

"I'm gonna be late," I pant, though I don't really have it in me to care all that much.

"Good," his breathing is labored.

There is a knock on my door and then it opens as Shay walks in.

"Never mind," she smiles and turns to leave.

She comes in almost every morning to hang out with me while I finish getting ready. Judging by the amused look on her face, she approves of my morning rendezvous.

Unfortunately, I can hear when Jenevieve's heels stomp down the corridor to give orders to the maids. Even with the sound of her heels clicking, Jonah doesn't relent. Sitting up, he pulls me onto his thighs, gripping my hips as he rocks me back and forth.

I can feel the sweat coating his chest as my back rests against him, and it turns me on even more.

When I hear her heels abruptly stop, I stiffen.

Jonah must have felt it because he grabs my neck firmly, turning my face toward his, and presses his mouth to mine.

"Where is she?" I hear Jenevieve question and my stomach sinks knowing it's me she's referring to.

"She will be a little late. Mr. Everett approved it," I hear Shay respond.

"Ugh," she screeches, and her stomping heels move quickly toward my door until my door is swinging wide open and she storms in.

I try to react, but Jonah's hold on my jaw tightens as he keeps my face to his, his other hand going between my slit and he circles my sensitive bud, eliciting my hips to rock faster on him. Stifled moans from me fill the air as he groans with each sway of my hips.

Jenevieve scurries out of my room, shutting the door behind her and then silence. Until I hear her start barking orders to everyone and her heels clicking quickly down the hall.

Flipping me over onto my back, he positions himself between my legs, thrusting in and out of me quickly as he takes his release.

I'm so humiliated that all the maids just heard us having sex, I sort of fake an orgasm just so I can distance myself from this situation.

As he climbs off me and retrieves a towel from the bathroom, he cleans me up and I just lie there.

"Can I ask a favor? And if not, I completely understand, don't feel obligated to say yes," I tell him. I don't think I can face any of the staff today after that little show we just performed.

"Of course," he says, sitting on the edge of the bed looking down at me.

"Do you mind if I clean your office today?" I ask, hoping I can just hide in there with him.

A grin spreads across his face. "Please do," he agrees.

Smiling, I get up and head to my closet with him following behind.

"Skip the uniform, babe. Wear something comfortable," he beams.

"Really?" I ask, thinking it would be nice to not wear work clothes today.

"Really," he confirms.

When I am dressed, we walk hand in hand to his office.

Of course he didn't actually let me clean anything, instead we talk about random things until he has phone calls in which case I just sit at his desk in one of the chairs on the opposite side, reading a book.

For lunch, Gladys brought both of us our food. I don't know how she knew I was in here, but she somehow knew and seemed thrilled about it.

After work he takes me to the observatory where dinner is waiting, and we watch the sunset.

As the night approaches, the temperature drops, and it becomes cold.

"Ready to get to bed?" he smiles.

"Ready," I stand and hold out my hand to him.

We have spent all day together, and I love it when he leads me to his room. I prefer his room much more than mine. As we settle in bed together, he falls asleep quickly. But my mind decides now is the perfect time to become active.

Taking a moment to survey the room, I'm struck by his impeccable taste, it's truly impressive. I'm also in awe of how immaculate everything is. I also can't comprehend how clean and tidy he is. I can't recall ever seeing anything of his in disarray. Is this how he was raised or is this a type of OCD that he has?

I ponder about the lucky maid who gets to clean in here. Changing his bedding, doing his laundry, cleaning his shower. No one ever talks about it, but the long-time cleaners seem to frequent this end of the mansion. A thought crosses my mind—what if I asked him if I could clean his room? He'd likely resist at first, claiming he doesn't want me to work at all, but deep down, I sense he would relent if I insisted.

Oddly, the mansion is situated in the middle of nowhere, and I've never encountered a single bug inside. I begin to entertain the thought of whether he might be scared of bugs. The image of him, with his composed demeanor, being frightened by a tiny insect strikes me as amusing. I detest bugs—can't stand them. Every relationship needs someone who can bravely handle bug duty when necessary. I wonder if he harbors any fears or aversions.

My mind swirls with these random questions, but as his breathing remains steady, I decide to slip out of bed quietly. I intend to return to my room briefly to fetch my phone. I plan to be back beside him before he even notices my absence, providing a quiet moment to scroll through social media while I wait for sleep to finally overtake me.

Slipping out of his bed, I cautiously make my way to the door, tiptoeing so I don't create a single noise. The mansion's peculiar silence strikes me as odd—it never creaks, not even when wandering through it late at night.

The cold floor feels refreshing against my bare feet as I traverse different halls, eventually winding back to the maid's quarters.

Suddenly, the screech of Jenevieve's voice pierces the air: "You stupid little bitch," and before I know it, she's grabbing me by my hair, yanking me backward. I lose my balance from the sudden attack and fall to the ground. Her shrill screams intensify as she climbs on top of me, straddling my waist as she hits and claws at me relentlessly. "He is mine," she shrieks louder.

"Jenevieve, stop!" I scream, attempting to push her away, but she shows no signs of relenting. The assault continues; it feels like my skin is being slashed open with knives, and her threats escalate. "I will fucking kill you, whore."

Amidst the chaos, trying to block her claws, she is pulled off me by large hands. Jonathan is who intervened, while Shay rushes over to help me up. Despite being held back, Jenevieve continues her barrage of insults and even spits at me. I wipe the saliva from my chest, which feels worse than the blood trickling down my forehead, cheek, neck, and shoulder.

Instead of breaking down, an unexpected reaction takes over—I break into a sinister grin that escalates into full-blown laughter. Shay, Jonathan, and Jenevieve stare at me in disbelief as if I've lost my sanity. Through gritted teeth and a twisted expression, I declare, "He licks my pussy in ways you'll never feel.

His cock fucks me in ways you'll spend your entire life wishing he would have fucked you, his semen is still inside my pussy. You're nothing, Jenevieve—a forgettable fling he used to entertain. But now, you're obsolete, unwanted, and insignificant. A disgusting, cheating, baby-killing psycho. You'll never be anything to anyone, just a classless, cheap thrill. Even then, you could never truly be anyone's thrill." I revel in the moment, finding a perverse humor in exposing her pathetic existence.

My chest heaves with anger and I turn toward my room and continue down the hall. "Oh, and Jenevieve," I turn back to look at her, whom Jonathan is forcibly escorting away. "YOU are the stupid, fucking bitch..." Wiping blood off my lip. Her yells only grow louder, reverberating through the corridor.

Shay accompanies me back to my room, visibly shocked. Once behind closed doors, she demands, "What the fuck was that?"

I examine the claw marks riddled across my skin that are oozing blood.

Turning on the sink, I wet a towel and blot it on the wounds. Meeting Shay's gaze in the mirror, I smile. "Jenevieve walked in on Jonah eating me out. She was horrified," I laugh.

"Shut the fuck up," Shay grins, jumping up to sit on the counter next to me. "What did Mr. Everett do?" she asks, clearly intrigued.

I continue cleaning the blood, adrenaline still coursing through me, numbing the pain of the cuts. "He ignored her, and quit fucking me with his tongue, sat up, and started fucking me with his cock, then he yelled at her to put a file on his desk and get out," I recount. "You know," I reflect on her interruption. "In that moment, I was terrified she walked in on us. But then I felt exhilarated, knowing she witnessed him doing things to me he never did to her. Fuck her," I conclude, the resentment finally bubbling over as the stinging sensation from the marks starts to pierce through.

I'm tired of her being a bitch, I didn't choose for him to want me. I didn't choose him not wanting her. I didn't choose her to treat me like garbage since the second I walked through those doors. I tried being nice. I have spent too many months with her abusing me and I am done.

Shay's smile radiates pride and then she starts checking all the marks on my face. "Mr. Everett is going to murder her," her gaze focused on the injuries. "Let's go stay at that cottage you love so much. At least until you heal a little bit."

"I'm not letting her run me out of here after attacking me." I dab some Neosporin on the marks before heading into my bedroom. "I was just coming back to grab my phone, but I'm definitely not going back to his room tonight." I don't want Jonah to wake up and see me looking like this.

Walking over to my bed, I pull the covers back and climb in. Shay follows suit on the other side. Reaching across, she laces her fingers with mine. "I am so proud of you, Kal. That was badass, the way you stood up to Jenevieve like that," she commends.

It did feel pretty amazing finally getting to tell her off. I almost wish this confrontation had happened sooner. Now I find it comical that Jenevieve walked in and saw Jonah going down on me. Screw her.

A knock on the door precedes Jonathan's entrance. "Hi, babe," Shay greets him. "Did you throw her to the wolves?" she teases.

He is in no mood for jokes or lighthearted jabs. He just walks up to my side of the bed. "Are you okay, Kal?" he asks concerned as he leans in to inspect the marks.

"Yep," I assure him, and a glimmer of humor briefly lights up his eyes

"You sleeping in here tonight, hun?" Jonathan asks Shay, who nods and then rolls over, wrapping her arm around my waist. He laughs and mentions he's heading to his room, ensuring to lock the bedroom door on his way out.

CHAPTER

Thirty-Nine

As the morning alarm jolts me awake, I notice a burning sensation on my skin where Jenevieve had clawed me. Getting out of bed, I head to the bathroom to find that the scratches are not only bright red but also swollen, with slight bruising surrounding them.

"She's like a damn cat," I mutter to myself as I inspect each mark. The more I stare at them, the more anger builds in me, contemplating how she thinks it's okay to lay her hands on me. It occurs to me that I need to find a way to avoid going to work today. I'm not prepared to run into Jonah and have him questioning how I got these injuries. Especially when he fell asleep thinking I was safely in his arms. I don't have the energy today to lie about Jenevieve attacking me like a rabid animal.

"Hey Kal, I'm heading to my room to get ready for work," Shay's voice calls out as she moves toward the door. I hear the click of the lock, the door opening, and then closing again.

I pull out my makeup, attempting to conceal the scratches on my face. Despite my efforts, they remain visibly prominent. *"Well, I will for sure be a treat for everyone to behold,"* I muse to myself as I finish braiding my hair. Giving myself a quick once-over, a subtle chuckle escapes my lips upon seeing all the claw marks. What a loser.

Changing out of my pajamas, I put on my maid uniform, pondering whether I should bring some sort of weapon with me, considering Jenevieve's inability to keep her hands to herself.

Exiting my room, I see the other maids already leaving the maid's quarters for their assigned chores. I am confused about what's happening and why Jenevieve isn't here giving orders. Maybe Jonathan really did kick her out. Or maybe security has her wherever they were holding the intruders.

Shay is waiting for me, smiling when she sees me. "Dusting duties," she says as we exit the maid's quarters behind the others. We gather our cleaning supplies and head to the grand entryway leading to the front door and the massive living room straight ahead. While we're all cleaning, Jenevieve's heels click into the room. I guess she isn't locked up.

Without saying a word, she stands in the doorway, fury in her eyes, her makeup noticeably thicker today, likely an attempt to conceal that she spent the night crying. I feel satisfied that she got a small taste of her own medicine.

Making eye contact, she looks like she's contemplating ways to kill me, and I respond by grinning at her. I want her to know I am no longer afraid of her. Just as she seems to muster the courage to approach me, a loud commotion erupts from somewhere else in the house. All of us turn our heads in the direction of the noise, at the same time Jonathan walks into the room looking for Shay, from a different area.

"Oh, fuck!" Jonathan exclaims as he rushes toward the commotion. We all stand there, and then it becomes clear.

Jonah storms into the room with Gladys, Giles, security, and at least ten other house staff trailing behind him. The moment I spot him, I drop my duster and rush towards him.

"Babe, calm down," I frantically try to coax him into taking a second to breathe. He stops walking and glances at me briefly, his eyes scanning each scratch mark, before his nostrils flare even more, and he makes a beeline for Jenevieve.

"You told him?" I screech at Jonathan, anger coursing through me that everyone's day is about to be ruined because of this.

"He didn't say anything, Kal," Shay defends.

We all watch as Jonah walks up to Jenevieve, grabbing her by the throat and shoving her against the wall with a loud thud. A hushed stillness envelops the room, the silence so profound that it feels as if time itself has come to a standstill. Every person here is immobilized, their eyes fixed on the unfolding spectacle before them. Everyone holding their breath, anxiously awaiting the outcome of Jonah's confrontation with Jenevieve, and if he will kill her right here in front of all of us.

Rushing to him I try to get his attention before he harms her. I frantically plead for him to let her go. My hand grabs his arm that is holding her, and she stands frozen in place. I reach up, grabbing his face and forcing him to look at me.

"Baby, I'm fine. Come on, let's go to your office or back to bed. Do you want to go back to bed?" I offer my best reassuring smile, attempting to calm him down. Despite my efforts, his breaths remain labored, as an internal war rages inside him, torn between how to deal with the emotions of how he feels toward Jenevieve's latest assault on me and how he should be handling it. His chest rises and falls as he grapples with how to react.

He turns back to Jenevieve, bringing his face down to hers, with an intensity that has my bootyhole puckering. "Get the fuck out of my house, and don't ever come back," he seethes before releasing his grip on her roughly.

"It's okay," I reassure, grabbing his hands and pulling him away from her as she stands there looking pathetic. His intense gaze remains fixed on her. My attention stays resolute on him, and I extend a soothing touch to his hip, attempting to guide him away. In a moment of realization, he blinks back to the present, turning his head to look down to me. Cupping my cheek, his eyes roaming over the marks she left, then he reaches down, takes my hand, and starts pulling me out of the room.

Jenevieve adjusts her composure, her tone sharpening with anger. "I can't help but wonder how your family will react to this. You know we are to be married, Jonah. Your family will never approve of you and the hired help," she declares, her words dripping with resentment. "Rest assured, your mother will know all about this," she seethes, her threat hanging in the air.

He stops walking and turns to look at her for a brief moment, a devilish grin crossing his face before he shifts his gaze down to me. Tilting my chin upward with his hand, he presses his lips to mine. Our mouths part, and his tongue slips inside as we passionately kiss right there in front of everyone. His arm reaches around my waist, pulling me closer, as he grabs a handful of my ass, squeezing it. Pulling his mouth off mine, his eyes have a flicker of arousal as he playfully spanks my butt. "God, I'm gonna fuck you."

Before we escape, he addresses security, "Get her the fuck off my property," and then pulls me out of the room.

His breathing is heavy as we walk the corridor to his office. The tension is palpable, evident in the painful grip he has on my hand, pulling me along with determined force. Upon reaching his office, he forcefully thrusts the door open, ushering me inside before slamming it shut with a resounding click.

Restlessly pacing, his mind appears to be a whirlwind of thoughts, and I wonder whether his anger stems from firing Jenevieve or if he's contemplating how I got entangled in the situation. With his relentless pacing, I discern that the silence between us has stretched long enough. I take a breath and decide to interrupt the quietness.

"You were sleeping so peacefully, and my mind started to wander. I thought about how clean your room is and whether you're scared of bugs, given that I hate bugs. If we both do, who would kill bugs in our house? Then it hit me that I've never seen a bug in here. So, I figured maybe bugs are scared of you. I realized I wasn't tired, and you were sound asleep. I just wanted something to distract my thoughts, so I went to grab my phone, thinking I'd be back in bed with you before you even knew I was gone. Then Jenevieve must have seen me and attacked, and I didn't want you to wake up seeing me like this. I'm sorry, Jonah," I admit, realizing at this point I'm just word vomiting all over him and I need to learn when to shut the fuck up.

His restless pacing comes to a halt, and his gaze fixates on me. "I'm not scared of bugs. I don't like them, and I don't want to see them in my house. If there is ever a bug near you, I will kill it for you," he asserts, his eyes unwavering.

I can't hold back a smile at his declaration. "Good," I respond as if his assurance alone brings comfort. Then, with sincerity, I add, "I'm sorry again for leaving your room last night."

A shadow crosses his features, signaling an underlying concern. Finally, he divulges, "She was waiting for you." His words hang in the air. I'm puzzled, and he must see the confusion on my face. "I watched the security cameras to see where you went. She watched us when we left my office and went to the bathroom last night," he explains. My mind connects the dots—she was the person I glimpsed in my peripheral vision when we were leaving the bathroom. "She went to your room, and when she didn't find you there, she began looking around. Not finding you, she waited for you to come back. Lucky for her, she only had to wait an hour before you were slipping out of my bed and walking back to your room," his anger resurfacing at the thought.

I stand there momentarily rendered speechless. What kind of psycho prowls around for someone just to attack them? It's chilling to think about the lengths she went to.

"I don't know if I'm supposed to apologize. I understand you didn't want her here and that you were forced to keep her around. But firing her is going to cause huge issues with your family, and I don't want to be the cause of that," I let him know my concerns. I am acutely aware that coexisting under the same roof with Jenevieve is impossible. If she were to stay, my leaving would be inevitable. Yet, it's obvious he doesn't want her here, and the sentiment is shared by everyone in this house. She is the devil in stilettos. But now he will deal with her repercussions.

He strides over to the chair he occupied just last night and settles into it. Following suit, I choose the adjacent chair, perching on its edge, with my forearms on my legs and hands clasped in front of me. Having expressed everything on my mind, I find myself in a state of silence.

He speaks with a resolute tone, "I don't care what happens with my family, you are my family, babe—the only family I want and will ever need." He sits upright, his intense gaze fixed on me. "I'm the one that should apologize," he adds sincerely, but my gaze remains lowered, fixated on my hands.

Unexpectedly, he lowers himself to the floor, dropping to his knees in front of me. With his hands placed on each of my legs, he nudges his nose against mine, coaxing me to look at him. A smile blossoms on my face, mirroring the one forming on his. His hands trace a path up my legs, encircling my back, and with a gentle pull, he guides me onto his lap. I willingly comply, settling on his thighs.

My legs naturally wrap around him as I embrace his neck, holding onto him tightly.

Last night transpired so quickly, leaving me in disbelief that Jenevieve full-blown attacked me. It's quite comical how crazed she looked, her eyes on the verge of popping out of her face as she was gouging her long, pointed claws in me. I wonder how much damage she would have been able to inflict had she not been wearing those talons. I also realize I am in dire need of self-defense classes, and once I take them, I will fantasize about all the ways I'd like to kick Jenevieve's ass up and down these halls.

However, I know Jenevieve well enough, I'm sure she is currently on the phone with Jonah's family, shedding fake tears and strategically crafting a narrative where I am painted as the villain in this situation.

I briefly entertain the thought of the security room having Jenevieve's picture hanging on the wall, serving as a visual reminder for everyone to not let her enter. Yet, the reality is that Jenevieve has become an unforgettable nightmare etched into our collective brains, ensuring that she won't be easily erased from our memories.

In a seemingly choreographed twist of comedic timing, Jonah's phone begins to ring, he lets out an audible exhale of annoyance. I gracefully disentangle myself from his lap, returning to the chair I initially occupied. Typically, Jonah would insist on keeping me in place, enveloped in his arms, but today is different—we both recognize the incoming call is his mother.

With a faint, strained smile, he rises, leaving a kiss on my lips before retrieving his phone from his pocket. Walking toward his desk, he answers the call "Mother," sitting down in his desk chair, keeping his gaze locked on mine. The muffled sounds of yelling reaches my ears, revealing an unmistakable tone of loud anger. Feeling a sense of unintentional intrusion, I avert my gaze, fixating on the expansive windows before me. Gradually, the dialog between him and his mother fades into background noise, allowing only my thoughts to remain.

Why does he not have a cat or a dog? Maybe they would get lost in this ridiculous mansion. He has a large area with multiple horse stables and even a full-size racetrack for them. Also, why does he have twenty horses? I could see people riding the horses all the time while mucking stalls, but I've never seen him out there.

My mind conjures whimsical images of a fluffy white cat with giant blue eyes, reminiscent of Jonah's own. I'm not sure why this is even a mental image I would have. Maybe he doesn't have time with how much he has to travel. I ponder the potential drawbacks of frequent travel and whether it becomes tiresome. I've never been particularly fond of extensive travel. The whole experience tends to render me thoroughly exhausted upon returning home. Although I have never actually traveled very far.

Recollections of when I was younger come to mind and the frequent travels I shared with my mom and dad. The three of us were inseparable. However, after their passing, I found myself under the care of my dad's mom. Their relationship had been strained, largely due to my grandma's disapproval of my mom. Even with the tension, my grandma willingly took me in after my parents' untimely passing and embraced the responsibility of raising me, doing her best to provide a stable and nurturing environment for me.

She was a heavy smoker, and developed lung cancer, frequently in and out of hospitals during the time she raised me. Most of my days were spent with Sam and his family, who graciously welcomed me into their home. As I stayed for weeks on end while my grandma underwent treatments, I found solace in their company. They even allowed Sam and I to share his bed. And well, we decided to lose our virginities together. This choice resulted in a cringe-worthy incident involving Sam's mom mistakenly assuming I had started my period. In a well-intentioned yet awkward gesture, she went ahead and bought me a collection of pads and tampons. Despite my vehement denials regarding my menstrual cycle, she insisted, and it was Sam's dad who pieced together where the blood actually came from. Prompting Sam's family to move me to his sister's room for sleeping arrangements.

Sam is undeniably attractive, yet I never considered him as a potential romantic partner. Our shared intimacy muddled our friendship, especially when I found myself torn between declaring us as mere friends one moment and undressing him the next. In my teenage confusion and heartbreak, I believed that engaging in a physical relationship with Sam would somehow convey the love I sought from him. Looking back, I realize the flawed nature of my thinking during that time.

Initiating a conversation with Sam about all of that has always been a challenge for me. We've both seemingly moved on, treating the past as if it never occurred, and now, I struggle to find an opportune moment to address it. It seems easier to bury those memories in an unmarked grave and let them remain undisturbed, never to resurface again.

I catch the sound of Jonah ending his call with his mom, prompting me to glance over at him. He reclines in his chair, his arms resting on the armrest, lazily twirling his thumbs in circles as he seems lost in thought.

"That good huh?" I tease.

He meets my gaze, his features visibly relaxing, and he rises from his chair, making his way over to me. Positioning himself behind my chair as I look up at him, he leans down, pressing his lips to mine.

CHAPTER
Forty

KALYN

I find myself drawn to the serenity of the courtyard, needing a moment of solace. Finding a shaded bench, I lower myself onto it, allowing my gaze to meander across the meticulously crafted landscape—a view that has always captivated me. The sheer beauty of the surroundings stands in contrast to how I am feeling on the inside.

The storm brewing inside me finds its roots in the ongoing issues with Jenevieve. Time and again, her actions have ruined everything. Strangely, though, with each of Jenevieve's wrongdoings, I become the undeserving recipient of the repercussions. It's a confusing cycle, leaving me wondering how this keeps happening.

Jonah had to excuse himself to take care of some things and has been absent for five hours. Shay steps in to distract me by taking me to a section of the mansion on the second floor that resembles a casino. She had me bowl with her, and play some slot machines before I tire, and tell I wanted to go for a walk alone.

Unexpectedly, a voice startles me out of my contemplation. "May I sit with you?" I turn to see Antoinette standing there, her gaze fixed on me.

Taken aback by her sudden presence and a desire for her approval, I respond without much thought. "Of course, please," I gesture to the space beside me. A surge of nervousness overtakes me as I try to think of reasons why she is here. I even allow a small glimmer of hope, daring to envision that she has come to offer Jonah and me her blessing.

In my daydream, we would share a heartfelt moment, and hug, and she'd become the mother figure I've longed for. If this were a movie, the screen would cut, and we would all burst into fits of laughter at the absurdity of such a notion.

I recognize she must have something important to say since she not only flew here but sought me out. Clearing her throat she begins, "Jonah was *my* baby for twenty-eight years. You always think your children are special—Eliza and Ethan are both so special to us. Each pregnancy, each child, you always think you can't possibly love another human being more than the one you already have. When Jonah was born, it was different. Those blue eyes— like nothing I'd ever seen before—and the hair," she tips her head back as if transported to the precise moment she first laid eyes on him. "He had so much hair. We teased that he better come out with gobs of hair with the amount of heartburn I felt while I was pregnant. And he didn't disappoint. As he rarely does," she adds pointedly.

"His hair was this beautiful light brown, so long and thick, with loose curls, still matted to his head. He came out smiling, not crying, just absorbing the world around him. Everyone always says they don't have a favorite child, well, nobody ever admits it, but we all secretly do," she adds, clasping her hands together in her lap. "He was an extraordinary boy, so caring, and his love was fierce. Jonah never minded playing with his baby sister and her friends. At our dinner parties, he gravitated towards the younger kids, drawing everyone to him. My best friend often joined us, and as we sipped wine, Jonah effortlessly played with her little one. She was this lively, rambunctious little girl, and Jonah kept her and Eliza contained while the adults relaxed. Well, until Eliza and her friends decided they no longer wanted boys around. Undeterred, Jonah would cheerfully move on and contribute elsewhere. Our chef adored him and taught him the art of cooking, even though we were adamant he'd never need such skills. Then, one day, he transformed. Growing more serious and business-like, we just knew he would eventually take over his father's business. Beaumont tried instilling all his knowledge of business into Ethan, but he was always getting into trouble, chasing after fleeting desires. Jonah, on the other hand, exceeded our hopes as a future business partner. However, Jonah being the bullheaded man he is, was dissatisfied with his father's business practices, he believed he could do better, and indeed, he did. Jonah ventured into business on his own, and he excelled—outperforming not only his father but anyone we've ever known," she reflects, her voice carrying a mix of pride and nostalgia.

"In the world of business, being single can be a double-edged sword. Other powerful men often believe they can take advantage of you, and there's a sense of threat that you're enjoying the single life while they're tied down. So, in a way, they attempt to exploit the situation. Women, on the other hand, might pursue you because you're a big deal. However, when you're married, the dynamic shifts. You're perceived as powerful, stable—a person to engage in business with," she concludes the thought, her expression transitioning from one of understanding to a more businesslike attitude. "I'm sharing this with you because, while nobody takes Jonah for granted, he would be much stronger in the business world with a strong woman at his side, Jenevieve at his side," she says knowingly. "You're undeniably beautiful, truly stunning. I can see why he's captivated by you, but you're not his long-term, dear. I'll sit idly by while he plays out this fantasy with you. But these things only last a few months to a year with him. You could save yourself a lot of heartache if you ended things with him now, rather than dragging out the inevitable. He will marry Jenevieve. You understand that don't you?" she says, expecting me to readily accept the notion or perhaps hoping I'll decline an invitation to their future wedding.

"I'll bet he was an incredible little guy," I smile, reminiscing about what young Jonah would have been like.

"He was," is all she offers.

"I can see how much you love him." It's evident that her love for him is profound, but almost bordering on a level of control. "I just wonder how you can love someone so much and not want them to be happy?" I inquire, considering Jonah's disdain for Jenevieve and questioning how she could be so callous in wanting to impose a life of misery on him.

"The excited jitters, the constant sex, the thrill of sneaking around—it all ends eventually. Life truly begins when you have children. Jonah excels at his job, and he will produce strong children like himself. That's when he'll find true happiness. Jenevieve was born into our world; she knows how to navigate it. You, dear, would never survive it," she asserts as if she has a total understanding of who I am.

She discusses him as though he's a man bound by her orders, restricted in his actions and decisions. "Is Jonah weak?" I inquire, noticing her subtle flinch as I refer to him by his name.

She regains composure. "No, he's far from weak," she asserts proudly.

I maintain my gaze, seeking clarity. "Then how do you expect to remove me from his life without it being his decision?" I question sincerely, genuinely wanting to understand her perspective.

She appears momentarily stunned, unsure how to respond, but quickly recovers with a matter-of-fact reply. "You need to be the one to leave."

"That's the thing," I respond evenly, "I've already tried. The issue with Jonah is he always seems to get what he wants," I say, acknowledging the inevitability that, regardless of her plans, he will continue to pursue his desires unabated.

"I can tell how smart you are. I think we can help each other," she suggests.

"Why are you doing this?" I ask, wrestling with the realization that she might be right. I don't seem to belong in this world. I had to mend the pieces that Wyatt shattered, and Jonah meticulously restored every fragment until I felt whole again. How am I sitting here even entertaining the idea of leaving him? Tears stream down my face, and she reaches over, taking my hand. As pathetic as it may sound, her touch takes me back to my childhood—the warm embrace I once knew—and the tears continue to flow.

"I'll send a car for you tonight, dear. Spend an evening with him, enjoy each others company, take him to bed, release all your emotions, and desert them there. Jonah may be down for a day or two, but he will forget all about you in a couple days. This is for the best... For everyone. My driver will meet you outside at midnight," she squeezes my hand. "Let's get back. I'm sure he's pacing shoe prints into the marble."

A whirlwind of thoughts swirl through my mind, and my body seems to teeter on the brink of shock as we stand up and make our way back indoors, her arm unexpectedly interlocked with mine. Glancing down at our linked arms, I question whether I am hallucinating. Yet, to my disbelief, our arms are undeniably intertwined.

Stepping into the house, Jonah approaches, appearing as though he had been searching for us. Surprise flashes across his face as Antoinette releases my arm.

Did she do that just to put on a show for Jonah?

Holding her arms outstretched as she approaches Jonah, she envelops him in a tight hug. His eyes widen in a mixture of shock and confusion, shooting me a questioning look that mirrors his bewilderment about the recent exchange between his mother and me. "I love you, son," she declares, then redirecting her gaze toward me. With a nod she addresses me by name, "Kalyn," before briskly making her exit from the room.

Raising an eyebrow, he shifts his gaze from his departing mother to me, "What did I miss?" He stands momentarily frozen before crossing the room over to me, encircling me with both of his large arms in a comforting hug.

How do I even begin to explain what just happened? "Nothing," I murmur, gripping him tightly, my gaze fixed on the courtyard where Antoinette and I were just sitting.

The sun has begun its descent, painting the sky with ever-changing hues, and I observe the shifting shades of colors. We both stand, captivated by its beauty. He squeezes me tightly and then releases me. "Meet me back here at eight," he says affectionately.

I laugh. "Okay, where do you think you're running off to?" My playful tone masks my underlying curiosity about what could be so important for him to step away again after being absent for hours. It feels like this absence is more personal to me even though it's way less time. In his eyes, it's just another ordinary day with limitless time for us. Meanwhile, a quiet realization settles in—I sense that my precious hours with him are slipping away.

"I have a couple more work things to handle, shouldn't take longer than an hour," he explains, leaning down and pressing his lips to mine.

Returning to my bedroom, my mind is consumed by thoughts of the recent conversation with Jonah's mother. Why don't I harbor resentment towards her for seemingly pushing me out of his life? Could it be because she genuinely believes she's acting in her son's best interest? Or perhaps it's because I lack the guidance of a mother figure in my own life, making it easier for me to go along with what she believes is right. It feels like I'm missing out on crucial lessons and insights that a mother could provide.

The contemplation fades as I step into my bedroom, only to find the bathroom casting a warm glow across the kitchenette area and spilling a soft illumination into my room. There's movement inside, catching my attention. I approach the door cautiously and peek inside, discovering Shay busy arranging items on the counter.

"Oh, good, you're here," she greets me, plugging in a curling iron and adjusting its temperature before setting it down. "Come, sit down," she pats the chair.

I find myself staring at her, a mix of excitement and confusion on my face. "What are you doing?" I eye the assortment of makeup and brushes neatly laid out, resting on a towel.

"Your hair and makeup. Isn't it obvious?" Her joy fills the room as she delicately guides her hand above the array of makeup.

Guiding me into my vanity chair, I sit down, allowing myself to relax as she runs a comb through my hair. Grabbing a clip from her tidy collection of supplies, she secures the top half of my hair and starts skillfully curling the lower section into loose, cascading curls. My thick hair requires meticulous attention, and she works through it in three sections, brushing the curls afterward for a natural finish.

Effortlessly navigating her way around the makeup, she applies a thin layer to my face. Once she finishes, she turns me towards the mirror so I can witness the transformation. Staring at my reflection, I'm taken aback—I look... beautiful. The colors she chose accentuate my green eyes. "Wow, Shay," I murmur in disbelief at the stunning mirrored image before me.

She gazes at her handiwork impressed. "I know," she begins to clean up the makeup. "It makes it easy when you have a pretty canvas to start with. I picked out a dress for you, it's in the closet," she points a makeup brush over her shoulder toward the closet, as she continues the cleanup. Once she wraps up, she glances toward me. "Have fun," she coos before walking out.

I discover a stunning, form-fitting rose gold dress hanging delicately, accompanied by matching rose gold high heels on the floor below. In awe, I run my fingers down the soft material, then proceed to strip off my current clothes, tossing them into the laundry basket. Opting for a matching lace set of panties and bra, I slip them on before grabbing the dress, sliding it off the hanger, and slipping it on.

The dress hugs my figure, with a long slit up the front left side, a little above mid-thigh. With thin straps, I notice my bra peeking out from underneath. I decide it looks tacky, so I discard the bra, allowing my breasts to appear full and firm, though the fabric shows my peaked nipples through its thin layers.

Examining the open back of the dress, hanging just above my bottom, I notice that my underwear lines aren't flattering either. Quickly deciding that they too should go, I shed them, leaving them on the floor. As I stand up, I feel a newfound confidence, admiring my now flattering backside in the mirror. The roundness of my ass enhances the overall look, all thanks to good genetics.

Completing my outfit, I slip on the heels and gape at my reflection, I feel sexy… I look sexy.

Realizing that half an hour has slipped by past eight, I need to go find Jonah. "Shit," I murmur, casting one final glance in the mirror before exiting my room.

Upon my arrival, Shay and Jonathan are engaged in a conversation with Jonah at the front entrance. Their chatter halts abruptly, and all eyes turn towards me. Jonah's mouth hangs open in an animated expression.

"Sorry I'm late," I offer as I approach.

"It's okay, we all have to relieve ourselves sometimes," Jonathan alludes to me playing with myself.

I lock eyes with Jonah as he looks at me from head to toe, his gaze intensifying my newfound confidence. "Why would I need to do that when I have this hunk here to do it for me?" I remark, smiling as I join them, Jonah wrapping his arm around my waist.

"Shall we?" he smiles down at me, and my grin widens as I nod in agreement.

"Behave, you two," Jonathan calls after us playfully.

Leading me through the mansion towards an unfamiliar set of double doors, he swings them open to reveal a room I've never seen before. Stepping across the threshold, I'm immediately captivated by the breathtaking scene. It resembles a grand ballroom, bathed in warm lighting. A single table stands in the center, dressed in a white tablecloth adorned with shimmering patterns that catch the light from every angle. A large bouquet of vibrant flowers sits at the center of the table, adding an extra burst of color.

My gaze is drawn to the far side of the room where expansive windows dominate a large portion of the wall. Double doors stand wide open, welcoming a gentle breeze that rustles the curtains. My eyes linger on the doors, longing to step onto the patio and stare out at the night sky.

Jonah seems to sense my thoughts, tenderly pulling my hand, "Come on, baby, let's eat first," he leads me toward the table. As we approach, Gladys and a couple other chefs roll carts with trays into the room. It feels like a scene from a movie, with the trays topped with fancy metal lids being placed on the table. Gladys beams as she lifts the lids off the trays just as we arrive.

Jonah pulls out a chair for me to sit on, and Gladys is practically radiating joy. "You look beautiful, sweetheart."

"Thank you, Gladys," I respond shyly, then turn to Jonah as he graciously pushes my chair in for me. The surreal elegance of the moment is like a dream. A dream that has to have a touch of sadness, because a subtle hint of pain attempts to creep in. But I push it away, choosing to immerse myself fully in the present, and will deal with those feelings later.

We enjoy our dinner with lively conversation filling the room. As we finish, slow music begins to play over the speakers.

"Mr. Everett," I grin, as he seems to have put a lot of thought into this.

"Will you dance with me?" he rises from his chair, extending his hand toward me. Joy lights up my face at his request, and for a moment, I question if I've somehow slipped into a coma without realizing it. Everything feels too perfect.

Looking up at him, I feel a radiant warmth throughout my body. I place my hand in his and reply, "Yes," as he guides us to the wide-open space on the floor. Wrapping my hands around his neck, he encircles my waist, and together we sway back and forth, our eyes locked in a shared gaze. I wish I could snap a picture of us, so I can cherish it forever.

As the song concludes, he leads me to the terraced garden that caught my eye when we first entered the room. The sight is truly breathtaking—a large water fountain is the centerpiece out here, surrounded by an array of flowers and shrubs. I walk to the edge of the stone pillar rail, gazing out at the moon illuminating the lake in the distance.

He surprises me by lifting me, and a subtle startled squeak escapes my lips as he seats me on the flat stone edge. Wrapping his arms around me, I rest mine over his, leaning back into his chest, and let my feet dangle over the side, swaying them back and forth.

"Thank you for the most incredible evening," I say, feeling the blush on my cheeks.

He grins and turns his face to look at mine, offering a mischievous grin without saying a word.

"Why do you look like you're up to no good?" I playfully ask, aware that his thoughts revolve around getting me out of my dress.

"I'm always up to no good, baby," he finally responds.

A laugh escapes my lips. "I can believe this." I relax, enjoying the playfulness between us.

We sit in silence, holding each other. The chill of the evening air sneaks in, prompting him to wrap his arms tighter around me for warmth.

"I have a confession," I turn my head toward him.

"Can't wait," he says, his gaze meeting mine.

"I'm not wearing any panties," I whisper.

"I'm not either," he quips, leaning in to kiss me.

He scoops me up off the railing, carrying me back inside and setting me down in the ballroom.

"I was enjoying that," I protest.

"You are freezing," he laces his fingers in mine and pulls me across the room.

As we saunter along hand in hand back to his room, I decide to ask a question that has lingered in my mind. "Did you have this house built?" The entire estate baffles me. There are still unexplored areas of the mansion and property, and I don't understand who needs this much space.

When he answers yes, I reflect that it's not just him living here. Dozens of dedicated staff members call this place home—individuals whose stories of homelessness, recovery, or just down on their luck paint a picture of this beautiful man as a beacon of hope. He selflessly extends his generosity by providing shelter and employment, going above and beyond with generous wages for the staff.

I recall the surprise I felt when I checked my bank account after a month here, prompting me to contact the bank in disbelief. After a brief investigation, it became clear that the substantial deposits were indeed intended for me. At that moment, I felt like maybe I could retire that day, but came to my senses and transferred the funds to my savings account, deciding to quit checking my account after that. I figure I will have a large amount of money from the months of working here that I can go put down roots somewhere.

I've always wanted a dog, a small lap dog. Perhaps this is the time I will finally be able to get a furry little companion. Nonetheless, Antoinette was quite reserved with the details of my destination. I ponder the possibility that she might be chauffeuring me to an airport, where they plan on dumping me in the middle of the ocean where Jonah will never be able to locate me.

That would be a depressing end for me.

Entering his room, we both make our way to the bathroom. My gaze follows him in the mirror as he adeptly unbuttons his shirt, seizes the collar, and effortlessly removes it. The discarded shirt finds its spot on the floor at his feet, and with equal grace, he proceeds to unbutton his pants, peeling them away. The sight is nothing short of magnificent. His naked form embodies chiseled perfection, with rock-solid muscles defining every inch of his body.

He steps in the shower, and I watch him letting the water cascade over his face before he starts washing his body with soap.

I take a towel from the stack on my designated counter in his bathroom and begin washing the makeup off my face. I remove the majority before using my face wash to scrub away any lingering traces. I apply moisturizer as I make my way to the closet to retrieve some pajamas.

I sift through the clothing, choosing a delicate pink silk nightgown that's conveniently easy to slip off, as it's barely long enough to cover my ass.

Slipping my feet into the nighty, I draw it up until it rests comfortably on my shoulders. Returning to the bathroom, watching him as water cascades down his face, his thick hair tousled as though he had just washed it. Our eyes connect as I walk by, and I offer him an innocent smile, lazily trailing my finger along the glass, which is just beginning to fog up.

He gazes at me with a seductive intensity as I exit, closing the door behind me.

I settle onto the bed, reclining against an array of pillows. As I survey the room, a profound sense of sadness washes over me. It's unclear whether this stems from my looming departure or the unsettling feeling of allowing someone to create a divide between Jonah and me.

My mind wanders into the realm of future possibilities—marriage, children, a picturesque family with a white picket fence, and, of course, a small, lapdog. A wistful look takes over my features as I daydream about the prospect of having both a son and a daughter. Would my daughter be like me? And would my son mirror Jonah?

Reality hits with a pang. Why am I envisioning a life with Jonah's likeness in my son? Jonah won't be my husband. He will be Jenevieve's husband. Recalling Jonah confronting her against the wall, a surge of anger was visible on his face. Strangely, for a brief moment, she appeared aroused before fear crept in. A tear escapes my eyes, but then I find myself laughing. "Fuck that bitch," I mutter to myself.

Reflecting on this situation, the phrase "Hindsight is 20/20" resonates perfectly. If I could revisit the night she assaulted me, I would seize her by that absurd hair of hers and deliver a resounding blow to her face. The hatred I feel for her is overwhelming. It's hard to imagine her experiencing any emotions other than a sense of superiority over everyone else. How did Jonah fuck her? And he did it with the same dick he fucks me with.

Well, that's not a pleasant thought.

Next.

Resolute in dismissing any lingering thoughts of her.

How do I leave without telling Shay goodbye? God, I'm a shitty friend. Sam forgave me for doing this exact thing to him, but

Shay has no reason to ever talk to me again unlike Sam who is practically family.

I'm not ready to lose Shay as a friend.

What kind of idiot goes along with a plan they don't even agree with? How am I going along with a plan when I don't even know what it is? Antoinette didn't tell me anything other than she would have her driver pick me up tonight. And then what? I don't have anywhere to go. Not only that, but I want Estelle and she's parked in Jonah's garage, and he never gave me the keys back. So, she had better have a plan of getting my keys and car back to me.

I hear the shower shutting off, prompting me to tuck away all the wild thoughts swirling in my mind. Wiping away all traces of my tears with the back of my hands, I settle into the bed. I need to enjoy the night and not seem bothered, or Jonah will suspect something is wrong.

It's showtime, I remind myself as the bathroom door opens and he emerges. The steam from his shower permeating the bedroom. Pausing briefly in the doorway, he appears angelic, and my heart melts at the sight. I recline as he leisurely advances, wearing only a towel snugly wrapped around his waist. With a prowling gaze, he uses two fingers, walking them down a path from my toes, down the top of my foot, and slowly up my leg as he approaches the side of the bed where I lie.

As he moves closer, I gracefully uncross my legs, which were previously stretched out in front of me. Slowly, pulling them up into a bent position, parting them open to reveal I'm not wearing panties. His eyes light up as he gazes between my legs, and a sheepish grin tugs at the corners of his mouth.

"Baby," he breathes out, placing his hand on my knee and begins to slide it down. I clamp my legs together, stopping his hand in its tracks, and elicit a wider smile from him.

Raising my hands above my head, I delicately rest them on the pillows behind me in a provocative pose. "What do you have under that towel, Mr. Everett?" I bite my lip and open my legs back up to release his hand.

Maintaining an unwavering gaze, he grabs the corner of the towel, releasing it from his waist. His thick, hard member springs free as he lets the towel drop to the floor, and my mouth immediately salivates at the enticing sight. "What do you have under this?" he playfully counters, tugging at the edge of my nightgown.

Staring up at him, "Take it off and find out."

He reaches for the hem of my nightgown, delicately pulling it off me. The way he stares at me every time he sees me naked is a sight I could never tire of witnessing.

He leans down firmly pressing his mouth against my nipple, drawing it into his mouth. His tongue delicately licks the hardened peak, causing my breath to hitch in my throat. My hands clutch the pillow behind me, relishing the blissfulness of him on my sensitive flesh. Then, with a subtle nip and bite, he pulls away, releasing before he causes too much pain.

He grins down at me, climbing onto the bed, situating himself between my legs, resting his hands on my knees, and pushing my legs wider apart. Willingly, I let them fall open as he slides closer between them. Planting his hands on either side of my body. He bends forward, placing a kiss on my lips. Drawing away, he looks at my lips and then into my eyes before leaning in again, rekindling the connection with another press of his lips. Our initial kiss is tender, gradually intensifying into a more passionate exchange.

"Jonah," I whisper between our fervent kisses.

"Yeah, baby," he replies, returning to my mouth with heightened urgency, his tongue lapping at mine as he breathes into me.

"I want to feel you," my eyes silently pleading, hoping he understands my unspoken desire for tonight to be more than just physical pleasure but an intimate connection.

He must understand. When his mouth descends to mine again, it's with a tenderness reminiscent of our first kiss—a gentleness that transcends the physical act, signaling an intention to make love rather than merely satisfy our shared carnal desires.

He supports himself on one arm, while his other hand ventures between my legs. Looking down, he delicately traces a finger along my leg, moving from my outer thigh to the inner, and then gradually progressing toward my center. Smoothly, he glides the wetness up the exterior of my slit. The sensation of his touch intensifies as he continues trailing my wetness up and down, sliding his finger inside my folds, and moving upward to my swollen bud. He applies slow, circular pressure, prompting my head to fall back onto the pillows, lost in the pleasure coursing through me. He persists in creating soft circles, not quite enough to bring me to climax but sufficient to elicit a starry-eyed response.

This is exactly what I had in mind. He is taking his time while all his touches are soft.

Removing his hand, I sense the bed shifting as he readjusts himself, maneuvering his hand between us, gripping his thick member. Placing it at my wet center, and tracing circles around my entrance before pressing the tip in. The familiar tightness initially resists his penetration, but the wetness allows him to gradually push through. This time deviates from our typical routine of intense thrusts and passionate screams. Instead, he opts for gentleness. With a slow and deliberate rhythm, he leisurely inches his way in until fully immersed, and then withdraws.

With every inch, his cock moves back into me, a blend of intense pleasure and a fleeting worry—once he withdraws, he won't be able to fit himself back in because he is too big. However, he counters my concern by pressing all the way back in, causing my stomach to tighten with the exquisite sensations he effortlessly extracts. These delicate thrusts, mixed with his length and girth, cause my toes to curl.

My arms wrap around him, holding on as if my life depends on it. While he continues the rhythmic motion of gently pulling out and then softly pushing back in, quiet moans escape my throat at the electrifying intensity. My pussy clenches around him each time he delves deep and then withdraws, causing my body to instantly need to feel him again. A dance he does over and over with each delicate thrust in and each slow withdrawal, a mesmerizing rhythm in and out.

Throughout our months of intimacy, we have never had sex like this. Each time remains special, yet this present moment carries a distinct sense of affection and love. I leisurely glide my silky legs along his, as I reach his outer thigh, I press the soft sole of my foot against the back of his leg, tracing the path back down. Each caress against his skin ignites electric sparks within me. His touch is extraordinary, his skin irresistibly smooth.

Leaning down, he takes my nipple into his mouth, softly nibbling on it before trailing his tongue around the sensitive area. He creates a suction, biting and sucking, then releases with a tantalizing touch. Subdued moans escape my lips. The moisture from his shower has now transformed into beads of sweat as he continues skillfully working himself in and out of me.

He sits back on his heels, lifting me with him onto his lap. As if guided by its own rhythm, my body starts rocking back and forth, feeling his girth stretching me wide, each gyrating motion causing his cock to hit my G-spot. Our tongues caress one another, and his hands wander my body, cupping my ass, squeezing firmly, and then releasing. His jaw clenches in a primal instinct, the urge to lay me down and drive into me with the force we both enjoy, but then he loosens his grip, and his jaw relaxes as he returns to the current moment filled with tenderness.

My fingers glide into the nape of his hair, applying pressure, and then I remove my mouth from his, bringing it to his ear. Softly biting his earlobe, trailing down his neck, indulging in gentle sucking and biting. A low, rumbling groan escapes his throat, a sound that's like music to my ears. Licking up his neck, I nibble at his sculpted jaw, eliciting another moan. Pressing my lips to the same spot, he removes one arm from around my waist, bringing it between us. He presses his thumb onto my swollen bud, expertly applying circular motions to my clit.

The sensation of him entirely filling me and rubbing my sensitive bud sends every sense into a frenzy of heightened arousal. Each movement and touch intensify the electric connection, deepening the pleasure that courses through my body. Peeling myself off his chest, I sit back, allowing us both to witness his skilled touch. I continue gyrating my pussy on his cock, the synchronized movements heightening the pleasure coursing through our bodies.

Locked in a gaze, we hold each other's eyes until a blink interrupts the connection, prompting us to shift our gaze back down at the mesmerizing movements unfolding between us as I continue to rock my hips rhythmically on him.

The intensity of my orgasm builds as my movements gain speed. Closing my eyes, I grip my fingers into his shoulder, my breathing quickens, and he skillfully maintains the perfect circular movement between my legs. Moans escape me as my orgasm reaches its peak, and waves of pleasure cascade over me.

"Fuck!" I moan, my pussy tightening around him with intense pressure as I ride out the exhilarating surges. I continue gyrating on him, each contraction of my orgasm elicits moans from him, the shared pleasure intensifying until I feel the cascade of his climax flowing out. His face falls between my breasts, and I hold onto his head and shoulders while our bodies continue working against each other until they gradually cease movement. Both of us panting heavily, immersed in the aftermath of ecstasy.

He firmly holds my waist and guides me back onto the bed, my arms instinctively returning to the same position they were in when we began, resting above my head as I seductively gaze up at him. With deliberate slowness, he withdraws himself, sending final jolts of my orgasm rushing through me from him pulling out. He leans down to the floor, picking up his discarded towel and proceeds to wipe me clean.

Collapsing to the bed, lying on his back, he stretches out beside me, his arm looping under my back, drawing me onto his chest. A soft laugh escapes me as I settle against him. With an exaggerated happy sigh, he utters, "Right where you belong," planting a kiss on my forehead. A yawn escapes him, and he puts his forearm over his eyes, and the world stands still.

I lie there, delicately trailing my fingers up and down his chest, exploring each muscle on his taut stomach. My fingers slow, and I gaze up at him, etching every feature of his face into my memory, determined to sear this moment permanently in my brain for the rest of my life.

As his breath gradually settles into a steady rhythm, I ease myself off his chest, placing a soft kiss on his lips before slipping off the bed. Moving silently into his bathroom and then his closet, I slip into a pair of my clothes that I discover he's been keeping in here. Returning to his bedroom, I stand by his bedside, quietly observing the peaceful rise and fall of his breathing. Stirring a whirlwind of emotions within me.

Sitting down beside him, I resist the urge to touch him, instead I admire this captivating man, imprinting his image in my mind. Summoning my courage, I make a conscious effort to move, not allowing doubt to hold me back. Almost inaudibly, unsure if the words ever truly escape my lips, I whisper, "I love you, Jonah," hating how that is the first time I've said those words out loud to him and they are also my final words to him.

I gently close the door behind me as I step into my room. Once inside, I lean against the door, taking a moment to absorb the familiar surroundings. It's here that Jonah first slept beside me, holding me in his arms, and where Shay and I shared countless conversations, laughter, and tears. The memories within these walls weigh heavily on me, and I'm not ready to say goodbye.

In my mind, I had envisioned packing my bags only to move into Jonah's room, not leave the mansion entirely. Tears well up as my hands tremble, and my legs feel like lead, rooted to the spot by the weight of the memories. Despite the emotional turmoil, I know I need to pack. With effort, I peel myself away from the door and head to the closet, grabbing my floral bag and filling it with clothes and essentials. Retrieving the rest of my belongings will be something future me can worry about. I wonder if Antoinette has already made arrangements.

'Move, Kalyn,' I scold myself, my heart pounding in my chest, as I step out of my room, closing the door softly behind me. Navigating through the house with purpose, I am driven by an urgent need to avoid being seen by anyone.

Descending the stairs at the front of the house, I spot a black car waiting for me. Just as Antoinette said there would be. As I approach, the driver, an older man with gray hair and a bald crown, dressed in a black suit, steps out. He walks around the car, opening the back door for me. "Thank you," I gracefully slide into the remarkably spacious back seat. A blacked-out window separates the front seats from the back, a subtle indication of Antoinette's desire to maintain a distinction between herself and the "hired help," as she often puts it. He shuts the door behind me, in my lap at my trembling hands, I don't allow myself to turn back and bid farewell to the home and the man I've grown to love.

It doesn't hit me until we veer onto the main road, the weight of my actions sinking in. I try to suppress my emotions, reassuring myself that everything is okay, but a sob escapes, quickly followed by another, each one filled with raw pain. What have I done? Tears stream down my cheeks as I pull my legs onto the seat, wrapping my arms around them, burying my face in my knees as my sobs continue. Fumbling through my bag, I grab a shirt to wipe away the tears, but the waves of emotions continue to crash over me as we travel in silence for three agonizing hours.

I cycle through sobbing, trying to compose myself, then berating myself, only to succumb to tears once more. Suddenly, I'm hit with waves of nausea, my voice trembling. "Sorry, could you pull over please?" The driver obliges, and I barely make it out of the car before I'm doubled over, retching on my hands in knees in the dirt and rocks. Tears blur my vision as I sob and vomit, feeling utterly out of control. In a moment of frantic self-awareness, I realize how unhinged I must appear to the driver—first sobbing uncontrollably, then requesting a sudden stop so I can puke, followed by more tears and me pacing back and forth down the road behind the car, and then gathering myself enough to return to the car.

"Sorry," I murmur, unsure if my apology reaches him through the tinted window.

Emotions whirl through me, each surge as fleeting as a blink. Confidence accompanied my departure, tinged with nervousness about the possibility of being caught. Exiting the driveway, a wave of dread swept over me, quickly followed by the piercing ache of my heart crumbling apart. Leaving Jonah without a word was a painful choice, but I knew he wouldn't allow me to go willingly.

Antoinette surprised me with kindness in the courtyard. Instead of the expected scolding, she shared anecdotes from Jonah's childhood. Rather than swaying my feelings for him in a negative way, it only intensified my feelings for him. Deep down, I acknowledge that Antoinette genuinely desires what's best for her son. Jonah has been instrumental in helping me get back on my feet, and I will continue making progress long after he has moved on and forgotten about me.

Perhaps one day we can cross paths and catch up over our once blossoming love.

The driver continues on for another forty-five minutes, the only sound being the gentle hum of the tires on the road. My stomach has rumbled a few times, and I don't know if it's from hunger or letting me know I made a huge mistake, but either way, I have no intention of eating; the discomfort can become familiar for the next few days, at least.

When we pull into a hotel parking lot and come to a stop by the front entrance, I sit motionless, unsure of the reason for stopping. I stare at the hotel. "What are we doing?" My voice still carries traces of tears, but the realization dawns on me—it's 4 AM, and the driver must be exhausted, in need of rest before continuing wherever we are going. Maybe I can sleep, and the bed will swallow me whole.

I hear the driver's door open then shut, and he walks around the car.

However, he doesn't open my door. Instead, he opens the front passenger door. In slow motion, I watch as a towering figure steps out and walks to my door, pulling it open and extending his hand. "C'mon, baby," Jonah says, reaching out to me.

To Be Continued

ACKNOWLEDGMENTS

A very special "Thank you" to the two people who complete my 'Tripod': Wissa and Jane.

You encouraged and supported me to write, and gave me back-aching laughs in the process.

EXTRA, extra special thank you to Wissa for reading and rereading all my rough drafts, revisions, and more edited versions before this.